Paul Marzeky Mystery Thriller

EXCELSIOR!

Stefan J. Malecek, Ph.D.

EXCELSIOR!

A Paul Marzeky Thriller.

Stefan J. Malecek, Ph. D

COPYRIGHT

Stefan J. Malecek, Ph.D.

ISBN: 978-1-7349047-2-7 (eBook)

ISBN: 978-1-7349047-3-4 (Paperback)

Website: https://www.stefanjmalecek.com/home-page

First Edition – March 2020

DISCLAIMER

The author of this book does not dispense medical advice or prescribe the use of any technique as a form of treatment for physical, emotional or medical problems without the advice of a physician either directly or indirectly. This book is a work of fiction. The names, characters, places or incidences are all a product of the author's imagination or are fictitious in nature. Any resemblance to actual people, events, or locations are entirely coincidental.

OTHER BOOKS BY STEFAN J. MALECEK, PH. D

Crucible of Shame: Healing the Societal Roots of Addiction and "Mental Illness"

Trauma And Transformation (Read For Free)

The Paul Marzeky Mystery Series

Crazy Tales of Combat Psychiatry

Spirals of Time

Unwitting Witnesses

Alchemy's Angel

The Gilded Edges of Shadow

Excelsior

Get them all here

https://www.amazon.com/author/stefanjmalecek

About The Author

Shop The Full Series Of Paul Marzeky Mystery series

https://www.amazon.com/author/stefanjmalecek

Excerpts From Crucible Of Shame: Healing The Societal Roots Of Addiction and "Mental Illness"

Excelsior!

CHAPTER ONE
MOVEMENT

San Francisco   Saturday, November 11th, 1995: 1322

P aul did a double take as he walked up Columbus Avenue through North Beach. He could have sworn he'd just seen someone who was dead, long ago in Vietnam. By the time he looked again, the specter had disappeared completely, leaving Paul with only fleeting memories of the 'Nam and present tense sense impressions—the shape of the nose, the tilt of his wool cap, his stride. Paul shrugged his shoulders and dismissed it as another flashback.

He'd met Doc Roach at a late-night set. Camp Evans RVN, sitting on a chopper pad surrounded by dozens of comrades all getting as blasted as possible—primarily on Southeast Asia's finest marijuana, though there was no dearth of other drugs circulating — speed, heroin, all manner of pills, even cannisters of nitrous oxide purloined from Medical Supply. They were all carrying, every manner of automatic weapons, handguns, knives and other implements of destruction. Their convocation of brothers was sacred, held in a kind of wild reverence beyond the stolid contrivance of "military regulations."

Paul took a deep hit from the foot-long Esmerelda-papered joint

1

filled with high potency red Laotian weed that somebody had brought in from Saigon that very day. The resinous smoke went deep into his lungs. In a manner honoring Gnossos Popandoupoulis, he kept the smoke in until he breathed out empty air. That single hit was all he needed to amplify every bodily sensation, wave after electric wave resonating through him before handing it off to the rugged-looking man who sat down next to him, holding a bottle of tequila. Paul scanned the man, noticing the black Airborne Wings and the Combat Medic Badge sown above his left pocket, and the man's severely pinpointed pupils.

They dapped open-handed, and Paul held up the joint.

"Roach. Charlie, 1st of the Oh Deuce," he said, and they dapped.

"I'm Jay!"

Roach took a deep hit from the joint, and started coughing.

"What the fuck is this?"

"Upcountry red, brother!"

"You spiked this shit!"

"Because you're coughing?"

"No, man! Seriously!"

"No! Straight business!"

"Wow!"

Paul took another glug from his bottle of Russian vodka. The lettering on the bottle was in Cyrillic, so Paul assumed it was

2

genuinely Russian. Stolichnaya. Far smoother than American vodka that inevitably tasted more like dishwater. Roach sucked on his tequila, then took another hit and passed it back managing to keep the smoke in.

"Some of these guys are in my company. We're going back to the A Shau tomorrow."

"'Going back?'"

"Yeah. I was with my platoon last time. This time I'm going in with Battalion Aid."

"I heard it was hairy," said Paul.

"Fucking NVA had tanks and tracks!"

"Jesus!"

"And a fucking surgical hospital five stories underground!"

Paul couldn't speak.

"We lost forty-three KIA, 140 WIA."

"Fuck!"

Then Roach sighed.

"What?"

"What 'what?'"

"I'm the psych consultant. I get paid to pay attention."

"So?"

"Brother, you look boo-coo strung out. Then you sighed, so you must be depressed too."

"That's pretty sharp, man."

"And?" said Paul, suddenly feeling like a Father Confessor. He felt the heaviness in the other man.

Roach swiveled his neck and surveyed the controlled chaos spreading all around them, then looked directly into Paul's eyes.

"I... I'm missing thirty-nine morphine syrettes! I signed 'em out. They're gone! I heard CID is investigating me!"

"Shit! That's fucked!"

"Amen, brother."

"What are you going to do?"

"I just fucking die in the A Shau?"

It was the last time Paul had seen him. And now he could have sworn he'd seen him twice in the past two months! Elsewise he'd been hallucinating. What a great news story that would make— psychologist admitted to psych unit with acute hallucinatory syndrome, or some other such media-created nonsense!

Now that he was lurching into middle age, and still seeking self-redemption, or at least rehabilitation of his heart and memories, he was frequently reminded of the Jefferson Airplane line: "You achieve the stability you strive for in the only way that it's granted, in a place among the fossils of our time." His entire life, and the small stability he had achieved, was rooted in the continuous emotional release that was his hallmark, releasing ancient, twisted memories and emotion.

Still ruminating about the possibility that he had seen Roach, he decided to brew a cup of his favorite of his favorite blend—two-thirds French Roast, one-third Mocha Java drip-ground at Graffeo's in North Beach, just a few blocks from where he lived on Fielding Street (off Powell, between Chestnut and Lombard). He had a magnificent view of Coit Tower and the Embarcadero, with the East Bay in the distance—a view of which he never tired, the constant panoply of ships and boats, the ever-refreshing currents and tides accompanied by the tang of the salt air and the intricate patterns of birds, masters of the air.

He'd been very fortunate in its location. The way the space was laid out—and the rather immense privacy it allowed him. He was able to rent out his therapy office for a portion of the week to Tomas Chavez, a half-Mescalero Apache, half-Spanish Mexican Indian, a former classmate who was working through his supervised employment. He therefore had all of the referral resources attendant to that, including agency referral sources. This latter was yet another beneficial aspect of their former association. It put Tomas in the position of referring what he called his "overflow clients" to Paul, who certainly benefitted, despite seeing them at a discounted rate.

Using his certification as an Alcohol and Drug Counselor (CADC) and his National Provider's Identification (NPI), he had been able to get referrals from some of the smaller hospitals and bill the appropriate insurance companies at the full rate (which was one hundred dollars an hour). So, altogether, he was doing reasonably well.

He considered his anti-APA stance as a kind of badge of honor. It began earnestly enough when he was working as a Licensed Psychiatric Technician (LPT) passing meds on both sides of an Acute Crisis/Geriatric facility. He attended a Network Against Psychiatric Assault (NAPA) meeting with a fellow LPT, after which the both of them decided that the patients had a right to know what the side-effects of their prescribed medications were. That decision set in motion a series of events like tumbling dominos that resulted in almost half of the patients refusing their meds. It had almost cost him his job—and left him bitter about the APA ever after. For him, the psychopharmaceutical industry was just another for-profit business that preyed upon people's fears and social pressure to induce belief that individuals "needed" psych meds to "fit in" with the extant dysfunctional society.

But then, it was just one of many selections from the library of his encyclopedic "rants," most, if not all related to his discontents with contemporary society. They fed the core of his desire to write, to communicate, especially in that he so often felt that he was unheard, especially in that he believed he had lived a very extraordinary life, and saw the world in a highly idiosyncratic yet universalistic way that he believed could lend a certain modicum of relief to a suffering humanity. Of course, the frustration with finding a wider audience had led to his developing the quasi-delusional belief in being destined to be a widely acclaimed, world-class author, and a deep streak of being disgruntled with, variously, having to "endure" daily normal practicalities or "manage" the lesser intelligences and abilities of "most people."

He wished so sincerely that he were able to effectively eschew living in a society that put a premium of making money, rather than expending its energies to serving its citizens, and deepening the collective resonance of connectedness and global service. Underneath of it all was the desire to live in love, immersed in love, surrounded by love, interacting in and with love all the time, instead of vainly seeking that all-embracing realm of inclusiveness somewhere, anywhere, everywhere, outside of himself. He longed so to be infused, effused, enervated, with the power and the glory of pure heartedness and heartfulness.

Essentially, he longed to be love.

Ideally he could have a grace period of five years off just in order to write, to create some portion of the many books, articles, chapters, poems and magazine pieces he was carrying around in the hard drive of his mind. His journals were chockablock with different pieces of narratives, dialogue bursts, characters, plot twists and multi-colored schools of herrings including red.

The vision was intimately intertwined with his longstanding, almost Asperger's-like longing to write, expressing the inwardness that he seemed incapable of merging with what most called "reality." It was deeply rooted in what he had learned was called "alexithymia," the inability to put words to his emotions. He had always felt so emotionally obtunded, retarded almost, furthered and complicated by the utter lack of respect, love and nurturance with which he had been treated in the Auschwitz-like surroundings of his childhood. It always reminded him of a line by John Bradshaw: "It's worse growing up in an abusive home than it is to be in a concentration camp because, at least in a concentration camp, you are allowed to hate your captors."

His writing was precious, the most poignant, most prized and finest of his gifts. He resonated with Anais Nin, who perfectly described her relationship with the written word and the art of producing it:

We write to taste life twice, in the moment, and in retrospection. We write, like Proust, to render all of it eternal, and to persuade ourselves that it is eternal. We write to be able to transcend our life, to reach beyond it. We write to teach ourselves to speak with others, to record the journey into the labyrinth. We write to expand our world when we feel strangled, or constricted, or lonely. We write as the birds sing, as the primitives dance their rituals. If you do not breathe through writing, if you do not cry out in writing, or sing in writing, then don't write, because our culture has no use for it. When I don't write, I feel my world shrinking. I feel I am in a prison. I feel I lose my fire and my color. It should be a necessity, as the sea needs to heave, and I call it breathing.

CHAPTER TWO
SPINNING THOUGHTS

San Francisco **Monday November 13ᵗʰ, 1995: 0833**

Paul awoke relatively early. Veteran's Day had a paradoxical effect on him, both ameliorating and reinforcing his lingering memories—now even more focused upon the possibility that he was actually catching peripheral glimpses of Roach. Additionally, it triggered his convoluted (he disingenuously called it "schizophrenic") thinking about the relationship between war and business. Chomsky referred to the process of entire societies being driven by the profit motive as "the permanent war economy." Art always seemed juxtaposed to "business," under which rubric any number of crimes were regularly committed and justified.

The specter of money surrounded everything, camouflaged the deeper layers of essence that he knew must be held in trust by Life. His personal prejudice tracked it as starting with Robot Reagan, but he knew that it had been deeply entrenched long before that. Walter Lippman praised subtrefuginous government in his1922 book "Public Opinion." Paul could not help but remember hearing as a child Eisenhower's infamous (and duplicitous) 1954 warning about the "military-industrial complex" when it had already been long before established—including a fifty-thousand dollar "loan" made by defense contractors to pay for his famous farm in Gettysburg, Pennsylvania, a "loan" in name only, never expected to be repaid. As far as Paul could discern, business and government had always been incest partners. It had always violated the presumed trust that was supposed to exist between citizens and "government" (upon which the media and other propogandists played incessantly). The relationship had always been between government and its biggest stake holders—the military as an enforcement arm, media as a propaganda arm, and major industries as an economic resource.

He remembered an astute piece by a fellow named Rao who perfectly summarized the roots of this toxic relationship reflecting on the British East India Corporation:

The essentially sociopathic nature of modern corporations worldwide is easy to explain when one remembers it originated in the needs of professional opium traffickers. To see it as anything other than the expression of a criminal mind-set is catastrophically naïve. They grew opium in India and shipped it to China under armed escort until twenty million Chinese were addicted by the nineteenth century... The entire British Empire would have gone bankrupt without the narcotic.

He had been exploring the idea of predatory economics as the root cause of both addictions and "mental illness" (what he called "traumatogenic" childrearing that was inherently "addictionogenic"), and that shaped the entire of such a society. Such machine-like, automatized behaviors seemed to drive the bulk of the planet's governments and economies, creating soulless societies that functioned on fear and fostered the delusion of achieving happiness through external rewards and the sacrifice of one's inner resources.

Paul really felt drawn to work with others who had experienced serious addictions, but always with the caveat that they be at least a year clean first. He had found that the first year would solidify an individual's recovery in such a way that doing the deeper work would be much easier by creating a greater comfort and openness. During the many years he himself had been in therapy, he had never felt emotionally complete with strictly "talk oriented therapy," all of which was based in some form or fashion on Freud's original "talking cure." Of course, the latter had always been meant to elicit catharsis, an emotional release, not just more intellectualizing and verbal babble.

The current "therapy culture" demanded the quickest and most economically efficacious methods. Treatment bean-counters were infatuated with Dialectical Behavioral Therapy (DBT) or Cognitive Behavioral Therapy (CBT), both of which were oriented to simply making mental changes to address one's behaviors without purposely aiming at eliciting an emotional release. The net result was relatively superficial, focused more on behavior than essence. Paul did not believe that true healing was possible without emotional integration. It simply allowed the world-as-usual to roll on unabated and get worse—in fact, it allowed consumer culture to create further tentacles of co-optation by including therapy as a profit generator.

Providing strictly mental health treatment was often not as appealing, primarily because people who had been to "the bottom" tended to be more available to healing than those who were imprisoned within the chains and walls of "mental illness." The expectation with this latter group was generally that a treatment provider would seek to have their symptoms medicated, and only secondarily receive psychotherapy. Paul usually refused to take new clients who were medicated, unless they were willing to work with a medical doctor he knew to titrate their way off of them. Side effects of psych drugs could be very dangerous. They also interfered with an individual's ability to feel and express emotions (especially because they impacted the prefrontal cortex).

Paul had evolved treatment methods out of his own experiences, engendered by his belief in and aim for emotional unblocking. Traumatically driven behaviors were, for the most part, pejorative as aberrant and the clients marginalized. Paul worked in his own idiosyncratic manner, utilizing therapeutic approaches to healing that had worked for him, and tended, no matter how apocryphal the evidence, to be both far more efficacious and potent. He had lost track of the number of clients he had had through the years who had expressed their gratitude to him, and even those who had said he had "saved my life."

CHAPTER THREE
GRATITUDE

San Francisco   **Thursday November 16th, 1995: 1201**

Paul was excited to have a new client. Beyond the income (which he sorely needed), it was always fun to start painting on a new blank canvas.

Sylvia Santos had come to his office right on time. She was quite good-looking, with firm, supple skin that hinted at her being younger than her stated age in her early forties. Her hair was black and shoulder length. Her skin was cocoa-colored and she had emerald green eyes. She was five foot seven and her carriage was dancer-fluid. Paul was very aware that she emanated a sexual frisson from her well-proportioned and very fit body. She was casually but immaculately dressed in jeans, a silk blouse and knee-high black leather lace-up boots. She came into his inner sanctum and made herself at home immediately. She seemed very comfortable in her skin, and Paul wondered why she might have requested a full eval at his cash rate.

"So, tell me a little about yourself," he asked in an open-ended rather than directive manner, a small test to see how perceptive his new client might be.

"It's a little convoluted. My soon-to-be-ex-husband is hassling me. We are definitely going to be going to court. He's claiming I'm

13

'mentally ill' (she said, making air quotes around the term). He wants to take my daughter away from me."

"Do you have an attorney? I'm not qualified to deal with legal issues."

"I have a very good attorney. She recommended you, in fact."

"Oh? Who's that?"

"Shirley Stephenson!"

"Shirley's representing you?"

She had represented Paul previously. She was held in both fear and reverence by law enforcement community, especially as she had successfully represented a number of people who had sued SFPD, The City and County of San Francisco, and the State of California for a variety of infractions related to civil liberties violations—and won handsome settlements from them all.

"How do you know Shirley?"

"We sit in some of the same women's circles. And we're both on the board of both de Young and the SF Symphony."

"Excellent!"

"She said you were a 'fierce advocate' for your clients!"

"I would have said the same of her! I've always deeply admired her!"

"I'm glad! I really need an advocate."

"Tell me more."

The young woman paused for a moment, gaze turned inward, and then answered.

"First off, Phoebe is <u>my</u> daughter. She was born a year before Chad and I met. He and I have been together eight years and only married for the last five. There is no legal bond between Phoebe and him. None."

"OK."

"He wants to take her away from me to punish me."

"'Punish' you? Why?"

"I'm no longer willing to put up with his cheating."

"This has been going on for a while?"

"I suspect even before we were married. But since we've been married, I'm certain."

"We may be getting ahead of ourselves a little here. Let me have you fill out the basic paperwork and Releases of Information."

"I do not want him knowing anything! Nothing at all!"

"I will completely protect your confidentiality. But if this goes to court, and the judge issues an order, I will have to cooperate."

"But..."

Paul held up his hand in a crossing-guard gesture. "I will make minimal notes, so there will be very little for them to prey upon."

"Oh. OK," she said looking somewhat mollified.

"Since you're paying cash, I can follow your instructions and keep no notes at all. If we're billing your insurance, I am required to keep progress notes and provide a Treatment Plan along with the formal Evaluation to them."

"I... I hadn't thought of it in those terms. But I need a formal evaluation, especially for when we go to court. It's inevitable, I'm afraid."

Paul furnished her with the requisite forms on a clipboard and she set about filling in the blanks. She stuck the end of the pen in the corner of her mouth as she concentrated, a gesture he normally found repulsive (especially when the damaged pen top was left behind as a kind of contaminated "gift"), but with her he found it oddly intriguing, almost as if she were a small child. He did make a mental note to himself to make sure she took the pen with her.

Paul had seen far too many clients who had great resources (physical, financial or artistic) who, as their work progressed, proved to be emotionally unstable or simply a mess. It was with this large chunk of salt that he reined in his immediate attraction to this woman. He also did not immediately accept or dismiss the implications of her story. After all, part of his job was to investigate what he called the "givens"—that which was presented up front, the often expected-to-be-accepted initial information of clients that, frequently, even almost always, proved to be quite different. He suspected that there was a countervailing story that would be, or could be told, that emphasized her husband's relative innocence and emphasized her own culpability. Nonetheless, she was his client and he would do the best professional job he could.

Paul went through the paperwork page-by-page, asking small questions for clarification; pointing out spaces that she had failed to initial; and continued to listen to the feedback from his intuition. His immediate assessment was that his new client was not looking for any kind of treatment, but was wanting to present him with the best picture of herself that he would, in turn, formalize in a legal document about which he would later testify in court, showing her in the best possible light—and eventuating in her getting what she wanted. He knew he could be wrong. She could be a genuinely forthright woman and telling a great portion of "the truth." It remained to be seen, but he had always been a big fan of first impressions.

"Let's talk a little more about this situation with your husband. Do you have actual proof that he's cheating on you? Not that I am doubting you for a moment, but legal proof is tricky. It speaks to credibility, especially if I'm to use your accusations as some portion of my evaluation."

She sat for a moment, as if absorbing a blow. Then she jumped up out of her chair and started pacing.

"Shirley said I could trust you!"

"You certainly can. But you must also be prepared to have your ideas, especially your accusations, closely examined. I cannot simply re-state blindly what you tell me. If I put it into a legal document, I must be prepared to defend what I've written."

The young woman stopped in mid-pace, then whirled and said, "I thought you were writing me off!"

"No. Not at all. But you should start thinking about how you're going to respond to cross-examination in court."

She lowered her head, then inhaled deeply before replying.

"I... guess I'm pretty sensitive."

She used the word in the way that most clients did, denoting reactivity rather than how he might use it in the more clinical sense of being aware of energy.

She stopped in mid-stride. A tear escaped her left eye and streaked through the light coating of her make up.

"I... it's just been so...difficult lately. Chad is such a bastard! First he cheats on me and now he wants to steal my daughter!"

"I understand."

Turning to face him, she asked, "So, how does this work? Is there any therapy included in the five hundred?"

"No."

"But..."

"There's a great deal of work involved in the eval. Once we get the basic historical information on paper, we'll take a little break. Then I'm going to give you a battery of psychological tests. The court will expect me both to administer and interpret them, and then write a small report just on that information that will be included in the eval. Then, after I have gotten that far, we'll reschedule a shorter appointment for you to read it over—not to change my mind or argue with me, but to clarify the information. That's why I am billing you for three hours for today. It includes my time writing everything up."

"What about court? Will you be subpoenaed?"

"Very likely. I will give you a break on my court appearance fees, depending on how long I am on the stand. It's likely to be less than two hours."

She resumed her seat and seemed to be contemplating him.

"You must forgive me. I had no idea it would be so expensive."

"Consider me to be a highly specialized tool. If the job I'm doing is important, and you want it done properly, then you must employ the proper tool to do the job. Elsewise, you might just as well not bother."

"And why are you the 'right tool' for this job?"

Paul took a deep breath before responding.

"I'm local. I've been around psychiatry here in San Francisco for decades and I know many of the major players. Also, in the court system—lawyers, prosecutors, even deputies in the jail, I'm well known. Additionally, I have testified dozens of times and I'm aware of some of the tricks that attorneys use. I'm very clear and comprehensive. I'm not vague or murky. My word is trusted. Judges and attorneys trust me. They know I do not lie."

"I see. That makes a lot of sense. Let's get this eval completed."

"Works for me."

Paul continued the social history; filled in the blanks concerning medical and psychiatric history (nothing significant); family history (she denied any abuse or neglect despite having a workaholic father and a questionably codependent mother); two older siblings, both happily married with families in the Bay Area; employed for twelve years as the manager of a financial consulting firm on Sansome Street as well as working as a sculptress; making a very good salary, and not dependent on her husband's income (he was the manager at the local Porsche agency and made a very good wage with excellent benefits). Her daughter was quite bright and had been double promoted twice. She was currently two grades ahead and there was talk of her being able to complete high school in three years. Emotionally, Sylvia described Lily as being very aware of her intelligence; that she read at a very advanced level; she played piano and, in keeping with her early accomplishments, was skeptical of the behaviors of her same-age peers and their preoccupation with what she considered to be "childish" pursuits.

They took a small break, during which time she smoked a cigarette on his front porch, admiring the views. He declined to join her. He really could not stand the smell. When she returned, he walked her through the intricacies of the Weschler Adult

Intelligence Scale (WAIS), The Minnesota Multiphasic Personality Inventory 2 (MMPI 2), and the Beck Depression Inventory. He considered administering the Thematic Apperception Test (TAT), even the TOSCA (Test of Self-Conscious Affect), but decided he would evaluate the results of what he had already administered and then see if more testing were indicated.

She asked to smoke another cigarette. Paul sighed, knowing this to be a prelude to her wanting to ask therapeutic questions, usually accompanied by "it'll only take a few minutes" or "I just need a little more information." Paul had learned long ago to write it off as a minor artifact related to basic human greed, though it still rankled him.

Besides, she had been very task oriented as they proceeded through the battery of tests. She had completed her testing in record time, and even with the extra time built-in for evaluating and writing up the formal document, he could afford a little largesse.

He had already begun forming his clinical opinion, and while he would certainly note her previous treatment for depression (she had been prescribed SSRIs), he had half-way decided to downplay the impact of that by calling her an Adjustment Disorder while citing her various stressors, including being, in effect, a single mom stressed further by a hostile, cheating husband who only had minimal interest in, and took little responsibility for, her daughter Phoebe; and who now had the temerity to want to claim full custody, despite having never advocated for adoption either.

"So, what do you think?" she asked when she returned.

It was the kind of question that clients often asked immediately following a session, long before any competent clinician would have fully formulated a solid diagnostic equation. Besides which, it would not be ethical of him to answer such a question. With her, he decided he might need another short session in the next week or so to further clarify some areas that he felt might be helpful to explore, especially given the importance of the outcome in terms of a young girl's life. (Secretly, he had already decided that the husband was a creep, and that, while remaining as clinically objective as possible, he would subtly slant his findings in her favor).

Even though he explained all this to her in foreshortened form, she nonetheless reformulated her desire to hear Paul's opinion.

"I understand all that, but" she paused before flashing him a radiant smile and then asked, in a kind of goofy, almost cartoon character voice, "Am I crazy, doc?"

Despite himself, Paul laughed, then smiled and answered.

"'Crazy' is not what we are talking about here. What civilians call 'crazy' refers to what the court calls 'insane.' In criminal court the concern is being able to differentiate between right and wrong and being able to choose one over the other. What I believe you are asking is, do I believe you are mentally ill; and are you being, and capable of being, a competent and caring parent?"

She suddenly turned very serious and nodded her head.

"Absolutely!"

"Again, it's too soon for me to comment officially. Especially since you might repeat a casual comment to a friend, or in court, that might be misconstrued."

Disappointment flashed across her face, and then he said, "However, not on the record, and totally between us, your responses about your daughter seem genuine and caring. I am, therefore, at this early juncture, inclined to believe you." He was tempted to tell her that he might petition the court to grant him the opportunity, (and hence the payment, of course), to interview the little girl—though that got sticky because Paul would not want her mother present when he did so (too much opportunity for emotional contamination, vis a vis the nearness of the mothering person). That, in turn, required the presence of an authorized (and paid) court-approved competent adult. The work would not be anywhere nearly as extensive as with his client, but it would and could add a decidedly informative perspective. The court was sometimes reluctant to grants such opportunities, especially when the initial request had been concerning the mother's mental status.

"I do have a recommendation for you, though. Please tell Shirley that I suggest that your husband be required to have a Psychological Evaluation as well. If he is suggesting he is a more fit person than you as the child's natural mother, he'll have an extremely difficult task in front of him."

"Shirley and I talked about that. It seems to me that turnabout is fair play."

"So, is she proceeding with the request?"

"She hasn't yet, but we have plenty of time before our court date."

"If your husband's attorney claims that there's too little time, the request might get derailed, or your court date might get extended."

"I see her the day after the day before Thanksgiving. I will definitely bring it up again."

"That might be wise."

She started to reach up as if to kiss his cheek, then hesitated and held out her right hand to shake.

"Happy holiday to you."

Paul smiled, and said, "We'll talk again soon."

CHAPTER FOUR
FURTHER DEVELOPMENTS

San Francisco   **Monday, November 20th, 1995: 1221**

He had really made good progress of late. He was proud of his recent production, indeed, he often gauged his self-worth, his very beingness, by how much work he had done and the quality thereof. *Brotherhood* had now been re-named *Crazy Tales*, the new title giving a kind of ironic twist to the material, incorporating the insanity of the 'Nam and his duty as a psychiatric functionary—even though the latter usually just meant his being a paperwork flunky feeding what Paul felt was the hidden agenda of the military establishment—to eliminate all (combat vets and others) who refused to carry the party line about "winning the war" and maintaining "military discipline." The net effect was to deny them GI benefits and aftercare under the specious auspices of AR-635-212, the so called "Undesirable Discharge" claiming that these men, who had endured the rigors and terrors of combat, were being blithely dismissed with no consideration since what were considered their "problems" (often stemming from combat experience) had "existed prior to service." As such, the military declared itself not culpable and ergo, not morally or financially responsible, for what damage had been done. As was true of veterans throughout all time (the first documentation of PTSD was over three thousand years ago), and were considered "expendable," discarded

25

after they had given their blood and brains for the Empire.

He had divided loyalties when he originally started the book. In part, he wanted to show a side to war and combat that had rarely been portrayed, especially from the psychological viewpoint. His other intention was to rail about the utter insanity and excremental idiocy he had experienced while expurgating his incandescent rage about all of it. He had also meant to display, graphically portray, the aftereffects of war that were now termed Posttraumatic Stress Disorder (PTSD).

His writing, as always, as ever, had been his sacred refuge, the very best therapy he had ever had. Writing this book, his very first novel, had carried him through the decades in increments since he had come home. He could no longer remember the number of drafts he had written and edited since 1979, when he had first synthesized three small short stories into a tentative first draft. (He had to admit a certain fondness for the massive 563-page version he had once produced).

He had always believed his own PTSD had developed from a very early aged and had been transformed into a full-bloomed monster by his experiences in Vietnam (he still hated the new, politically correct spelling). Even his many years of recovery from cocaine, and thousands of hours of therapy, he was still at least occasionally pissed off with the Creator, blamed Him/Her/It/All That Is for the torment and tumult of what he deemed to have been an extremely agonizing life filled with tremendous suffering that had engendered self-hatred and lack of self-respect that had formed the core of his early years and seemed ineradicable. He had always felt "forced" to endure every single moment, every single day of his life, that had held on tenaciously even through the fires of his most extreme drug abuse, only to surrender slowly as he aged and the blessing of time's passages assuaged his parched soul to be integrated.

He was now beginning to be able to see the distinct possibility that self-loathing and all of the other devastating and debilitating artifact of his life were absolutely necessary to unwind and integrate—the perfect counterpoint for self-development, pushing him to the absolutely maximum of his limits (what he called the "fifty-ninth minute of the twenty-third hour") in order that he might discover the hidden treasures he carried within himself, and ultimately allow him to fully experience the love and glory so many others had seen in him, access to which beauty he seemed unable to access. He had always fought against his own recalcitrance, had for so long desired to live in that supernal light sequestered within him, treasured like a last match lit in the midst of a typhoon. He carried that Light Eternal and it was his sacred Herculean duty to struggle mightily to open himself to the awareness of its presence and allow it to shine forth in its awesome clarity, joy and wonder—not only for whatever warmth and comfort it might bring him, but for the inspiration and uplift he could bring to assist in easing the struggle of unworthiness and cupidity from which a suffering humanity had so long endured.

The answer was always the same: Love.

Unconditional love. It was always a matter of seeking within himself for what he had rather than seeking something outside of himself he had not. The conundrum for him was that, if one felt truly whole with oneself, the desire for anything or anyone would disappear. He'd read a blog post that said:

I am not waiting for a hero. I saved myself long ago. I don't need someone to complete me. I am whole alone. I just want a weirdo to go on adventures with. Someone who will dance with me, kiss me when I least expect it, and make me laugh.

To which someone responded:

Sounds simple, but it may not be as simple as it seems. If you're truly whole alone, that means you have all the self-worth, self-love and self-respect you need. In that, you will not accept just any weirdo. You will only be available for someone who is truly right for you. You have to genuinely be interested in being around them. There has to be inherent growth and purpose behind the adventures and a mutual respect and healthy intent behind the time spent connecting intimately. In essence, your own wholeness precludes you from finding that special weirdo just anywhere. We say "that's it" but really, if we're honest, "that's it" isn't something small. It's something big. It's something not so easy to find. But that's OK, because you're whole and don't need it. Waiting to find that right weirdo will be worth it, just like you're worth it.

This was, indeed, the crux. It was almost tautological, in that the proposition seemed to circle back onto itself. If it really were so, it could be dismissed as just a mind game, and he could allow it to not haunt him as constantly as it did, to seek evanescent wholeness through another.

But Paul was as much of a fool as any man when meeting a new woman, especially when he believed that there might be a spark that led him to fantasize (yet again) that he might have met "the one." Paul had even considered that he might be afflicted with the vicious entanglements of de Clerambault's Syndrome (popularly known as erotomania). He was so hungry for female attention that his internal meters jumped high up into the red zone when he felt a desirable woman paying attention to him, that she might be his soul's mate. The women were invariably good-looking, if not always beautiful, and intelligent enough to keep him engaged in bright conversation. The attention, no matter how fleeting, was enough to inspire thoughts of possibility. He always convinced himself that they embodied all of the wonder, grace and joy for which he hungered, as if they possessed vital nutrients that he needed to racinate his life.

He decided to go have a quiet drink by himself, and walked down to Gino and Carlo's, the renowned watering hole located at Columbus and Green since 1942, and in the hands of the Rossi family since 1954. It was a true community centerpiece, for sports events, competitions and darts tournaments, a place to celebrate joy and commemorate sorrow. It got rowdy sometimes, and although Paul was not a terribly heavy drinker, sometimes it was the perfect anodyne for malaise or the occasional funk. He found it to be stimulating for his writing.

Most of the seats at the bar were occupied and both pool tables were busy, with a long string of quarters lined along the upper edge of the cushioned sides of the tables. The amount of alcohol being consumed always boggled his mind, as did the relative paucity of violence, despite often-loud verbal exchanges that happened from time to time.

Paul picked a table where he could keep his back to the wall, sip his snifter of Drambuie, and continue his rumination. He thought about all of the research on the history of both Southeast Asia and the drug trade. He was continually shocked by the psychopathic underlayment of it all.

The unfeeling exploitation of other humans for profit was sickening. The magnitude of the greed quotient was staggering. He was constantly struck by the enormity of the lack of empathy involved when it came to most humans and the fruitless search for enough—especially money, but food, sex, comfort, anything that could be bought and sold, anything that seemed as if it were vitally necessary to sustain an inflated lifestyle. He owned the extraordinary power of his projections. He worked all the time to ameliorate it, seeking down often-tenuous vine-like lines of thought and emotion to find the roots of his discontent and perceived deficiency. It seemed that most humans externalized inner needs and desires, then sought them outside of themselves.

It reminded him of an old creation story that spoke of the gods living a grand and lavish life in the heavens while proto-humans suffered relatively in a form of slavery—until the gods suddenly noticed that the humans were becoming increasingly organized and were starting to demand god-like qualities. The gods had a conference and decided: "Let's cut each of them in half! Then they will spend all of their time looking for their other halves and will leave us alone!" And so, they did, and the rest is history.

He knew that theoretically, everyone was completely responsible for all of the events of their own lives, including pre-birth artifacts such as choice of parents and the circumstances of birth. This line of thought was excruciatingly painful for him because he did not want to believe that he had chosen all the suffering he had endured. It was simply incomprehensible. No one in their right mind would have chosen such an egregious and anguish-filled life.

His investigation invariably led him to utter despair either at being responsible for a highly toxic pre-birth decision; or that he was delusional prior to birth and his entire life had been spent in psychotic denial. Either way he wasn't entirely happy with the results, and so far, had been able to integrate the possibilities.

He had at least occasionally dreamed of having killed thousands of people through the course of his timeline, in every manner possible, but often quite bloodily and with maximum violence. He had dreamed of it so many times that he felt it was true, as if it were a curse he'd carried like his unmoored dead who came to him like spectral figures appearing out of the late-night fog, or as flashbacks in a crowded street in The City, his city.

He looked up from his aromatic snifter and realized he had drifted off in a reverie. His journal still lay open before him. Looking up and focusing his eyes, he spied a fleeting, almost phantasmic figure walking out through the front door of Gino's. He stood as if to follow, but instinctively knew he would be far too late. When he looked back down at the table, he noticed a small piece of paper folded neatly in half sitting next to his black-pebble covered journal.

CHAPTER FIVE
GIVING THANKS

San Francisco   **Thursday, November 23rd, 1995: 1431**

Machiavelli had written many succinct gems during the course of his life, but one of Paul's favorites was that "The victors write history." That was how it came to pass that the distorted version of Thanksgiving came to be embraced as official. There had been no equal exchange of food and gifts. The plain truth was that the native folk had saved the goddamn Euro settlers from utter extinction, people who had absolutely no idea how to live in the wilderness and fend for themselves on land whose use had been granted them initially by the indigenous people who had occupied it for thousands of years. Paul had also refused to acknowledge the primacy of Columbus after hearing the truth about him that had been recorded by the Dominican Bartolomé de Las Cassas, (and suppressed by the Vatican for over 500 years) about Christopher Columbus. Murder, rape, torture, all manner of hideous crimes committed by and permitted by him and his alcoholic crew.

But for Paul, it was far simpler. He truly loved the "traditional" turkey dinner and the surrounding gathering, even though he despised "the holdase" generally as specious, irrelevant opportunities to create hysterical spectacles of often maudlin content, based upon stories created by White people to frame themselves as "saviors of the savages," who had thousands of years of culture and history in the Americas long before the arrival of the Europeans. The stories as well as the culture of the Whites were simply used to justify the genocide of indigenous peoples, and brand them in a Christianized format so as to exploit them for profit—the White man's greatest sin and disease, greed.

Greed was a rampant infection that antibiotics could not cure; that kept feeding on itself and getting stronger like a cancer, more virulent, more pervasive, insatiable. No matter what the context, no matter what arena in which it showed itself, it was unstoppable, fed by the deep underground wellsprings of unrequited and unintegrated shame—all in service of attempting to alter one's consciousness to feel "better." It was an epidemic, an international phenomenon, sullying every soul it touched, propelled by the never-ending struggle of individuals to regain their birthright of autonomy and unconditional love, warped and stolen by toxic, fascist cultures.

It was the most pervasive of all addictions, yet it was rarely acknowledged or treated clinically because of the common assumption that everybody is greedy; that everybody is "out for Number One!"; that most people lack compassion and the desire to connect—yet this insidious artifact underlay all psychiatric symptoms and the entire nosology of "mental illness." Psychiatry kept adding to the vast number of "diseases" inferred from behaviors while the vast majority of practitioners never even touch upon the intensity of shame as a precursor for all of the symptoms for which were prescribed the latest and greatest drugs *du jour*. As all of these drugs directly impact the prefrontal cortex (PFC) of the brain, whatever "effects" they might have on behavior were always at the cost (ultimately) of creating widespread brain-damage. The process totally aligned with the for-profit society, and making extraordinary amounts of money both directly through psychiatric services and pharmaceutical dispensing, as well as such services as aftercare, residential treatment, police services, the prison industry and even by funding agencies like the Psychiatric Security Review Board (PSRB) used to force reluctant or recalcitrant "clients" to take meds and shock treatment against their will. All in all, it was a true cash cow.

Paul sighed and truly wished he had not awakened to this particular old rant, but he was, as now, so often struck by the general miasma of denial and indifference that most people embraced, accompanying the slow erosion of civil rights sacrificed for the specious notion of "security." If it were the only corrupt venue with which one needed to deal, or that required changing in order to set a true course of relative sanity, it would be a relatively simple matter to clean it up and allow a mature, sane, sensible and caring society to emerge from its chrysalis and fly free like a butterfly. But, instead, every caring and concerned citizen had to face an interlocking web of toxic relationships conspiring together to develop a cohesive influence that impacted all parts to create a profit scheme by manipulating the citizens into becoming production-and-consumption machines without their willingness or consent—"good little consumers."

Paul had raged as long as he could remember against the nature of the society into which he had been born. Driven by his angst and the ever-accumulating pressure of what he felt, he was driven to tears at least once a week. The more he investigated, the more he despaired of finding a solution to the vast conundrum with which he (and all of humanity) had been presented. He felt it very personally, no matter how many times other people said to him "It's just business," or told him to "Let it go!" because it was beyond his pay grade, he was unable to stop worrying it like the proverbial dog with a succulent bone. And what drove it all was the fear and frustration that he would never be able to manifest his true potential, the burning, aching love that lived in his heart, and the desire to somehow influence humanity in a positive way; to go counter to the seeming eternal subjugation of humans to a machine-like overlay that had developed into a heroin-like relationship. The programming was incredible! Even before birth, parents start mapping the lives of their children, believing that a symbiotic relationship with the existing order was necessary to survive; that one must bow down in fear and praise to the great god-idols who both demanded and controlled their fealty and owned the actual products created—and kept the bulk of the money for themselves. He remembered a line from ones of his old poems, called *Eco-Promise*:

There is a day of reckoning coming

For all of us who for so long have worshiped

The great god Technos

Have knelt in obeisance at his polished metal shrines,

Have bent our knees in fear and awe and trepidation

At his massive mechanical altars.

It struck him again and again how ineluctably intertwined the artifacts of daily life were with the inner states that preceded them, that birthed them into manifestation. It always led to the question of which conditioned which, as there seemed to be a continuous flow between what he saw as two halves of the same seamless whole constantly impacting the other.

He remembered reading the classic three-volume series by John Bowlby on *Attachment*. Following his research on vervet monkeys, chimpanzees and other mammals, Bowlby concluded that all mammals have a natural tendency to seek the safety of their mothers by moving into closer proximity when threatened or in the presence of danger. Such a sense of safety inevitably leads to developing healthy emotional expression and the ability to regulate internal states. He called this *secure attachment* and said that it applied to 70% of all humans. The rest of humanity developed some form of an *insecure attachment* that manifested in a variety of ways, including anxious-ambivalent (when the mother is unable to soothe the infant after an absence); anxious-avoidant (when the infant avoids or rejects proximity); and disorganized (in which the infants acts oppositionally or fearfully, in reaction to the relatively boundaryless attentions of a caregiver with substance abuse or violence issues). Zerbe's work influenced his thinking too, especially a classic passage that referenced a mother maintaining a too-close tie to her child, creating a "highly pathological nexus with the baby fulfilling many of the mother's needs for care, warmth and attachment... and with the child fulfilling the function of an addictive object." This so perfectly described his relationship with his own mother that had informed and shaped all of his later strategies with women. Paul thought of it as his own particular brand of "emotional retardation."

CHAPTER SIX
FURTHER DEVELOPMENTS

San Francisco   Tuesday November 28th, 1995: 1633

Paul shook his head, sitting at his writing desk, and re-read the scrawled notation. It was just a phone number (he absently noted that it was an Inner Richmond exchange), and the simple words: "Call me."

He vacillated between calling because it might just be humbug and a burning curiosity that had driven him to look at the note over and over and decide to not act on it.

It was intriguing. It could just be a severely mentally ill person, or a total stranger. If it were actually Roach—Jesus, what might that mean? If it were he, that meant that he was still alive; that he had survived the A Shau and the 'Nam; and that he was alive in San Francisco. Whether he was well as well was yet to be determined.

And if so, what the fuck? How had he managed to track Paul down? And why? Jesus, it was just a chance meeting at an obscure chopper pad twenty-seven bloody years ago!

Paul made another coffee of his favorite blend and prepared to pick up the narrative flow of the manuscript simply by re-reading the previous paragraph or two.

Of course, in and of itself dismissing Roach was not a solution,

especially as it took him back in space and time to Camp Evans—
and of course, brought him metaphorically face-to-face with Roach
and all of thousands, tens of thousands of memories he carried,
would always carry, though he had managed to shed much of the
pain associated with them, washed away in oceans of cleansing tears
and untold quantities of drugs.

He worked for intensely two hours without any awareness of time
passing, deeply immersed in the flow as the memories took him back
in time, captivated by the flashing, sparkling neural connections that
lit him up and flooded his nervous system. He felt as if he were on
an old school, out-of-control Tilt-A-Whirl. He surrendered in to the
unfolding of the libraries in his skull as they unfolded
simultaneously at both regular speed and super-slow motion, such
that he was able to capture all of the sights and sounds, even smells
and tastes, that were endemic to the original, imprinted moments—
and he was able to retrieve and record them in exquisite detail as
both speeds unfolded together.

It had been very purgative. As he emerged from his demi-trance,
the material simply unfolding as if it had been held, waiting for him
to arrive at the proper intersection of awareness and openness to tap
into the correct sequences in his brain as it facilitated or suppressed
the proper hormones and neurotransmitters, and allowed the magical
material to seemingly simply appear in his consciousness as clearly
as on a television screen.

And then the decision presented itself again, as if it had been on hold. Could it possibly be Roach? It seemed impossible, yet...

It was still relatively early and he chose to give himself another half hour to sort through his feelings. It was one of his favorite avoidance tactics, setting a time in the future at which to act on something in the present with which he felt incapable or unwilling to do. It did help sometimes, treated like a good piece of beef that had to be marinated and given a long, slow cook in order to be delectable. The more deeply he went into his own healing, the more he was able to release increments of traumatic material stored in his "vault," held there as if sacred verses scripted and stored in sealed clay containers against a future day when their intent and content would be better appreciated and appropriate. He had come to believe in the value of everything, including his own worst memories and experiences.

This was an enormous departure for him, after having endured many years of holding the rigid and implacably doctrinaire belief in the victimization in which he had been so long entrenched, a stance that allowed for his constant vigilance and rage at the circumstances of his birth and the consequent unfolding of the events of his life. In a client, he would have called it obsessive, even delusional. There was a certain logic to this progression of thoughts and the resulting conclusion, as there always was in any good delusion. It was only the initial false premise that distinguished it. There was no denying the original traumatic experiences.

In her parasitic grasping to redeem herself, to make herself surreptitiously more relatively whole, his mother had worked assiduously to parasitize his autonomy. He had learned to win by losing; to suppress his autonomy was the twisted solution she had molded—a perfect solution as far as she was concerned.

He had been resisting intrusion his entire life, seeking space in which to operate, to move within himself—especially since he had internalized so much of her poison (a process called "introjection"). Working through these psychic entanglements had been the continuing work of his lifetime. All of his work had paid a handsome dividend. He knew he was a true seeker after the truth; no longer doubting his own sincerity or open heartedness; secure in his identity and his sensitivity. His intuition was stronger than ever; he was able to practice his own idiosyncratic path to utilizing his healing skills based his mood-altering processes to a land of abstinence and a modicum of inner peace. He was living proof of William Blake's famous dictum from *Proverbs of Hell*: "The road of excess leads to the palace of wisdom."

CHAPTER SEVEN
THE DOOR OPENS

P aul steeled himself, more against his own anxiety than the actual fact of making the phone call itself.

He had totally torqued up the tension about making this call! He chided himself briefly, then sat down on his favorite leather couch, set his cup of coffee on a coaster on the teak end table and called.

The phone rang. And rang. And rang again. He remembered once letting a phone ring just to see how long it would take before he got disconnected. This was, of course, in the good old days of Ma Bell's rule, and listened for a full three minutes. Not so in this case.

"What?" answered a gruff, menacing voice.

"What do you mean 'What?'"

"What do you mean by 'What do I mean What?'"

"You fucking gave me this number! Who is this?"

There was a silence that reigned for the better part of twenty seconds, and then an almost whispered "Oh."

"'Oh' is all I get?"

"I wasn't sure you would actually call."

"Well I did! And I ask again 'Who is this?'"

"You know who it is. Or at least you suspect."

"Not good enough. Who is this?"

"Did you ever have a nickname?"

"Not since I was a kid. I don't like nicknames."

"No. More recently. Say, in a foreign land."

This particular inquiry struck Paul, and he felt his anger and anxiety dissipating somewhat.

"Ah. You mean a long time ago, 'in another world so far away,'" he said, citing an old Van Morrison line.

"Yes. Now you're getting it."

"Then tell me your *nom de guerre*! Even better, you could tell me what the fuck you want!"

"'*Nom de guerre*,' huh?"

"If you're who I think you are, you'll know exactly what I am talking about."

"I do, brother. It's Doc Roach here."

"When did I last see you?" asked Paul, testing further.

"Sitting on a chopper pad at Camp Evans, I-Corps, RVN."

"Jesus! It really is you! You been ghosting around in my peripheral vision! I thought I must be hallucinating!"

"I had a hard time believing it was you too."

"I must have made a hell of an impression on you, to remember me after all these years!"

"Actually, it was that fucking red weed!" And the both started laughing.

"Jesus, Roach? What the fuck?"

"I'd like to get together and... have a little chat."

"OK," said Paul, though the way he articulated it made it sound like it had five vowels.

"No place too public. And not my place. Not now. Not yet."

Considering possibilities, Paul had a tinge of concern about what seemed to be the man's excessive wariness.

"When?"

"How about tonight? I'm usually up pretty late."

"Me too. Where?"

"You live anywhere near where I saw you?'

"Yes."

"How about the midnight show at the Great Star Theater? On Jackson?"

Paul laughed, remembering a long stretch in the early Seventies when he had regularly attended Chinese Kung Fu films at the theater owned by Run Run Shaw to show Cantonese and Mandarin films that he and his brother produced. Now it featured occasional four-hour long Chinese opera performances.

"Is it still even open?"

"The Chinese National Opera Company is in town and putting up a production. I'll meet you out front and we'll go from there. I really need to talk to you."

"You're on, brother."

Built in 1925, the building retained many of the trappings of the original theater, even after the remodel. Paul walked up Grant toward Jackson and then turned east. He checked all four quadrants as he approached the building. He failed to see Roach, though he passed a man mid-block who resembled a drunken down-and-outer transplanted from the Tenderloin. As he passed him, the fellow muttered "Follow me!" out of the side of his mouth.

Paul simply did a double-take and then followed him twenty feet behind down Jackson, watching his wool-capped head bob and disappear down the nighttime streets—they passed Kearney, Montgomery, Sansome, as the crowds thinned and shifted in quality. By the time they reached Battery, they were the only people on the street. Roach led confidently, never once looking behind to see if Paul were still following. They went past Front, then Davis, until Jackson ended at Drumm, where they turned south and walked down Washington to the Ferry Building and caught the ferry for Sausalito. They still had not acknowledge each other, though Paul followed the enigmatic figure to the upper deck as they crossed San Francisco Bay in the fog and mist, in the rain and enveloping crispness of the

46

hibernal night. They could have been a thousand miles away on another continent, or on a rocket ship to another planet in interstellar space. They were alone in the open air, standing at the rail on the upper deck as the gallant ship plunged through the white-tipped waves that slammed against her bow.

Paul just waited, watching and wondering if this was to be a journey of adventure or misadventure. He stood there quietly questioning his sanity, not in a self-scathing, caustic way, or in the pseudo-jocular defensive way he normally used to fend off those who questioned his credentials or his mental status. This latter group irritated him intensely, especially as the inquisitor usually had far less education and/or experience than he. Plus they had the temerity to attempt to take the high ground in questioning Paul's "radical theories" (especially about shame-based childrearing and the emotional retardation that inevitably results), and taking refuge in stale and outworn theories, hiding in what Kuhn called "normal science" in the *Structure of Scientific Revolutions*, and not doing any cutting edge work or translating the data of their own experiences into real and enduring work as expert witnesses in and of their own lives.

No, he considered that he must have taken a flyer into genuine madness. Maybe he really was crazy. Elsewise what was he doing here on the midnight ferry heading to Sausalito on a winter night in the fog and rain? Many would question his judgment. Why not he?

CHAPTER EIGHT
UNFOLDING

San Francisco   **Sunday, December 3rd, 1995: 1123**

It was several days later before Paul had an uninterrupted span of time to process that windy, foggy night. He'd had another new client, preparation for a potential court testimony and two evaluations to complete. Appropriately enough, it was the ferry *Marin* that they had ridden to Sausalito.

They'd been alone on the upper deck, watching in reverent silence as the brooding hulk of the former Federal Penitentiary Alcatraz loomed up out of the fog to their north/northeast. Originally called "La Isla de los Alca traces," (the archaic Spanish word for "pelicans"), it had been a breeding ground for various types of pelicans, including the California brown for centuries, maybe millennia.

Paul listened to his intuition and allowed Roach to approach him. They had stood on opposite sides of the craft looking back at The City as Angel Island materialized out of the ethers, by which point they had both moved to the same rail, though still standing a number of feet apart. The island was almost entirely in jurisdiction of the city of Tiburon, but Fort McDowell, a small sliver at the eastern end, was claimed by the City and County of San Francisco, separated from the Marin County mainland by Racoon Strait.

Paul had had the foresight to add a hooded sweatshirt to his usual nighttime ensemble, so that, coupled with his Levi's jean jacket, he felt chilled but not cold. Roach seemed immune to the environment, standing stalwart as he gazed back at the skyline wearing only a t-shirt and a windbreaker. By the time the man finally spoke—*sotto voce* out of the side of his mouth, Paul had just about exhausted his patience.

"You've fucking dragged me the fuck out here to the middle of San Francisco Bay! Now what the fuck is going on?"

"I wasn't looking for you. I was here takin' care of business and I saw you on the street. So, I followed you around and found out you were a shrink."

"Actually, I'm a psychologist. I am not a psychiatrist!"

"What's the difference?"

"If you're looking for a prescription, you've got the wrong guy!"

"No! No! It's not that, man! I... I'm in trouble! I need some help!"

"I have seen you in beaucoup years, and now I'm supposed to help you! What the fuck?"

"It's, what do you call it? Serendipity!"

"Last time I saw you, you were blasted on tequila, weed and morphine! I'm surprised you remember anything at all!"

"It was that red weed you turned me onto!"

"That weed kept my memory alive all these years. I call

'Bullshit!'"

"When did you first see me? Around here?" Roach asked archly.

"I don't know. First time...maybe two weeks ago."

"I've been shadowing you for two months!"

"What?"

"Sneaking and peeping, brother!"

"Jesus! No?"

"I had to check you out before I let you see me."

"But why?"

"I told you, man. I need some help."

"With what?"

"I'm...on the run."

"From who?"

"I can't tell you that...yet."

"I'm supposed to take you at face value? You could just be boo-coo dinky dau!"

"No! Square business! Once we have a confidentiality agreement, I'll tell you everything!"

"Are you asking me to be your therapist?'

"I... really need some help."

"I'm a therapist, not an attorney!"

"I'm really worried, man! You got to help me!"

"But how?"

"Are we confidential?"

Paul pondered for a moment, and replied, "There are some caveats."

"What?"

"Standard stuff. I'm a mandatory reporter, so, if you admit to child abuse or elder abuse; or if you are actively homicidal or suicidal, I have to notify the authorities."

"I... I've killed a lot of people...in the 'Nam."

"That doesn't count. Actively homicidal."

"No, not that."

"How about the rest?"

"What? No! None of that!"

"OK. Provisionally, we have confidentiality. I'll need you to sign some official paperwork, at some point."

"So, we can talk?"

"Confidentiality is one thing. Whether I'm going to take you as a client is another."

"Oh, fuck you!"

"You fucking act like I owe you something!"

"I've got money! I can pay!"

"I'm expensive!"

"How expensive?"

"I usually charge $100 an hour."

"I'm boo-coo fucked up!"

"Tell me what you're experiencing."

"I'm on the run. My memories are kicking my ass! I can't sleep!"

"It could be any number of things!"

"You're the fucking expert! Help me!"

"My usual approach is to deconstruct the client's experiences so that I can assist the client in letting go of old pain, and make better choices freed of the pain."

"And you really think that method will work for me?"

"Are you clean? Right now?"

"I drink too much and smoke a lot of weed. But, no, I'm off the hard shit!"

"How long?"

"Have I been clean?"

"Yes."

"Sometimes when things get really bad, I do a little run. Two, three days. But not now for twelve...no, thirteen months."

Paul's standing rule was to never take a client who was not at least a year clean and/or sober. His long experience with his own addictions, as well as those of hundreds, maybe even thousands, of clients, had convinced him that the client had to have relinquished his or her dedicated, codependent relationship with the substance of choice to be able to benefit from doing the necessary deeper work.

He and Roach moved into the cabin of the ship, especially since it was deserted, and they could continue talking without being overheard. It seemed especially important to Roach.

"We really gotta keep this on the down low," said Roach in a more normal tone, though still subdued.

"I'm with you, brother. Where do you want to start?"

"There's boo-coo stuff I need to sort out."

"Sound like you definitely have PTSD. Do you have a disability rating with the VA?"

At first Roach looked stung, the jerked his head back and broke out in a maniacal laugh bordering on a shriek as Paul looked on, caught between bemusement and concern.

"I'm so fucking tired! I've been running for a long time. If I could get a disability pension, I'd be in fucking heaven! I might finally get some rest."

"Obviously it goes a lot deeper than that."

"So, what are we going to do?"

"I think the more relevant question is: What do you want to do?"

"Are you going to help me?"

"Yes, but with some more caveats."

"What's that mean?"

"No more midnight ferries to Sausalito!"

CHAPTER NINE
THE DEVIL IS ALWAYS IN THE DETAILS

Sausalito   Monday, December 4th, 1995: 0112

T hey disembarked in Sausalito and made their way to Bridgeway. Roach didn't seem to know his way around, so Paul led them to the No Name Bar.

"What are you having, gents? Gotta be quick. Closing time soon."

"Just need a couple of quick pops to warm up. Thanks. I'll have a Drambuie. A double. In a snifter. Unheated."

Roach got into a brief discussion with the bartender about single malt scotches. After being told they did not have Talisker, he asked for a double Laphroig neat with water on the side.

They procured their drinks and moved to a Naugahyde-tufted banquette deeper in the room.

"OK, man. You've impressed me with your stealth skills and your knowledge of good scotches. Now tell me what this is all about."

"This is not the most confidential of settings!"

"Give! Now! Or I'm gone!"

Roach was silent for several long moments, and then looked up and cracked a crooked smile.

"I thought I was boo-coo fucked up in the 'Nam, but it's worse now."

He sat silently while holding Paul's eyes, then spoke.

"I really like morphine, the pins-and-needles rush, but there was always smack too, goddamn cheap and easy."

Now his smile took on a distinctive aura of dissonance, his eyes dimming as his speech slowed and grew softer. He seemed to be receding, withdrawing as recalled the littered path of his past—and the retrospective loss he was only now, feeling, and the attendant remorse that was just surfacing.

"It <u>was</u> a whole different life. You know how it is, being strung out," he said, presuming on the unwritten history that was inscribed on Paul's face and in his eyes.

"Only too well, man. My big trip was *cocaine*."

"The only time I got into that was skimming off loads in in Central America."

"I thought you were a skeg head!"

"I am. Always have been."

"And?"

"It was a situational thing. I did it because it was easy, close at hand."

"You stopped using smack because the coke was free and easy?"

"Temporarily. I never did like it. Made me too jumpy."

"And?"

He looked into the far distance for several long moments, then back at Paul, and said "Look man, there's a lot to this story. And you may find some parts of it unbelievable. But it's all true."

"So far you haven't told me shit!"

Again, Roach's voice was *sotto voce* as he replied.

"I'm not all that sure this is a secure location."

"What the fuck, man? It's a fucking bar!"

"I know. I know. But I have to be careful."

Paul allowed his anger to infuse his voice when he answered.

"Look, man. I haven't seen you in what, twenty-six years? And suddenly you come into my life acting like I owe you something."

"I have to be careful. My life could be in danger."

"And you're dragging me into this mess of yours, whatever it is? I don't think so!" Paul said throwing a twenty-dollar bill on the bar and started to rise.

Roach immediately put a hand on Paul's left forearm in a restraining gesture.

"OK. OK. I'll tell you the whole story. But not here. Let's walk."

They got to the sidewalk and started walking down Bridgeway, looking at the skyscape of The City sparkling in the far distance.

Paul was still angry. And he was not at all convinced that Roach wasn't just another messed up vet and that his story was a quasi-paranoid tale of woe.

"So, your life may be in danger. What else has changed in the last quarter-century? First thing I want to know is: what happened in the A Shau? And when did you get home?"

The other man took a deep breath and sighed, once then again.

"It was the usual clusterfuck! The so-fucking-called 'intelligence' was pretty worthless. You remember Hamburger Hill—the book, the film?"

"I left May 5. That didn't happen until after!"

"Intelligence fuck ups in the A Shau happened over and over before that!"

"OK. OK. I got that. So?"

"We got our asses handed to us on a plate—again! They kept using massed ground assaults like it was fucking World War Two again! Even Senator Edward Kennedy told Congress said it was 'senseless.'"

"All of the fucking 'brass' refused to take what we reported as accurate!"

"I remember! I remember!"

"We found a three-inch wide cable that supposedly led all the way over the border into Laos, and a sophisticated communications network all over the hill! It's how they could coordinate their attacks. And they fucking told me I was crazy when I said they'd penetrated our radio net! The NVA knew exactly what we were doing!"

"This is where it gets a little bit sideways."

"Quit stalling!"

"After the NVA withdrew, and things started winding down, calling in Dust Off, I decided to go get loaded, just a taste."

"Jesus!"

"You never used any junk, have you?"

"Just a little taste once or twice."

"Not the same. You know the old saying: 'You don't know what it is about until you get strung out.'"

"I say the same thing about cocaine."

"OK, so you kind of understand. I just needed a little taste to keep going."

"Got it."

"It must have been stronger than I remembered, or I was more fucking wiped out than I thought."

"What happened?"

"I thought I'd sit for just a little bit—and I actually nodded out."

"And?"

"I guess Battalion thought I was with my company, and the company thought I was with Battalion."

"Oh, shit!"

"I don't know how long I was out, but I woke up tingling."

"'Tingling?'"

"Yeah. Someone was watching me."

"Oh, shit!"

"I peeped out from under the brim of my boonie hat and didn't see anyone. But I couldn't shake the feeling."

"And?"

"Here I am in the fucking jungle, and I don't hear any human sounds—no troops, not helicopters, nothing."

Roach stopped for a moment, his eyes glazed and far away.

"Before I moved a muscle, I did another, really slow scan—and then the fucking tree line started moving—and here's these eyes in the middle of it, and suddenly somebody stepped out! Perfect camouflage! All I could only see was the whites of their eyes!"

"Gooks?"

"A Marine Force Recon team!"

"No shit?"

"I swear to God!"

"What the fuck were they doing there?"

"They'd been cross-border in Laos, and were working into the A Shau, sneaking and peeping. They'd heard us from way off, and laid doggo!"

"Jesus! Why?

"It wasn't their mandate. We had more electronic resources than they did anyway."

"Wow!" said Paul, genuinely stunned, as he always was by true tales from the boonies. He made a "come on" gesture with his right hand.

"They were all in black pajamas with camo paint on their faces. I didn't even see them until the trees and weeds started moving."

"One guy put a finger across his lips. Then another came close and whispered to me. The Navy corpsman assigned to their team was injured—and they needed my help." Everyone in Force Recon had some medical training, though only the Navy corpsman assigned was considered a Class One medic. A six-man team may or may not have had a Class One medic, whereas a twelve-man team always did.

"How'd they know you were a medic?"

"They could see my CMB. Plus I was carrying a .45. Most enlisted guys didn't."

"That's right. You're right. Crew chiefs and officers."

"I did some quick calculation and said to myself 'Fuck it! There's worse options.' And I went with them."

Paul laughed. "Oh, Christ!"

"Their guy was just writhing in pain, but keeping his mouth shut, keeping sound security. They'd applied pressure dressings to stanch the bleeding, but the guy was boo-coo fucked up."

"What'd you do?"

"I told them we needed a Dust Off immediately."

"And?"

"They said 'Fuck no!'"

"What? Why?"

"They were the blackest of black ops, man. And their radio had been shot to shit too. So, they were making their way back as best they could when they ran into me."

"We'll get him to an LZ, but we're just infiltrating. You're going to have to come with us until we complete this mission."

"Holy shit!"

"I was freaked! Then the guy looks at me and says, 'We're only sneaking and peeping.'"

"What did you say?"

"What could I say? It sure seemed like a better option than returning to the shit storm waiting for me at Evans."

"What about their medic?"

"I didn't have any syrettes," he said guiltily, "so I told them to get me some."

"And?"

"'No sweat, GI!'" he says, and hands me half a dozen syrettes."

"I must have looked really spooked. And the jarhead says to me, 'Hey! We're Recon. We get anything we want!'"

"'I'm fucking glad of that,' I said. And they kept me very-well supplied."

"I looked at their corpsman and he knew he was in the shit big time. He looked back at me and said 'You got to get me a doc. I can't lose my arm.'"

"I looked him in the eye and said, 'I'll do my very best, brother.' It sobered me up. Instantly clear and alert. I wasn't loaded anymore."

"Adrenaline overrode."

"Right. Gangrene had started to set in. He smelled it too. I see that the bone hadn't been set properly, so I had to take a chance on re-breaking it to set it properly. It couldn't wait. I'd seen it done at Battalion Aid..."

"Jesus!"

"It was either that, or doom the man to losing his arm, maybe his life."

"Pretty fucking bold, man!"

Roach was silent, his body language clearly enunciating that he was re-living the details of that day so long ago, so far away.

"So, what happened?"

"We had to hump a bit to get to a secure spot. I needed to build a little fire—to boil water, sterilize my instruments, wash my hands."

His face slackening even further, then he continued.

"They scouted out a little cave, pooled all of their water for me to use, set up a perimeter."

"How'd the corpsman do?"

"I just got him really loaded first. He did fine."

"What's that mean?"

"He didn't feel a thing! The bone wasn't as bad as I thought. I cleaned it up, sprinkled on a lot of sulfa powder and reset the bone."

Paul laughed. "God!"

"We had to lay doggo for two days, keep a secure perimeter. We were just maybe a click and a half from Laos!"

"Jesus! What did you do?"

"We kept him loaded up the whole time. We took two hour turns on watch in pairs. And the rest of them patrolled constantly."

"So? Tell me! What happened?"

"Two days later one of them contacted a Ruff-Puff patrol. He used their radio, one of the restricted channels, and got us some transport."

"Did you save his arm?"

"The doc at Battalion Aid wrote me a Letter of Commendation! He told Division I saved his arm and his life!"

"That saved you?"

"Division had me as MIA. Thought I might have been captured."

"Damn, man!"

"Then the fucking CID really ramped up the pressure around the missing morphine syrettes."

"Did they hassle you?"

"Word got around. I was a hero. The FR guys offered to take out the CID assholes!"

"Excellent!"

"So, I kind of got a break for a while."

"And?" asked Paul. He knew there had to be more.

"They couldn't give me a ceremony because it was all so underground, but they gave me an Army Commendation Medal. Then I got a promotion and they offered me an E-6 slot at Battalion Aid."

"No shit? Quite the celebrity!"

"Yeah, but it was fucked up! Too much attention!"

"Things cooled down, but I was still using. I started buying wholesale and piecing it off."

"'Piecing off?'"

"Break it down, sell smaller quantities."

"Oh. Dealing!"

Roach looked at him as if he were another species.

"Yeah. Right. I had access to Battalion Aid's equipment to measure out the dope, but I wasn't going to sell tenths. (A tenth of a gram is the usual Stateside heroin user's sale). I was making more than enough profit to support my habit."

"Of course."

"But I made sure everybody knew it was pure."

"Got it."

"So, it went from grams to eight balls (eighth of an ounce, or three and a half grams). I swear to God I never intended to get too deep into it!"

"When I first got home, I had to start selling weed because I couldn't find anything, but shit weed that cost too much. Then it was pounds, and hundred-pound bales!"

"Everybody at Battalion knew I was strung out, but I was untouchable!"

"And?"

"How did you know there was an 'And?'"

"Had to be! Everything was going too well!"

"Fuck you! You can't possibly know that!"

"I'm smarter than you look!"

"Fuck you, man!"

"Very articulate! Very intelligent!"

Suddenly a Marine K-Bar Combat Knife was in his hand, pressed tightly against Paul's throat.

"Shut the fuck up and tell me how you knew!"

"Back away with the knife, man!"

Roach let up slightly on the pressure but held it steady.

"It's part of my job to know things that others don't tell me."

He withdrew the knife further but continued to glare at him.

"I'm as good at what I do as you are at what you do."

Now he pulled the knife back completely, and it disappeared into the sheath up his left sleeve.

"Sin loi, motherfucker!" he said, reflecting. "Tell me more."

"If we were to look at your life, there would be a series of tumbling dominos leading up to this moment. If you had never experienced traumatic events, we wouldn't be here today. You wouldn't need my help. It's really that simple—but based on decades of education, training and experience."

"You're a very strange man."

"Thank you, said the kettle to the pot."

CHAPTER TEN
OF COURSE

Sausalito to San Francisco Monday, December 4th, 1995: 0243

They continued to walk, down Bridgeway to the Sausalito Yacht Club, all the way past Waldo Point—then reversed directions and walked back up Caledonia, past Pine, Bee, Litha and Napa Streets, deeply immersed in conversation—flashing back and forth through the decades, across longitudes and latitudes, traversing the continents; through the jungles, alluvial plains, deserts, frozen tundra's, and immeasurably deep oceans.

"How ever did you escape the malicious attentions of the CID?"

"By getting even more strung out than ever."

"You are a crazy motherfucker."

By the time they had traversed the little burg's back streets, they were both still animated and far from ready to call it a night. They wandered down to the hub at the center of the town and both of them decided they were hungry. Paul had not been sleeping mentally in mistaking this meeting simply as a reunion. It was clearly an interview with a potential client. The reunion side was going fine, a good connect. Other than vague generalities though, they had not yet gotten to exactly what the man wanted. He was truly the master of circumambulating storytelling.

"As good as it's been, our having this little reunion," said Paul, when they had settled into the back seat of a taxi that was taking them to the Peppermill Restaurant in Corte Madera, a 24/7 establishment that served excellent food—and had the benefit of being staffed by very hot looking hostesses in sexy outfits.

It was busy, even at 0300. As they entered, several heads turned. The restaurant had a longstanding reputation as an after-hours gathering spot for dope dealers and other underground characters. Paul knew that the intensity of their energy made them more visible and interesting to others, their shared past containing a unique power that bound them through time. Roach had ducked his head as they entered and headed for the furthest corner booth in an alcove on the left. He took a corner seat, facing the room, and Paul slid in to his immediate right with a similar but slightly more obtunded view. Paul flashed for a moment that they were still deep in a Southeast Asian jungle.

They were quickly given set ups, menus, water and coffee. From long acquaintance (dating to the days of the cocaine flow), Paul was already well-versed in what was on offer. He decided to have a Belgian waffle (crisp), three eggs over quickly and a double side of sausage patties. Roach ordered the mushroom and cheese omelet, side of crisp bacon and two well-toasted English muffins. He inquired about lemon marmalade but agreed to raspberry jam instead.

Having refused to talk in the back of the taxi, Paul now prodded

Roach to continue his monologue.

"What did you mean you got more 'strung out than ever?'"

"I stopped giving a shit about anybody knowing!"

"What the fuck?"

"It was such freedom to not pretend!"

"Jesus! How the fuck did that work?"

"There's a missing piece here. Something I didn't tell you about!"

"So, tell me."

"I developed a kind of immunity from ordinary bullshit."

Roach fell silent as their luscious waitress approached, both arms lined with plates full of victuals. When she moved out of earshot, Paul set to immediately after saying a Native Indian-flavored prayer of gratitude for the food and all who had had a part in its coming to him. Roach did not bother with such niceties and had finished almost half of his plate by the time Paul finished praying. The other man ate with his head bent close to the plate, eyes constantly scanning by quadrants.

"But how?" Paul felt he needed to prod the other man yet again.

"I became important, to certain people."

"'Certain people?'"

Roach took a deep breath and sighed.

"There's so much...You can't understand what happened next...

"So, again I ask, what do you want from me?"

"There's more you need to know, or it won't make sense."

"Just give me the short version."

"I got involved with ...the people..."

"Just tell me!"

The young waitress approached with the coffee pot and they both took a grateful refill. Paul nodded his thanks.

"The fucking drug trade is so much bigger than anyone knows!"

Paul sat quietly and waited for Roach to go on.

"I...my military job became a kind of joke."

"What's that mean?"

"I started moving lots of smack."

"And?"

"I kept getting...pushed up the food chain. I had good connections and I spoke fluent Viet."

"And?"

"I've got some stuff here you might not want to hear."

"What? You think I'm white bread or something?" Paul felt insulted. His innate intelligence always led him to believe that he was at least as knowledgeable and worldly experienced as anyone.

72

"No! Hell no! It's just that, well, I been places and done things you might find unbelievable."

Paul huffed heavily, then responded "I am aware of the global drug trade and how the United States has been participating for boo-coo long time!"

Roach looked down his nose coolly and asked "How long?"

"I know about the Opium Wars in the Nineteenth Century. And about the deal the CIA made with the Thai Mafia after the French lost at Điện Biên Phủ in 1954."

Roach looked at him again appraisingly and said "Then you know more than most people."

"So, are you going to educate me some more?"

They again both fell silent as the waitress checked to see if they wanted anything else, and Paul could not help but quip "Only if you have 911 on speed dial!"

As she retreated, having left the check on the table half way between the two of them. Paul waited to see if Roach would make any effort to grab the check.

"The missing piece is what the Green Beanies were actually doing there."

"Tell me more."

"Protecting and guarding the opium crop."

"And?"

"That means that 'The G' is, and has been, involved in international drug trade for a long, long time!"

"Since the US made a deal with Lucky Luciano before the invasion of Naples?"

"Absolutely! Straight up trade! For help infiltrating resistance groups, Luciano would get 'ten years with no interference with his heroin trade after the war.'"

"And that fucking rotten scumbag J. Edgar Hoover claiming to Congress for what? Thirty-three years? That there was 'no organized crime in America!'"

"I got a 'special assignment' to go out with a black ops team to 'an undisclosed location.'"

"Why you?"

"I had been wanting to start moving more product. This was supposed to be me getting my hands dirty. Or dirtier, I guess."

"I'm not sure what you mean."

"They called it a kind of initiation. A welcome to the brotherhood. I was being asked to join kind of a crime family."

"But why you?"

"I was known and trusted. I had access to Army vehicles; got as much time as I needed to go where I needed; had armed escorts and drivers; I hardly had to report for duty. They liked me, liked the fact that I was a combat vet; liked the fact that I was strung out but keeping the business part tight."

The waitress brought the coffee pot again and refilled their cups. In his head, Paul added five extra dollars to her tip for her being circumspect and polite.

"Who?"

"Ah. I really can't name names."

"Again, why you?"

"Let's just say that I had proven to be trustworthy. Certain people liked me."

"Aww, come on man! You keep dancing around any question I ask that has any depth!"

"I fucking told you! I cannot name names! And it's not really, whatchamacallit, germane to the story!"

Paul took a deep breath and sighed.

"Maybe we have come far enough for now. I kind of need a break. To get home, get some rest. Where are you staying?"

"Why?"

"I want to get back to The City. I've got shit to do tomorrow."

"Why do you want to know where I'm staying?"

"OK. I will make this a lot clearer! Are you coming back to The City with me or what? Because I fucking want to go. Right now!"

Roach froze momentarily, scowling, and then smiled a wry smile that slowly spread to his entire mouth. He grabbed the check unceremoniously, looked at the total, reached into his pocket and pulled out a huge roll of bills. Then he peeled off a fifty-dollar bill and laid it on top of it.

"Let's call a cab and sky up!"

"I'm with you, brother! Are you coming back to The City with me?"

"And even better. I'm gonna pay for the cab!"

"You don't have to do that, man!"

"No! Fair's fair. Plus, I want to do this," he said, and pulled the thick roll out and peeled off six fifty-dollar bills.

"I want this 'relationship' between us to be straight up. You are worth my time. Let's ruck up!"

There must have been a cab cooping in the parking lot, because as soon as Paul and Roach emerged from the restaurant's front door, they were able to settle into the back seat of a very comfortable Marin Cab—and made the driver very happy when Paul told him that their destination was North Beach.

"Just sit back, gentlemen, and enjoy the ride!"

CHAPTER ELEVEN
NEXT STEPS

Paul had felt so exhilarated when he got back to his place that all he wanted to do was write. But as soon as he walked through the door, he realized that he was quite exhausted, and barely managed to brush his teeth before he dropped his clothes in a heap and fell in bed, musing about the long, strange night it had been.

As he drifted off, he had an intuitive flash that he was ripe for incubating a dream. He started breathing deeply as he drifted off, and formulated the question he was going to ask the Universe (or his deepest self at least) to answer: was it in the best interest of all concerned that he continue working with Roach? He also added addendums as to likely outcomes, which usually came to him in some form of a branching road, or a diagram broken into layers.

He awoke groggy six hours later, infused with the remnants of a series of dreams. The primary stream was extremely clear: The brief but ancient bond between he and Roach was still in effect, exponentialized into the present as an insistent reminder that there was work between them still to be done. He breathed deeply into the quasi-lucid fog that hovered around the edges of his consciousness, and then caught the tail of a trail that led to an opening, as if from a game trail into a forest glade or clearing filled with filtered, dappled sunlight. He was immediately struck with numerous lines of awareness that seemed to ride the energy of the sunbeams into a deeper clarity.

As if he were being initiated into the Great Mysteries, his brain flooded with streams of information more pictures than words, each containing a depth of knowledge thick like a bag full of packed cells flowing into an insensate body, absorbing the long-awaited nutrients. Today's dream was unusually clear, even for he who usually garnered hidden, mystical knowledge from his dream journeys. There were several vectors that ended in pools of golden sunlight that infused him with effusive and effulgent light. In yet another pathway, Roach disappeared into, and was absorbed by, the encroaching future. There was yet another line that confirmed his suspicion that Roach was well and truly delusional. There was one line that was shrouded in an even deeper darkness that emanated from a cavernous opening, emitting a malevolence presence that was repelling, even in memory, and filled Paul with an ominous foreboding. The dream showed Roach lying on the ground, not breathing, inert and lifeless. It frightened him, yet it passed through him without his attaching any added significance. He knew instantly that he would withhold it from Roach.

Roach had kept the cab when he had dropped Paul off, leaving Paul no way of getting a hold of him or where he might be living. Nonetheless, the dream was extremely clear that, while Roach undoubtedly had PTSD, there was a distinct possibility that Roach had gotten immersed in a delusional fantasy. Conversely, it might all be absolutely true, and he was about to get involved in the most complex case of his life.

Paul decided to immediately seek consultation assistance, to discuss his quandary confidentially. He admitted that he needed expert assistance and utter confidentiality to sort through the many possibilities being presented. He felt intuitively that he needed to speak with Karen Farrington. She was a brilliant, pert, lively, beautiful and intelligent woman who completely belied the stereotyped thinking that was projected upon her (almost exclusively by men)—that because she was beautiful and had a great mind, that she should be relatively easy to manipulate and cajole with charming manners and sweet talk. The truth of the matter was far, far different. Not only was she bright and articulate, she was one of the few clinicians (male or female) with whom he could discuss anything on his own level, and very rarely, if ever, have to explain himself. She had gone immediately from her Doctoral program into private practice, and now did primarily consulting work with other clinicians.

"Karen Farrington."

"Hello, Karen. Paul Marzeky here."

"Paul! Good to hear you!"

"It's good to be heard!" he quipped.

"What can I do for you?"

"Actually, I was hoping you might have some time available to meet with me. Soon."

"Not today. But if you were willing to break your iron clad rule about not getting up early, I could sneak you in before my regular schedule. Can you be here at 0800?"

Paul groaned inwardly. Paul never saw any clients until 1200. Conversely, he often held open appointments for 2000.

"Wow! You are a hard task mistress!"

"You called me! If you don't want that appointment, it'll have to be next week."

"Oh, hell no! I'll be there!"

Paul spent the rest of the day preoccupied with thoughts of the previous evening. He would never have imagined that he'd go drinking with someone who was becoming a client. That would have to stop, of course, once they signed the paperwork and they formalized the therapeutic relationship.

Since he was up early (relatively speaking, since any time before noon was early for him), he decided to make the most of it. After brewing a single cup of his favorite brew, he sat savoring it while he contemplated what for him was the core of his creative life. The manuscript was moving along, even though he had gotten kind of frozen. It wasn't a real block, but his production was less than prodigious. It was frustrating. He had not been "in the flow" very much recently, devoting the bulk of his time either to building up his practice, attending to his clients or the minutiae required to keep the machine running—writing case notes, treatment plans and evaluations; billing and answering the inevitable inquiries from other clinicians and invitations to workshops and seminars, all of which were invitations to attend at an exorbitant price, none an invitations to speak.

He had seemingly been working intermittently on the newest novel, *Spirals of Time*, though he was considering yet another re-write of what had previously been *Brotherhood* (and was now re-named *Crazy Tales* as a kind of double entendre). He had decided to shift the point-of-view of the protagonist to that of himself working in combat psychiatry rather than the adopted (and therefore false in many ways) perspective of a combat infantryman. He was re-counting some very dark days in his earlier life when he had been too depressed to work (on an in-patient psychiatric unit, of all places!) and had been on medical leave for a year. He remembered it so vividly, punctuated as it was by vast and unrelenting oceans of tears and sorrow, flushing out old toxins while building for a new future. It was the prelude to an awakening (great title, that!).

The true magic of the process lay in the evocative remembering and the lyrical writing that grew out of it. It was transformative of both his emotions and the work in an alchemical kind of way—as if it had been necessary for him to suffer the trials and travails that he had in order to return like Jason with his personal Golden Fleece as a talisman of his journey, a gift for his people rather than a personal implement for him to keep and cherish in a kind of twisted masturbatory process. It was a deeply cleansing process that allowed him to move more fluidly within himself, more completely expressing his heart's deepest needs in a liberating way that delivered him into realms previously unseen and unknown (even intuitively), transported him to previously unconceived realms of freedom and imagination. It was a journey into love in its purest sense, the most complete sense of recognition and validation he'd ever had. It allowed him to work more relatively freely without inhibition, fear of recrimination or having to pay slavish obeisance to cultural mores and social mandates. He felt fully released from the straightjackets of a lifetime, catapulting him into a process of continual homecoming for and to himself.

As the book continued to unfold magically under his fingertips, he always found himself expressing profound gratitude for having the opportunity to write, to express himself in words filling him with a musical urgency that would grace both his heart and his page. His real work, as he called it, allowed access to vagrant feelings and obscure emotions that might otherwise have escaped notice, especially in the common light driven by the format of ordinary life, and detailed to meet the hidden agendas of the oligarchs who ruled tyrannically over the furtive lives of everyone else like feudal lords, subjecting all others to the capricious whims of fickle whims, condemned to the vacuous, wretched twisted impulses of the darkest hearts of a cancerous humanity.

His writing was a blessing from the gods and goddesses, the eternal lords and ladies who oversaw the fates of humanity, and allowed individuals to be diverted by their own devious devices, serving capricious drives and voracious appetites for hidden and forbidden treasures kept from the hearts and minds of ordinary citizens, as if the entire planet and all of its citizenry were its private play toys.

Paul so disagreed with the popular belief that one should not speak to one's aches and pains, the injustices and petty ignorance that seem to infuse daily life. In much the same vein, he completely disagreed with those clinicians who argued that abreactive work on traumatic memories was dangerous because it "might exacerbate" trauma instead of helping relieve it—as if putting band aids on an arterial laceration were the treatment of choice.

After a timeless time in the mystical, mythical zone where it did not exist, he looked up and saw that the clock had moved forward three and a half hours, yet it seemed to him but fifteen minutes. Clinically, it could be considered to be dissociative; or a measure of absorption that was an aspect of the autohypnotic state. It was a celebration of his gift, being able to become so focused, so immersed in the glory of his thought-dreams and visions that he lost all normal sense of the passage of time, while his mental and emotional faculties graduated into higher states—though strictly speaking the latter was his interpretation of his altered states, albeit induced by joy and wonder, even reverence, as opposed to those on the darker end of the menu, like delirium-induced dreams and hallucinatory experiences brought about by numerous illicit (actually illegal was more to the point, according to his thinking) drugs.

Legality was yet another aspect to be considered in his proposed treatment plan for Roach. He was going to explore with Karen, whether, beyond the requirements of mandatory reporting, that he might in any way be liable if he did not report other criminal activities that the man might mention. The new fascist direction in which the country was moving did not yet preclude mandatory reporters being required to become extensions of the State, even though the new egregious professional practices approved by the AMA and the APA encroached upon previously sacrosanct territories and heralded the deepening of the Therapeutic State in which patient's rights were routinely trampled in service of more "effective" or expeditious "treatment," such as happened regularly with "involuntary holds" that denied a person's civil rights if they were declared "Danger to Self, Danger to Others, or Gravely Disabled" in the august opinions of psychiatric authorities; and were therefore to be made available to the latest "accepted practices" that were actually experiments proposed by those whose medical and professional degrees obscured often malicious and fascist strains of thinking and feeling—allowing such barbarous practices as "electroshock therapy" (ECT) and drugging with brain-damaging chemicals in order to induce or produce what were considered to be the desired behaviors in people who were often intractable in their belief systems, frequently about the very authorities who were imposing their aberrant wills upon them vis a vis "repairing their broken brains." It had happened before. One only had to view the many eminent "scientists" who enthusiastically endorsed and promoted eugenics beginning near the end of the late Nineteenth Century.

Of course, Paul believed that all such intrusions were in service of an even darker, more sinister goal, of micro-managing the lives of the entire citizenry in order to keep them industriously involved in producing and consuming, creating ever more profit to be funneled upward into the coffers of the "owners" of society." As he thought of this, he swiftly enumerated a list that he was compiling for *Crucible,* a direct bleed-through from his excavation of the toxic corporate structure that drove contemporary life.

1. Corporations commodify the artifacts of addiction; create the actual substances of addiction (tobacco and alcohol); provide places where addictions are practiced (casinos);

2. Corporations advertise and/or sell addictive substances and deny their potential toxicity—including all variety of pharmaceutical products, such as thalidomide and Phen-Fen;

3. Corporations create and profit from institutions that "treat" addictions (private "treatment" facilities), many that support the medical model whose treatment model is well known for simply recycling clients.

4. Corporations "own" a share of the criminal justice

"industry" in that they build and maintain privatized prisons.

5. Corporations perpetuate the myth of "mental illness," and profit from it by owning and maintaining "treatment" facilities that use brain-damaging, addictive chemicals; and promote the use of barbaric techniques like electroshock and lobotomies.

6. Corporations manufacture and advertise "medications," often knowing that the substances are toxic in their effects as well as their "side effects;"

7. Corporations benefit broadly from a variety of both service and

8. manufacturing industries that support war and the permanent war

9. economy—arms, and all other manner of products designed to more efficiently kill, maim, or injure. Corporations also profit greatly from supplying the government with such "needs," as well as from such businesses as "private security."

Even without considering a grand conspiracy theory, there was an interlocking web of connections linking everything. No matter how seemingly disparate or disjointed, everything ultimately fit. Everything feeds everything else—animal patterns, for example. When the veldt gets plenty of rain and the grasses and brush are lush, antelope, wildebeest and zebra herds flourish, and, in turn, lion and other predator herds grow exponentially larger because there was more nourishment available; and the females produce more young critters as they would have an increased chance of survival.

The human world was far more dysfunctional. Since humans had at least minimal access to their prefrontal lobes (despite the poor use they made of them), their depredations were far more egregious and widespread, allowing humans to ignore natural patterns and rhythms; and be delusional convinced (via media hype) that anything that was possible could or even should therefore be manifested.

No matter how strange or bizarre; no matter how unethical or moronic; no matter how self-destructive or ecologically unsound; no matter how expensive or insane; no matter how weird or antiquated; no matter how odd or draconian; no matter how unhealthy or ludicrous; no matter how inane or paralyzing; no matter how corrupt or violent; no matter how discordant or shocking; no matter how incredible or subliminal; no matter how monstrous or costly; no matter how shameful or wounding; no matter how beautiful or magnificent; no matter how elegant or ill-formed; no matter how tasteful or malignant; no matter how gross or incredible; no matter how tenuous or paranoid; no matter how toxic or noxious; no matter how ephemeral or wonderful; no matter how valid or incongruous; no matter how virtuous or banal; no matter how magnificent or absurd; no matter how terrible or flavorful; no matter how awesome or dangerous; no matter how tangential or threatening; no matter how splendid or virulent; no matter how satisfying or cavitating; no matter how lustful or abstemious; no matter how glorious or aromatic; no matter how unpleasant or vital; no matter how unctuous or tyrannical; no matter how trivial or fragrant; no matter how egregious or smooth; no matter how tremendous or wicked; no matter how stupendous or relentless; no matter how onerous or calamitous: no matter how taunting or cruel; no matter how tormenting or prejudicial; no matter how sweet or igneous; no matter how powerful or musical; no matter how tenuous or odiferous; no matter how admirable or tantalizing; no matter how lively or truncated; no matter how obdurate or deniable; no matter how incredible or tangy; no matter how obtunded or comfortable; no matter how tedious or nonpareil; no matter how smooth or obtunded; no matter how hot or twisted; no matter how obscure or juicy; no matter how tortured or digestible; no matter how bitter or strong; no matter how pungent or obscene; no matter how creamy or tactile; no matter how odious or prickly; no matter how beauteous or warm; no matter how damaged or true; no matter how sharp or false; no matter how slow or fluid; no matter how balanced or sticky; no matter how antiquated or basic; no matter how ironic or hysterical; no matter how attuned or massive; no matter how tonic or constipated; no matter how organized or pileated; no matter how chronic or temporal; no matter how gorgeous or dissipated; no matter how buxom or purposeless; no matter how unbound by gravity—it could all be manifested.

CHAPTER TWELVE
EARLY MORNING ENCOUNTER

San Francisco   **Tuesday, December 5th, 1995: 0755**

Karen lived on Argüello near the Jefferson Airplane's old mansion at 2400 Fulton Street. She had inherited the house from her mother's only sister and remodeled it extensively to create an office space with a separate entrance so that her clients could come and go without invading her private space.

Paul purposely awoke early enough to drink a cup of his favorite brew and then made his way down to Columbus to have breakfast at a funky little shop called Curley's, the owner/chef who was, of course, bald. He cooked up a mean breakfast, including freshly made hash brown potatoes, a particular favorite of Paul's. In spite of being in North Beach—home of Café Trieste, Malvina's, Graffeo's, Café Roma and Peet's Coffee Roasters—the coffee was pretty terrible.

He launched himself into a huge double order of crisp hash browns and sausage patties accompanied by two over-easily eggs and local sourdough toast with real butter and raspberry jam. God! He loved breakfast, any time of the day!

Since she lived more centrally than he, it became a matter of how to get there expeditiously. He generally liked to walk. He was totally in love with The City, and had carved walking routes all over. Today he decided to walk to Mason and Vallejo to catch the cable car to Market Street where he could catch the #5 Fulton directly to his destination. Many of his out-of-town friends questioned why he did not have a car. He always responded that he loved walking this city of his heart, and he was therefore not saddled with parking spaces, parking tickets and/or fees for garaging a vehicle. He knew his way around quite well on public transportation, which, in this particular case, took him to within thirty feet of his location. It also allowed him time to think unrestrainedly about other matters than traffic or querulous drivers or pedestrians, and simply enjoy his current book selection.

Despite the early hour, it was an easy journey and he was in a bright mood, and arrived five minutes early. He took a deep breath and then walked down the side of the main building under the overarching trellis of currently recumbent wisteria vines, and back toward the small cottage at the rear of the property. It had been constructed in a way that was congruent with the original architectural style of the main house. It still looked new, but the wooden cladding had started aging nicely aided by the Mediterranean climate of the Bay Area.

Karen was standing in the doorway and greeted him as he came toward her. They had met several times socially and exchanged business cards—and, despite a mutual attraction, had not interacted socially. Paul noticed that she too had some small symptoms of anxiety at this their first professional meeting. She had dusky skin, dark eyes and hair and radiated a deep friendliness and welcome that seemed innate. She wore a purple silk blouse over a pair of black linen slacks, with huarache sandals on her feet. He looked closely at her face and noticed again how really lovely she was, and could not, in his typically male manner, stop himself from admiring her physical features and imagining touching her. But then she smiled and extended her hand in greeting, and he repurposed his thinking to align with his intentions in being there.

"Thank you for seeing me on such short notice."

"I'm glad I had an opening."

"I imagine you're pretty busy."

"I work two days a week part-time consulting with the Psychology Supervisors in the Outpatient Psychiatry Department at Kaiser. I really enjoy the work, but they're constantly talking about 'budgetary restraints.' I have to do my paperwork to reflect fifteen-minute increments for billing. Legally, if I work seven extra minutes, the client has to pay for the next fifteen-minute increment!"

"Boy! That's tight!"

"But I love doing supervision! So, all in all, it makes it worthwhile. And it helps me financially."

"Nice place you have here."

"Thanks to my Aunt Olivette. She left it to me. She was ninety-two."

"You've done a great job fixing it up."

"I have been so fortunate. She always just really loved me! Then, she left me the house and enough money to fix it up."

"What a grand legacy!"

They stepped into a large open room with four multi-paned windows on each of the street-facing walls. In the forefront was a small, floral-print covered love seat that fronted a teak coffee table and a pair of what looked like genuine Bauhaus leather chairs opposite. Paul reflected that, if they were original, she was doing very well for herself. Paul loved their simplicity and classic lines. He himself had considered getting a pair of reproductions, but even their price was beyond the reach of his budget at this point, perhaps ever.

The bantered lightly, and Paul briefly sketched in the back story to what had brought him there. He made a point of strongly stressing the need for confidentiality.

"Please don't misunderstand. I trust you completely, but this situation is so strange that I am especially concerned—certainly if what he is telling me is true and not a delusion."

"You say you hadn't seen this man for twenty-six years? And suddenly he appears wanting you to 'help' him?"

Paul looked at her for a long beat and then said, "I know. I know. It sounds absolutely nutty! But I'm inclined to think it might be true!"

"How do you know? How can you really know?"

Paul sighed deeply and leaned forward with his elbows on his knees. They had both taken seats in the Bauhaus chairs, and he turned slightly toward her and said, "I know it sounds crazy, but it really is him. I met the man on a chopper pad at Camp Evans in 1969 in circumstances that are forever imprinted in my mind. Look, you just have to understand that every Vietnam vet develops a bullshit detector. And I know he's real. Totally real! I know you might find this hard to swallow, but I recognized him! Immediately! It's really him! No doubt!"

As if taken aback by the relative vehemence of his reply, Karen's face closed slightly, and she looked away from him into the far distance for a moment. Then she looked up, directly into his eyes with all the beautiful clarity she could project, nodded her head and said, "I believe you. I do. Do you feel that you might be in danger too?"

"I've been considering that. And it might certainly be true, depending, again, on whether or not this is delusion or not."

"And by extension, if we continue supervision, I might be as well?"

"That's certainly possible."

"So, the crux of the matter balances on diagnosis."

"To some extent, yes."

"And?"

"'And?'"

"'And' what have you decided so far?"

"As I told you on the phone, we spent almost four hours together. My overall impression is that he has lived a very...powerful and unusual life, one that has shaped him, like Life shapes all of us. He hasn't yet divulged a lot of his experiences yet, and I believe he will as treatment proceeds." Paul paused and then said emphatically, "I almost totally believe him."

"'Almost?'"

"I'm holding out the possibility that he may be delusional."

"Your doubt concerns this adventure in which he may or may not have been involved?"

"I have absolutely no doubt about the breadth and depth of his combat experience. That it might have influenced him to adopt a suspicious, even paranoid, preoccupation is not beyond the pale, of course."

"You trust your own judgment in this?"

Paul felt a flash of anger that infused his reply and he slammed his right hand, palm down, on the arm of the chair.

"Damn straight! I came here seeking guidance! Not to have you critique my professional judgement!"

Karen gave him a long look before replying.

"That certainly seems to have pushed one of your buttons."

"Buttons or not, I'm neither inexperienced nor uninformed clinically!"

"Thank you. I quite agree. My comment was a bit over the line."

Paul breathed deeply and looked at her, face flushing.

"I apologize. It is one of my oldest, strongest 'buttons!'"

"Do you want to talk about that?"

"No. Not now. Thanks."

"Just as long as you are clear that I will be...questioning, let's say, aspects of your therapeutic methods."

"Of course! Of course! I... I'm sorry. I'm still...touchy, still triggered."

"Your own PTSD, of course."

Yes, precisely."

"Are you working on that yourself?"

"I'm between therapists right now. I need to take a break every once in a while."

"I don't know you all that well, but I do know that you seem to be highly intelligent, and, by all reports, a fine therapist, especially with trauma cases."

"Wait a minute! 'By all reports?' What does that mean?"

"This city is really just a small town! The therapeutic community is very tight. Word gets around about who's competent and who is not. That's especially true when one is a therapist seeking therapy or supervision!"

"I fucking hate it when I get so defensive around any hint of invalidation! It still so reminds me of my father! He constantly eroded my self-worth!"

"We should perhaps take that up at some other time."

"Yes, of course. Perhaps when I'm ready to pursue another round of therapy."

"So, more to the point. You say Roach is, or has been, a heroin addict. Is he using right now?

"He says not. And I don't get the feeling he is. I can almost always tell. When I used to work with vets extensively at Swords, I was always called upon to tell if someone was using. I was kind of a living lie detector."

"And you've retained your skills?"

"If anything, they've gotten stronger."

"And you're convinced that he's clean...currently?"

"Ninety-five percent, though I have been known to be wrong occasionally!"

She had the good taste to laugh politely and he joined in, always entertained by his own humor.

"And so, you're going to work with him?"

Paul laughed. "I must be. He paid me for three hours last night!'

"Oh really?"

"Yes. Cash."

"So, he has money?"

"Seems to."

"Hmmm. That puts a different spin on things, at least peripherally."

Paul made a "come on" gesture with his right hand.

Karen blushed a little, and touched her mouth with her right index finger.

"The picture you're painting is changing. At first, I thought he might be some kind of scruffy drug dealer type."

"I thought that might be the case," he said and laughed.

"I really don't know you that well. I didn't know exactly what to expect."

"So, what's your first impression? Vibe wise, I mean?"

"So far, I agree with you that it could be delusional."

"Or, conversely, this all could be totally true. He could be being hunted by organized crime and or the CIA."

"Also, true. And?"

"'And' I cannot wait to see how things unfold!"

"So, we're on? For supervision? I really would appreciate being able to talk with you about this case."

"Works for me. Good to see you again."

"Should I call you, or should we do next week? Sometime later in the day? Afternoon please!"

"I'll call you."

CHAPTER THIRTEEN
ONLY IN SAN FRANCISCO

San Francisco   **Tuesday, December 5th, 1995: 1002**

Paul felt completely energized when he left Karen's. He saw a small break in the fog as a precursor to it lifting, as it often did before noon, though not always in the winter. Nonetheless, he decided to walk back to North Beach and enjoy the city he loved above all others. It also afforded him the opportunity to further reinforce the conclusions to which he had arrived— primarily telling Roach about the necessity of his supervision sessions with Karen. He knew Roach wouldn't like it, but he'd convince him of its importance, at least in part to get him to pay for it. It was a necessity in a case as complicated as this.

He decided to walk over Arguello, then turned north and followed it all the way to the Presidio where he turned east and walked over West Pacific Avenue. Then he took Lyon down to Union Street to get a late lunch (actually a second breakfast) at La Cucina where the coffee was superb. After eating, he considered walking up either Pacific or Broadway over the top of the hill, but as he was feeling a little logy from the food, he decided to take the #41 Union instead. He knew he'd be hearing from Roach soon, very likely even today. He was intrigued to hear more of the man's unfolding story, delusional or not. His practice was a little slow anyway, so the extra cash would be welcome.1

He emerged from the bus at Washington Square Park and decided to amble (loved that word!) home. It was a semi-day off with nothing concrete planned, so why not? A side effect was that it allowed him to absorb the effervescent beauty of North Beach as he made his way home. He loved counting the number of languages he heard spoken in any given day. His personal record still stood at twenty-five!

He could have ridden the bus further but opted for a post-prandial walk to settle his meal. He went up past Filbert and Greenwich, then Lombard where he turned onto Fielding and his little hide-away that was his hidden little corner in a truly great city that had so many trippy places to live. So much depended upon one's neighborhood of choice. Each district offered different flavors, different textures. He had lived all over and enjoyed every place in which he had lived. It was such a joy to walk the haunted, vaunted streets of her heart. but he loved North Beach best of all.

A nap, he thought, a nap and then phone calls. He expected to hear from Roach today. Their first face-to-face encounter had opened old doorways of a bond of trust yet had left a gap of memory and experience to be explored to further create the therapeutic alliance.

Stripping off all his clothes, Paul fell asleep almost as soon as he lay down. He felt a little chilly, so he pulled the duvet over himself for added comfort. He took a moment before Lethe stole him away to ask for a further dream about Roach and his entire situation. In only moments he was plunged into a maelstrom of flashing pictures and heaving emotions. He was riding in an open rowboat down a turbulent river with small waves crashing over the bow as he held onto the sides of the boat for dear life. There were no paddles, no anchor, no motor. He was completely at the mercy of the rushing torrents. The water was murky and grey where it met the black, turbulent sky. Everywhere was the most treacly light. As he sank down through the layers of his excessive emotions, he was terrified; but that terror was superficial, like a liqueur float on a cocktail. He dove deeper, seeking respite, relief of any kind, and realized that he was in fact quite calm and even anticipatory, awaiting the next moment in his personal drama, not unlike the first anticipatory rushes when LSD was in the internal pipeline; it was not unlike shivering and quivering in a bunker as rockets and mortars pounded in like freight trains falling; or the tense moments just before he and the staff converged on a berserker patient who had to be taken down, restrained and secluded. Though he was filled with angst, there was always a frisson of confidence, even a thrilling chill, despite the fact that he might be injured, even killed. He was floating on the edge, flirting with Death itself, though attempting to make an ally of that imperious golden eye filled these moments like the soft toffee cream center of a dark chocolate candy.

Then, out of empty space, a massive wave swept in tsunami-like and lifted his small boat so high in the air that he felt he were in an airplane, sailing through the skies above the swollen river so quickly that he was unable to distinguish it as a separate aspect of his journey. Before an even more extreme terror was able to register on his sensitive consciousness (while still magnificently conveying moment-by-moment information to his neural networks), he was able to react without thought or volition, as if aloft on a sailboard, shifting his weight to properly maintain a perfect balance and landed smoothly back in the water, glimpsing a rapidly receding dark cloud bank as he was gently pushed into calmer waters. He awoke, his whole-body pulsing with incredible gratitude for his marvelous blessings, of body, of heart, of mind, even though he had not yet cognitively processed what had transpired. He was utterly suffused with a wondrous glow of joy and extraordinarily peace. His sheets were soaked through with perspiration. He leapt, catapulted almost, from the bed and headed to the bathroom before any of his other bodily fluids eclipsed his physical limits, while still maintaining the edge of the ethereal glow with which he had been endowed.

Paul quickly stripped the bed and replaced the fitted sheet before falling back onto the bed to bask in the hypnopompic glow that still surrounded him like an invisible yet psychically palpable cloud of cotton wool. Without a bidden thought, he had a sudden vision of a naked Karen in bed with him. He had never thought of her that way before. They always seemed to have enjoyed each other the few times they had met, but suddenly she materialized in his altered state as an object of desire. The curious part was that he was not sexually aroused so much as feeling her deeply intimate presence as they lay in bed together and cuddled, speaking quietly and laughing, kissing occasionally or holding hands without any sexual energy attached.

102

It was a gorgeous, tender scenario filled with tenderness and deep intimacy, just a truly lovely afterglow. And then the phone rang, its clamorous clang slicing through the delicate, ethereal images he had so been cherishing like a scimitar slicing the unyielding air.

CHAPTER FOURTEEN
BATTER UP!

San Francisco   **Tuesday, December 5th, 1995: 1635**

He hesitated to answer, but he had failed to ask his service to pick up, so he knew it wouldn't stop ringing, no matter how strongly he willed it. He knew intuitively that it was Roach, so he answered. His floating, dreamy state was already ruined.

"Hello, brother!"

"How'd you know it was me?"

"Just a feeling."

"I called a couple of times earlier."

"I didn't check my messages. Just came home and took a nap."

"Are you...I mean, can we get together and talk some more?"

"Of course. But not immediately. I just woke up and gotta have some coffee."

"Of course. Where shall we meet?"

Paul had been considering this very topic, and, although he used his spare bedroom as an office, still wasn't quite ready to invite Roach over yet.

"I know you're not one for sitting too very much, so I'm up for a walk-and-talk session, if you are."

"It's not raining, so where do you suggest?"

"It's going to be dark in an hour or so, so why don't we meet at Washington Square Park and stroll around there. Then if we're still going strong, we could come back to my office for another hour or grab a quiet corner in a restaurant."

"Isn't that a little bit of an unusual approach to psychotherapy?"

"I admit that it's not 'traditional.' We'll only do it if we can have privacy and confidentiality. I admit that the American Psychological Association would likely frown on such an approach, but if you're comfortable and agree to it, then I don't see it as an ethics violation."

"Works for me. Washington Square. How about half an hour?"

"You're on, GI!"

Paul was being extra-cautious, not-quite-yet entirely comfortable in Roach's presence, particularly if he was "an old Asia hand," expats who had acclimatized to the culture and mores of Southeast Asia and just stayed, making a living any way they could, living underground and surviving off of various black market enterprises—many of which were overlooked as just being normal business practices there that had been utilized for thousands of years before the false premises of the "Western way" had even been conceived and enforced through violence and coercion.

If there were more to pursue that night after their "walk and talk," they could go to his office. Roach was, after all, a client. After the incredible dream he had had, he knew he was in for a stormy ride fraught with danger, but one that would result in his winning through the challenges of this latest Hero's Journey he had entered. His gifts were his to use and give away (even if he got paid). They were not his to keep and gloat about or own like a bloated billionaire with a hidden collection of Old Masters.

Paul pulled on his favorite long-sleeved emerald green t-shirt and a chambray shirt. Then he put on a worn pair of old Levi's jeans and his hooded, knee length London Fog car coat. His feet were shod with a pair of black suede Sketchers with waffle bottoms. Perfect walking around clothes. He took a last sip of his coffee and walked down to the storied, historic park.

Juana Briones grew potatoes and raised cattle there, before Jasper O'Farrell laid out San Francisco's street grid in 1847 and designated this block a city square. Against the background of Saints Peter and Paul Cathedral, there's a smaller-than-life-size bronze statue of Benjamin Franklin, by an unknown sculptor, that stands upon an ornate granite base and contains a time capsule. There are inscriptions on all four sides of the base where once spigots dispensed drinking water into three stone basins as a memorial to the streams that once ran freely through the area. In the aftermath of the 1906 Earthquake and Fire, the park sheltered six hundred refugees. Due to the efforts of neighborhood preservationists, after almost 150 years, Washington Square is the only one of San Francisco's three original parks that has not been made into a roof top for an underground parking garage.

There's also a sculpture of two firefighters commissioned by Lillie Hitchcock Coit and erected in 1933 to commemorate the volunteer fire department of San Francisco from 1849-1866. Coit Tower was built as a memorial to her, who was an honorary member of the Knickerbocker Volunteer Fire Company Number Five. (Contrary to popular myth, it is a representation of a fire hose nozzle, not male genitalia, of which Ms. Coit was ostensibly also quite fond).

Roach was sitting on a bench facing Union Street and observed Paul approaching from afar. He too was wearing jeans and a canvas car coat, with sturdy boots on his feet and a battered-looking hat that could easily have been an ancient boonie hat.

Paul laughed as they met and dapped.

"That fucking hat looks like it's from the 'Nam!"

"It serves the same purpose and for good reasons."

"I kept my old one for years. And my boots!"

"So, what's up?" Paul asked.

Roach looked around, quartering the immediate vicinity with his eyes, and said, "Let's walk."

They started up Union, intending to walk around the circumference of the park. When they turned up Stockton, Roach began to speak, continuing to tell his story as if he were simply picking up the thread where he had left off the night before.

"I couldn't leave. I didn't want to leave. There was no fucking way I could ever live in CONUS (Continental United States). Too many rules, too many laws."

"What did you do?"

"I just ghosted around Southeast Asia. I had all these connections. There were corrupt officials everywhere. The 'G' was in deep. There was too much money to be made. Millions. Billions."

"I heard about that Command Sergeant Major of the Army, Blackwell, who got busted for black market activities."

"He was stealing money from the PXs too."

"I heard he was extorting money from all the locals, and the Filipino women entertainers too."

"He was a fucking piker compared to the Command Sergeant Major of the 101st."

"Hoxley?"

"He was a big part of the command chain for the dope trade."

"Hoxley? That motherfucker!"

"Did you know him?"

"He was the son of a bitch that got me court martialed!"

"You got court martialed?"

"I was AWOL and he tried to get me sent to LBJ."

"What a fucking hypocrite!"

"How's that?"

"He was the bag man for the 101st!"

"How's that?"

"He took care of all of the payments, the kickbacks, and passed the money on to senior military who were in the food chain."

"No shit?"

"No shit!"

"So, what happened to him?"

Roach turned silent and seemed to be pondering something, perhaps imponderable, as if much weight lay upon its utterance.

"I need to ask again. Do we have confidentiality?"

Paul explained again about the limits imposed upon his granting total confidentiality.

"So, let me make sure I've got this straight. If I were proposing a murder, you'd be required to report me to the police. And give a warning to the potential victim."

"That's correct. It's called a 'duty to warn,' a Tarasoff warning."

"What about an old murder?"

"You mean one that you already committed? And for which you were not held accountable?"

"Yes, exactly."

"First of all, I am not a lawyer. So, what I tell you is in the context of my being a psychologist in the State of California. I am not required to report an old murder as long as you are not currently homicidal. What you say here, stays here. It is important to me that you know this. The things we talk about remain confidential except under very specific circumstances."

"So, I can talk to you honestly and openly about everything?"

"With the exceptions I have already noted. Everything I'm telling you now will be in the paperwork I'll have you sign when we get back to my office. You're free to ask any questions you have at any time."

"What about cops and other 'authorities?'" he said making air quotes underlain by heavy sarcasm.

"No one can call me up and ask about you. If they do, I tell them I cannot confirm or deny knowing you. As soon as I get a call like that, I will contact you and tell you. Your records are confidential, as is the contents of anything we talk about in session. If you give me permission to release information about you to someone, and we agree it is in your best interest, I will do that. I will release information without your permission if you are a risk to self, risk to others, disclose abuse that I am mandated to report, or if your decision making is impaired based on the symptoms of a mental illness. Short of that, it would take a court order from a judge for me to be required to release information. I am not required to hand over medical records based on a warrant or a subpoena. Since you're a cash client, I will not be required to submit case notes or information to an insurance company—therefore there will be nothing in writing other than the confidentiality agreement which protects me."

"I'm glad you know what you're doing. I'm going to entrust my life to you. I'm a bit paranoid and it's kept me alive all these years. If I get even a whiff of something going sideways, I'm out of here."

"So, what happened to that asshole Hoxley?"

"He was part of a network. When they found out he was ripping them off—false reporting, sending money to Liechtenstein—they ordered him eliminated."

"Wow! Seriously?"

"As Dylan said, 'To live outside the law, you must be honest.'"

"Wow! That motherfucker!"

There was a protracted silence then, and Roach looked at Paul long and hard.

"I guess I did you a big favor, brother."

"How's that?"

"I took the motherfucker out. Two in the face, and we shipped him out in empty jet fuel drums and dumped him in Laos."

"No?"

"I don't lie!"

Paul felt a flush of both gratitude and guilt wash through him.

"Thanks, man."

"That's why I kept asking about confidentiality."

"I see now. Again, thanks."

"Don't mean nothing." He said and they dapped.

"There is one other small thing we need to talk about. I have a colleague with whom I consult. She has the same arrangement with me as I have with you. Nothing in writing. Cash pay. Total deniability."

"Why do you need her?"

"I'm just a human being too. I can make mistakes or get too involved or misinterpret things you tell me. She is my backup, my support. She ensures I am giving you my very best at all times."

"She can't tell anybody what we talk about?"

"No, and she can't tell anybody what she and I talk about either."

"Ever?"

"Never. Plus, she doesn't keep paperwork either. So, other than the confidentiality agreement, there is no record ever."

"Do you trust her?"

"Totally. Otherwise I wouldn't work with her."

Roach looked away, eyes glazed and distant for a moment. Then he looked back sharply at Paul.

"I'm trusting you, brother."

"You're totally safe with me, man."

They had walked over Filbert and then down Powell, making a loop of the park. They went around again until they returned to Powell a second time, when they turned north and headed for his office. There was part of him that didn't want Roach to know the location of his house, but the man was a client, after all. Paul mused that he was still a long way from deciding whether he was mentally ill or just involved a very complex posttraumatic stress process. Either way, the man's presentation was fascinating. Until he knew for sure, he was going to give the man a break. After all, he was a brother vet.

CHAPTER FIFTEEN
THE BEAT GOES ON

San Francisco   **Tuesday, December 5th, 1995: 1845**

He walked Roach through the living room and ushered him into his office. He had bought a new chocolate-brown leather couch, intending to put it in the living room for his own use, but decided that his office deserved the added presence more than he needed it for his own personal use. He had had the good fortune to find a matched pair of nearly-new fabric-covered chairs that he'd had re-covered in black silk. They sat on either side of a mahogany table he'd bought on sale at Macy's Stonestown.

Roach looked around slowly as he entered and did not comment until he sat on the couch with his back against the wall. He continued to observe and said, "You've come a long way, brother."

"Every day I wake up breathing is a celebration," Paul said, referring to the old maxim that his best friend Macallan Da Besh always used.

"Amen, brother!" he said and they dapped.

"I always remember a great quote from Shakespeare."

"Which one?"

"One that reminds me of you," Paul said, "from *Henry V*." Then he quoted from memory:

- We few, we happy few, we band of brothers,

- For he today that sheds his blood with me

- Shall be my brother. Be he ne'er so vile

- This day shall gentle his condition

- And gentlemen in England now abed

- Shall think themselves accursed that they were not here

- And hold their manhood's cheap while any speaks

- That fought with us upon St. Crispin's Day.

Roach reached out a hand and they dapped vigorously. They laughed again and he handed Roach a clipboard with all the proper forms to be filled out. He decided that Roach looked better rested and less frantic than the last time he'd seen him. Perhaps the little walk around the park had helped restore some of his vitality. Paul knew for a fact that it had helped brighten his own mood, reinforcing the contents of the dream he had incubated.

"So, tell me. What else do you want to talk about today? I'm not totally clear about your goals and intentions."

"This would be by way of the 'treatment plan' you mentioned?"

"Well, that too, but primarily I'm not exactly sure how I can help you, because I'm sure what you want."

Roach took a deep breath, then closed his eyes for a moment

before answering.

"Look, I told you...a bunch of stuff...before. It's all true."

"And?"

"It's so fucking weird. For the first time in my life, I find I... need to ask for help. It's not easy."

"I understand."

"No. I'm not sure you do."

"Say more."

"I've done stuff you might find...unbelievable."

"I'm willing to admit that you may have gone beyond the beyond of my personal experience, but clinically, I have far more expertise than you do."

"I'm willing to trust your judgment. Some of the stuff I know...could be dangerous, to you too. So, you might want to consider how much you really want to know."

"I'm pretty jaded."

"Not nearly as much as me."

"That may be, but here we are!"

"I'll buy that. So, 'danger?'"

"You have no idea how much money is involved! They're willing to kill, ruin people's lives, do anything to protect the flow of profit. Anything!"

"I know you want me to be scared."

"You should be! This is massive! To some extent the economy of many nations is involved!"

"Especially the U.S.!"

"Especially, not exclusively!"

"How can that be?"

"Before the drug trade, slavery and human trafficking were the mainstays of numerous European nations—Germany, The Netherlands, France, Spain, Belgium, others. Then the United States stepped into the breach."

"And?"

"You have no idea what the drug trade is worth, how many people are profiting! Or how much!"

"So, enlighten me!"

"Are you sure you want to know?"

"Of course!"

"Once you know, I can't take it back! You cannot un-know!"

"I'm willing to trust you...to a certain extent," Paul said, and laughed. "Here I am declaring my trust in you when I should be working to allow you to trust more in me!"

"Why don't we consider it to be a mutual interaction, with each of us holding parts of a puzzle that could potentially benefit each of us?"

"That subverts the entire principle of the therapeutic alliance! It reduces my ability to help you!"

"You...need me too! You need me to fill you in on some aspects of...Life that are missing from your view of 'reality.'"

"'Reality' is such a fluid word! So totally misunderstood! So poorly used!"

"So, what's your take?"

"I believe every individual has a 'reality' that they refer to as capital R reality, though it is clinically called 'naïve reality.'"

"I'll buy that. But what then is 'capital R reality?'"

"I don't know. No one does."

"But you have some ideas?"

"Yes. Of course."

"And?"

"As close as I have been able to come is: The combination of everyone's 'realities,' plus more."

"'More?'"

"I think there is a kind of container that 'holds' all of these 'realities,' and coordinates them harmoniously in such a way that everything, absolutely everything, works together without friction, everything benefits everything else—no matter how otherwise fucked up, painful, shameful or whatever things may look or seem to be, there is an underlying harmony that unites everything!"

"How do you account for greed?"

"'Greed' is just a distortion, no matter how it might seem, no matter how painful it might feel."

"Why do you keep saying 'seem?'"

"Because everything is a matter of perception. What may seem like a deficiency to one person, leading to obsession, lust, craving, need, whatever, may, for someone else, seem like a requirement, a necessity, for managing life as that other individual experiences it. The missing piece is having a large enough perspective."

"Say more."

"As Bob Dylan once said, 'I am right from my side, you are right from yours.'"

"And?"

"I believe he was alluding to everyone having a perspective from which they believe themselves to be 'right,' and therefore entitled to act as if whatever they did was 'proper' because it accorded with being 'proper and correct' for them."

"And?"

"And, therefore, in some sense every person, every perspective, is correct within the limited perspective of that individual."

"Even when it conflicts with the perspective of others?"

"Of course! Because that larger container, the more encompassing perspective that holds every other perspective; and must, of necessity, be larger or greater in order to do so; and hence be of a completely different nature and quality as it is 'more completely whole,' if you will."

"Shit, man! You've woken up my brain in a way that I haven't experienced in years! You've got me thinking I've been off-track! That maybe there is something larger for me to integrate than my own life experience!"

"I think we can work together."

"I'll still pay you!"

"I appreciate that. Quite honestly, I really need it."

"Even knowing where my money comes from?"

"Ultimately, all money is dirty! What's that old saying? 'Behind every great fortune is a great crime?'"

"Who was that?"

"Honoré de Balzac."

"He was so right! Even just in the U.S., look at all the industrialists and bankers who profited from 'Manifest Destiny' and the 'Westward Expansion,' killing millions of Indians to steal their land. And all the ultra-rich who profited from WW II, both before and after—including the Germans like I.B. Farben and Krupp, who bailed out the bankrupt Nazi Party in 1932."

"Americans too, though."

"Of course! Ford. Standard Oil, Chase Bank and members of the State Department. At the center was 'The Fraternity', all associated with the Rockefeller or Morgan banks, all linked by the 'Business as usual' ideology!'"

"I didn't realize you were such a historian!"

"Sidebar to trauma! I've had a lot of time to study and do research, especially when I've been hospitalized for detox. I've had a few of those!" he said and chuckled.

"How many?"

"I don't know. I've lost track. I've always had to go to 'special treatment facilities' that were both extremely private and expensive; where discretion was of the utmost importance."

"Can you name any of them?"

Roach laughed again. "I could name an ex-president's wife, if I were to be indiscreet."

"I see. But that didn't work?"

"Neither time—if I had been there at all, that is."

"What finally worked?"

"Look, I told you I've been clean for a pretty long time now."

"You said thirteen months."

"Since I've been strung out."

"Just so we're on the same page—you mean using every day?"

"Exactly."

"So, what finally worked?"

Roach laughed again, slightly louder this time.

"I have so many secrets, but this one will be kind of fun to tell you. We do have confidentiality, right?"

"As I have explained before."

"I had all of my blood supply replaced. In Switzerland."

"What's so confidential about that?"

"I was in the same clinic as Keith Richards."

"Rolling Stones Keith Richards?"

"That's right."

"What was he doing there?"

"Same as me. Complete blood transfusion."

"I knew he was strung out."

"I heard he was staying clean."

"It's easier when all of the heroin metabolites are flushed out; when you get a fresh blood supply."

"And you?"

"The only thing that's ever worked."

"Don't you get tempted sometimes?"

"Not like I used to, but sometimes, sure, of course."

"I have a theory about addictions, one that evolved out of my own experience."

"Tell me more."

"It's all related to being totally honest."

"What's that have to do with being strung out?"

"I believe every human being is born exquisitely sensitive. And we shut down our feelings from the moment we're born because adults can't handle their own sensitivity and a child's truth. The child's sensitivities remind the adults of what they've lost. They can't stand it, and they use shame, purposely or otherwise, to distract the child, to get him or her, to be quiet."

"And then what happens?"

"The energy has to go somewhere. Any kind of pain or hurt or shame that doesn't get expressed—especially as an infant or child—is turned inward and stored."

"And?"

"At first, it sets a pattern of being suppressed. And then any time after that, any kind of negative feeling or trauma triggers the original trauma and gets stored. It just keeps building on itself. Eventually, the body gets overwhelmed with trying to contain the energy. Addictions develop out of the need to stop feeling, to stop being sensitive."

"So, you're saying that expressing the original pain heals the addiction?"

"Only if one connects emotions with memory."

"And you're saying what? I'm going to start using again because I haven't remembered my original pain?"

"I'm offering you a way out of the pain."

Angrily, Roach replied. "I...my fucking life is a mess and I want to change."

"That's all well and good, but I need you to help me figure out exactly how, so we can develop specific, tangible goals towards which to aim."

"That sounds a little like psychobabble!"

"It's really not. Let's say you want to go sailing. Do you just go out and rent a boat, put it out on the ocean and hope that you won't drown?"

"No! Of course not!"

"Same same here! If you want to arrive at a particular destination, then we need to create a map to get there."

"That sounds complicated."

"It could be. Isn't your life complicated right now?"

"Why the fuck else did I come to you?"

"So, I need to ask you some more questions before we can make a plan."

"Got it."

"You are going to need to spell it out for me in great detail, so I can make a really good map to get us there."

"'Us?'"

"In some ways, I am the good captain of your ship temporarily. You're trusting my years of experience sailing and my knowledge of maps and currents to take you through whatever reefs we might encounter. And I guarantee you there will be reefs and shoals, maybe even a monsoon or two."

Roach smiled at the analogy and held out a hand to dap. "So, exactly how long is this going to take?"

"I cannot honestly tell you. And the one thing you can always count on with me is that I will not lie. Ever."

"'Ever?'"

"'Ever.'"

"That's a big promise."

"If you sign up for the ride, I will prove it to you."

"I'm supposed to trust you?"

"Not blindly and not 100%, at least not yet. But enough to do homework assignments."

"'Homework?'"

Paul sighed. Why did so many people balk at doing preparatory work on themselves and for themselves when, even if he were to start meeting daily with a client, it still left a significant number of hours daily, weekly, monthly that the client could devote to their own healing. It was yet another artifact of the consumer society that led people to believe they did not have to do any work themselves, just go to the expert and get fixed without any effort of their own!

Paul explained this concept to Roach who seemed to get it immediately. Then he expressed the rest of his thought train.

"Of course, this, again, assumes we have a plan and a direction we're following."

"If you fail to plan, you plan to fail!"

"That old saw is as true now as ever. So, depending on what direction you choose to have me help you move—and depending, quite honestly," he emphasized, looking directly into the man's eyes, "on what I decide is your diagnosis, there will always be different lists to be assembled, exercises to try out and so on."

"My diagnosis?"

"I told you I wouldn't lie to you. Here's my truth right now. I know you've told me that you are on the run from organized crime and the CIA. That brings up a number of questions for me, the primary one being—don't be offended here, but I am being completely honest—I'm tossed between complex PTSD, secondary to the 'Nam."

"And?"

"I'm holding out the distinct possibility that maybe, as a result of all of the trauma you've experienced, that your mind has created a story for you to explain to yourself your suspiciousness and your fear."

"'A story?' Are you fucking saying that I'm making all of this up? That I'm lying?"

"That is the last thing I'm saying!"

"Then you better explain it better. I'm getting pissed!"

"I told you I'd be totally honest."

"And you're saying I've made all of this up?"

"I'm not saying you did," he said, "just that it's one possibility to explore."

"But it is true! It's all true!"

"That still leaves us having to sort through all of some pretty scary shit through the years, not even to mention your military background."

"So, are you saying you believe me?"

"Absolutely! And it doesn't matter what the diagnosis is, there's still a great deal that I can do to help you. That is, ultimately, what you want, isn't it?"

Roach was silent for a very long time, a kind of deep, almost oppressive silence that seemed to stretch the barriers of ordinary time, as if what he were experiencing was beyond ordinary counting or recounting, even to one who had been there and shared at least part of it, some section of it. Then he spoke, slowly, as if through cotton batting.

"There's a book, by Michael Andrews and David Widup, called *The 'Nam*."

"I have it."

"There's a chapter called *In Country*, and there's a quote I memorized because it says so much so succinctly—and it applies to me, to my life, so perfectly:

The reason that all stories about the Nam involve hyperbole is because it was so alien a universe that no one who was not there at that time will ever grasp the experience, the smell of it, the feel, the taste, the terror, the moral outrage, the pure out-of-this-university of it. It is simply beyond art, language, and translation. It is ineffable. It is incommunicable. In our desperation to tell our fellow humans about what happened in the republic, in order to communicate the truth of the emotional, psychological, factual, and spiritual impact, our stories must dwell on the most intense, the most bizarre, the most horrific—and in pursuit of the reality of it, we are forced to utilize the power of hyperbole, myth, fantasy, and the blackest of black, black humor.

Paul took several moments to reflect, and then replied, "So, you're saying that unless one has lived your life, 'walked a mile in your moccasins,' as it were, no one could really understand who and how you are?"

"Precisely."

"That kind of understanding is my stock-in-trade. Extending my understanding to embrace the life experiences of others so that I can intuitively blend, give another perspective."

"There are some things I do not want to change! I... must admit that I like being intense. And my 'suspiciousness' has saved my life many times."

"I'm not trying to take anything away from you. That's why I keep asking you questions, trying to pin you down a little, to get a more solid idea about where you want our work to go. That's what I am trying to get at, and why it's important to understand what drives you, your motivation: We can only go toward what your stated goals are."

"Whether you decide I'm crazy or not?"

"'Crazy' is not a clinical term."

"You know what I mean!"

"Yes, I do."

"So, if you decide that, for whatever reason, I made this up, then you 'treat' me a certain way; think of me in a different way than if you truly believe me, truly believe that everything I have told you is true."

"Every person has a perceptual bias that shapes how he or she sees things, interprets experience. When you use a word like 'crazy,' you're implying that there is a sort of imaginary line, on one side of which is 'sane' and on the other is 'crazy.' It's not set in stone like that."

"But you're still holding out the possibility that I may not be 'realistic.'"

"Look, brother, I know you are real. Otherwise I would not have invited you here. This is not just my office, it's my home."

"OK. OK. You're right."

"And whatever I decide, your symptoms are still your symptoms. No matter your motivation, I will help you to the very best of my abilities."

Roach reached out and they dapped.

"Thanks, brother."

"How often do you want to meet? I mean, I can give you a little break on my hourly rate if that helps."

"No, the money isn't an issue. I really like it that we can meet for two hours, if that fits your schedule."

"Like I told you, my schedule is pretty loose right now, so that will work for me. You want to try every other day for right now?"

"Works for me."

CHAPTER SIXTEEN
DIVING DEEPER

Roach had called the night before and they had set an appointment for the next afternoon. He had shown up early. Paul had suggested a short meditation, but Roach had demurred, stating that he felt too restless to settle. He said he'd made the attempt once in a monastery in Thailand (though he had actually been in there for other reasons).

"What would you like to work on?"

His face looked grey and ashen as he replied.

"This is really hard for me to admit, but I am truly afraid...and really worried."

"Wow! What brought all of this on?"

"I decided to trust you."

"I thought you already did."

"I do. I did. But there's a deeper level, one that almost...that I almost never open up."

"What's that about?"

"I'm usually too...paranoid."

"Being paranoid means being afraid to the point of great

suspicion; or fear of being injured. Is that accurate?"

"I... yes...I don't know."

Roach's face started to regain some color, then nodded his head, unable to speak.

"What's shifted for you in the last few days?"

"I... decided I...don't want to run anymore."

"I understand. I've been there myself."

All Roach was able to do was nod.

"Here's a great quote for you, from John Bradshaw from *Creating Love:*

We are here because there is no escape, finally, from ourselves. Until a person confronts himself in the eyes and hearts of others, he is running. Where else but in our common ground can we find such a mirror? Together we can take root and grow...not as the giant of our dreams or the dwarf of our fears, but a man/woman...part of a whole with a share in its purpose.

"That...that's beautiful! Who was that? John Bradshaw?"

"Yeah. He's one of my favorites. I did a workshop with him once. He's a powerful presence."

"But that quote? It's so much to the point. I don't want to run any longer."

"You said that. What's that mean for you?"

Roach again turned silent, looking as if he were far, far away. He nodded, then spoke.

"I'm going to tell you something I've never told anyone."

"What?"

"I've killed...a lot of people."

"Before or after the war?"

"Both."

"And you want to tell me because...?"

"They say confession is good for the soul."

"Bullshit! You don't buy that!"

"No! I was just fucking with you a little," he laughed.

"So why? Why now? Why me?"

"I told you. I've decided to trust you."

"You don't have to tell me, even if it was sanctioned by the government."

"I've never really had the desire...or the opportunity...to tell anyone! Plus, I learned never to trust anybody!" he said and laughed.

Paul laughed in spite of himself, then chided himself for chiding himself. It was a perfectly natural reaction. He never had really believed in the Freudian psychoanalytic bullshit of being a silent observer who withheld personal reactions (and all human feelings) from their clients, in keeping with the very antiquated notion of the quasi-pseudo feudal society that had ruled humanity for centuries.

"I apologize. It's just the way you put it. You can be very funny!"

"Thanks, man. I don't usually get opportunities to make jokes!"

"I imagine. And most likely only the darkest humor at that!"

"'Combat vet humor!'"

"Or 'morgue humor' or 'ER humor.'"

"Exactly! Only those who have been to the depths really appreciate it!"

"I'm hip! I remember very clearly when I first got home. I made the mistake of telling a joke about this gook who came running out of an NVA bunker on fire after somebody had thrown in a Willie Peter (White Phosphorous). Anyway, the entire squad opens up on him. He just kept bouncing around from all the hits. And somebody said, "Live from the boonies, it's the Arthur Murray Dance Show!"

Paul busted up laughing, and then saw from Roach's face that there was more to the story.

"Then what?"

"I was laughing my ass off! I thought it was funny! But both my sisters and my mother just turned pale and looked like they were going to shit a biscuit!"

This got Paul to laughing even harder and Roach joined in.

"There's just no accounting for taste!"

"Amen, brother!" And they dapped.

"So, you were saying you've killed a lot of guys."

"True, so true."

"Do you mind my asking...?"

"I don't know. Maybe a hundred."

"I've had other vets tell me that they're haunted by the dead; that they sometimes appear in dreams."

"Not so much anymore. It used to be worse. It's...I think it's gotten better since I stopped using."

"Why do think that is?"

"I'm not as preoccupied."

"Preoccupied?'"

"It's very consuming. Well, you know how it is when you're...immersed in the business."

"I've never been as deeply involved as you. But I have some small idea."

"If you are less 'preoccupied,' does that mean you're less stressed?"

"I... the...it just started not working. The junk."

"Wait a minute. I don't understand. If you are less stressed...did that lead to a lessening of desire, or...?"

"I got burned out. Tired of all the fucked-up people I had to work with!"

"I must admit. Working with you is certainly unique."

"Thanks, man. Can we take a little break? I need a smoke."

They went out to the deck, basking in the view of Coit Tower and the Bay Bridge in the far distance.

"It's really awesome, isn't it?" said Paul.

Roach looked pensive, withdrawn almost.

"I... It's hard being so...open."

"Artifacts of a former life," Paul declared and snapped his fingers. "That would make a great title!"

"It's very uncomfortable. I... don't know if I like feeling so much."

"And we haven't even opened you up yet!"

"I'm not sure I want that!"

"The only way to heal is to let go. I'm living proof of that!"

"I just want to stop running! I'm so fucking tired!'

"I know it may not seem like it, but you're really only running from yourself!"

"Bullshit! There's some bad-ass individuals out there who mean to do me harm!"

"I'm not disputing that. And I am also saying that perception is one thing and reaction is another."

136

"What does that mean?"

"The people chasing you are completely real, but they are stimulating—we call it 'triggering'—your old emotional stuff. They are reminders of other, older fears of being harmed."

"Listen, brother, I've been being 'harmed' my whole fucking life!"

"Exactly my point!"

"So, what I need help with is getting the fuck out of harm's way!"

"And I am saying that how you react to the potential danger creates what we call 'reality!'"

"Wait a minute! Wait a minute! The danger is real! Completely fucking real!"

"I don't disagree! Not for a moment. And, if you change your perception as a victim, you will change how you react!"

Paul could see the anger and tension rising in the other man's face. To his credit, the took a deep breath before he responded.

"I will never be a victim again! Ever! I will never sit still for being fucking tortured ever again!"

"Whoa, man! Who 'tortured' you?"

"My goddamn father! And you will never fucking convince me that I was responsible for that! Or for the motherfuckers chasing me!"

"You misunderstand what I was saying. How you react to a threat makes it better or worse. Of course, you don't just sit there and allow yourself to be harmed! That would be crazy and irresponsible!"

"But what about other people? Their motivation to harm me?"

"They're responsible for what they think. You're only responsible for how you react."

"It still sounds like I'm responsible for the abuse!"

"I didn't say anything about 'abuse,' but it's the root of it all."

"Fuck you, man! My fucked-up childhood is why these people want to take me off the board? That's crazy!"

"I believe our earliest experiences condition our later reactions. That you are on the run from seriously dangerous individuals—that didn't just happen yesterday."

"OK. I'll buy that."

"So, if we trace the feeling of being endangered, we would probably find the roots of it in your 'fucked-up childhood.'"

Roach nodded his head, and said, "I always hated my asshole father! I did everything I could to not be like him, and stick it in his face every chance I got."

"I don't imagine that helped very much."

"Fuck no! But I never let that bastard see me cry! No matter how much he beat me!" Roach said, as an admixture of fury, shame and pride flashed across his face.

"And where, brother," Paul said softly, "do you think all of that

138

pain went, even when you didn't express it?"

Roach looked shocked, confused, even a little crestfallen. In an entirely different tone of voice, he expressed his incredulity, being presented with this new tack. His eyes conveyed confusion and distress, even though he didn't speak.

Paul spoke again, softly into the silence.

"I know this must be a shock for you."

Suddenly his client, his brother vet, responded, his voice angry and a bit bewildered.

"Is this all I can expect? The longer I'm clean, the more fucked up I get?"

"It always gets worse before it gets better!"

"That sounds like psychobabble bullshit!"

"No. When you stop hiding from yourself; when you start not being afraid of being real, then the shit starts pouring out! It feels worse!"

"Then I'm not so fucking sure I want this!"

"You've been defending yourself with rage and violence, with smack, for decades!"

"It's kept me alive all this time!"

"And it's brought you here. Congratulations! Now you have an opportunity to have a different life, if you choose."

"I... don't know if I'm ready."

"What's the alternative? More of the same old bullshit?"

"I'm really afraid of being too open. I'll get hurt!"

"It will be a daunting journey."

"I'm inclined to trust you because you've been through your own shit!"

"I'm still a work in progress, but I've done a lot of work."

"That's why I trust you. And you were at Evans."

"I can only share with you what I myself have experienced; what I know is true."

"I... feel like I'm overseas and I don't know the language!"

"There's this professor, University of Houston I believe, by the name of Breen Brown, who said 'Owning our story and loving ourselves through that process is the bravest thing that we'll ever do.'"

"And you believe that?"

"I think she's brilliant!"

"But do you believe that?"

"Yes! I'm a living laboratory for what I believe."

"And what's in it for me?"

"I don't know, man, who you might become. What is it that you really and truly want for yourself, above all else?"

"I don't know. I've always like to draw. I might like to paint."

"See? There's always something we hide from ourselves when we're strung out! It's too scary to be that honest!

"But you live well. Nice house. Must have some bucks."

"Probably a lot less than you think. This work is the only thing worth pursuing. And I'm not obsessed any more. I love and respect my life."

"Then why are you helping me?"

"You came to me and asked for my help. That's one of my standards. I do not recruit clients. I never intervene with others unless it's an emergency."

"Why?"

"Because it more-or-less guarantees that a potential client is ready to do the work; that they will be relatively cooperative with letting go and do homework."

"So, you have faith in me?" he asked, only semi-mocking.

"I believe you have great potential—to arise from the ashes of your own making and become the man you always wanted to be, the man you have always been in your heart of hearts."

"I... don't know how to respond to that."

"I don't expect you to. I am just laying out what I believe. It will apply to everyone at some point, but most of humanity is not ready yet."

"Why not?"

"First, I think it requires great suffering, and then recovering from the effects of that ordeal. At least it has for me. It seems to be a universal process of what my Indian friends call 'carrying medicine.'"

"'Medicine?'"

"Healing ability. One becomes medicine through the process of learning to develop whatever kind of healing power is given to one."

"What does that mean?"

"As my friend Macallan Da Besh always says, 'You don't choose medicine. Medicine choose you.'"

"Say more."

"I have been gifted the ability to help others because I have healed a lifetime of 'mental illness'—what drove me to drugs in the first place."

"'Gifted?'"

"It's a gift, brother. Granted by the Universe. All you can do is heal yourself, heal your own injuries. Then, maybe, you can help others."

"It sounds like you're talking about recovering from addictions."

"Yes! Absolutely! Though in a larger sense. That's why humanity isn't ready yet. Most people are immersed in addictions because we live in a toxic soup called 'society.' We get manipulated to 'fit in' rather than being encouraged to think for ourselves, to attempt to become who we truly are. Joy is our birthright, and it's denied to us through the systematic application of large doses of shame and degradation from the very beginning, reinforcing the mandates of the pre-existing society."

"Quite a speech, man. I know you really believe what you're saying, but it's beyond me right now. Can we take this up next time?"

"Surely."

"Do you have any homework for me?"

"Certainly, grasshopper!"

"I certainly hope you don't expect me to call you 'Master!'" and they both laughed and then dapped.

"I want you to make a list of everything that is bothering you; everything you'd like to change, not matter how impossible it seems. Then, go back and assign a number to each of them, prioritize them so we're both clear about what's most important."

"All right," said Roach, who peeled off four fifty-dollar bills and placed them on the coffee table.

"Saturday? Same time, same place?"

CHAPTER SEVENTEEN

IMMERSION

Immediately after the session with Roach, Paul called Karen, on the off chance that she might be willing to meet with him. He knew it was nominally her day off. She told him that she had gone out early and done her errands, then took a five-mile hike through Golden Gate Park. She had just returned a few minutes before he called.

They had agreed to meet at 1500 and he arrived with minutes to spare. The skies were clear and the temperature was fifty degrees, with a ten-mile an hour wind that permitted him to be comfortable wearing just his jean jacket over a long-sleeved t-shirt and a pair of corduroys.

Karen greeted him at the entrance to her office wearing jeans and a black silk t-shirt. Paul took a seat in one of the Bauhaus chairs (they were really comfortable), then closed his eyes and took a deep breath.

When he opened his eyes, Karen was sitting quietly, observing him. She smiled and said "OM to you too!"

Paul laughed and said "Thanks so much for seeing me. We should just set up a regular time. I'm seeing my client every other day, so the day of the week we meet might need to shift. I have a lot more information and I want to sharpen my focus. I also want to talk to you about the legal aspects of this case."

"Good! I'm ready! I've done some research."

"Excellent!"

"So, let's review just a little bit. The greatest blessing of the therapeutic relationship is in the beginning when a client can talk about whatever they wish—their fantasies, fears, hopes, traumas, crimes. All we have to do is listen. This helps establish the basic trust without which no client would ever feel safe exposing the contents of their minds, hearts, and souls."

"I agree with you."

"With my clients, I lay out the parameters of confidentiality and the conditions under which I may break it. I explain that psychologists have a duty to protect people from abuse, and a duty to protect patients from committing suicide. I tell them that this doesn't mean that I will immediately hospitalize them if we talk about having a dark night of the soul or wonder what it would be like to not be alive. I tell them that many people talk about suicide and contemplate their own deaths; that many people are chronically suicidal and never require hospitalization. I tell my clients that we can talk about this any time, and that we'll work together to make sure he or she can talk openly about any feelings they have about suicide while also making sure they are safe."

"Good standard stuff so far!"

"I also tell them about psychologists having a duty to warn and protect intended victims of homicide. I use the example of someone who says, 'Oh my boss, I could just kill him.' Just a figure of speech. They wouldn't be hospitalized for that. However, if the client should have planned and have intention to commit murder and tells me about it, and identifies an intended victim or victims, then I will have to take every action at my disposal to protect him or her from committing this crime and protect the intended victim. And I tell them that I may have to secure him or her in a psychiatric hospital. In addition, that I am required to warn the intended victims and warn the police.

"Tarasoff warning."

"Precisely!"

"Now we come to the part that is of the greatest interest to me."

"Yes, I know. Sorry if I was boring you."

"Not boring. I know you're extremely thorough. So, no, not boring. Pray, proceed."

"I can tell you that the information I gave you last time is correct. But I want to amplify it today."

"Sounds good. I want to make sure I'm on the right page with all of this."

"Totally!"

146

"And thanks again for all the good work."

"It didn't cost me anything. There's this attorney—you don't know him—who's been asking me out."

"And?

"He's nice enough. So, I finally said 'Yes.'"

"And?"

"We had a nice lunch and I asked him a bunch of questions. He never knew my motivation."

"Very smart. Very, very smart. And cunning!"

"Thank you, kind sir!"

"You are a trip!"

"*Merci beaucoup!*"

"As he—Raoul is his name—explained it to me, most discussions of this subject fall under the general category of 'misprison of a felony,' the presumed general obligation of all citizens to report felonies that come to their attention. Courts have consistently interpreted the federal misprision statute to require active concealment of a crime, not merely the failure to report. Most states reject misprison as a common law crime, because it's incompatible with the contemporary notions of justice. There is no statute of limitations for murder, and therapists are never required to report them except as we've noted. In almost all jurisdictions, however, the fear of prosecution for failure to report a past crime should not be a factor in deciding on a course of action."

She paused and asked, "Do you want to hear more about this?"

"Is it relevant?"

"In for a penny, in for a pound!"

"Neal v. U.S. created a four-part test for establishing that the crime of misprision has occurred: (1) the principal committed and completed the felony alleged; (2) the defendant had full knowledge of that fact; (3) the defendant failed to notify authorities; and (4) the defendant took an affirmative step to conceal the crime. The mere fact of the therapist's reporting the commission of a federal crime under the Farr vs. Neal test would not, in itself, expose the therapist to legal jeopardy. It would appear to be true regardless of the crime involved, including threats to federal officials and even treason."

"'Treason?'"

"'Misprision of treason' is addressed by a separate statute, but the wording of the section 'conceals and ... does not disclose' is the same as misprision statute."

"Jesus! These bureaucrats! They create these so-called 'laws' to keep people under the yoke. Always acting *in loco parentis*!"

"You are so incredibly political!"

"I just love the way you explained the law to me! This is just vital information!"

"You're most welcome!

"Wow! Would you think I was weird if I said that was sexy, the way you laid it out?" Paul said and laughed. The truth was that her passion, her grace and the depth of her intelligence was very attractive, so this mild flirting seemed appropriate.

"Thank you yet again, kind sir. It's cute of you to flirt with me!"

"We're both adults, despite the legal proscriptions of our relationship."

"Granted. Now for the rest."

"I'm ready!"

"Next is what is called the 'Crime-Fraud Exception.' In California, there's an exception to the therapist-patient relationship when the patient is seeking, or obtains the therapist's services, in order to commit a crime, or any form of fraud. For example, a client making a deceitful statement to a psychiatrist in order to obtain controlled substances, is not privileged. That doesn't mean that all statements by that client over the span of therapy would be admissible in court, probably only those related to the crime."

"Say more about that please."

"This applies in cases where the defendant seeks to use, or did use the psychotherapist's services to enable himself or anyone else, to commit a crime, or to escape being caught and/or arrested after committing a crime."

"If a client were to wish to plead 'not guilty by reason of insanity,' or 'incompetence to stand trial,' confidentiality is erased."

"That totally makes sense. Any other conditions?"

"Only those that would apply if the therapist, or any Qualified Mental Health Professional (QMHP) were to judge an individual to be a 'Danger to Self' or 'Danger to Others'; anyone who would otherwise qualify under the auspices of Welfare and Institutions Code Section 5150 for a 72-hour hold."

Paul took a deep breath and exhaled heavily.

"Now, at least I'm comfortable enough to tell my client he can safely unload any and all of his past crimes on me!"

"Within the parameters!"

"Of course! Indubitably!"

"Has he told you he's killed anybody?"

"He was a Combat Medic. He was in the 'Nam for like eight years. So, what do you think?"

"I would think so. But you don't want to tell me."

"Is it relevant?"

"I don't know. Maybe."

"Well?"

"I shouldn't have to mention this, but..."

"Confidentiality."

"Absolutely!"

"You should know you can trust me."

"I do."

"Well?"

"He told me he's killed a lot of people. He guessed 'a hundred!'"

"Oh my God! Do you believe him?"

"I have no reason to doubt him. To some extent it depends on the circumstances."

"Such as?"

"In combat, it is totally legitimated. But he has revealed a great deal of other activities."

"'Activities?'"

Paul breathed deeply again, then sighed. "'In for a penny, in for a pound!'"

"Yes?"

"Heroin."

"'Heroin?'"

"International drug dealing. He implicates the government."

"Our government?"

"My answer would be: in as much as it was ever 'ours,' but yes."

"Really?"

"No. I'm making it up!"

"And he purports to be able to detail his accusations?"

"He claims to have lived everything he's telling me. And he has not yet even told me some of the deeper shit that happened after the NVA took over!"

"But he stayed in Asia?"

"Apparently. We haven't got that far yet. But it's important for me to have you in the loop, especially because there's at least the possibility that I may develop counter-transference since we have some significant history."

"I really appreciate your faith in me."

"It's only given because you deserve it. I don't necessarily trust, even clinically, very easily. I find that most clinicians are too immersed in the old methodology, in the so called 'traditional' beliefs about so-called 'mental illness.'"

"I want to keep earning your trust."

"I'm touched. I really appreciate the feedback, especially because I haven't yet made a decision about whether he's delusional, or if this is the absolute truth. I just don't know yet, but I do know he has a serious traumatic history. He's like a lot of vets I've with whom I have worked. They have traumatic histories from childhood experiences that make their PTSD exponentially worse from being in country."

"I know you told me that your father is a WWII combat vet. Do you think his might be?"

"I don't know, but it makes a lot of sense. I wonder if the current crop of Iraqi vets had Vietnam vet fathers."

"That would make a really interesting study."

"Yeah, if you could get the funding. I mean, I would love to do such a study, but the costs could prove to be onerous."

"Too true."

"I could arrive at the diagnosis of Substance-Induced Delusional Disorder. But then, I would have to differentiate between the situational suspiciousness related to using illegal drugs and pre-existing conditions."

"Excellent razor, Occam!" and they both laughed.

"May we talk a little about differentiating between delusional disorder and actual lived life experience."

"Wow! Huge topic!"

"I know, but it could be the basis of part of our ongoing conversation."

"As Freud used to say, 'First we must have a definition of terms.'"

"I guess that depends in part upon who you read."

"How very true."

"The old saw about a delusion being a fixed idea to which an individual actively clings, and that has no external referent of validation, is so outmoded. Jaspers calls these only the 'external characteristics' of delusion."

"All you have to do is listen to two opposing politicians arguing with each other, or members of two different religions. They fit all of the categories but, at least in the popular parlance, they're not considered delusional."

"By your standard, both the politicians and the religious are delusional!"

"Absolutely! But we're speaking clinically here."

"What both the religious and the politicians are using is what Jaspers called 'overvalued ideas,' unreasonable ideas that a person holds, but about which the affected person has at least some level of doubt as to its truthfulness and validity. They're also quite easy for psychologically unsophisticated individuals to invest in because such folks are unaware of the deeper currents of human consciousness; too easily manipulated by the 'popular press.'"

"Go on."

"Delusion is just never a mere object which can be objectively detected and described, because it evolves and exists only within subjective and interpersonal dimensions, however 'pathological' these dimensions may be."

"I agree."

"Jaspers' book, *General Psychopathology,* marked a major step in establishing psychopathology as a scientific discipline. Experiencing mental states by the patient and understanding those experiences by the physician were his central tenets. He totally denied the biological orientation. He declared that mental events can never be accessed directly, but only through the expressions of the person experiencing them."

"So, we're talking phenomenology here, the study of subjective experience, the empathic access or understanding of the patient's experience—the therapist's ability to enter into the client's experience through using their own experience. That's the value of undergoing one's own therapy during training and graduate school. It sharpens the intuition and broadens the empathy base as well as alleviating one's own emotional blocks."

"I love this conversation!"

"Jaspers emphasized that the phenomenological approach enables the therapist to recreate the client's experiences within themselves through empathy."

"Rather than staunchly holding onto one's own views and calling them 'reality!'"

"Precisely."

"I feel like this sort of relates to your theory of psychic weight being attached to the mind as physical weight attaches to the body, though the former is related to trauma and the latter is related (such as with compulsive eating) as an effect of trauma or secondary to the irresolution of trauma."

"Wow! You really do get me!"

"I take that as a compliment."

"You should. I love it when someone really sees me. I feel really validated!"

"I love the distinction between overvalued belief and delusion."

"It cuts closer to creating a clear definition."

"Which then makes it easier to create a differential diagnosis."

"Absolutely! That's exactly what we are talking about here—discerning between overvalued belief and delusion."

"Even though you say he has lived a very heavy-duty life."

"True. Too true."

"In either event, we are talking about the manifested effects of life experience."

"There is, of course, the subjective interpretation of lived experience."

"I personally believe that all delusions, indeed all 'mental illness,' is a direct result of internalized, unintegrated trauma."

"Jaspers referred to it as 'the primary delusional experience,' and being 'the *direct, unmediated* intrusive knowledge of meaning, not considered interpretations but meaning *directly* experienced. In fact, the primary delusion is essentially not a belief or judgment at all but rather an experience.'"

Wow! That's it exactly!"

"Thought you'd like that."

"Though it really doesn't change the treatment approach too much. I still have to help the man sort out his longstanding pain—whether it is delusional or based on complex PTSD."

CHAPTER EIGHTEEN
THE NEXT ROUND

San Francisco   **Saturday, December 9th, 1995: 1502**

Paul had had a really fine morning at the keyboard, knocking out eight fresh pages between 0930 and 1400. Then he took a shower and brewed a fresh cup, deciding to sit quietly simply to contemplate until Roach arrived, partly at least, his growing attraction to Karen.

He and Roach completed their usual ritual greeting of a quick dap. They laughed, when Paul recounted a story of seeing two Black guys in Qui Nhon do the most elaborate dap he had ever seen—first palms, then hands back and forth, fist bumps followed by elbow knocks; then turning around, it was shoulders and hips, and, when they both fell on the ground, tapping the soles of their feet before they stood up laughing to a round of applause.

"That's funny, man."

"All kinds of crazy shit happened on Support Command Compound. It was so quiet, so safe there. I used to go into the ville three or four times a week to eat dinner!"

"Pretty slack."

"It was loose-o, for sure."

"I apologize. That wasn't the most professional exchange I've ever had."

"You keep opening up areas that I've always kept hidden."

"Sounds like a pattern to me."

"In what way?"

"Keeping things hidden; being suspicious all the time; acting as if they were true; going around armed and ready to kill people all the time."

"Comes with the territory."

"But that's been a choice too."

"It's worked for me for a long time."

"But now you say you want something different."

"Yes."

"In accord with Einstein, I say that doing the same thing over and over and expecting something different is the working definition of insanity."

"I've heard that before."

"But it's true! If you really want to change, you'll have to shift some of your entrenched beliefs."

"Is that what we're doing? 'Shifting my beliefs?'"

"Only with your permission, of course."

"I just want to stop running."

"Good. We're on the same page."

Roach sat silently for a moment, contemplating, and then looked up abruptly and asked, "So, what's next?" as if they were wasting time talking about anything that did not give him immediate relief, as if he were sizing Paul up as his next fix.

"Tell me what you want to talk about today. Did you do your homework?"

"You told me to make a 'list of all of the people or arenas' that were bothering me."

"That's right."

"I do have a list, but I hesitated to make it too comprehensive or detailed."

"Because?"

"It could be incriminating, if it...fell into the wrong hands."

"I will, of course, defer to your wishes. My hope was that it might give us a sort of map by which to navigate our work together."

"I'll use it, but I'll keep the list itself."

"As you wish. Where do we start?"

Roach turned to him and looked him fully in the face. Paul thought for a moment that there were tears in his eyes, an unprecedented event if that were so.

"I... I've lived what seems like such a long time, more than one lifetime in this body. And I am tired. Very, very tired," he said as he slumped into his chair.

Paul squelched his first impulse to lay a hand upon his shoulder, and instead simply followed his own trail.

"Brother, I've been there in my own way, when I quit cocaine."

Paul thought it unseemly, perhaps even unethical, but for Paul's methods to work effectively, it required that his clients have faith in him, and empathically resonate with his experience. His greatest asset had always been his ability to feel the suffering of others. His credibility turned on his lived life experience. Since Roach (it was weird that he didn't even know the man's name) and he had shared a brief, but extremely poignant slice of history, and he felt strongly compelled to enlist the man's trust and connection more strongly in order to break through the walls that guarded the vaults of his shame and perdition.

Something in Paul's tone alerted Roach. He looked more intently at Paul.

"Can you...tell me more?"

"This is unusual, but then, so is our connection."

San Francisco   August 1982

Paul had never intended to get strung out. Certainly, had never intended to progress from snorting to free-basing, and thence to putting needles in his arm. Certainly, never intended to become a complete slave to the tune of a $1000 a day habit. Until, came the day, when he had had to utterly abandon all else he had ever held dear for the specious ecstasy of his sweet lover—and quit caring about clothing, cleanliness, food, or sex.

Looking back, Paul realized how dazed and confused he had been before he finally surfaced, leaden, lethargic, anergic. He only really quit using because he self-destructed around caring about money—using all of the money from fronts to pay off other fronts and finally just using it all up in a kind of Gotterdammerung blast that left him broke, unable to pay back anyone's front, physically damaged, and his reputation in tatters.

The rent was long overdue (the manager was one of his connections); the gas and electricity were turned off for lack of payment—and he had completely alienated everyone he had ever known. And the only thing he could think about was cocaine. The only thing he wanted was cocaine. The only thing he needed was cocaine.

As all of the struts and supports of his world disintegrated, he took to sleeping as a refuge, for what seemed like months, sleep and delirium absorbing 16-18 hours of every day, the remainder devoted to ruminating about, or castigating himself for, the catastrophe he had created (oh how glorious the familiarity of self-loathing!). He categorized anything else that happened during the day as "lost." Even his delirium dreams were related to cocaine, to craving, to scheming, to grieving—none of which made any difference to the debt-collectors and arm breakers on his trail.

Since there were people camping out in the park across from his apartment house waiting for him to emerge, he could only come and go carefully through the basement service door. His reputation was in ruins. No one would even give him a line, despite the thousands of dollars' worth of product he had freely dispensed. He had awakened from one delirious sleep-and-dream session with a most severe craving he'd ever had cutting through him like shards of broken glass in every cell—crying, shaking, depressed and exhausted. At length, he threw his hands in the air, fell to his knees and cried out nakedly.

"I need some coke!"

His disorientation led inevitably to utter despair. In the depths of the darkest dark, the compassionate, ethereal voice of a woman spoke to him from the very air itself.

The Voice of Divine Mother. Unmistakable.

He had first heard from her in 1970 when he was in extremis, severely tortured and depressed by the deaths of Janis Joplin and Jimi Hendrix. He'd had a fantasy of stabbing himself in the heart, and sat down to write a death poem, sobbing uncontrollably. Then the atmosphere of the room changed, infused with a luminous, numinous light—when SHE came.

Thrilling ripples trilled down his spine when she spoke.

"You may not yet leave. You have work to do.

He was unable to convince himself that he was not hallucinating.

He was willing to sacrifice absolutely anything for even the smallest measure of cocaine this time when SHE came—and spoke from the juncture of the ceiling. The harshness of the words was tempered by a deep compassion.

"IF YOU USE AGAIN, YOU'RE GOINGTO DIE!"

Paul shook his head repeatedly, then fell back onto his bed and slept. Resurfacing from his quasi-coma, he shook his head and decided that he had been hearing voices. He decided to ignore what he knew to be patently true, to go in search cocaine without any money. He was shrugging into his disarrayed clothing when SHE spoke again.

"IF YOU USE AGAIN, YOU'RE GOING TO DIE!"

He was awake enough to start cursing, while contemplating whether he cared enough whether to live or die.

HER voice had penetrated his armor plating, and he fell to the floor sobbing—deep, wrenching blasts of despair, wave after wave of uncontrollable tears, a river of mucous splashing down his cheeks and chin, face contorted in a rictus of desolation, his outbursts so strong that he tore an intercostal muscle on his left side.

SHE had broken him open, ineluctably and forever, as if a giant cleaver had laid bare his skull. He simply sobbed and wept, sobbed and wept as a life review scrolled through his memories in excruciating detail. He begged for forgiveness, for release from this life bereft of self-forgiveness. He was gasping for breath and made a Herculean effort to stop crying, though the slightest vagrant sensation triggered him again and again, as if a deep river of toxins and corruption were flowing uninterrupted out of him, and purple stars appeared against an infinite black background.

When he could manage to get his feet under him, he stood and threw his hands in the air.

"Please help me!" he cried. Divine Mother poured a flood of soothing syrup through him. In that scintillating moment, he decided to live! No matter what a shitty mess he had made, he wanted to live!

The words of Joe McDonald's song "Who am I?" came forcibly to him:

"What a nothing I've made of life

The empty words, the coward's plight

To be pushed and passed from hand to hand

Never daring to speak, never daring to stand

And the emptiness of my family's eyes

Reminds me over and over of lies

And promises and deeds undone

And now again I want to run

But now there is nowhere to run to."

CHAPTER NINETEEN
A HUGE BREAKTHROUGH

Revealing his traumatic history had led Roach into revealing details of many depredations and abuses he had experienced as a sensitive young man at the hands of his violent and sadistic father. He confessed that he had survived by shutting down emotionally and channeling the bulk of his malignant rage into an early life of petty crime. It started with stealing small amounts from his mother's purse (his sanctimonious father counted every penny in his pocket, every bill in his wallet whilst his mother did not); then it was cigarettes from either of his parent's packs, escalating to packs and cartons from the small, local grocery store; then stamps and coins to bulk up his collections; when he got a little older, it was 45 records and LPs from shops and to which he bicycled with his next door neighbor partner-in-crime; eventually, anything at all in a rush to feel momentary fullness, to chase away the terrible emptiness—until, at the age of twelve, he succumbed to his father's favorite demon, alcohol, the most advertised "legal" drug of modern times. He indulged daily throughout high school, though still managed to do well in the life sciences, had even though briefly of medical school, though he did not do well with the more abstruse subjects like math.

"I started hanging out with the 'hoodlums.' They were all heavy drinkers, and we just didn't give a shit! They called us," here he chuckled, "'miscreants!' We called ourselves 'The Shit Disturbers!'"

"Sounds familiar!"

"I started smoking weed when I was fourteen, and every day by fifteen."

"Did it help?"

"'Help?'"

"With feeling shitty and disconnected?"

Roach thought for a moment, and then nodded his head.

"For a while, but of, course, it was never enough."

"But you kept smoking anyway?"

"It worked better than anything else. But then I hadn't found the shit yet."

"When did that happen?"

"Not for a while. We all took diet pills. That just took us deeper into crime. We started doing muggings, shaking kids down for their money—not just the joke lunch money crap. We went to the higher-class schools where the rich kids were. They had real money. We stole cars, first for joy rides, then started turning them over to professionals, guys older than us. We made a lot of money."

"Then what happened?"

"I would never have started using narcotics, if I hadn't gotten busted."

"For what?"

"I swiped a Mercedes. A gorgeous, gold 280-SE convertible."

"And?"

"The cops wanted me to snitch out whoever gave me the order."

"And?"

"Fuck them!"

"And?"

"The judge gave me a choice: Three years in jail or three years in the Army."

"Oh, Christ! Unfortunately, I've heard this all too many times."

"I did really well in Basic, after the first week or two. I excelled at hand-to-hand combat and on the rifle range. I thought for sure they were gonna want to make me a rifleman, except I had high marks for life sciences—so they sent me to Fort Sam for Combat Medic training."

"I see."

"And I excelled there too. They offered me 91-C training but I didn't want to enlist for the extra year."

"And then?"

"I went airborne for the adventure—and the extra pay. I wanted excitement!"

"It sounds like self-hatred lies at the heart of all of this! You couldn't 'stand yourself,' like James Brown used to say!"

"I really never looked at it that way. I just never felt...comfortable in my skin."

"It does make total sense, choosing a drug that blanks you out."

"Good way of putting it. Blessedly numb."

"I believe that when someone is experiences anxiety, they choose heroin or benzos. Whereas someone who's depressed, they'll choose speed or cocaine, to excite the mesolimbic dopamine reward system, to create the illusion of being high, as if they had done the work necessary to actually relieve the pain."

"So, recovery is actually recovery?"

"Yes. Releasing the toxic materials and reviving the initial state of wholeness that existed before the damage."

"How did all of this start?"

"I do have a theory."

Roach just grimaced and twirled his hand in a "come on" gesture.

"It all begins with a corrupt, dysfunctional society that uses shame to control children and as a means of social control. Individuals then grow up with an inbred sense of deficiency, of needing something—sex, food, money, drugs, whatever. It creates a greed that feeds on itself. It keeps getting bigger and bigger until it grows out of control, until there are no longer any boundaries. Everything is legitimated. Everything is allowed."

"I understand that really well. I've been living that way for years."

"You've been a junkie for a long time, brother—long before you found heroin."

"The heroin trade is a way of life. Even the most fucked up shit is just another day at the office!"

Paul took a deep breath and addressed the man.

"Let's look at your list. Unless there's something in particular that's up for you today?"

"I'm pretty acquainted with PTSD symptoms, and I've got all of them."

"And?"

"I think I need to go deeper, to the symptoms behind the symptoms."

"What in particular do you want to address?"

"You said that there's shame behind all of all of what I'm feeling."

"And healing the shame will, in my opinion, heal the anxiety and the underlying material that leads you to want to use."

"I don't care so much about using. I mean, I do. But what I really want is to feel good about my life. I want to get off the fucking treadmill."

Paul considered for a moment, then responded.

"In my cosmology, that's going to require dismantling the structure that's maintained you all these years."

"What's that mean?"

"Again, when you internalize trauma, it's stored, and repeatedly acts as if it were still happening in the present. It's the traumatic affect that creates symptoms. Addiction is a symptom that helps you keep your fears and anxieties in check."

"That sounds right."

"The problem is that once you quit using, then you have to deal with the underlying issues that have always existed."

"Like my goddamn father!"

"Like your 'goddamn father!'"

"And what does that require?"

"You're gonna have to allow yourself to feel all the shit that you've been hiding from all these years!"

"FUCK THAT!" Roach shouted. "I DON'T WANT TO REMEMBER THAT SHIT!"

"It's not to torture you, or punish you."

"THEN WHAT?"

"You have to be willing to feel the original pain so that you can let it go!"

"I DEALT WITH IT ONCE. I DON'T WANT TO DO IT AGAIN!"

"That' the point. You didn't get the chance to 'deal with it.' You were a little kid."

"I've been dealing with my PTSD from the 'Nam all these years!"

Paul roared. "BULLSHIT!!"

"FUCK YOU!"

"You been shooting smack all these years! You call that a good adjustment?"

That stopped Roach, who simply stood and stared at Paul.

"No. I guess not, huh?"

"So, as I said 'You have to be willing to feel the original pain so that you can let it go!'"

"How do I do that? You have some kind of plan?"

"Like I've said: 'You have to be willing to feel the original pain so that you can let it go!'"

"Re-experience all that horrible shit? How do I know that will work?"

"I can only talk about my own experience."

"And you are a fucking glowing example of recovery?"

"I have been clean since 1982. That's almost thirteen years. And, for the most part, I abstain from obsessions and compulsions across the board. I'd call that a pretty fucking good record of recovery, wouldn't you?"

"Well, then, I guess we should at least look at my fucking list!"

CHAPTER TWENTY
THE BEAT GOES ON

A t the end of their last session, Paul reminded Roach to continue his homework. Before his next session, Paul looked over what Roach had written and then made a very cryptic list of his own, having promised him that he would burn the original afterwards.

Paul had always considered himself to be somewhat jaded, inured to cruelty and savagery in many forms, but he was unprepared for some of the atrocities enumerated by Roach:

Pushing the head of a recalcitrant village headman into a boiling pot of cooking opium after a dispute.

Shooting a rogue CIA man in the face after he had threatened Roach's native wife and kids.

Participating in a large number of "thousand-foot interrogations," in which reluctant-to-talk individuals were questioned at a thousand feet over the jungle in a helicopter (it usually only took one man being tossed out to convince others to talk);

The many eyes and ears, noses and teeth he had removed in the course of his "days in the office" in order to punish or simply

174

intimidate others to get his way.

Uncountable, unauthorized cross-border excursions in pursuit of business.

Exiting and re-entering Laos, Cambodia, Burma, Thailand without official authorization.

Flew thousands of hours in black helicopters guarding body bags filled with heroin all around Viet Nam, and to ships and planes for export.

Wearing civilian clothing while serving as a military service man.

Making deals with opium warlords while acting as a sub-rosa agent of the government.

Transporting thousands of kilos of heroin.

Decapitated dozens of NVA (mostly men) and putting their heads on stakes as a warning to their comrades.

Shepherding and delivering tens of thousands of kilos of raw opium to the Thai Mafia for processing.

Routinely eliminating anyone who got in the way of his duties as he saw them.

Inadvertently killing an undercover NYC cop (who had been posing as a bad guy);

Had his blood supply completely transfused at government expense several times. (He did, after all, have a government health care insurance card with no limits).

After numerous pages of this, Paul had had to stop. He was exhausted. He felt as drained as if he'd been working manual labor for ten hours. He needed a shower and a change of clothes, followed by a nap. When he awoke three hours later, he set a pot of mixed Brown, Black and Red rice to cook that was just ready to eat by the time his food was delivered. The indulged in Ginger Crab, Beef in Black Bean Sauce, and Spicy Eggplant. It always struck him as odd that he had to order his meals delivered from a Richmond District restaurant when he lived within walking distance of Chinatown.

He ate as if he hadn't eaten in weeks, then cleaned up, and fell into a deep, deep slumber punctuated by dreams of some of Roach's experiences that gave way to a guided tour of the Underworld, burning pictures of the 'Nam flashing like urgent messages down blazing telegraph lines to the very heart of his DNA. It reminded him of an early version of *Brotherhood* (entitled *Born in Hell* at that point) and watched the re-enactment of a thirty-page description of torture he had planned for Hoxley...

...And awoke crying, in a cold sweat, sheets soaked, wave after wave of old tormenting memories sweeping through him like a diarrheal river.

And he knew, *just knew*, exactly how he could help Brother Roach.

CHAPTER TWENTY-ONE
WE MEET AGAIN, MY FRIEND

San Francisco   **Wednesday, December 13th, 1995: 1101**

Paul looked at Roach for a very long time before he felt able to speak coherently. He felt "hung over" from his previous evening's journey. Despite the powerful cathartic effect of his dreams, the night had left a shadow hovering around like a spectral shroud, even while it lent itself to his approach to working with Roach.

"Let's do a little meditation first, just to better clear the air."

Paul led him through the systematic process of centering his consciousness. When Paul felt they had both reached a greater level of inner quiet, he allowed the silence that was nowhere else available to linger for just a few more moments.

Roach sat quietly too, then, as if breaking a spell, he shook like a wet dog emerging from a puddle. The beatitude that had informed his face fell away too, and his "usual" face dropped back into place, like a rigidified stone effigy, the protective mask he had worn for so many years.

"Pretty trippy, huh?"

"I'm...I don't know if I especially like it. It feels...weird."

"'Weird?' How?"

"I just…I'm just not used to feeling so…exposed, so helpless."

"What does it remind you of?"

"Oh, fuck you, man," he replied.

"Why are you being so reactive?"

"You keep wanting me to remember my fucking childhood!"

"Only because it still owns you, brother!"

"God damn it! I suddenly feel like using!"

"No wonder! You've always avoided your feelings and living on the nod!"

"Fuck you, man! You don't fucking know anything about it!"

Paul wrestled with himself for a moment. Even after having shared his cocaine adventures, he was torn between ethics and credibility, and decided he might have to go more deeply into his own personal story. Theoretically, he should not offer, as he had done several times with this man, personal information in support of credibility. There was only a moment of hesitation before he responded.

"Fuck you too, man! I do!"

Roach shrugged and made a waving gesture with his right hand as Paul took a deep breath and plunged on.

"When that fucking Hoxley set me up, I spent five weeks smoking opium every day!"

"Five weeks! Big fucking deal! You weren't even really strung out!"

"Fuck you again! I was using five grams a day!"

"It wasn't skag!"

"No, but I do know where narcotics took me—especially when I had to kick!"

"Say more."

"I got seriously immersed in erasing the world. I just wanted to be sedated!"

May, 1969   Phu Bai, Viet Nam

Though he had ten grams of black tar stashed in the hollow leg of his bunk, he was determined to keep his word to the good Captain, his attorney, not to use again and be as straight as he could the following morning. He knew he was gonna start kickin', but he would have a little help from his friends. Restless and twitchy, he kept hitting the shitter. His belly alternatively cramped and turned liquid as his vision filled with an array of dragons, serpents, gargoyles and demons wearing lurid, psychedelic colors as the worst migraine he'd ever had twisted through him, metastasizing to his inside out stomach, his spasming spleen, and quivering liver; his inner highways flooded with an ocean of napalm. Even his toenails felt ill. He was vomiting from all his pores and orifices simultaneously, as vital fluids streamed and steamed through him spilling viscous gouts of tears and fears, singeing his cilia and villi. His throat closed. He felt like he was having total organ failure. Every muscle and tendon was infected by an icy fire; his brain pan was afire with the only currency his body understood—the unworldly excruciating pain that was the price of his addiction to pure opium—or rather the tormenting, unrelenting lack of it as he kicked, cold, cold, bitter cold turkey.

He felt like ten pounds of shit in a five-pound bag. Cold perspiration poured out of him as hot urine ran down his legs and he cried: "Oh sweet Jesus, help me! Make it go away!" He prayed to die, and found a most unexpected empathy with William Burroughs' rhetorical question from Naked Lunch: "I'd kill my own mother for another shot of heroin, wouldn't you?"

He kept purging and puking as an existential madness excoriated him. He was beyond fear, immersed only in the shattered moments exploding throughout his body.

HE WAS GOIN' HOME!

Nothing could harm him any longer. He was beyond the pale of normal human understanding and experience, walking in the Underworld, immersed in his ordeal, tortured by the demons and other residents of all the Hells! His exhausted sphincter let loose over and over, and he filled his pants with multiple times. He felt dirty and defiled. Did not want to be touched! Could not stand to be touched!

HE WAS GOINGHOME!

180

Jed, his good brother Jed, approached confidently, striding toward him, overriding his signals as he held out his hands palms out in push-away gestures.

"It's OK, brother! It's OK!" he said and drew Paul closer, lifting him.

A whole bunch of good brothers dragged him pissing and shitting, and puking and gagging, into the showers and stripped off his clothes. HE WAS GOIN' HOME! Mother Kali ravaged his very soul with the darkest visions as sheets of white hot phosphorous flashed up and down his spinal column. HE WAS GOIN' HOME! He was castrated and eviscerated by syphilitic gophers; crucified and quartered, stretched on the racks of a thousand lands for unknown crimes and deprivations. HE WAS GOIN' HOME! Thick, black, torpid ropes of unidentifiable toxins and viscous fluids poured out of his every pore as incandescent flame of ecstasy and exquisite agony danced through his muscles, tendons, and nerves. HE WAS GOIN' HOME! Numinous flames of holy convulsions consumed his heart and shut down his airway. Jed jumped in and cleared it, waters of initiation pouring over them in a soul baptism, brothers forever. HE WAS GOIN' HOME! Rockets and mortars slammed into the compound, shattering buildings, choppers and people, but no one cared. No one abandoned him, not even for a moment. His good brothers stayed with him, cared for him in the most tender and perfect ways, as he cursed and spit, raged at them to kill him, to help him kill myself, to give him some dope, to make it stop. HE WAS

GOIN' HOME! HE WAS GOIN' HOME! HE WAS GOIN' HOME!

———————

Paul sat back, exhausted, tears still falling from his eyes—fucking ethic be damned! This was his life, his practice, his brother-in-arms! He rarely shared this harrowing adventure. Even now, through the immense sorrow and sadness, he felt a euphoria rising from the recall and recitation. Now, for him, it was just another story, another selection from the *persona dramatis* of his writer's life. Roach sat silently. He was observing Paul now with noticeably less of a gimlet eye, perhaps even with a glimmering of compassion, but that might have simply been Paul's fantasy.

"I'm buying it, brother! You do know!" He paused for a moment, then asked.

"Now what?"

"I told you that story because having it's critical to our work together. Your trusting me and the process are essential—what Bradshaw called 'the social aspect of healing,' the ability and willingness of the client to trust the therapist. I hold space for you so you can work out your old pain in a safe container where no one gets hurt. Not me. Not You. No one."

Roach again sat silently as if absorbing Paul's words as if he were osmotically taking them in through his skin. Then he nodded and spoke.

"I trust you right now. Beyond that, I can't say."

"That's fair. As you grow stronger, get clearer, we'll see what's next."

"We are on the same page, brother."

CHAPTER TWENTY-TWO
BLOSSOMING

San Francisco   **Thursday, December 14ᵗʰ, 1995: 1401**

P aul recounted his most recent sessions with Roach as he sat back on Karen's very comfortable love seat. He was still emotionally affected by the impact of the previous day's work. He always experienced the unmitigated power and emotional depth of re-telling this part of his story, but he had only very rarely revealed himself to a client in a therapeutic relationship. He noticed that he felt softer, gentler, less inclined to be guarded, today with Karen. Making a diagnostic choice suddenly didn't seem as important. He felt as if he had crossed the Rubicon like Caesar, in defiance of the Roman Senate, remarking, "*Ālea iacta est.*" In Paul's declaring "The die is set," he was putting his mark on the therapeutic alliance he had created with Roach, and was, therefore, much less concerned about the ostensibly delusional nature of the man himself.

"You sound different today. What's happened to you?"

Paul elucidated the amazing changes he'd been experiencing. He shared the story of his awakening that he had shared with Roach. He cried again as it resonated through him, chilled and thrilled him yet again.

Karen was clearly moved, put a hand on his forearm and looked at him softly.

"Wow! Thank you for sharing. I always knew you had a heavy history!"

"It's not something I talk about very often."

"Is it the Vietnam connection that brought this out of you?"

"It's pretty giant."

"You identify with him?"

"Deeply."

"Is there a bit of a countertransference developing here?"

"I may have crossed the line, but I don't see eye-to-eye with APA standards anyway. I argued in graduate school against adopting an APA standard because I was opposed to the profit motivation of the APA, not only in allowing, but encouraging the use of neuroleptics."

"Was that all of it?"

"No. The whole medical model grates on my nerves. I do not for a moment agree with the biological basis of 'mental illness.'"

"I know this isn't supposed be personal therapy for you, but I have to ask, why are you always so oppositional?"

Paul thought for a moment, taken aback a bit, not expecting this particular tack. He considered not answering, but then replied, "It's a legitimate question. My attitude does have the potential to flavor my approach with clients."

"Thank you. Are you going to be more specific?"

"I've been resisting my whole life. Fighting to stay alive, to preserve what little self-esteem I could to shelter myself in childhood. It really rubbed off on me."

"But you continue to fight, always opposing established rules and order."

"More against mandates. I am virulently opposed to the existing order. As George Bernard Shaw once commented:

I am, and always have been, a revolutionary writer, because our laws make law impossible; our liberties destroy all freedom; our property is organized robbery; our morality is an impudent hypocrisy; our wisdom is administered by inexperienced or mal-experienced dupes, our power wielded by cowards and weaklings, and our honor false in all its points. I am an enemy of the existing order for good reasons.

"That's a great quote! Sounds a lot like you!"

Paul sighed deeply, and then looked directly into her emerald green eyes. He had always been attracted to her, but had, wisely he thought, deferred his feelings in favor of cultivating her excellent work ethic and intelligence, her professional presence. He was again reminded of that decision, and currently sharing far more of his personal history than he had intended.

"This is taking us into my personal history, way more than I had intended, but you're right. This does have a direct connection to the work, so..."

Karen sat silently, patiently awaiting whatever revelation was coming next

"I do identify with him. He had a really brutal father. He was a WWII vet too."

"And why is that relevant?" Karen just had to ask.

"I identify with him, but that allows an even deeper empathy in me."

"And?"

"Being oppositional has been the way I've always survived. Even if I reject that approach without coming to some kind of peace with it, it still retains a strength and vitality for me. It always allows me to feel safe. It has an impact on my soul."

"Sounds very Jungian." It was Karen's primary orientation as well.

"I buy a lot more of his work more than I do Freud's."

"Are you acquainted with the work of Jeffrey Moussaieff Masson?"

"Oh my God, he's an excellent writer!" Paul felt a strong frisson of excitement run through him. Masson was rather esoteric, and that she knew of him, was exciting.

"I really resonate with his work. He really exposed Freud."

"Especially since Freud put so much emphasis on 'penis envy!'"

"He's one of the few men in the psychoanalytic community

who's actually written favorably about women. Or rather, spoken honestly about the damage done by patriarchal psychiatry. Have you read *A Dark Science: Women, Sexuality and Psychiatry in the Nineteenth Century?"* Feminist psychology was one of the arenas that Karen had specialized in from its inception more than twenty years before. She had always considered herself to be an empowered woman. Paul, in turn had always struck her as being amenable to the feminist perspective.

"Very powerful. Men just can't seem to help being sexist. It's an old agenda that's been pushed for centuries. Men grow up inheriting their father's shitty attitudes and passing them on. Society is just a larger version of that same patriarchal subterfuge."

"Freud blamed children for sexual abuse, too."

"Did you read *Assault on Truth: Freud's Suppression of the Seduction Theory*?"

"Yes! Freud was panned by the critics and the professional circles when he first started writing about psychoanalysis."

"And Masson exposed all of his shadow stuff, when he published *The Complete Letters of Sigmund Freud to Wilhelm Fliess, 1887-1904.*"

"Somebody told me that Fleiss and Freud were actually lovers!" exclaimed Karen.

"Peter Gay talked about that when he edited *The Freud Reader*. 1989, I think."

"That was incredibly revealing! Masson was shunned by the psychoanalytic community after that."

"Protecting their sacred cow!" Paul said scathingly.

"He kind of blew them all up after they de-frocked him. I loved *Final Analysis: The Making and Unmaking of a Psychoanalyst*."

"One of the most compelling books I have ever read!"

"I agree!"

"Wow! This is exciting! I'm finding so concordance with you!"

"But we've gotten off-topic!" Karen said, then re-assumed her role as holder of the container for this session.

Paul sighed. It was often a come-down for him to have to focus on practical matters when he would most naturally delve into abstruse metaphysical matters.

"You're right. All of that was triggered by us talking about oppositionality. And thinking about an impoverished sense of self that develops from a lack of early nurturing, often accompanying some form of violent abuse that furthers the sense of the unworthiness of being loved."

"And you identify with that?"

"As a matter of fact, I do."

"As long as you don't let it contaminate your working relationship."

"I operate using my empathy, so there's always a certain level of 'blending,' or 'joining.'"

"'Blending' in therapy doesn't mean blurred boundaries!"

"Having a too set rigid set of boundaries leads to the whole idea of 'objectivity' so touted by 'traditional' treatment. As if such a thing were even possible!"

"I agree. I'm just reminding you that this is therapy, not friendship."

"Thanks! I appreciate that."

"Are you are getting in too deeply? A bit too personally involved?"

"No! I really don't! What I've shared of my personal story has increased my credibility and deepened our therapeutic bond."

"Are you going to be able to stand apart sufficiently to treat him without counter-transferring?"

"That's why I'm here!"

"Now, is there anything else we need to talk about today?"

"I feel we're pretty much up to speed."

"Well, then, there is something I believe we need to talk about."

"What is that?"

"It sounds like you're no longer interested in establishing a diagnosis. Have you abandoned the possibility that he might be delusional?"

190

"It's not as important as I originally thought, especially since he's opened up to me."

"And?"

"It's totally germane to keep working with him, to allow him to release stored toxic emotions. At some point, when he's clearer, it might be time to delve more deeply into diagnosis."

"I see. But isn't it dangerous, in case he's not delusional? In case Organized Crime is really after him? It might put your life in danger too."

"I've entered into a contract with him, expended a great deal of time and energy with him. Besides, this is exciting and intriguing."

"I can see that. And, I admit, I like working with you on this case."

"So, let's keep close track of the counter-transference. I so sincerely appreciate the acuity of your eye and your heart."

CHAPTER TWENTY-THREE
A PERSONAL INTERLUDE

San Francisco   **Friday, December 15th, 1995: 1111**

Paul had taken the bulk of the day to himself, sleeping late and lying in bed to read after he awakened. He was reading José Argüello's *Transformative Vision,* and it was fascinating. The author firmly believed that our current period of time had been prefigured by the ancient Mayans, a time when the "arrogance of homo consumeritis" would be transformed by an incoming wave of higher dimensional energies that would lead to massive changes on the planet as a whole. He further predicted the awakening of humanity, and that a vast number of men and women who would undergo initiatory ceremonies (and the concomitant rebirth experiences) necessary for them to embody the cosmic power of this higher dimension of energy. They would in turn become the healers and guides for an emerging humanity.

It was totally inspiring, especially as he believed he was one of those described in the Theosophical texts of the 19th century as the "New Group of World Servers." It described an awakening from what Charles Tart had called "the consensus trance," the aberrant, though "normalized" state in which most people exist that legitimizes all dysfunctional artifacts of contemporary society. (It was, in part, why he considered his book, *Crucible of Shame:*

Trauma and Transformation, to be his version of Freud's 1919 classic, *Civilization and its Discontents*).

At length, he somewhat reluctantly willed himself out of bed (mainly to use the bathroom again), and then decided that his day should officially begin. He made his way to the kitchen and pushed the "Start" button on the coffee maker, preloaded with six heaping teaspoons of Sumatran ground for drip, and the appropriate amount of water to make two ten-ounce cups of steaming brew.

He woke his computer from its sleep, checked his e-mail, then moved to the spot at which he had left off working on his latest manuscript. It was the way he could readily pick up the thread of the narrative easily and apply the inspiration he'd gotten from that morning's reading.

Argüello's writing was simultaneously lyrical and deeply logical, reflecting the fact that he was both a scientist and a musician, both a philosopher and an artist. He so intimately embodied the living truth that he had seen—and provided Paul with many golden nuggets.

He spoke of the many dimensions of the Hero's Journey, the initiatory process he himself had experienced during his weekend experience with the Mankind Project. The process was ancient, universal and eternal. Argüello noted:

Just as the embryo recapitulates biological evolution, so the individual life recapitulates the history of civilization; at one point, apocalypse is inevitable and natural. Apocalypse is what the visionary or shaman must undergo in order to come into his own revelation of his own integral wholeness of things, for apocalypse is catharsis...post-history [will be] a collectively altered state of consciousness, a radical shift in human perspective.

Argüelles' writing called to his soul in a way that very little else ever had, to a new way of seeing, as if liquid knowledge had awakened in his soul and fed to his heart and brain directly, a holy revelation that transported him into the ever-effulgent Light that transposed every molecule of his consciousness into integrated accord with the One Law, the One Word that had always existed and always would, beyond all space and time, incorporating everything. Nothing was hidden. It was all available with each intake of a single breath.

Argüelles continued (he couldn't put it down):

To pass through the center of this apocalypse is to embark on a new stage of growth. Once the test of personal and historical catharsis is met, true individuation becomes possible. The visionary experience presents itself as a necessity for survival, as the purpose of life on Earth inexorably unfolds...The road is hard, and only those who are ready for individuation, the reunion of the psyche and techne, will themselves become the path that must be traveled in order for humans to realize their full humanity. The vision-seed has already been planted in their fertile consciousness. Through these beings of transformed vision, the earth and heavens may experience reunion, and the world may be returned to a mythic space to be divined and explored by humanity in full consciousness.

He was so excited that he just kept reading, deciding that this incredible literature so well informed his own work, so enriched his worldview and gave him answers he had long sought, solidifying numerous strings of his often disparate life experience into a more coherent and comprehensive whole that sang in his heart and brightened his interior vaults, illuminated his awareness and his desire to share his work with the world in a much larger way than previously, in ways that he had only rarely considered possible. He felt like he had crossed a threshold and was taking the first tentative steps into a completely new and unexplored Universe.

It reminded him of one of his favorite and most cherished passages from Ken Wilber:

And comes to rest that Godless search, tormented and tormenting…gone the madness of a life committed to uncare, and gone the tears and terror of the brutal days and endless nights where time alone would rule. And I—I rise to taste the dawn and find that love alone will shine today. And the Shining says: to love it all, and love it madly, and always endlessly, and ever fiercely, to love without choice and thus enter the All, embracing the only and radiant Divine: now as Emptiness, now as Form, together and forever, the Godless search undone, and love alone will shine today.

CHAPTER TWENTY-FOUR
BATTER UP!

San Francisco   **Friday, December 15th, 1995: 1904**

P aul grilled a rib-eye steak and a pile of crisp French fries, with which he drank several glasses of water. Though he did occasionally indulge in a glass of fine wine or the happiest beer available, he never did so prior to seeing a client. He went to his office to sit quietly and breathe while awaiting Roach's arrival.

Roach looked different when he arrived. He was clean and neatly dressed, but that was no different. The change seemed more internal, as if something ineffable or ethereal had bloomed in his heart. Paul commented on it without naming it, hoping that Roach might choose to elucidate on his own initiative.

The more Paul looked at the man, the more he himself had changed too, and might simply be seeing Roach through his own changed perception. No matter. Paul knew he had been changed, even for a small space in time; had been led to a place he had always been seeking, albeit without necessarily carrying an awareness of his own true north; baffled and battered many times, but keeping his head down and pointed into the heart of the storm, driving toward the golden goal that had been planted in his brain like a lodestone, always keeping him pointed to it magnetically, always pursuing what had been born in his heart; toward what had been hidden from him for a very long time, and was just now beginning to manifest—and he had no idea what form it might take.

Paul took another deep breath and shifted into clinician mode before addressing Roach. He considered different approaches to open the session, but it was just too much work not to just be natural and follow his intuition.

"Did you further refine your homework?"

"Well, no, man. I've been...pretty busy."

"Do you have any idea how fucking inane that sounds, man?"

"What do you mean? 'Inane?'"

"Do you know the definition of 'inane?'"

"You're saying I'm silly; stupid; not making sense."

"Partly."

"'Partly?'"

"How I'm using the word is more along the lines of silly; lacking significance."

"And that applies to me how?"

"You come to me claiming to want my help; agreeing to do your work; and when I give you homework, you don't do it and then you give me some bullshit about being 'busy.'"

"Fuck you, man! I'll kick your ass!"

"Isaac Asimov said that 'violence is the last refuge of the incompetent.'"

"Now I'm incompetent? You fucker," said Roach rising from the love seat.

"What do you think, brother?" Paul asked. "I push you a little bit and you go all fucking Rambo on me!"

"Why is it 'silly' or 'incompetent' of me to not do my homework? What the fuck difference does it make?"

"Listen, man. I do not do anything without a reason. I give you homework so we can go deeper into cleaning up your shit—that is, if you really want to 'stop running.'"

The last word from Paul's lips stopped the man's until-then-confident approach.

He looked at Paul as if seeing him for the first time, then shook his head and looked nonplussed.

"I see. I been fucking up. I'll own that. OK?"

"Good by me. Are you ready to go further?"

"What do we do?"

"Let's start with your homework. I'll sit with you and we'll go through it together."

Roach nodded and moved back to his seat.

Paul sat down in the chair immediately adjacent to the love seat, and deposited Roach's list on the table. Roach looked up then and said, "By the way, it was George Bernard Shaw who said 'Politics is the last resort for the scoundrel.'"

Paul laughed heartily and offered a dap, which they shared.

"Now. Let's look at this list, and prioritize it together. That way we can work on what's most important to you."

"What does that mean for me? In practical terms?"

Paul sighed, then looked up and smiled.

"Therapy is exactly like everything in life. You get out of it what you put into it."

Roach watched as Paul went on.

"In this particular case, that means, if you're really interested in changing, we're gonna have to go a lot deeper than we have. We're going to really open you up. 'Fire your rep,' as we say in Mankind Project."

"What's that mean?"

"That all of your bravado bullshit, no matter how well-earned and merited, is just that—bullshit!"

"It's kept me alive all these years!"

Paul felt a flame, definitely a non-professional one, leaping up his spine. It exploded out of his mouth in a laser beam of focused anger and frustration.

"You can't hide behind your façade any longer! Your junkie insouciance is bullshit!"

"Fuck you, man!"

"There you go again! Rather than admit that you are in deep pain, you attack! To keep me further away! Just so you don't have to be real!"

"What the fuck does that mean?"

"I look at the list of shit that you claim haunts you, but I don't feel any fear or shame or pain, no remorse! It's more like fucking pride!"

"My human emotions got killed off years ago in combat!"

"No! It was long dead before that. Combat made it worse!"

"Oh, here we go! The childhood shit again!"

"You goddamn right! My shit didn't start in the 'Nam. Neither did yours!"

"Look, motherfucker, I've been in charge of my life for a long fucking time!"

"And now you tell me you want to change!"

"I do!"

"But you refuse to address your past!"

"Fuck all that! It was over a long time ago!"

"So, you want me to put band-aids on your spurting arteries?"

Roach only hesitated for a moment, then sighed and said, "No! I... need help!"

"But?" Paul felt it implied in the lingering silence.

"I don't want to bring up all of the old childhood shit!"

"Then, you should just go back to the smack!"

"Why are those my only choices?"

Paul sat up as one of his many illustrative metaphors sprang to mind instantly.

"OK. Here's an idea for you," he said after he drew a glass of water from the tap. "I'm going to put one drop of potassium cyanide," he said and shook a brown glass bottle that actually held lavender oil, "in it. And then, I am going to challenge you to drink around it."

Roach looked at him in an admixture of incredulity and disbelief.

"Im-fucking-possible!"

Paul opened his hands at his side, arms wide, palms up.

"Precisely!"

"So?"

"The more of the poison you hold onto, refusing to release it, believing in the mistaken notion that it keeps you safe, the sicker you stay!"

"Like you're a fucking paragon of virtue!'

"I don't claim to be! I'm 'making my own way through my own day' as Buffy Saint Marie once sang. I have almost fourteen years clean Christmas Day. I've done a shitload of work, hard motherfucking emotional work, to get clean and stay clean. I am a changed man! And I'm still changing!"

"And you think your way will work for me?"

"I don't know. All I can do is share my way, be an example of all that I believe in. If you choose to apply what part of that that works for you, it may help you. I cannot change you!"

"OK. And?"

"I'm here to help you awaken your heart. You'll find your own unique way to continue to stay clean."

"That's it, huh? For a hundred dollars an hour?"

"You have to do your homework. You have to go through your own suffering, your own trials."

"Relive them? Fuck that!"

"The difference is that I'm your witness, to hold space to support your healing."

"That's it?"

"It's your work. I'm just your living instruction manual."

CHAPTER TWENTY-FIVE
THE BEAT GOES ON

San Francisco　　　**Friday, December 15th, 1995: 2034**

T hey decided to take a little break after their two-hour session, and to get something to eat while continuing less formally though maintaining the contextual integrity. They decided to go down to Sam's Black Sea Restaurant. It had opened in 1947, the same year Ben Friedman started buying up the entire block of Columbus Avenue from Green to Grant that included his flagship store, The Postermat as well as the US Restaurant and a large number of apartments and other businesses.

By comparison to the bulk of eating establishments in North Beach (all tending to further and further gentrification), Sam's had stayed more-or-less the same since about the mid-1960s (Paul was guessing), even though the marquee, in plain black letters against a white background with red trim, looked to be original. Some people might have called it a dive.

Paul had eaten there many times, and had cultivated a relationship with "Sam" (the sobriquet he had adopted as a close proximation of his own, nearly unpronounceable real name). Paul introduced Roach who had apparently already been taking many meals there. The food was fresh, the coffee strong and the prices reasonable. Sam greeted them both warmly in a two-handed shake that belied his small stature, and exuded the radiant warmth that was so characteristic of him. He brushed his moustache, first one side and then the other, before gesturing to the counter where he could converse with them while he prepared their order in the open-style kitchen. As soon as they were seated, he served them water without ice and a small bowl of çorba, a thin Turkish soup often eaten as an appetizer. He also put out a platter of simit, a crusty circular loaf of bread, to nosh on while they studied the menu. Paul usually told Sam what he was hungry for and allowed the older man to follow his unerring instincts. If it hadn't been for that willingness, he would not have tried a large portion of the menu, all of which had delighted his palate.

Roach had similarly adventurous tastes, and they discussed that which each of them was craving that night.

"I'm having a taste for some fish, like this one here with the sumac berries."

"That sounds good! And some kind of eggplant, maybe that stuffed one Sam calls 'The Imam Fainted!'"

"With all of that sucuk, the spicy sausage and vegetables."

"And what, rice pilaf or potatoes with peppers and yogurt?"

"Maybe both!"

"Excellent! I'm glad you're hungry too!"

In very short order, their side of the conversation dissipated as Sam filled the counter with numerous dishes and side dishes (many

204

of which they did not order but he provided anyway, as was his gracious custom). The he started telling some of his origin stories, about growing up in a small village and the closeness of family life there; of fishing with his father and uncles and brothers; of storm-tossed seas and bulging nets filled with sardines, mackerel and other fish; of growing up swimming and diving from a very early age, for lobster, crabs, squid and octopus; of the years during the war when he lived in Istanbul, and then Constantinople, when he was a bit of a spy (though he downplayed his roles) and black-marketeer and smuggler (mostly cigarettes, alcohol and precious foodstuffs, though he admitted that there had, of course, been guns and munitions too—on a rare night under the influence of too much raki, ("Lion's milk" that turns white when water is added).

Despite their vast consumption, they both felt compelled to have a piece of Sam's homemade baklava along with several cups of strong Turkish coffee. Tonight, they would consume no alcohol, as there was still much work to process, albeit the need was somewhat less urgent after their fine meal. Roach paid, as usual, and Paul tipped lavishly.

They bantered as they walked back to his office. When they had settled in their respective places, Paul took the opportunity to do some deep breathing with Roach. One became two became three, and when they opened their eyes, they shared a small laugh and the sense of being on the same page.

"That was pretty cool, man," said Roach.

"Amazing, isn't it?"

"How does that work?"

"I only know that it increases oxygen and decreases carbon dioxide. Personally, I believe that it opens the margins of the skin, what Alan Watts called 'the skin encapsulated ego,' to embrace the larger reality that always exists."

"That sounds so 'New Agey.' Do you really believe that?"

"I don't say things I don't believe."

"So, for you, there's a reality out there," he gestured, "beyond the senses, beyond science?"

"Absolutely!"

"Do you find it comforting?"

"'Comforting?'"

"You know, like religion. Something lingers after you die and all that."

"Not comforting in that sense. I know something is out there that's tangible and accessible. If you learn how to reach out for it, to trust that that which we call 'reality' is SO much bigger than we're taught."

"What does all this have to do with me?"

"You're going to have to reach out beyond everything you've ever believed in, everything that you've relied upon. Everything you've done to this point has led you here, to who you are now. If

206

you want something different, you are going to have <u>do</u> something different."

"If I give up what's worked for me no matter how 'dysfunctional,'" he said, making air quotes, "I also give up what's kept me alive."

"It all depends on what you're guarding, what you're 'protecting.'"

"You were there, man! You know the kind of shit we had to put up with!"

"All that was a long time ago!"

"And don't fucking tell me you don't have flashbacks too!"

Paul sighed, and said, "You're right. I do. I've worked for a long time to let go of all the pain and traumatic associations."

"How the fuck <u>do</u> you change 'associations?'"

"Being willing to let go."

"But then what?"

"You start safely letting go of all your old shit. I emphasize 'safely.'"

"It won't do any good to relive all that shit!"

"It hasn't done you any good to re-create all of that shit either over and over!"

"I'm alive, man! I'm still fucking alive!"

Paul had reached the limits of his tolerance, and spoke what he was feeling, momentarily abandoning any pretense of being therapeutic.

"Yeah, and you're just doing oh so fucking well, aren't you?"

There was a stunned silence, and it appeared as if Roach might lunge at him, even attack him. But then the other man fell back in his chair with his hands in front of his face as if ashamed, his cheeks and forehead totally inflamed and cherry red.

When, at length, he looked up and spoke, it was in a considerably quieter voice.

"If I were to pick you as this "safe person," and decide to trust you, then what? I spill out my guts to you—at a hundred dollars an hour! And then what? What will I be left with? Nothing! Less than fucking nothing! I won't have any defenses! Everybody could take advantage of me!"

"You really think I'd just leave you out there without any protection?"

"So far all you've done is sell me a box full of promises!"

"What do you really want?"

"Something tangible! Something real!"

"I don't make promises I can't keep."

"You claim that you've made progress, that your life has changed tremendously!"

"Yes."

"And that you managed to kick cocaine twice!"

"That's so."

"And you've stated—as a fucking fact—that you've done what you're asking me to do! Right?"

"True!"

"Give me some kind of proof, tangible proof!"

"Remember, I told you that you only get what you're willing to give?"

"So, what?"

"If you pick something that is really bothering you, and open up, really open up and tell me about it, we'll mark the date. Within a month, I will guarantee that you will experience marked relief."

"What's that mean?"

"You will say to me that you are 'better,' maybe even 'improved!'"

"What if I pick sleep problems?"

"Too complicated off the bat. Something else. Something more...accessible."

"Like what?"

"Flashbacks? Craving for smack? Nightmares? That last one won't go away, but I can teach you some techniques to reduce their intensity."

"'Craving for smack?' You can really help me with that?"

"Yes."

"How?"

"One technique involves you allowing yourself to feel <u>exactly</u> what you're feeling. You quit fighting the urge and let yourself go into it. When you're full of the feeling, you release it from your body. I will show you how to flush it out of your body. But you'll have to keep working it. It's not a cure! It won't work forever! But it's a tool you can use anytime, anywhere."

"Sounds too simple."

"Deceptively so."

"When do we start?"

"Next session."

"You're on!" he said, and peeled six fifty-dollar bills off his seemingly never-exhausted roll.

CHAPTER TWENTY-SIX
REFUEL

San Francisco   Saturday, December 16th, 1995: 1403

Karen had agreed to come to North Beach for their session, and they decided, semi-whimsically, to eat at the Rosé Pistola on Columbus (that had previously been the Café Roma). They declined alcohol, but Paul ordered a house coffee and Karen a gingerade.

"Are we breaking protocol again, or are we just going to have a pleasant lunch?"

"How about both?'

She shot him a quizzical look.

"We can keep the conversation fun and light, yet still touch on some of the relevant topics without breaking ethics, without naming names."

"Sounds like a deal to me!"

"We can talk in therapeutic generalities and theories without breaking confidentiality."

"Agreed."

Being a committed vegetarian, she decided on the angel hair pasta with fresh mushrooms, peppers, garlic and oil. Paul ordered the osso Bucco with rice pilaf. They decided to share a Salad Niçoise since she liked the vegetables (and Paul had both portions of the tuna). Both being hungry, they dived into the basket of fresh, hot bread, dipping it into olive oil and salt.

"So, what's the latest?"

"I'm really getting into this case. He's more willing to listen."

"What does that mean?"

"This guy has more resistance than any client I've ever had."

"Given what you've told me, it makes sense. Have you gotten any further in deciding if it's straight up delusional or substance-induced?"

"I've pretty much decided that it doesn't matter. There's no insurance to bill, and I don't have to formalize an evaluation."

"But still..."

"I'm not saying that I don't juggle with both of those considerations, but to some extent it's a separate issue. Helping him get a better perspective is far more important."

"But how can you successfully treat him if you haven't defined the issues?"

"I am very clear about his issues, especially the underlying roots. I don't need to put him into a category to work with him."

"But isn't the approach to a substance-induced delusional order different than if it is straight up delusional disorder?"

"The underlying issues are the same. The roots are in earliest childhood leading to a dysfunctional adaptation."

"I'm familiar with your thinking."

"Do you have an alternative line? Are you going to fall back on the old 'biological psychiatry' bullshit?"

"You know I don't buy any of that!"

"I know. I'm sorry. It's such a hot topic for me."

"Then why did you mention it?"

"You didn't exactly give a rousing endorsement for my beliefs!"

"I just think you're pretty radical."

"Because I've based my therapeutic approach on my own life experience and learning?"

"Even though it contradicts current accepted practice?"

"Arthur Schopenhauer once said: 'All truth passes through three stages. First, it is ridiculed. Second, it is violently opposed. Third, it is accepted as being self-evident.'"

"And you see yourself as some kind of progenitor, a forerunner for the human race or something?"

"No, but I do believe that there is a universal process that every human being will eventually experience. The Krishna people call it 'returning to Godhead.'"

"Is this the evolution/devolution thing you always talk about?"

"That's right. Some people are devolving, down into matter. Others are rising up out of matter into the higher realms of Origin."

"Returning to Source?"

"Yes! Exactly! That's precisely why I am so opposed to the current system in psychiatry, trying to put all of the emphasis on the brain, on the physical as the root of what are essentially emotional traumatic occurrences that leave a taint; scarring, if you will."

"And?"

"The emotional scarring magnetically attracts other energies of the same ilk. In Sanskrit, it's called *samscars*, literally past life emotional scars. So, if one is wounded, one continues to attract wounding in a similar manner."

Karen laughed then, and smiled. "You know I'm just playing Devil's Advocate with you again."

"Outside of myself, I know you are the most attuned therapist I know! That's why I come to you for consultation."

"I appreciate you too. It's always good to have a friend who speaks Psychologist!"

"Amen to that!"

"One of the many things I love about you is that I can speak freely with you about anything. I... You always help me feel more connected, like I'm less alone."

Karen's voice caught in her throat as she started to speak, and

Paul watched a faint rose blush rise from the base of her throat, and a single tear escape the orbit of her left eye and roll down her alabaster cheek.

"Paul, I don't know what to say."

Paul felt tears of empathy welling up in his eyes that infused his voice when he finally managed to speak again.

"I... didn't plan that. I guess I feel closer to you than I thought. I'm glad it came out, no matter why."

"I... I'm very touched, Paul."

"I love how you say my name, like you're tasting something you really enjoy with your tongue."

"You can be quite poetic."

"I've written a lot of poetry. You inspire me!"

"That must mean I am some kind of muse."

"I'm tempted to make a bad joke about you're being a-musing, but that's another tack."

She giggled, then laughed deep-throated.

"Thanks," she said, then paused. "Paul, I have to say something here. I... I admit... that I have some attraction to you..."

Paul sighed, having clearly heard the subtext, then said "But..."

"I'm sorry. I am attracted to you. It's just that..."

"There's somebody else...Of course."

"We used to be poly-amorous. A while back, we took a vow to be monogamous with each other."

"I understand. I don't like it one bit, but I understand."

"Until today, you and I've kept our relationship strictly professional. Now, I don't know what to do."

"If it's not too painful for you, I'd like to continue working with you!"

"How about you?"

"Everything professionally is still the same. But personally, I admit that I'm disappointed. But the real work goes on. I owe it to my client to give him the very best. And you give me the best feedback I have ever had."

She smiled again. The wattage of it lit up her face and the space they were in.

"Thanks for not making it more difficult."

"I don't want to lose your guidance...or your friendship!"

Lacking anything better to say, she said, "Shall we walk back to your office and continue this?"

"Sounds like a deal to me" Paul replied as casually as he could manage, working to balance all of the conflicting emotions he was experiencing.

They continued chatting as they walked through the incoming fog and the increasing wind as the afternoon deepened.

"So, you feel like you're making progress with this fellow?"

"Sometimes it feels like swimming through molasses."

"What's next?"

"He's gonna keep resisting, but I aim to get him to cry."

"'Cry?'"

"'Cry!' Because he's carrying so much grief, so much rage!"

"And crying's gonna change that?"

"Oh, come on, Heath, you've always been an advocate of therapeutic tears."

"Rosemarie Anderson's work introduced me to this at the Transpersonal Institute."

"I always forget you went there too."

"I had the good fortune to meet her once. She's got an article coming out in the *Journal of Transpersonal Psychology* early next year."

"Cool! Is Tom Greening still the editor?"

"And going strong! He's indefatigable! And brilliant!"

"Truly a gentleman and a gentle man."

"Indeed!"

"You figure you can loosen your client up enough to get him to cry?"

"It's the only way I know to genuinely relieve human suffering and open the door for integration. I mean, the crying will be the release of the emotions he's holding."

"Do you really believe it's possible to be integrated?"

"Maybe not totally. Some people say that, no matter how enlightened one becomes, one has to retain some portion of ego or shadow simply to stay in a human body."

"I tend to agree with that. It'd be extremely difficult otherwise. But there are degrees of healing, of awakening."

"I see it as part of my job as a healer, to alleviate human suffering as much as I can in every form—even though I truly know I can't do it completely, maybe I'm not even supposed to. No one has that power, but it's only in the context of the greater cosmic wholeness that suffering exists. It's an integral part of people's growth and illumination. It has been in my own."

"Are you saying you're enlightened?"

Paul laughed.

"Oh, hell no! But I am making progress."

"Like climbing a ladder?"

"If you will. I believe it's a process to be experienced, not a status to be achieved."

"Say more."

"I used to believe that 'attaining enlightenment' was a sort of goal after which one no longer had to struggle; that one would be on a kind of natural automatic pilot; that everything would be easy, effortless."

"And now, you no longer believe that?"

"No. I still believe it's possible to be attuned to one's relationship with the entire Universe in such a way that there is no longer a 'me' or 'I' with which to be concerned."

"And?"

"And, while one may remain functionally separate—eating, for example—one is informed by the needs of the whole. One, in effect, becomes the servant of the whole. As the I Ching says, 'To rule truly is to serve.'"

"To function as a Ram Das."

"Servant of Ram. Vishnu."

"Precisely!"

"Yeah. Like that."

"What happens to the individual?"

"What is called 'individuality' is actually just separatist egotism. When one is absorbed in the awareness of the greater whole, it still exists as a distant thread, but it is irrelevant. My immediate path is individuation."

"Say more."

"You know, Jung's ideal. True embodied authenticity versus

accenting superficial differences in personality."

"Wow! That was poetic!"

"And very much to the point clinically. Individuation is nothing less than what Maslow referred to as 'self-actualization,' integrating the conscious and the unconscious."

"And?"

"Look. I know you're not as simple as you're trying to seem. Please get off the 'Devil's Advocate' stance for a minute, will you?"

"I apologize. It's second nature for me to be skeptical."

"I understand. It's almost too easy to dismiss the truth, to hide tender feelings behind a skeptical, disbelieving stance."

"So?"

"Almost every human being does that, mainly because it's too goddamn painful to admit how shitty we feel, from the time we're children."

"Back to your primary theme!"

"As always, because it's always true!"

"You honestly don't believe anyone has a happy childhood?"

"I admit that it's a statistical possibility, but so small as to be approaching irrelevance!"

"Never?"

"'Never!' I cannot tell you how many times I've had clients tell me how happy or wonderful their childhoods were! And then later, in treatment, they tell me about beatings and torture, rape and abuse! Every single time! Without fail! Or else they quit the work when I apply the heat!"

"And so, you approach every client as a kind of liar?"

Paul thought for a moment, then replied, "I never really thought of it that way, but you're right. I am very skeptical when anyone tells me about a 'happy childhood.'"

"And then, you treat the client as if he or she were lying, probing for the underlying truth of the matter that you're convinced is the case."

"Only because I think that uncovering the emotional truth about one's life and releasing it is THE key to healing every emotional disturbance—ultimately all planetary dysfunction."

"So, when you get to this nugget of truth, then what?"

"Once someone gets free enough of the prison of the past, they are then free to start telling the truth. Like Shakespeare said, 'To thine own self be true, and it follows as the day the night, one canst not then be false to any man.'"

"Wait a minute! Wait a minute! As far as you're concerned, telling the truth is the key to healing all dysfunction?" She could not keep an edge of incredulity from her voice.

"Of course! Underneath of all 'dis-ease' is lies!"

"So, your antidote is the truth?"

"Think about what would happen if everyone told the truth all the time?"

"Civilization as we know it would fall apart!"

"Precisely! The entire façade of what we know as 'history' and 'civilization' is built on lies and obfuscations! Remember your Machiavelli: 'Only the victors write history!'"

"I thought that was Josef Goebbels."

"Misattribution. Or plagiarism."

"As always, you leave me with much to think about."

"I love to be an inspiration."

CHAPTER TWENTY-SEVEN
THE NEXT ROUND

San Francisco   **Sunday, December 17th, 1995: 1502**

Roach looked simultaneously perplexed and inquisitive when he arrived for his session.

"I must admit I am intrigued by the possibility that you mentioned last session."

"About reducing your craving for heroin?"

"Exactly. Can you show me it's true?"

"I can teach you a technique and walk you through it, but you have to keep applying it. That's the key. It won't go away if you just use it once."

"Today?"

"You bet!"

"How do we start?"

"First, I'm going to tell you about it and why I think it works."

"All right."

Paul took a deep breath and continued.

"Let's start with the nature of craving. A habit develops initially because the substance or process, like gambling or compulsive sex, seems like it will give relief from emotional agony, of any sort. For example, I feel anxious and depressed, I smoke a joint, and I feel better. That seems like a good solution. After a while, though, it starts working less well; or, I start having more anxiety than ever, smoking more weed and getting less of a response. I'm still having anxiety, so I try something stronger. And eventually I build a tolerance to that and need more."

"I understand. I've done all that myself."

"Of course. And what seems like a solution suddenly becomes a problem of its own. Now I've got the anxiety and the addiction I adopted to deal with the anxiety. I've compounded the problem."

"I'm with you."

"The natural reaction to the now-increased anxiety is to attempt to shut down and not feel, to ignore the problem and act as if it doesn't exist. And when it comes, to attempt to shut it down and not feel."

"That's right. Why should I invite more pain?"

"The real problem is that attempting to shut down the pain also shuts down the opportunity for pleasure."

"Hmmm."

"Trying to shut it down does not eliminate the source of the pain. It only causes it to grow stronger."

"So, what am I supposed to do? It sounds like I can't win."

"There's only one way to 'win.'"

"What's that?"

"You're going to hate this, but you have to embrace your feelings."

"What? What does that mean?"

"Instead of trying to get rid of how you feel, you have to give yourself permission to feel <u>exactly</u> what you're feeling. Feel your true and exact feeling; suffer through them; get to the real source of the pain, then embrace it and let it go."

"You're fucking crazy!"

"Square business, brother!"

"What feelings?" Roach muttered in a huff.

"All your feelings. Not just what you believe you're 'supposed' to feel, but what you actually do feel."

"Good or bad?"

"'Good or bad?'"

"And then what?"

"Once you allow your feelings, then you no longer have to fight them. Then whatever you feel is just what you are feel. It's legitimate. It's just you, and it's OK."

"Just like that, huh?"

"It's actually more complicated than it sounds. But essentially, yes."

"And what do I have to do?"

"Basically, just tell the truth. Especially to yourself."

"And how is that supposed to make me feel better?"

"Being honest allows you to feel what you really feel. You don't ever have to lie. You don't have to figure out the 'right' response anymore. You just get to be."

"What good is that?"

"We start lying as children because we're innocent. We try to protect the ones that injure us."

"Sounds normal to me."

"But it's not! It's totally screwed up! We keep creating generation of abused kids. Then they have kids and abuse them— and the world keeps getting worse."

"And telling the truth changes that?"

"Changing yourself changes the entire Universe."

"What does that mean?"

"Simply this: If you tell the truth to yourself, you can stop carrying around all of the shitty baggage of your childhood. You can quit defending yourself as if you were constantly being wounded over and over like you were still that little child."

"How do you know I was abused as a child?"

"You had Posttraumatic Stress Disorder long before you went to the 'Nam?"

"So, I have PTSD, huh?"

"Have had for a long time. That's part of why you keep repeating self-damaging patterns. Like using smack."

"Wait a minute. I use smack to keep from feeling old pain.

"Yes."

"I hide from old pain because I don't tell the truth about the beatings every single day of my life?"

"Not because of the beatings, but because you weren't allowed to tell the truth about the terrible, terrible pain and suffering you experienced. You had to hide it from yourself."

"If I had told the truth in any way, or to anybody, he would have killed me."

"Exactly!"

"The only time I ever fought back, when I was a little kid, I kicked him, as hard as I could after he beat me up."

"And what happened?"

"He beat the shit out of me again and threw me in the closet! He locked me in for a whole fucking day!"

"Pretty fucked up, huh?"

"Yeah. That was the last time I ever cried in front of him too. I swore I would never let him see how hurt I was. Never!"

In spite of himself, Paul jumped to his feet and exclaimed, "That's it exactly!"

"What's 'it'?"

"You stopped feeling! You shut down! How old were you?"

"Five."

"When did you start using?"

"What, smack?"

"No! Anything!"

"I don't know. I started...soon after that."

"Using what?"

"I started sneaking cigarettes."

"Five?"

"Yeah."

"Then what?"

"'Then what' what?"

"What else happened around that time?"

"'What else?'"

"What else happened in your life around that time? How else did you change?"

Roach was silent for long time, then looked up and shrugged.

"I don't know exactly! I just never got along very well in school."

"How? School work or the other kids?"

"School work was never a problem. I... sometimes older boys would try to steal my lunch money or push the little kids around."

"And?"

"I would always fight back, fight for the other kids too."

"Why did that get you in trouble?"

"I got kind of a reputation. Even if it was a really big kid; even if I was getting my ass kicked, I wouldn't stop! No matter what!"

"And?"

"Any time any shit got started, they automatically came looking for me!"

"Wow! That really sucks!"

"I just stopped giving a shit about what the fucking adults wanted. My goddamn father blamed me for everything anyway!"

"Jesus! What a travesty!"

"I really...now that you got me to talking about it, I guess I've never really got over it. It just kept getting worse!"

Paul took an intuitive leap and asked, "How do you feel about it now? How does it feel that you can tell me the whole truth?"

Again, Roach went silent. Long moments went by before he responded.

In a rare instance of emotional display, Roach looked up and screamed.

"AHHHHHHHHHHH! That motherfucker! I am fucking hate him!!'

"Wow!"

"I wish I could kill him a thousand times! Dig up his bones and piss on them!"

"Wow!"

Roach sat quietly though his face remained red. Paul could have sworn he saw a tear in his right eye.

Paul silently joined him in that sacred moment, an instant that occurred with every client who would prove successful in healing. It was that magical flash, that brief glimmer of a far deeper truth yet to be revealed, one that would be revealed in the course of time, but that itself precured the revolution of a heart and soul that was hidden, buried in the deepest recesses, protected by innumerable layers guarding the most delicate and precious truths against any and every assault or depredation; that could only be unlocked through the client's willingness to feel and honor his or her truth. Of course it involved the credibility of the therapist, and his or her willingness to maintain an aura of safety, protection and care that could not be spoken of or advertised in any other way than by the direct perception of the client. There was no way to fake it.

Both he and Roach sat there, a bit befuddled, looking at each other, not speaking. They were both aware of the import of what had just occurred and shared the altered state like a doorway into another dimension that had opened between them.

Roach breeched the silence with a small "Wow!"

Then his face hardened slightly, as his more usual consciousness began to return, flooding his neurons. Paul breathed into the floating altered-space and embraced it.

"Great, brother!"

Roach immediately started smashing his right fist into his left palm and growled. Paul brought out a small pile of pillows and a small plastic bat from behind the couch.

"I have to ask you not to yell too loud. But, if you can channel your rage using the bat, you can bash the shit out of your father! Imagine his face on the pillow every time you strike!"

For the next twenty-seven minutes, that is exactly what the man did. Paul only had to remind him twice to keep his voice down. The intensity of the pounding remained steady until all of a sudden it looked as if all of the electricity in Roach's muscles failed him, as if he had been stricken with tetany. He fell flat, weak and drained, across the pillows onto the floor. He lay there silently for some minutes, glassy-eyed but breathing steadily. Then he looked up at Paul with a tear-stained face and opened his mouth soundlessly several times before reaching for the tissue box.

Paul remained a compassionate witness to his client's release, and simply allowed the man to be with himself—likely a brand-new experience for him, representing the possibility of a new framework for living through which he might come in time to love and be loved.

CHAPTER TWENTY-EIGHT
MOVING FORWARD

San Francisco   **Monday, December 18th, 1995: 1017**

P aul wasn't surprised when Roach called and cancelled their next scheduled appointment, claiming he was still feeling "a little overwhelmed" and needed to reschedule. He said he would call "in the next few days."

Since Paul had no idea where Roach lived, or any idea what his phone number might be, he had very little option but to agree and offer support and encouragement.

"Call me if you need to chat. I know this is an especially hard time tight now. I been there too!"

"Thanks, man. I will."

"The key piece is to stay true to you, to your truth."

Paul then set about clearing his desk of phone messages, requests by potential clients, tallying unbilled client hours and filling out the billing forms. He worked through lunch into the early afternoon. When he felt called to eat, he rummaged through his fridge where he found three slices of cold extra-sausage pizza and the makings of a great salad: fresh spring greens, roasted red peppers, feta cheese (his favorite Bulgarian sheep-milk kind), pecans, cherry tomatoes and some marinated mushrooms he had bought at Molinari's Deli along with some pitted Kalamata olives. He ate with great relish, having completed most of the more jejune tasks that had been facing him.

Paperwork and bills were like a psychic weight that hung around his neck, as if he were bound in an ancient cangue the longer he failed to attend to them. Getting the petty details squared away freed his mind to focus on things he considered to be far more important. It had always been so for him. He had always framed his life around his essential need to write, taking afternoon or midnight shift positions to do so. This allowed him to spend his vitality on his own work—whether it was poetry, polemics or the ever-growing number of books in what he envisioned as a series of novels whose protagonist' experiences loosely paralleled his own, but in ways that Henry Miller would not have recognized as classic autobiographical novels.

But they were his own. He wrote *Crazy Tales* as a kind of purgative for Vietnam. It was with *Spirals* that had brought out the first had a glimmering that he could write an autobiographical novel series, though it all made perfect sense. One of the insights that fed this was the realization that he would never be the urbane, well-heeled man of the world who could speak with ease about the best restaurant on the West Bank of Paris or the best bathhouse in Pest. But he knew the ins and outs of psychiatric units and the politics of psychiatry. He had lived them and discoursed endlessly about them in his own mind many times—and imagined all variety of characters, witty dialogue and incredible narratives. His immersion in psychiatry had formed the skeletal backbone of his life, as if it were, in fact, his legacy, a career, a lifestyle, an education, an entire encyclopedia, waiting to unfold, waiting in time for him to arrive.

In more grandiose moments, he described his books as a safari into a new literary genre—or sub-genre, to be more correct, since he was actually treading in the relatively well-worn path of such literary luminaries as Charles Dickens, Gregory David Roberts and Tim O'Brien, all of whom had used the very real and actual events of their lives and presented them in a fictional context; all of whom—Sylvia Plath, William Burroughs, Jack London—wove their real events into a fictive context to share the real treasures of a life well-lived and filled with grand adventures; Jack Kerouac, Leo Tolstoy, James Baldwin might not otherwise have either reached the page or been received in the same way; James Joyce, Charlotte Brontë, D.H. Lawrence all of whom had been recognized, elevated and celebrated for the deeds, real or fictive, much like Ralph Ellison, F. Scott Fitzgerald and Marcel Proust.

He took it as an omen, as certain as grace, that he had been granted a day off by the Universe from what would have been the ordinary course the day might otherwise have taken. He granted himself the luxury of lingering over a third cup of coffee, letting his mind drift, recalling the latest session with Roach, imagining all that the man might be going through at that same moment—and how intricately, how perfectly Paul's own process of unfoldment, his deep personal work, had fitted him perfectly into his role as a healer of souls.

Paul laughed aloud as if there were an unseen audience in attendance, guffawed at another example of his grandiosity, based on a single breakthrough moment with one client—though it had been inspired by his memory of other clients who had proclaimed that he had "saved my life." In some cases, it had been actual and factual. When working in crisis (as he had for five years), he had frequently encountered individuals expressing suicidal ideation, though a much smaller percentage had true intent. There had been those rare occasions when he had directly intervened with someone intent on destroying their sacred vehicle—it being a rather common *accoutrement* of severe depressive symptoms, the illusion (actually delusion) that "killing" oneself by eliminating one's body would be a solution to stopping maddening effects of the sorrow and the Grand Canyonesque feelings of despair and worthlessness. Paul had been there too, and therefore able to provide his heartfelt opinion and support.

It was so convoluted. The pivot point for all of the continuing planetary dysfunction seemed to be the unwillingness (and concomitant inability) of most individuals to do deep personal work, healing the illusory rift between self and body, or mind and body as some would have it. Again, Argüelles magically came to his aid. Paul worked constantly to reconcile his own lived experience with the larger, skewed format touted as "history," especially the deeply engrained penchant for war:

When art, or any of the means of knowing and expressing ceases to be a rung on the ladder of greater evolutionary development, and instead becomes an end in itself, the individual becomes a parody of his labors: how much more so for entire cultures? When culture becomes a refinement rather than an integral expression of internal necessity, it blinds and dulls the senses rather than educating them; when the senses are sundered from the wholeness of innate experience, when the cumulative power of culture distorts perception more than aids it, and distracts attention more than serves it, when knowledge deludes rather than enlightens, and when social mores are used to rationalize rather than uplift, then it is inevitable that war should become civilization's most distinguishing feature— that activity, finally, to which all other modes of knowing and artistic practice must be subordinated.

Wow! The man continued to impress him with the acuity of his thought and the erudite understanding he applied to the broadest scope of "modern civilization," which, he believed, was neither modern nor civilized. Paul's experience in the military, especially in Vietnam, had re-oriented his life onto the path that he had pursued ever since. (Of course, there had been precursors. In some sense, it could be said that the arc of his entire life had been such that he was only now treading ground for which he had already always been preparing, or for which he had been being prepared). Part of his recovery from the military was to immerse himself in an intensive study of the recorded history of Southeast Asia. He had become very acutely aware of the massive distortion that had been officially sanctioned and reported—especially in the "official" recording of the activities of the U.S. government, slanted to paint the rosiest of pictures and claiming the most humane of motivations for all of the scurrilous and degenerate practices by a succession of leaders and political manipulators, always couched in terms of pseudo-benevolence displayed toward "the savages." It was all, of course, a gigantic package of lies and dis-information aimed at camouflaging the true intentions and the utter depravity of Empire building.

Cogito ergo sum was usual summation of intellectual and cultural life used to emphasize the split from integral wholeness that was used to persecute indigenous cultures for thousands of years: Descartes' dictum explicated civilization's orientation to fragmented consciousness, which, of course, only echoed Da Vinci's orientation to art, who, in turn, reflected Aristotle: "The sense which is nearest to the organ of perception functions most quickly; and this is the eye, the chief, the leader of all others; of this only will we treat in order to not be too long." This totally framed the left-hemispheric visual bias of the European worldview. As Argüelles further noted: "Leonardo confounded this truth with an inherited Platonic-Christian prejudice that denigrates the body and elevates the eye, whose medium of information is *light*, symbolic of the spirit, above all other senses and modes of knowing...*Owing to the eye the soul is content to stay in its bodily prison, for without it such a bodily prison is torture.*"

Paul looked up from the keyboard to find that nearly three hours had passed. He basked in the awareness of his accomplishment. He sighed and sat back in his chair. These periods of reverie, of blessed intervention—from what he considered to be the higher dimensions—continued to amaze him. He looked at them as extended communications from his Higher Self that allowed him temporary access to a timeless realm to which he did not normally have admittance, bound as he was, in the machinations of time and schedules and other mundane bullshit with which this corrupt and comic "civilization" was afflicted—focused almost exclusively on maximizing production and profit, the bane of a true spiritual life. Paul's clinical self then chimed in with antiquated concerns about "loss of time" being symptomatic of dissociation, perhaps even severe "mental illness," but he had hashed through these so many times that he was unconcerned, especially, like Krishnamurti had said (echoed by pundits like R.D. Laing): "It is no measure of good health to be well adjusted to a profoundly sick society."

That extremely profound observation lay at the base of much of his own sense of dislocation and his decided lack of interest in and enthusiasm for much of what the current world model touted as "beneficial," even "necessary." Of course, he had always felt distanced from the enticing and enthralling events and experiences of "normal" everyday life, of investing one's precious life energy in what he considered stupid, banal and superficial—in a word, almost everything associated with modern life. (He always figured he'd end up a crotchety curmudgeon in due course).

He had grown up dissociated. The experience that had sheltered him to survive the egregious abuse he had suffered (in pointed contradistinction to his younger sisters' opinions, who seemed to have grown up in a totally different household). Withdrawing inwardly had always been the wisest, perhaps only, move he could have made in the face of the daily hostility and emotional violence he had experienced. He knew many others who had endured worse physical, even sexual, abuse and had come out strong and powerful. Some were able to advocate for, and embrace, the kind of love and support they themselves had never had. A recent New York Times article had made note of a peer-reviewed clinical study that had pointed to emotional damage as being at least as damaging (or worse) than physical or sexual abuse.

He had always stayed in the shadows as much as he could, yet always nurturing an extraordinary longing to be seen and heard while being deathly afraid of it. The interventions of his mother had often been the only barrier between he and his death at the hands of his father—though she had her own motivations were equally dark and tangled as to the disposition of his self and his autonomy.

On yet deeper and continuing reflection, he always felt as if he had always lived in a different time zone, set apart from others—not just in the Cartesian sense, but more as if he were literally from another planet. (He had had many dreams about Alcyone in the Pleiades as well as sitting in Council and making a pre-birth decision to come to Earth). He felt that he had passed his entire childhood enveloped in a shroud-like leaden shield that deflected some, but not all, of the vicious, toxic emotional energy away from his acute awareness, and left him aching in every cell and neuron to feel a sense of connection with others. Part of his acute separateness had led him to stealing his father's porn and to compulsive masturbating from the age of eight. His desire to connect was so intense, despite it feeling so *verboten,* that it left him even more emotionally impotent.

This inwardness had led him through the ordeal of drugs and alcohol to the land of incredible healing adventures. As the old saying went, the only way out is through.

He believed that trying to modulate one's addictive desires ("manage" them), was a total dead end. It was the equivalent of walking down lower Market Street on a beautiful late September afternoon, and seeing a man wearing a hat, sunglasses and a top coat approaching. Odd, but not necessarily incongruous. As he got closer, the man whips open his trench coat and reveals a glistening, scimitar-sharp machete. Before he can react, he slices the misbegotten pedestrian from the shoulder to the crotch. As he falls, exsanguinating, to the sidewalk, a well-meaning (but delusional) old lady comes running up with a box of Band-Aids, yelling "There, there, dear, I'll fix you right up!"—as if, when needing immediate emergency surgery, such an intervention could be deemed appropriate.

It was similar to the approach pushed by book-learned "experts" to use cognitive approaches to re-train one's desires to be "moderate." To which Paul shouted a resounding "Bullshit!" It did not work and never would, mainly because most people never really indulged in their desires and addictions to the maximum; and therefore, never really touched the roots of their insidious cravings; and hence, could never truly heal their souls. This was the quintessence of true healing, this embrace. Until one had the courage to reveal oneself to oneself in the total light of day, holding nothing back, unfearful of what might be exposed, willing to embrace whatever was shown in an all-embracing love and courage to accept it as the remnants of one's selfness that have strayed and now been found, and welcomed back to the flock as an oracle or messenger from beyond the ordinary. Until then, one would never be unified with oneself. Anyone who had not experienced the depth of an addiction (and therefore missed experiencing the depth of one's own peculiar nature in that way) could not (even should not), speak to the issues involved, and certainly not prescribe or provide treatment for others.

It was similar to an old argument frequently touted in the early days of LSD. One could not authoritatively speak about it if one had not taken it. Conversely, one could not do so if one had taken it. Therefore, there is no such thing as objectivity. Or, as Ken Kesey once commented, "You're either on the bus or you're not" referring to "Furthur," the iconic school bus in which the Merry Pranksters toured to deliver their Electric Kool Aid Acid Tests.

He always looked to his own experience as a living beacon, to his own memories and experience to find exactly what might be required in almost any situation. He was well-versed, yet not at all closed off to new information or input. He liked to think of himself as an osmotic vessel, in which and through which nutrients and such could easily enter, and the detritus and discarded elements of digestion, aerobic and anaerobic work, could pass to be eliminated. He applied this to himself emotionally and mentally, though it was also true physically.

He had encountered a countless number of ostensible "caregivers" and others calling themselves therapists or counselors or psychologists or Mental Health Professionals or healers or shamans or curandero. Many, almost to the person, were convinced that what they had learned from books or with their august degrees, was the real life equivalent of lived experience tempered with suffering and wisdom. It was another aspect of the cognitive orientation that the contemporary machine society had adopted, endeavoring, as much as possible, to eliminate or negate, actual lived human experience from every realm of human life, allowing human-created machines to attempt to replace empathy and compassion and the human emotional touch. Paul had even heard that there was software in development that was intended to replace clinical judgment in making diagnoses simply by ticking the appropriate boxes from drop-down menus on one's computer. What utter bosh!

He laughed aloud as he imagined a cartoon representation of himself shouting "Excelsior!" as he trudged up an endlessly high mountain strewn with rocks and boulders, covered with vast stands of trees and foliage, that was simultaneously inside and outside of himself, echoing Tennyson's epic poem. He saw his journey as exactly thus: The world outside of him perfectly matched the world inside of him, and his journey not only created but required that he embrace any and all obstacles as part of his spiritual path. Only then could he, reflecting the Buddha, "take refuge in the dharma" because it was all dharma, even the most sub-atomic portion of his journey. He believed he had reached an understanding with the Universe. As much as possible, and with as little grumbling as he could manage, he worked at maintaining a certain balance and stability in his daily life, embodying with himself, whilst still incomplete, the spirit of equanimity, love and devotion as might a genuinely loving parent with an errant child. All of his work had led him simultaneously deeper within himself and further into the world of experience that applied to all. He saw that he was gradually changing the world with his new attitude and actions—all simply by changing himself, settling ever more deeply into the new grooves that were being incised into his heart and soul by what he now considered to be a loving and benevolent Universe.

He was not in denial or delusion about the extant harshness or brutal exactitude that "The Big U" could exhibit. He was just more resolved with himself now, and therefore nowhere near as needy or hungry as he had been for so many decades. In some ways, he actually lived in a different world than many others, dictating different choices both personally and professionally that, in turn, mediated different outcomes that were far more tuned-in and idiosyncratically suited to him than might have been the more random or machine-generated ("popular") ones.

His innate sensitivity had grown exponentially. More and more he found himself having to divert energy to things that the world took for granted: rude people; intrusive behaviors; loud and demanding advertising and commercials; telemarketers (across the board—he didn't care if they "had to make a living"); the ongoing genocidal treatment of Native Indian and other indigenous peoples globally; the criminal orientation and behaviors of the food industry pushing sugars and raising obesity with false advertising; all in collusion with the US government endorsing high sugar, low fat diet and food choices; the arrogance of "experts" (in every field) proclaiming that the population as a whole was either ignorant or had child-like mentalities; loud intrusive music; uncaring, reckless drivers (especially those who routinely drove over the center line); Jehovah's Witnesses (and any and all "messengers" who showed up uninvited and unannounced at his door); bullshit politicians who egregiously proclaimed their ignorance and lies as being in the "public interest"; venal bankers and other fat-cats who manipulate the "market place" as if it were their very own kingdom; the ignorance and arrogance of most men in their attitudes and behaviors toward women (even though he had been guilty-as-charged himself for many decades); enforced poverty upon vast segments of the population in order to build Empire; military intrusions into other countries to enforce US power and presence, most especially engineered by the CIA, NSA and other alphabeted agencies. Paul decided to cut off his all-too-familiar rant before it consumed him (again) and took him off-track from his real work and the beautiful, sun-dappled attitude that fed it.

Even though it was now getting to be late afternoon, he was loath to leave his keyboard for the day. He felt filled, uplifted with brightness and a numinous energy permeating his every cell, as the pages seemed to just fill themselves. He had almost eight fresh pages, the cornucopic horn flowing with bounty and inspiration.

He was considering getting some exercise in, perhaps one of his pre-mapped walks through Golden Gate Park, measured from the Arguello Gate into the park proper. North Beach had a plethora of fine parks (Ina Coolbrith Park; Russian Hill Park; Pioneer Park), but sometimes there was much to be said for living more centrally as he had for many years. Of course, there were plenty of great walks in and around Columbus Ave, the cultural hub of The City (or one of several, at least). He couldn't help but think of all the districts in which he had lived: Haight, Mission, Lone Mountain, Noe Valley, Twin Peaks, Forest Hill, Inner and Outer Richmond, Russian Hill, Ashbury Heights, Pacific Heights, Nob Hill and even once (briefly) The Tenderloin.

Jesus! Unbelievable! He laughed (he could now) at the frequency of some of his moves of residence—once he had a place for three days and moved again because he thought he was being surveilled. Still, he gave thanks for every aspect of his journey. Since it was getting rather late and it was winter. He decided to take a quick walk to the Filbert Street Steps and down to The Embarcadero, and then back. A fun walk, and the perfect topping a productive and creative day, like fresh whipped cream on hot crepes.

CHAPTER TWENTY-NINE
CONTINUING UNFOLDMENT

Returning from his walk, he stopped at Il Pollo and picked up a roasted half-chicken with coleslaw and an order of extra-crisp fries. Walking in the door, he checked his answering machine and saw that Karen had called, but Roach had not. He had a fleeting concern that Roach might have had a relapse, having opened up his psyche with Paul. He knew how enticing might be the draw of shutting down fresh awareness, using again to tamp it all back down.

He knew his blood sugar was falling precipitously, so he decided to eat before calling Karen. Any conversation with her was likely to be an extended one, albeit fun and interesting. She was one of the most intelligent women he had ever known and inspiring (he was tempted to call her a muse).

"Haven't heard from you recently, so I thought I'd give you a call." She sounded bright and airy, a zephyr across the telephone wire.

"We've been meeting once a week, but my prime client cancelled his next appointment."

"Have you spoken to him at all? After the big breakthrough, he might be fragile."

"'Fragile.' Beautifully put. I know you're going to think this is weird, but I don't have his phone number. Or address, for that matter."

"That does sound a little strange. Why not?"

"I'm complying with my client's wishes."

"He didn't want you to have contact information?"

"That's right. I believe he has a mobile phone, but I don't know the number. He always calls me from pay phones."

"That is rather unusual."

"Despite our long acquaintance, he's more comfortable that way."

"Now what?"

"I've been concerned that the breakthrough might have given him a 'good reason' to use to stuff his feelings back down."

"Exactly! So, what are you going to do?"

"There's not much I can do. I've been busy writing and catching up on my other clients."

"What if, theoretically, you never heard from him again?"

"That would be one of those enduring mysteries!"

Though she chuckled, she asked again, "No, seriously?"

"I'm not going to panic over one missed appointment."

"But what if he's using again?"

"That's his choice."

"You don't feel any responsibility for not following up?"

"I'm in compliance with his wishes."

"Still..."

Now Paul felt a frisson of anger rising in his belly and his voice.

"Which would be more ethical—tracking him down against his wishes (which I would not know how to do anyway)—or waiting patiently, maintaining my composure and holding space for his next decision?"

There was silence on the line and Paul waited her out, knowing his own ground was solid.

"It is a bit of a conundrum, isn't it?"

"Certainly."

"Kind of a double-bind, huh?"

"It is. And I know this guy. We're brothers. We share a certain realm of experience and the residue of it."

"PTSD?"

"That certainly, but just the overall-ness of it."

"'Overall-ness?'"

"You know, the ambiance of having been there and the weltanschauung that develops from having been in a combat zone."

"You've never talk too much about your experience."

"I detailed some of it in my first book, *Crazy Tales*."

"I haven't read it."

Paul laughed and said, "You and millions of others!"

"I'd like to."

"Really? I'll have a copy printed and gift it to you. I would love to hear your observations and feedback."

"You're on."

"I'll let you know when I hear from him so that we can, hopefully, get back onto a regular schedule. I really appreciate working with you."

"Me too. You, I mean."

The call left Paul a bit unsettled, riding the wave of connection and yet longing to have more with her. Despite the fact that she had proclaimed herself committed and unavailable, he couldn't help but think how it might be to be involved with her intimately. More and more the craving for a solid, loving, intimate relationship had begun to appeal to him—yet he knew that, somehow, finding that kind of situation required that he be aligned and available for it.

The conundrum was: how did one prepare for such an exigency? He could only be who he truly was in his heart of hearts and hope/pray that the munificent powers of the Universe find him worthy. Of course, some of that was being clean, healthy, nicely dressed and at least semi-intelligent and willing to listen, really listen. At least superficially, he seemed to qualify. His many years in psychiatry had attuned him to be a good, if not great, listener. It all hinged on self-feeling, as did so much else in life.

He had spent such a large amount of time investigating his emotions, with the aim of becoming more modulated rather than being constantly assaulted, torn asunder by wildly vacillating, tempestuous moods and waves. He had never really learned self-soothing or how to best utilize emotional energy in the most appropriate ways. He'd always felt inundated by the power of his inner oceans and trying to navigate without a compass or astrolabe.

The vagaries of his life had led him to become more "emotionally fluent, gifted by the Universe with being exposed to a vast variety of altered states. This had paved the way to his compassionate understanding of the realm of "mental illness" (and even "ordinary" emotional states). It had become the very bedrock of his life, the foundation upon which his life work, paid or unpaid. It was so natural for him, like a second heart infusing his every thought, his every action.

Notwithstanding their previous acquaintance and Paul's enduring penchant for assisting veterans, it was what had led him to say "Yes" to Roach initially. He had to admit that he may have been precipitant in taking him on, and pushing him too hard. But he could not, would not, be anything but honest with any of his clients—and be unrelenting in maintaining quality and consistency. He debated how much and how far to go with Roach, if the man even ever showed up again.

In the meantime, he decided to devote some energy to being nicer to himself, give himself some of what he was craving from another. At the top of that list was an early night, to bed to rest until sleep stole him away, hopefully to fill his slumber with extraordinary dreams and refreshment for the following day—a day he planned on devoting to writing preceded by another longer walk.

His sleep was, for once, absent dreams though still quite refreshing. He had been awake until almost 0200 reading and slept until after 1000. After a hearty breakfast of scrambled eggs with feta cheese and two slices of heavily buttered cinnamon-raisin toast, he decided to follow his foreordained plan. The weather seemed to be cooperating with his intentions. There was only a small amount of precipitation predicted and the temperature would be around fifty degrees with a low wind velocity. He decided to make a sort of pilgrimage to one of his old haunts on Union Street, Tarr and Feathers, perhaps have a drink. Paul decided to walk all the way down Chestnut, up past the Academy of Art, to either Divisadero or Scott, and thence to Union, maybe check out some of the art work, have a late dinner and then take the bus home. Thank God for the #41 Union!

He walked, absorbing the innate beauty and radiance of The City with which he was so enthralling. He was always inspired by the abundance of love manifested in the architecture and people of this,

his city. He diverted from his original course to walk further down Chestnut to his favorite Thai restaurant, Rama Thai. It was run by a man he and his friend Dore had once christened "The Thai Pirate" because he had a dark, swarthy complexion, wiry black hair and coal-pit eyes, one of which was covered by an eye patch. He barely spoke, counting on his wait staff of beautiful south-Asian women to provide a friendly ambiance. Of the many fine Thai restaurants in San Francisco, this was the best. Paul always knew he could count on the very freshest curries and other treasured dishes like Green Papaya Salad and Beef Thai Basil. They also served a mixture of black, brown and red rice that was very tasty.

He was greeted at the door by an exquisitely beautiful young woman wrapped in a sarong of deep green and gold silk. She had luminous dark eyes and a clear and radiant dark caramel complexion. He knew from previous meetings that she was seventeen, Vietnamese and a distant relative of the owner. She spoke immaculate English ("convent school") and was extraordinarily polite and gracious, especially for one so young.

He was quickly seated and decided to check out the menu, wanting to try something different. He was SO in love with their red curry, but was thinking of seafood, and decided on Soft Shell Crab with Garlic and Pepper Sauce. He ordered the Summer Rolls with shrimp as an appetizer and a large Thai Iced Tea. As he waited—they were always super-quick and the food piping-hot—he again contemplated the state of affairs with Roach, and what might be next on that particular menu. It was perplexing. Maybe he had gone too far too fast. He sincerely hoped he was going to get a further opportunity to work with the man. After all, they were brothers.

CHAPTER THIRTY
ZEPHYR

What had been troublesome and preoccupying in last night's thoughts was today—upon awakening from a long, restless sleep filled with many brief awakenings and two trips to the bathroom—carried a stronger sense of acceptance and resolve. The data hadn't changed: Roach had asked for a break while acknowledging the breakthrough. It was enormous that he had allowed Paul to see him cry! It must have had an aftershock effect on him and he decided he needed some private time to re-assess. Even with all of the therapy and personal work he had done, Paul was still reluctant to let others see him cry—but he was not now, and never had been, as shut down and phobic about it as Roach.

He got the coffee brewing and some fresh hot Italian sausage from Iacoppa's on Columbus that he made into a thick, juicy patty that would form the center of a delectable sandwich on fresh San Francisco sourdough toast coated with butter and imported French fig jam. He ate sitting at the kitchen table, reading the *Chronicle*. All of it was carefully measured preparatory to his sitting down to write. Morning had become his "go to" time to write. He had always been the almost-stereotypical late night and after midnight scribbler. In truth, he did miss that old routine, those special hours when most of the world was sleeping. He always believed that it lent a poignant edge to his work, allowing him to go deeper and further than he might have otherwise. He suddenly remembered the chorus from a poem he had written in Sacramento in 1974: "I love the nighttime streets in the silence of the night." Now, though, it was beginning to feel like a vestigial artifact of another lifetime, half-remembered in the hypnopompic state of being freshly awakened.

He decided that "trusting the process" included not obsessing or ruminating about his client, and instead, focusing on his own health and wellbeing. This might even require that he take a day off from writing! But no! That was akin to not breathing! He rarely had "writer's block," or a slump of any sort. He decided he would shave and shower simply because it would feel good. He oftentimes felt as if he needed some external reason—meeting someone or hoping to—to shave and present his best face to the world. Today it would be all about enjoying himself.

He decided to give himself a treat, rent a car and drive across the Golden Gate, go to Muir Woods, then up to Mount Tam, go out to the ocean—perhaps to Jenner in Sonoma County, get some Indian food at a little place he knew there, and maybe spend the night. Just get away altogether. Leave whatever thoughts of trouble or bother there. There was really nothing tying him to The City, other than his reluctance to leave.

He called Karen and got her service. He left her a message about his plans, and that he would be in touch. He called his service and told them to take his calls. He told them he would be gone one night, maybe two. He called the car rental agency, set up for a mid-size, a Hyundai, and walked downtown to the rental place on Geary, a matter of fifteen or twenty minutes. Securing his paperwork, he headed west out Pine, then took Presidio Boulevard until it merged with Lincoln Boulevard through the Presidio and followed it to the entrance to the Golden Gate Bridge. Traffic was relatively light flowing north and he drank in the exquisite beauty of the passage, cross-wind blowing brusquely as massive cargo ships loaded with multi-colored shipping containers headed for Asia passed under him, and the bridge traffic set its own pace on just another incredible day in the Bay, all of the vehicles headed to spectacular destinations in Marin and Sonoma, to Mendocino and Humboldt, or further into the Redwood Empire.

While it was exhilarating to get away from The City, Paul had the same kind of anxiety he might have travelling to a foreign land. He was generally so locked-in to activities and work there that he sometimes forgot how utterly incredible the Bay Area was in terms of natural beauty and cultural opportunities. There was a time, of course, when he traveled broadly all over the immediate three-county area every day (San Mateo not so much). He used to brag that he had attended "a thousand concerts at The Fillmore"—every Thursday and Sunday night for many years, as well as occasional audition nights (for only fifty cents!). He had also attended many events at The Lion's Den in San Anselmo (where Van Morrison occasionally dropped-in, as he lived just a few miles away on Deerfield Road in Fairfax). He was a frequent habitué at such diverse venues as Freight and Salvage and the Community Theater in Berkeley; The Inn at the Beginning in Cotati; Sweetwater in Mill Valley. But it was always The City and its splendors that always drew him most: The Fillmore; Winterland; Avalon; Matrix; The Saloon; Great American Music Hall.

Yet he loved the natural beauty of northern California! He could live here a thousand years and not get enough!

He drove away from the beauty and joy, but also the chaos and confusion, of The City, the less he thought about Roach and his coagulated history. Of course, every once in a while, a thought stream pinged in like a sonar wave bouncing, but he counseled with himself to focus on his relatively untrammeled freedom.

After crossing the Golden Gate Bridge, Paul decided to take Pacific Coast Highway (popularly Highway One) instead of staying on the far more heavily travelled Highway 101. He took the turn near Mill Valley and stayed with the landmark twists and turns all the way to Olema. The Youngbloods had made it famous with their *Hippie from Olema* when responding to Merle Haggard's *Okie from Muscogee*. When the highway proper turned right to continue north, Paul took the left fork toward the Point Reyes National Seashore and the town of Inverness. Vladimir's was a Moravian restaurant there where he had dined occasionally through the years. He was always welcomed like a long-lost countryman with an impassioned burst of

Czech, even though he did not speak a word. The owner had originally escaped over the Alps on skis with his wife, trundling their children on their backs when the Nazis invaded.

After being seated in the warm ambience and watchful presence of the hundreds of Old-World knick-knacks, and original art drawings and portraits that decorated the walls, Paul ordered an on-tap Pilsner Urquell, remembering that it had been being brewed in the same location since 1842, and was the first truly hoppy golden ale, upon which almost all others since had been modeled. A basket of warm dark bread appeared almost immediately while he dithered about food choices: Chicken Paprikash, Beef Tongue or the Hot Roast Duck with Moravian Cabbage Rolls? But then there was the Garlic Rabbit...He knew that all of the entrees would come with fresh, homemade purple cabbage, and that he was going to order schnitzel noodles, no matter what he got.

Vladimir came over to schmooze a little bit—it had actually been a couple of years since they'd seen each other. Paul told him of his dilemma.

Vlad looked up, smiled and snapped his fingers.

"How about I fix you a nice plate with half a rabbit and some Chicken Paprikash?"

Paul smiled and said, "Excellent! And if I can have some schnitzel and an extra side order of purple cabbage, that would make it just right!"

The older man agreed and left Paul to contemplate the vast silence in the nearness of Mother Ocean. He had arrived near the end of regular dinner hours. Vladimir was taking care of him personally and he did not have to wait long. In the meantime, he dipped fresh homemade black bread into the virgin olive oil touched with just a little salt.

As he waited, his thoughts turned to his main hunger, what Spitz had termed "affect hunger." He had postulated that children reared without opportunities for early, frequent and consistent interaction and nurturing may develop a continuing hunger for affection and attention, may even seem incapable of getting enough. Such individuals tended to be very indiscriminate in their search. The lack of consistent attachment-figures may lead to failing to internalize models of attachment, that, in later years does not seem to retard physical or cognitive development. While not as severe as institutionally-reared children, Paul himself had developed a kind of affect hunger that had driven his life. He was now so much less driven sexually than he had been, having blunted some of the urgency during his cocaine days when had access to many and frequent sexual partners. Emotionally though, he was still afflicted with a voracious need to connect with women that drove him to often indiscriminately seek connection in self-defeating liaisons—with married, unavailable, lesbian or indifferent women. He remained convinced that his twisted attachment to his mother continued to haunt his less-than-conscious awareness that had always embodied tragic consequences for him.

It stung him, like ice pellets in a blizzard blowing into his face. He felt his own separation so acutely sometimes, the distance between himself and connecting with "HER," the seemingly impossible-to-find-woman-of-his-heart. Perhaps she didn't really exist. Some said it could be any woman if his own heart were open enough to receive her. In spite of all of his achievements; in spite of all of his training and education; in spite of all of the thousands of hours of therapy and other personal transformation work he had done; in spite of all the good he had done for others; in spite of all the intense suffering and personal cleansing, he seemed completely unable to realign the trajectory of his life; could not seem to rectify his profound impotence in the arena of a loving relationship with his abilities as a healer and facilitator of the grief and needs of others; could not seem to rectify the heights to which his spirit had soared into numinous realms with the utter degradation of soul he felt in his most raw acidic moments; as if all that he had seen and done and suffered had simply been a kind of sadistic play for a disgruntled Creator who delighted in Paul's misery and dissatisfaction.

Yet, in his heart of hearts, he knew he was intimately connected to every molecule, every speck of dust, in the Universe; to that the magic power that held all things together that lived in his heart as well; and in some mysterious way, it was this same indefinable essence that drove him ever onward every moment, every second, seeking the goal of his heart's desire, no matter what the odds, no matter what he had to endure to be made whole with his love, to be held once again in her arms, and, as Bob Dylan once sung, "And

262

only if she were lying by me, would I rest, in my bed, once again."

Paul had been so preoccupied with his own thoughts that he couldn't eat at first, but the magnificent aromas enticed him back and he set to ravenously. It was superb—hot, crispy, tasty. After his meal, Vladimir asked if he wanted coffee and dessert. The man's wife made fresh apple strudel every morning, and he just couldn't refuse. As he was finishing his second cup, Vlad sat down and thumped down a bottle of *slivovice* (damson plum brandy) on the table along with two small glasses he called *panák* (literally: a dummy).

"Oh no, sir! I'm driving!"

In his fractured English richly interspersed with Czech, Vladimir expressed how disappointed he would be if a "fellow countryman" didn't share at least one drink with him! Paul decided he could have one and still drive safely. The problem was that Vladimir was just getting started, and he had selected Paul as his erstwhile drinking companion and the audience for some of his encyclopedic tales (told in English, Czech, Moravian, German, Polish or Russian—usually in some combination of them all).

"Na zdravy!" (To your health!) they toasted, threw down the potent alcohol in one toss.

It became evident that the older man intended to indulge deeply. Paul told the older man that he could not accompany him on his forthcoming sodden journey.

"Then, of course, you must spend the night here!" the older man replied

"I had planned to stay in Jenner tonight!"

"Ach! Jenner! Here is much better! You stay!"

"But where?"

"Right here! We fix you up a room!"

Paul decided "Why not?"

He rarely drank to intoxication, and by the third drink, he was melting around the edges—and did not want to journey to the land of unconscious decisions and unaware behaviors where he had been too many times before.

It took both Vladimir's wife and daughter to get the besotted man to stop pushing repeated drinks on Paul, who, though he was trying to be gracious, had become increasingly irritated with the intrusion (reminding him of his father), and he himself went off to his rented room to pass out, barely able to get his clothes off before he fell into bed.

CHAPTER THIRTY-ONE
ANOTHER ADVENTURE

Inverness, California   **Wednesday December 20th, 1995:**
0743

As he drifted off to the Land of Lethe, Paul knew he would be having weird dreams, and he did. Interspersed with bathroom visits were visions from the "spirits" (not the alcoholic ones!)—lurid, sometimes greasy neon images of pipes and tubes and scattered ancient artifacts, yet amazingly vibrant and haunting, leaving him craving for ever further contact as they flitted through his brain, and then raced off almost as quickly as he approached them, only to be immediately replaced by another barrage. What was significant though, was the feeling they conveyed: a familiarity that seemed to embody messages (as most of his dreams did), though his disinhibited medulla seemed incapable of responding, as if, indeed, it were always a half-step behind in comprehension and elucidation.

Despite all this, Paul awakened to the sound of the ocean crashing on the shore and a remarkably clear head with no sign of his having over-indulged the night before. His nose was enticed by the smell off freshly baked bread and bacon crisping. He followed his belly to a grand breakfast at his hosts' insistence, including homemade peach jam.

He was welcomed by Vlad's wife who smiled and hugged him. There was no sign of the older man. Indeed, it seemed as if he might have continued indulging in plum brandy long after Paul had retreated, as there was an empty bottle and glass sitting on the sideboard as he entered—that his loving wife quickly swept away and took to the kitchen.

He was on the road before what little morning traffic there would be became too thick, and he -headed north on the Coast Highway. He crossed the Russian River heading for Jenner after passing through Marshall, Tomales Bay and Bodega Head. He knew he should at least check in with his service, to make sure there were no pending emergencies, but decided instead that he would wait until he stopped again for either coffee or lunch.

He was enjoying the rhythm of being on the road and the bright winter sunshine, that he decided not to stop at the Sizzling Tandoor in Jenner. As he drove past the original "planned community" of Sea Ranch, he headed to Point Arena to check out the tremendous lighthouse there,

The original lighthouse was so severely damaged by the 1906 San Francisco Earthquake that it was demolished. Rebuilt in 1908, it still stands today at 115 feet tall. It had previously featured a First Order Fresnel Lens, over six feet in diameter and weighing more than six tons, made up of 666 hand-ground glass prisms all focused toward three sets of double bullseyes. It was these bullseyes that gave the Point Arena Lighthouse its unique "light signature" of two flashes every six seconds. An automatic beacon replaced it in 1977.

He somewhat reluctantly decided to call his service. He was relieved that Karen had called and asked for a return call. Roach had called, but left no message and number, so Paul felt comfortable proceeding with his plan. He felt drawn to go to Mendocino, the old logging town turned "quaint," though totally enjoyable hip destination on the north coast. He made a number of phone calls attempting to locate lodgings for the night. He particularly wanted a working wood (not gas!) fireplace and an ocean view. Given that it was the middle of winter, the rates were lower and the choice of accommodations broader. He located what he wanted at the Sea Rock Bed and Breakfast that, of course, included breakfast so he wouldn't have to go stumbling around in the morning to eat. (He would, of course, make coffee in his room before he ventured forth). He left his number with Karen's service, and then rearranged the room slightly to place a rectangular table squarely in front of the window facing the ocean so that he could open his laptop and write. The drive had been liberating and he felt a surge of energy that he wanted to devote to getting more thoughts on paper before they disappeared into the mystic.

He'd always felt that he would reach a time when his loneliness would more-or-less disappear into the flow of time. This was proportionate to the level on which he came to love himself more genuinely. He considered that he might be unwilling to give himself that deep level of affection; to admit to himself that he had redeemed himself from the slavering maw of his childhood and made of himself a mature male who was attractive. Some incredible woman would see it in him and appreciate him at some point, and decide to share her journey of discovery with him. Intellectually he knew all external "reality" was simply a holographic reflection. There was no escaping it—the Universe did not bullshit, even though humans frequently did.

It was such a relief to be away from his ordinary order of things. There was a certain freedom in not having the phone ring or having people asking intrusive questions, and needing or demanding potent, even life-changing answers.

He woke up very early and wrote for two hours. He wrote a small sub-section on catharsis and abreaction that he felt had been missing from *Crucible*. He was reminded of the origins of sacred theater. Plays had been written to trigger emotional release for the audience. They were an early form of community mental health.

Inevitably his mind jumped to comparing it to modern (especially soap opera/melodrama television) programming that not only suffused the airways but was punctuated by a plethora of insipid (Paul thought them moronic) commercials. For him, there was nothing better than the films from the American Movie Channel and the Turner Classic Movie Channel, classics from the 1930s and 1940s, especially film noir—though he had a secret passion for Busby Berkeley films too.

The innkeepers set a great table with eggs, bacon and sausage, and a toaster nearby so one could make one's own toast. There were hot pancakes made to order too with real maple syrup and a choice of several French fruit jams. Paul was impressed. It was true that one actually got that for which one paid. (He couldn't help but imagine that the cheaper establishments would be serving Instant Quaker Oats and frozen Eggs with Log Cabin syrup!)

He checked in with his service again, and found that he had had three calls, two more from Roach, one late last night and another at 0832 that day. Neither call carried a phone number. The other call was from a new prospective client who needed a full evaluation that had been court-ordered. (Pretty delightful, thought Paul. He could always use an extra $500, plus court appearance fees). He called her, chatted for a few minutes, and made a three-hour appointment for the following day at 1100.

He had not heard from Karen and anxious to discuss him further with Karen—to plot out the next territories of exploration. He was reminded of the integral relationship they had; and how he was now more able to assist others the more relatively free he became.

He tossed around the idea of taking Shoreline Highway back home, versus going down to Albion and Highway 128 over to Highway 101. The amount of time involved made the decision easy. The latter route would save an hour, maybe more, depending on traffic and the amount of lead in his foot. He might even stop and check out the Botanical Gardens before he left Mendocino. He'd easily be home by early afternoon, even if he stopped in Corte

Madera for a meal at the Peppermill.

Passed through Cloverdale, he was reminded of the time when he had quit his job in psychiatry to work as Head Roadie for Blue Cheer when they reformed as *Peterbilt*, with Dickie Peterson on bass and his brother Jerre on rhythm guitar. They'd opened at the Clover Theater for David and Linda LaFlamme of *It's a Beautiful Day* fame. What an absolutely fun night!

He shook his head in wonderment as he hit the outskirts of Petaluma, marveling at how much the town had changed. It had always been a small dairy farming community, and had now become a mini-metropolis of its own. The Institute for Noetic Science had relocated there and brought a much different level of attention and interest as well as variety of ancillary businesses—another example of the ubiquitous "progress" that Paul considered to be a disease, spreading like a cancer metastasizing without thought or care, embodying the constant growth required of advanced capitalism (according to Kavanagh). No one really seemed to recognize the inherent addiction associated with untrammeled greed obsession, or the incredible cost in human feelings and sensitivity it required to feed its insatiable appetite.

It was intriguing to him that the tunnel entrances into the San Francisco side of the Waldo tunnels were not painted with rainbows as were those leaving The City, implying somehow that one were entering a realm that was less enchanted and vital than that of the Magical Marin.

He had thought of Roach intermittently and what the man might be up to, but declined to parade all of his earlier speculations thorough his mind like a string of tired circus elephants. He rejoiced that he was returning with a much clearer mind and more open heart. He was not feeling the need to fill his mental spaces with distractions and spectacular images, carrying forward the usually empty and grandiose promises designed to elicit empty visions of a future more filled with excitement and varietal riches than the depredations of the present.

He felt freed of his nagging obsession with Roach's details. The cash flow notwithstanding, he no longer felt the need to continue treatment in such an intense vein. Of course, he had been allowing Roach to set the pace of treatment, dictated by his own needs, and simply flowed with it as it unwound since he had the superior healing skills and experience as well as the road map off of which they were working. He prepared his mind to retake his clinical cloak, reaccepting their arrangement. He had to admit that he was interested in extending the depth and clarity, plunging more deeply into the uncharted territory of his psyche. It was always the work. He was tempted to call it "The Work," as if what he was doing was pursuing a great alchemical process, which indeed, he was. From a certain perspective, assisting his clients to shift the grey wedges of leaden emotion and trauma into the bright and uplifting gold of cleansed and integrated emotion, opening the doorway to the ethereal realms of heightened awareness and spirituality.

He called in an order of Garlic Chicken with Spring Vegetables accompanied by a half-dozen small Chinese leek turnovers (*jiu cai he zi*) and added a bottle of Tsingtao beer from the rental agency. He decided to take a cab home. He was tired but exhilarated and just wanted some quiet and some down-time. He tipped the driver extra-well to insure continuing good relations with the taxi-driver community (especially since many of his clients took cabs to his rather obscure location).

He had barely made his way inside and secured the door when his phone started ringing. Hesitating for just a moment, he decided just to let it ring; to eat and get settled before having to deal with the world again. It felt as if he had been gone for a week rather than just two days. His buoyant mood quickly started dissipating when he thought of having to put on the yoke and take on responsibilities again. As much as he enjoyed the healing arts, and loved sharing his heartfelt discoveries and awakenings with others, there were still times when he truly wished he did not "have to" prepare himself to be present and pay attention to the needs of others.

Some thought it axiomatic, although it was more of a nostrum or colloquy: The idea that we give to others that which we ourselves want. He had always been driven, even compelled, to seek the satisfaction of others, finding pleasure in seeing others pleased—yet such a strategy invariably left him hungering for more for himself. He knew it to be a deeper measure of self-esteem to truly please himself, a measure that, even if others were momentarily discomfited, they would eventually recognize the honesty and compassion with which he delivered his truth. It was not his job to please others—it was only their own work that would give them what they wanted.

Paul decided to treat himself to a small snifter of Drambuie and reflected on the state and nature of his life, what he was doing, where he was going, where he wanted to go. As he sipped the last of his post prandial elixir, the phone rang again, and he sighed, smiled ruefully, then shook his head and answered.

"Dr. Marzeky? It's Irene at your service."

"Hi, Irene. And how are you this evening?" Paul genuinely loved chatting with the women who staffed his answering service. They always seemed to have such great tales to tell about anonymous individuals, of course. Confidentiality was the watchword.

"I'm very well. Are you officially returned from your journey, or would you rather wait until tomorrow for your messages?"

"Will they grow any less urgent or demanding by tomorrow?"

"I seriously doubt it, doctor!"

"Me too unfortunately. I guess you better give them to me."

As the young woman began to recite his accumulated messages and Paul recorded them on a slip of paper, he was struck by his growing popularity. Even in his absence, he had had nine calls that had gone through to his service. One was a telemarketer wanting to sell him "better liability insurance"; another was an ex-client he had not seen in four years who left a crazy message inquiring about his state of mental health with no return phone number; there had been a call from Karen inquiring about a possible consultation meeting, especially as she was "going away for a few days at Christmas"; another was a call from the new client who needed an evaluation (scheduled for the next day), calling to confirm; two calls from Roach with no call back number; and finally, three callers who had simply hung up when the service answered (for which he nonetheless had to pay).

"Well, I could be slightly maudlin and sing you 'Good night, Irene,' but I think I'll spare you both the rendition and the sound of my voice!"

"And I might have to charge you for service above and beyond!"

"Too true!"

CHAPTER THIRTY-TWO
ONWARD IS THE ONLY
DIRECTION

San Francisco   **Thursday December 21st, 1995: 0931**

He had not yet even had his morning coffee when the phone rang. His intuition told him to let it ring through to his service, and while debating the wisdom of this, it stopped—the decision was made for him by the Universe!

Or maybe not! Moments later the damn thing started ringing again!

He took a deep breath and exhaled purposely, then reached down and secured the handset.

"Dr. Marzeky here."

"It's about fucking time you answered!" growled Roach.

"Excuse me, sir, but 'Fuck you!'"

"What?"

"You heard me! You cancel our last appointment! You don't leave me a number to call you back and you disappear into the fucking ethers without a trace! And then you have the fucking nerve to call and act like it's my responsibility that I haven't heard from you!"

"You fucker! I'm your patient!"

"We use 'client,' unless you're in a psych hospital!"

"It doesn't matter! Where have you been?"

"Nice try. You disappear and blame me! No way, Jose!"

"I haven't been able to reach you!"

"You haven't left me any way to get in touch with you! And I have no idea where I could find you, even if I had made a search for you!"

"I..."

"What? I'm just human too! I'm not some goddamn machine you can just use when you want and then throw away!"

"I've been going through a lot of changes since we las spoke."

"I figured as much."

"And I really don't have an address either."

"Figured that too. You don't want to leave a trace."

"Exactly!"

"And?"

"'And' what?"

"What else?"

"'What else' what?"

Paul sighed and went on.

"I don't hear from you, can't reach you and you call me up, attacking me!"

"I can be an asshole sometimes."

"I agree. And?"

"I probably shouldn't have blamed you."

"And?"

"If we didn't have such a complex relationship; if you weren't my client; if this were some kind of ordinary relationship; I might expect you to show a little remorse for being such an asshole! But, given all of the above, nothing!"

There was a long silence, punctuated only by some fairly laborious breathing.

"So, now what?"

"I guess that depends on you."

"Well, if you're still willing to talk to me, I'd like to have an appointment."

"Thank you. I would be happy to talk to you."

"When?"

"I have a three-hour this morning at 1100, so how does 1600 look for you?"

"Thanks, brother."

"See you then."

CHAPTER THIRTY-THREE
RETURN OF THE WANDERER

San Francisco   **Thursday December 21nd, 1995: 1603**

The doorbell sounded particularly strident and demanding. It shook Paul out of his reverie. He knew he was feeling especially sensitive. He was grateful to have had the time to transcribe his thoughts and memories in such a literary manner. He took a deep breath before he opened the door, and was immediately struck by the difference in Roach's appearance. He looked younger, softer even. They dapped and then shook hands.

As they settled into their respective seats, both men found themselves gazing at each other. And then they laughed.

"You too," said Roach. "Look more relaxed, I mean."

"You've been going through some significant changes."

"Yeah, I've been wanting to talk to you about that."

"Say more."

"I hate to admit that you were right, but you were right."

"About?"

Roach sighed.

"I hate this!"

"What?"

"I feel better."

"You don't like feeling better?"

"I... it's confusing."

"Say more."

"Beating that fucking pillow...I never thought that would help."

"But it did."

Roach nodded.

"I understand now that I've been living off rage for a long time!"

"And?"

"Now I'm scared shitless!"

"Why?"

"The other day...that last session..."

Paul waited silently.

"I've been feeling disarmed! Helpless!"

Again, Paul allowed the silence to work for him.

"And?"

"And... now ...the other day..."

"You opened up...to your truth."

"And I... I'm not sure I want to go any further!"

Paul went silent again, contemplating this latest twist.

"And what? Go back to your old life?"

"I..."

"Can't, can you?"

"I..."

"Do you <u>really</u> want to?"

"I..."

Roach swallowed hard, then looked up into Paul's face. It looked as though he were age-regressing right before Paul's eyes, losing the hard, protective edge he'd always had, as his face seemed to get progressively younger and younger, until he simply sat there, limpid, unmoving. A single tear dropped from the innocence of his undefended left eye.

"I'll go get you a glass of water," said Paul and went to do so.

When he returned, Roach hadn't moved, though his eyes were open and tracking.

"Well," was all Roach could manage to say. Paul set the glass down next to him on the coffee table.

Paul nodded and sat down. Waiting.

"I'm fucking wiped out. And it's still really early in the day."

"Releasing old toxic energy is tiring. It's hard work."

"I'm glad you told me to keep going, beating that pillow—until the rage left me. I didn't believe you at first."

"It might take a couple more sessions—when you're ready!"

"Not now! Not today! Fuck! I can barely walk!"

"I see that!"

"No! You don't understand! I'm weak! I can't take care of business like this!"

"Healing is your real business!"

"That's easy for you to say! Where the fuck do you think all those fifty-dollar bills come from?"

Paul took a deep breath and continued.

"I must admit, I'm grateful for the money. But my real goal is to help you heal. That's why you hired me."

"I can't afford to take days off! From now on, when we delve deep, I need to schedule it—so I can have a day off afterward!"

"It won't always be as hard as the other day. It's like a muscle you haven't used for a long time. It aches more when you first start using it again."

"I certainly as fuck ache, all right!"

"Maybe we should take a walk. Generating some serotonin and dopamine will make you feel better."

"Right now, I think I just want to sit and chat a little bit."

"'Chat?' What does that mean?"

"Nothing too deep. I don't think I can handle it right now."

"We can just 'chat' and still be therapeutic. It's always good to erect a solid cognitive frame for what you've experienced emotionally."

"I'm cool with that."

"Especially since you've been very uncomfortably comfortable with your old way of being."

"Too true."

"And now it's not serving you anymore. Maybe even keeping you from being who you want to be."

"Maybe."

"You've had a huge breakthrough. You have seen a different self. It's still you, just a self you previously rejected. Now that you've seen it, you have the opportunity to change. You can shut it down, or you can nurture it!"

"Is it always black-or-white?"

"Of course not! But once you've experienced a greater awareness, let's call it, if you want to integrate it, you have to create a new framework in which to live it. So, we can talk about it if you like."

"Or not."

"True. You can reject what you've seen. You can try to go back to your old ways. Or you can choose to move forward in a new way."

"'Try to go back?' What does that mean?"

"Let's say you've never seen the ocean. Once you do, you can't pretend you haven't. It's impossible. You can deny it, even to yourself, but it'll be a lie."

"And?"

"Whether or not you judge yourself to be too 'vulnerable,' it's still a real possibility. You don't have to nurture it."

Roach looked thoughtful for a long moment, then nodded his head.

"Look what's happening to me! I'm so...fucking weak!"

"It's just temporary. In a couple of days, you'll feel stronger."

Roach shook his head. "You have no idea how much wreckage there is

"On some levels, it doesn't matter. Releasing it is the key."

"We could be here for years if I tell you all the details."

"The real core healing is for you to allow yourself to feel your own feelings!"

"What exactly does that mean?"

"As they always say, you have to 'feel it in order to heal it.'"

"Say more."

"It's like you're carrying around a fifty-pound dumbbell. When you drop it, you'll feel better?"

"Are you really trying to tell me that the 'answer' to all my problems is to simply, what, to acknowledge the pain?"

"Not necessarily to me, or the world, just to yourself! Look how much better you feel dropping some of your shit with your father."

"We keep coming back to my fucking father!" Roach exploded out of his reverie and his face flushed bright crimson.

"He seems to keep coming up."

"The motherfucker fucked up my whole life!"

"He certainly corrupted you initially, but you did a pretty good job since."

"So, I'm fucking responsible?"

"Only to the extent that you haven't healed what happened!"

"What happened, happened!"

"But your interpretation, especially if you beat yourself with it, is what's most important!"

"So, are you saying I don't really need you?"

"I just function as an intermediary, until you can hold space for yourself."

A prolonged silence ensued, then Roach looked up, confused.

"So, what the fuck am I supposed to do?"

"Just keep working at it—if you want to keep working!"

"You opened this fucking door! I'll be damned if I'll stop now!"

Paul laughed, and held out his hand to dap.

"I'm proud of you, brother!"

They dapped, and then laughed.

"You are a motherfucker, brother!" said Roach.

"Thanks, man. You're not so bad yourself!"

They laughed again and Roach gestured with his head, indicating that he wanted to go outside to have a cigarette.

As they stood on the front porch, looking out at the rain, Paul couldn't help but think of the rest of the refrain from Janis Joplin's song, "And something came along and grabbed me, and it felt like a ball and chain." It seemed incongruous, especially since Paul was feeling quite elated in the moment, but his quixotic consciousness always reminded him of the many of his generation that had been lost on the journey: Janis; Jimi; Jim Morrison; Alan Wilson; Brian Jones; and then, of course, one of the original members of the fated "27 Club," Robert Johnson himself.

"Wow! What a fucking life!"

"I'll say! The shit we've seen! And the people we've known!"

"A-fucking-mazing!"

They stood in a kind of stoned silence, induced by the brief piece of history that they had shared, and all of the experiences they had not.

Roach started wryly chuckling and made eye contact when Paul looked up.

"I must admit you may be right."

"About what?"

"I'm feeling less need to use. This shit is helping me."

"Excellent!"

"But it's putting me in a precarious position."

"How's that?"

"I'm not so sure I want to do this anymore."

"'This?'"

"My job. Moving the shit around."

"Ah!"

"It's all I've done for the last quarter-century."

"Can't you retire?" asked Paul quite naively.

Roach laughed louder and in a more prolonged way than anything Paul had heard from him, and then he started sputtering as he attempted to wind down and stop. By the time he did, copious tears were pouring down his face.

Paul's face had gone from quizzical to puzzled to sad to shocked to angry; then back to nonplussed, and then he started laughing too—at which point Roach stopped laughing and looked up.

"What the fuck are you laughing at, asshole?"

Paul was still semi-hysterical and barked out a couple of more squawks before he was able to stop.

"I... you crack me up! At first, I was confused, then I thought that I had offended you in some way. Then I got pissed that maybe you were laughing at me. Finally, I realized you were fulfilling a vision of mine, one I hadn't told you about."

"Yeah? And what's that?"

"I told her that my job was to get you to cry!"

"What the fuck?"

"Not quite in the manner you did. I figured that you genuinely started crying would be a sign that we had cracked through to your deepest shit!"

"And now?"

"We have broken through. Now it's a question of: will you continue?"

Before Roach had a chance to answer, Paul held out his right hand, palm outward, and said, "I don't want a knee-jerk reaction. I want you to really think about it, and we will pick it up next time. If you want. Or not."

"When is next time?"

"Call me and we'll set a time. I don't want you doing this unless you're ready. You've had a little taste and now you know it's gonna take some more hard work. So, call me."

"Works for me" he said and walked away.

CHAPTER THIRTY-FOUR
MEMORIES

P aul didn't have anything especially pressing, and so decided he could put an hour or so into combing through Sylvia Santos' MMPI and writing it up as a separate section. He already had an overall feeling, but wanted to check the "K Scale" (validity), though he had no reason to doubt her credibility. She seemed as relatively honest as he could determine from one three-hour session.

He brewed a fresh cup of coffee, and brought up his Eval template. Then, almost by rote, filled in the personal details, followed by social, medical and employment history sections. The truth of the matter was that he enjoyed doing the testing, interpreting and diagnostic work far more than anything else—though, the human element, especially seeing people change their lives as a result of their work together, was exciting. It was perhaps the ultimate payment for the work he did.

He was suddenly reminded of the time when he had been working at a local Community Mental Health Center. Even though at that point he only had a Master's, he had by far more actual working experience than anyone else in the agency, and was often called upon to intervene in, or even take over, difficult cases for other clinicians who might have been struggling or were simply under-prepared to manage sometimes difficult or unusual cases. He had also been asked, on occasion, to troubleshoot with clients who had threatened legal action against the clinic or were claiming some form of mis-practice. Mis-practice is less serious than malpractice, the major difference is that the prior is committed out of negligence or ignorance whereas the latter is committed with a greater awareness of the governing laws or ethics, or with purpose thereto.

Paul had managed to establish a bridge of trust with these troubled individuals by creating an empathic connection that previous clinicians had failed to establish and had thus left the client feeling ignored or mistreated. He had "saved" the clinic a number of times, as well as intervened with clients who were either mis-diagnosed or had otherwise "stalled" in treatment due to a less than comprehensive treatment plan and strategy.

One such client was referred to him because she kept failing to take her medications (which, at the time, included an antidepressant, an anti-psychotic, an anxiolytic and other assorted meds for a variety of ailments). Clients failing or refusing to take meds was not unusual. What was significant in this case was that she kept saying that she "forgot" to take them. As early as the first session, Paul was able to determine that she was not being disingenuous but was genuinely reporting her experience. She had been checked out neurologically and was determined not to be dementing, or to have any other vascular problems.

He had assiduously reviewed her file, and was aware that she had been shifted from one to another to another therapist during the previous year she had been being seen there, including a brief stint with the Clinical Supervisor who was reportedly "mystified" by the erratic medication compliance, and noted that she believed that the woman might simply be "purposefully non-compliant," but listed a rule-out of "malingering." She had recommended the ensuing neuro workup. The client had a husband who, by all reports (including a home visit), seemed very supportive and as nurturing as a man could be who worked sixty hours a week. She had a grown daughter from another marriage who lived in Sacramento and was in a graduate nursing program at the State University. Mother and daughter had infrequent, and mostly telephone contact, though both reported the relationship to be "friendly."

The woman appeared for her appointment a few minutes early, dressed rather dowdily in a plain dress and clunky-looking shoes. She sat stiffly in the chair across from his desk, answering all of his questions perfunctorily. Her voice seemed flat and her face appeared almost blank (he rejected the idea of her appearing "calm").

They spent that first appointment getting acquainted, and Paul made some small notes to himself about his observations and details he might add to her treatment plan. They shook hands as she left, and he asked her to make an appointment for next week at the same time if that were convenient for her. She agreed, gave him a fleeting smile and left. He was struck by a weird kind of vacuum she created when she departed, but he dismissed this as being his fantasy rather than a true psychic phenomenon.

When she arrived for her next appointment, Paul thought someone at the front desk had mis-scheduled. The woman who walked through his door stood two inches taller than the one he had met last time. She was stylishly dressed and well made-up. She introduced herself by another name and held out a manicured hand for him to shake.

Paul was perplexed but complied. When he addressed the woman by the name she had used previously, she smiled and shook her head.

"That's my sister. She's sick today so I asked her if I could come instead."

Paul was a little non-plussed, but simply smiled.

"Excellent. Maybe you can fill in some of the family dynamics."

For the next hour, he and the client who had shown up that day, had a very pleasant conversation, ranging from the weather to the 49er's prospects to the latest exhibition at the de Young Asian Art Museum. At the end of the hour, she promised to tell her sister how much she had enjoyed the session and would remind her of the next appointment. Paul stood in the doorway of his office and observed the woman walking down the hallway while he considered possibilities—though her intake form did mention that she had a sister who lived locally. He also considering a more extreme diagnosis—though he did not yet have enough evidence to make such an assertion. He decided to devote some portion of his non-billable hours' time to further research, with an eye to solidifying his nascent thoughts.

Paul anxiously awaited her arrival the following week, to see if he could verify his tenuous conclusions. When his client didn't arrive on time, he went back to his office to catch up on some overdue paperwork. About ten minutes went by before his phone rang. It was the receptionist, informing him, in a rather strange tone, that his client had just arrived. Pondering the off-note in her voice, he agreed.

The woman who walked in the door was yet another iteration of his client. She was dressed in a kind of trashy/sexy manner, with makeup that verged on the garish. When she spoke, her voice was deeper, throatier, than previously. And the content of her speech was radically different. When he greeted her by the name she had used originally, she snarled and sat back in her chair, revealing quite a lot of thigh.

"That bitch? Fuck her! She's such a prude, though she did tell me she thought you were cute!"

"I see. So, you know her quite well?"

"Yeah. She's such a prune," said his client, and leaned forward revealing the tops of her breasts as she did, the low cut of her gauzy gown seeming to part on its own. "Listen," she mock whispered, and he caught the scent of alcohol on her breath, "don't tell her I said so, but I call her "Church Lady." Paul immediately got the reference to the famous Dana Carvey characterization from Saturday Night Live.

"So, who are you? What name do I call you?"

"Well, by my name, you silly man!"

"And what name might that be?"

"You know. It's Es. Esmerelda!"

"Oh, I apologize," said Paul, treading very lightly, realizing that he had stumbled onto truly new territory with this client, all but confirming the diagnosis with which he had been considering—and yet not knowing exactly how to proceed.

"Please don't take this the wrong way, but could you tell me a little more about yourself."

The woman looked at him for a moment, then sneered.

"I know. I know. That prude Clara probably told you all kinds of stories about me. Well, fuck her! I'll give you the real lowdown."

Paul watched, fascinated as this previously unknown personality unfolded right before his very eyes.

"I bet she told you she doesn't like sex, didn't she?" the woman said, arching her eyebrows.

Paul could only nod his head, awestruck.

"I'm here to tell you, when I'm horny, I just take over her body and boy, can she scream when she's getting it! I'm the one who benefits because she's always so guilty afterward!"

"I imagine her husband is always happy to see you."

"He's such a stump! He doesn't even know it's me!"

"How could he not? You are so different!"

"He's just grateful she's having what he calls 'one of her moods!'"

Paul knew that her husband was a cable car mechanic and worked hard every day with heavy machinery, no doubt dulling his senses to potentially more subtle psychological and emotional clues and cues.

Esmerelda turned out to be quite the historian—very conversant across the personalities, informing Paul of several "others" who were with her "listening in" as the two of them spoke. She also told him what might have been biographical information about "their" history. (He had heard that different personalities frequently displayed different likes and dislikes, even to one having an allergy that others did not). He was now convinced that what he was seeing was a woman with Dissociative Identity Disorder (previously called Multiple Personality Disorder). How to effectively deal with it clinically was of a totally different magnitude. Obviously the seven previous therapists who had been assigned to her had entirely missed it, resulting in nine different diagnoses and a total of fourteen different meds prescribed for various reported aspects of her manifestation like depression and anxiety that might have affected one or more, but entirely missed being useful to the larger whole because the cause was not accessible to chemical ministration.

If he had a better connection with the Clinical Supervisor, he might have gone to her to discuss what he was thinking, but he believed she might only ridicule him (as she had previously) or otherwise try to dissuade him from his own intuitions. (Personally, Paul thought she was insecure and pretentious, and just not all that intelligent either. Conversely, she might simply be jealous of the fact that he was in a doctoral program, and she was more-or-less terminal with her master's and a load of student loans).

Paul kept his still-forming conclusions to himself and decided to pay for outside supervision with a psychologist friend of his in private practice who was very loosely assisting him (though without an official tally of hours) with guidance within the context of his program. Since he was only in the early years of his program, it would be some time before he was required to amass supervisory hours, but Paul had known Gloria socially for a long time so she was his natural choice.

"I still think you should talk to your clinical supervisor, Valerie."

"I know. I know. You've said that from the beginning. I repeat: First, I do not really trust her either personally or professionally. She has never treated me with any respect. She has always denigrated what I consider to be my superior knowledge base. She has less clinical experience than I do, and I trust my intuition."

"That may all be true. She is still the authorized supervisor for your agency. You could be putting the agency at risk by not sharing your findings with her."

"Yeah, and if I do, and am proven right, she'll find a way for me to take the hit. I can guarantee you the bomb will get dropped on me, not her."

"You sound a little paranoid."

"She's always treated me shiftily. When she was just a staff therapist, she was a lot friendlier. Ever since she got the promotion, she is rude and dismissive."

"Only with you? Maybe it's just part of her management style."

Paul took a deep breath and sighed.

"Look, you're not going to like this, but I believe it's reverse sexism."

"What do you mean?"

"She's dismissive of all the males, and almost saccharine sweet with all of the women."

"Oh, come on!"

Paul raised his hands in a gesture of surrender, and said, "I told you that you wouldn't like it."

"I know it happens, but..."

"I'm not being paranoid. I see it all the time, even in meetings she is dismissive of what most of the male staff discuss. And," he paused, "she favors the female staff with the best assignments. She doesn't distribute them randomly."

"Well, certainly some staff have better or more specific training-related skills..."

"But not consistently. I see the male staff getting almost all of the court-referred men. She almost always assigns all of the female clients to the female staff."

"A female therapist can bring a certain 'sensitivity' to a female client."

"I can see that sometimes, even the majority of the time. But in private practice, no therapist has only same-gender clients referred."

"Unless one chooses to set up practice is such a way."

"All right. All right. I agree. But at the agency, we're all supposed to be 'equal' in terms of seeing clients. There is not supposed to be a gender prejudice."

"Have you talked to anyone about this?"

"I've thought of going to the Director, but he would just refer me back to her. He's the one who picked her as Supervisor. Besides that, he's too busy scanning around being a junior media star—attending luncheons, press conferences, even going to Sacramento for state functions. I think he's angling to be the new Director of Mental Health for the state. He's only in the clinic one or two days a week."

"Have you enumerated any other symptoms? Does your client talk of lost time? Fugue states? History of suicide attempts? Headaches? Substance abuse? How is her sleep?"

"Wow! I see I'm not the only one who's researched this!"

"And?"

"She has cut her wrists several times, though not for years. An anti-psychotic overdose approximately ten years ago. She seems to have a binge-eating disorder, though she has never complained about it. Long history of depression, though no medication has ever seemed to really help. That was one of the first clues I stumbled on—no med has ever seemed to work. She's been on fourteen different meds that I know of."

"Have you ever witnessed her shifting?"

"She's has been consistent within the personality that shows up for appointments. Some of the personalities seem to be aware across the spectrum; she has spoken of 'others' listening in but refused to elucidate."

"Does she seem preoccupied? Or acknowledge having hallucinations?"

"Not so far."

"Has she mentioned any history of sexual abuse? Or other violence?"

"Not so far."

"So, what are you going to do?"

"I'm going to keep seeing her every week. Keep documenting what I am seeing. Since she has manifested three distinct personalities, I am going to start mapping them. The more she tells me about each of them, the better I'll be able to understand them and their functions within her, admittedly, idiosyncratic whole."

"Are you going to report your findings to Valerie?"

"For right now, I'm not going to say anything. When I finally bring up this case, I want to have really solid evidence. In the meantime, I'm going to count on your confidentiality and your support, until I'm ready."

"I'll respect your judgment, but only to the point wherein I sincerely believe you might be endangering the client's safety."

"Of course. I would expect you to broach that with me first."

"Of course."

CHAPTER THIRTY-FIVE
DIVING DEEPER

San Francisco   **Friday December 22, 1995: 1003**

Paul reflected on what a long way he'd come from the days when he was working as a Licensed Psychiatric Technician, especially in Crisis Clinics where the influx of clients was erratic and often shepherded by the Psych Police or other law enforcement personnel bringing in individuals who had come to their attention in various ways (unfortunately the bulk of these which involved violence in some form).

There was a rotation and it was followed relatively strictly, taking clients as they came. One of the few exceptions when someone who was personally known was brought in. It had happened to Paul once when the police dragged in his next-door neighbor who'd been standing on the sidewalk in his underwear yelling at an older woman who lived up the street—or rather at her little mongrel dog who kept growling at him, after the woman herself had dissolved into a welter of tears. The man was still angry and sputtering when he arrived at Westside Crisis Services (often called Mount Zion Crisis where they were then housed). When the man was ushered into the seclusion room (still in handcuffs), he appealed directly to Paul for intervention. Paul took a very harsh line with him that he hoped would have a sobering effect.

"Sir, you seem drunk. You have been hostile and angry with the officers and the staff. And now you're trying to take advantage of the fact that you happen to know me very casually. Where in any of that do you see a reason why we should cut you a break?"

The man screwed up his face in utter disbelief, expecting that his personal appeal would result in his being released forthwith.

"What? What do you mean? You know me!"

"Sir, in this situation our very casual acquaintance means nothing. I repeat: You are drunk, hostile and demanding, brought in by the police. How could you possibly believe that your behavior rates you any kind of special consideration?"

With that, he nodded to the officers who duck-walked the man into the seclusion room before pruning him against the wall after they removed the cuffs. Fortunately, he was compliant and did not need to be restrained, though for the next hour he kept banging on the door, demanding in a wheedling, whining voice through the door to speak with Paul—to no avail. Eventually the man slept for a couple of hours, and was re-interviewed by one of the other techs, and released by the supervisor with a referral for outpatient services and to AA.

Thank fucking God those days are over! Paul mused.

This morning had started out well. Exhausted last night, he fell into bed before 2200 with the intention of reading for a while. But shortly thereafter, he realized he was "reading" with his eyes closed, making up a story as he went along. He shut off the light and fell into a deep dreamless sleep and awakened at 0415. It was rather unusual for him to be awake that early, so he decided to take advantage of it. He jumped up, had a glass of fruit juice to prime his engine and took a long, hot shower, shampooing his hair twice. Given the advantage of being both clean and awake, Paul did not even bother checking his emails but went immediately to work. His intuition prompted him to do a little work on a long-neglected manuscript whose working title was *The President's Greatest Secret*.

He had written an early version some years before for the Weekend Novel Contest in Canada, wherein one wrote the first full draft of a new novel during the Labor Day Weekend between midnight Friday and midnight Sunday One was allowed to have sketches of characters, batches of dialogue and narrative, plot lines and such, and being held to assiduous honesty to maintain the time constraints. He had done a workmanlike job and actually believed he might have a shot at the Grand Prize of a professional edit and publication. But when the "Winner's List" was published, every single "winner," all the way down to the last and least of the "Honorable Mentions" was Canadian (despite the originator's claim to have entrants from twenty-three countries). Paul felt ripped off completely, especially at having sent in the entry fee of a hundred dollars. But he still believed that the premise of the book had merit.

He had done extensive research on Dwight Eisenhower, Jack

Kennedy and J. Edgar ("Mary") Hoover, and had amassed a substantial file folder full of info on each of them as well as developed what he considered to be an intriguing plot line.

The weekend before Kennedy's inauguration, JFK is "invited" to a "secret meeting" at Camp David by Eisenhower, who tells him cryptically that he is going to reveal to him directly the most closely-guarded secret of the United States Government. Kennedy's mind is, of course, awash with possibilities, especially since he neither likes nor trusts the older man, though that feeling is mutual. In fact, the only opinion the two men share is an intense dislike, bordering on hatred, for the "Director for Life" of the FBI, Hoover—who had asked repeatedly to be invited to the mini-summit and been pointedly refused by Ike and Kennedy both.

This, of course, set in motion a scheme on his part to illicitly surveil and record the proceedings. Using newly developed parabolic microphones, he intends to snoop on the meetings, especially since he considered his office to be, and referred to it as, the "Seat of Government." He took upon himself many plenipotentiary powers, including his infamous surveillance efforts against Drew Pearson, Martin Luther King, the Black Panthers and the American Indian Movement. (Paul had fantasized about what it might have been like to plunder Hoover's twenty-five metal file cabinets full of information that he had collected since the age of twelve when he started spying on schoolmates and recording the info in leather bound notebooks). Alas, upon his death the contents mysteriously disappeared, though it was all supposed to be destroyed.

Eisenhower asks Kennedy to sign yet another version of the Official Secrets Act, this one binding him specifically for the contents to be revealed that day. After that, he proceeds to present him numerous documents, movie camera clips and other assorted media (including autopsy photos and videos of aliens) that incontrovertibly prove the truth of the "Roswell incident" of July 1947: that the United States did recover still-breathing aliens as well as their craft and a great deal of physical materiel. He tells Kennedy that this was passed to him by Harry Truman in a similar manner prior to his own inauguration, to be personally passed from the outgoing President to the incoming.

Kennedy is apoplectic, repeatedly insisting that the material must be revealed to the American public. Eisenhower enumerates an extensive list of both powerful individuals and agencies who would be extremely upset to the point of violence if the younger man were to attempt to do so. Besides, the older man states, there is yet a deeper level to the cabal and the conspiracy of silence. He reveals to Kennedy that the US Government has established a form of "diplomatic relations" with the off-planet beings. Kennedy is speechless when he hears this and can barely form a coherent sentence.

"Whatever could we possibly want from them? If you're to be

believed at all!"

"John," said Eisenhower, using a name that Kennedy disliked, "there are things in play that effect not only our great nation, but the entire world. This is a matter of intergalactic politics!"

"Fuck you, General," responded the younger man, using a term of address that Eisenhower did not like either. "Are you mentally ill? Maybe you should be examined at Walter Reed!"

The older man kept his calm, and responded, "I guarantee you I am as sane as you are. It took me a while to wrap my head around this level of information too, I'll tell you that!"

Kennedy calmed himself as much as possible, taking deep breaths and then drank two glasses of water. He went to change his clothes yet again, necessitated by his Addison's Disease, a kidney disorder that resulted in his perspiring excessively. He usually changed his clothes from the skin out five or more times a day.

When he returned, he queried, "If you are to be believed, what exactly ...are we 'trading' with them? I assume this is some kind of business arrangement?"

"Ah! The very crux of the matter."

"What does that mean?"

"We have reached an arrangement. The Foreign Materials Desk at the Central Intelligence Agency has been reverse-engineering artifacts from the crash and feeding the results to private American companies to manufacture. It allows us, the government, to remain

'separate,' as if were, from these discoveries. In addition, we are being gifted with highly, highly advanced technology by the visitors."

"OK! OK! Enough! What we are giving them!"

It was Eisenhower's turn now to take several deep breaths before he continued.

"They...you have to understand that they are a very technologically advanced civilization."

"What does that mean?" Kennedy asked, both angry and impatient.

"Their evolution has led them to develop...highly advanced machines and tools."

"So fucking what? Will you get to the point!"

"They...we..."

Kennedy just glared at the older man, totally heedless of the fact that he had at one point been his Commander-in-Chief.

"They don't experience emotions...the way we do."

Kennedy's response this time was an arched eyebrow and a wry look.

"They...feed off our emotions."

"'Feed?'"

"They're able to...translate human emotion into food, the

nutrients they need."

"Oh bullshit, General! That's total crap!"

Now Eisenhower showed his anger and he slashed the air with the edge of his hand.

"Knock off the sarcasm! This is fucking hard enough for me as it is!"

Kennedy remained silent, but gave the older man an appraising look.

"We...I mean us...The U.S. government...at least some of us...there's a cooperative effort..."

"Oh Jesus H. fucking Christ, General! Just spit it out!"

"The surge in technology we've experienced in this country is a direct result of a policy decision...to feed the aliens with human emotions."

"What? How? What do you mean?"

"They like chaos. Upset. Anger. Violence."

"'They like it?'"

"It feeds them."

"So?"

"Our...arrangement is to create more of the energy they need. In return, they give us technology."

Kennedy shook his head, and asked "Like what?"

"Most of the technology that has been developed in the last fifteen years has been a direct result of intervention by extraterrestrials!"

"Are you on drugs, General?"

"GODDAMN IT! SHUT UP! I'M SERIOUS!"

Eisenhower angrily began enumerating items touching his fingers.

"Transistors! FM radio! Cable television! Nuclear submarines! The atomic clock!"

"Stop! Stop!"

"Microwave ovens! Laser beams! Weather satellites! Artificial heart! Polio vaccine!"

"Stop! Please stop!"

The older man stopped speaking, breathing heavily, complexion flushed from his mental exertions.

"Let's say, just hypothetically, that I believe you. Now what?"

"We've committed to providing a continuing supply of...food."

"What? How?"

"By creating opportunities for more and more tension, more chaos."

"How, General? How in the fuck are 'we' doing that?"

"It's a win-win!" the older man exclaimed.

"What do you mean?"

"It plays into our hands. We get superior weapons and technology, and it keeps the 'Rookies' on edge!"

"You're not telling me something here. How exactly are we creating this 'tension?'"

The elder statesman looked down and away as he answered.

"Racial tension. War. Financial unrest. Increasing law enforcement. More prisons."

"And this is an advantage for us how?"

"Because we're in charge! We hold the key positions in business and industry! We benefit directly from exploiting the population!"

"General, you fail to see that we're slaves too!"

"Somebody has to be in charge!"

"What a fucking mess! How in the hell did all of this get started?"

"We didn't want people getting upset, questioning our authority. Truman called together the top military and scientific minds to form Majestic-12, to develop a defensive shield against an alien invasion—and to keep the population quiet about all of the 'flying saucers.' Project Blue Book hasn't been terribly effective."

"It would result in revolution. Overturning the government." Then, in a snide aside, he mentioned, *"Toppling the Catholic Church."*

"If people stopped believing in the authority of institutions, we'd have complete chaos and anarchy."

"Precisely."

There was a long pause, a heavy stillness in the air, as the two men looked at each other from opposite sides of the room, followed by a shift in the energy, like the silent meshing of gears that seemed almost palpable to the both of them.

Kennedy sighed and said, "What do I have to do?"

"You signed the new Security Agreement. Just go along with the plan. It's your job."

There was more, so much more to be said by his fictional/real life characters, but he kept running up against what he called the 'tedium barrier,' of having to spend an inordinate amount of time doing the necessary research to get all of the personal details correct, all the meticulous miscellany of the lives of these well-known public figures. He'd read innumerable books about all of them, and still felt he was falling short, needing to do more, to make these tragic figures who had lived and breathed and walked the green earth, breathe again on the pages he produced; wanting them to be as dynamic in his fiction as they had been when influencing world events. The magnitude of details was overwhelming, especially the effort of portraying them as flawed individuals doing the best they could during the very difficult times in which they had lived, and yet introducing small slivers of his own critique, his own judgments (especially of J. Edgar Hoover, who he particularly despised). It was this tedium that gave rise to his working on it only incrementally.

CHAPTER THIRTY-SIX
ANNIVERSARY

San Francisco   **Monday**   **December 25, 1995: 0431**

P aul awoke far earlier than usual, but it was extra time to write, on what was going to be a writing day, a celebration of his thirteenth anniversary clean! Four thousand seven hundred forty-eight days! Almost unbelievable, but he had lived them, each and every one of them!

While the coffee brewed, he considering when and where to have breakfast. He considered Hopwell's on 24th and Diamond, but Café Roma was so much closer; and they had the mushroom omelet with sun-dried tomatoes and a side of chorizo or local Italian sausage. Of course, there would be the famous San Francisco sourdough bread toasted and served with butter and fresh lemon curd. Oh God, did that ever sound good!

But coffee first, always first! No matter what excellent blend a restaurant had (and there were many), he preferred his own home brew.

Sitting at his writing desk, he had the first robust sip, and the words just seemed to flow magically from his fingers. He was reminded of an ancient Religion class that he had had to endure during his Catholic grammar school years. Even though he had become disenchanted somewhere around age eight, he managed to endure attending Catholic ceremonies (including Mass) until he was thirteen. And now, for some reason, the image of the writers of the Old Testament sitting with their stone tablets and channeling the transcription of the Divine Word, occurred to him. And he had to admit, he felt a timeless kinship with them.

The further he went into the writing of *Crucible*, it was simultaneously strange to him that he was becoming both more and less angry and upset; becoming more and more enraged with the foul treatment to which every human (especially in "modern times") was treated, subjecting each of them to tremendous shame-enforcing mandates that channel all creative energy into the utter drudge of making money. It was interesting how the quality of his writing was feeding his spiritual development.

He dressed quickly and vacillated for just a moment too long (or, conversely, just long enough) for him to be caught by the telephone's demand for attention. He stopped, hesitated and then picked up when he was literally halfway out of the door.

"Dr. Marzeky here."

"Paul? It's Karen. I hope this isn't too early."

"What are you doing so wide-awake and early on X-Mas Day?"

"Calling to celebrate your anniversary!"

"At this hour?"

"No, seriously. Happy Day!"

"Are you sure you're not mistaking me with Jesus? Isn't it supposed to be his day?"

"According to who you read, or in whom you believe."

"As always."

"So, what's really up?"

"I know it's Christmas, but I wondered if we should meet?"

"Today? I thought you'd be having a big celebration dinner with what's-his-name?"

"We...we've sort of...split up."

Paul paused, unsure of how to respond. He felt split. On the one hand, he was glad because he had long fancied her. Conversely, he felt a natural human sadness for her loss.

"I'm sorry. Do you...I mean, if you want to talk about it…"

"Not right now. But I would like to talk."

"I'm sorry. I don't know what to say."

"I just thought...well, I know you live alone so I thought..."

"Ah!" said Paul, as the coin finally dropped.

"I'm sorry. This is awkward."

"No. I mean, kind of. Look, it's just a little early for me."

"I apologize."

"This all seems...out of character for you."

"I admit I'm a bit thrown."

"I was about to go out to breakfast. Would you...like to join me?"

"Not right now, but would you call me back, later? It's a little early for me"

"Of course! Of course!"

As Paul continued his quest for breakfast, he considered the swelling of his desire in the face of the lovely Karen's being potentially available. He usually resented anyone disturbing his early mornings. His usual practice was never to answer the phone before 1000. He really couldn't pin down why he'd answered today. Some kind of errant impulse, though now the possibility of being with the lovely Karen was enticing. After all, it was his anniversary! "Holiday" be damned! He generally ignored what he considered to be the "hysterical madness" that most people associated with such occasions. Such periods were always inconvenient for him, especially with business closings and public transportation on a holiday schedule that conflicted with own. The next level was, of course, that millions upon millions of individuals were enticed, seduced, manipulated into being obeisant to stringent, often draconian quasi-fascist rules and regulations meant to corral human feelings and channel them into pre-designed, conformist categories for the more machine-like "efficiency" (and enhanced profit) that had become the new contemporary standard.

Paul always wondered about the accuracy of the use of the term "modern." Was humanity simply re-discovering old technology, perhaps from millennia, eons, ago that the human brain was just beginning to be able to comprehend, and like small children, believing to have "discovered" it for the for the first time? It was very much akin to Creepy Columbus "discovering" the Americas. As much as he hated to cite "The Bible," it was there from whence he drew one of his favorite attributions: "There is nothing new under the sun" (though he always thought it belonged to Zeno the Elder for some odd reason).

He made his way down to Columbus and found his favorite corner seat with his back to the wall. The word had gone out on the North Beach silent telegraph that The Roma was going to do a holiday breakfast for regulars only, closing after 1100 for all and sundry to pursue more traditional Christmas plans. He decided to deviate from his pre-laid plans to simply indulge in the special of the day: waffle with maple butter, two eggs over easy and a sausage patty. It tasted wonderful, accompanied by three additional cups of fine strong brew.

As he meandered back to his place, he contemplated the odd conversation with Karen. It was not like her to propose a more personal contact, but then she was upset with her recent loss— though it had not been that long ago that she had been rather adamant about informing him of her unavailability. It could just be her woman's prerogative. He speculated that maybe things had not been as rosy as she had described. It was yet another mystery to unravel. No matter what, her input as a consultant was invaluable. He treasured her keen insights and willingness to explore almost any topic, to unravel the often deep and abstruse roots of knotty psychological puzzles to which they could apply themselves. It was one of her most intriguing and attractive characteristics. His physical attraction to her was exciting, but the empathic connection was far more primary and enduring.

He wasn't exactly sure how he was going to respond to Karen's gambit, but then decided he would follow her lead—professional or personal.

"Hello. Karen?"

"Paul! I'm so glad you called back."

"Of course! I said I would."

"I just feel like our earlier conversation was a little...strange."

"Not at all."

"Thank you. But I... we need to talk. In person."

"Surely. I understand."

"I'm not sure you do. There're things we need to talk about. Tonight? Can you come over? Please?"

He was non-plussed but kept his anxiety and excitement to himself.

"No! It's all good! We're friends and colleagues. I...shall we set a time?"

There was a short silence on the line, and then Karen spoke in a soft voice, "I don't want this to affect our relationship."

"We're solid as far as I'm concerned."

"Thank you, Paul. Will you come over? For dinner?"

"Absolutely!"

Then she laughed, a trill almost, girlish and bright.

"I'd really like to hear about your DID client! I'm actually dying to know!"

Paul laughed now too, relieved.

"I should have known. Inquiring minds and all that."

"How about two o'clock? We can talk while I complete preparations for dinner."

"Works for me. Should I bring anything?"

"Just yourself."

Paul's smile grew enormous and he swallowed it and put it in his belly. He already had it in mind to bring a good bottle of wine. He much preferred red, but it seemed that "traditionally" a white might be more appropriate. He did not have a good white on hand, and it being a holiday, even Safeway would be closed, so it was unlikely that he could pick up a good bottle on such short notice. His personal rule was that a wine had to be at least five years old before he would drink it. He had been told many times that it sounded kind of "snobby," but that was usually by people who didn't mind screw-top wine. He just didn't like young wine. He'd been nurturing a 1976

Sebastiani Vineyards Pinot Noir "Tail Feathers" (Tres Rouge). He had drunk all but this last bottle from a case he had bought years ago (he remembered paying $7.00 a bottle way back when). He'd savored a bottle with different groups of friends through the years on special occasions. This was the last.

Paul arrived ten minutes early, and she greeted him with a kiss on the cheek. She was wearing an apron over a pair of jeans and scoop-necked turquoise blouse. She led him into the kitchen where she continued her preparations. She had three different cutting boards in use, each holding different vegetables and other elements of what portended to be a grand feast. Paul inhaled deeply, the rich aroma of a turkey that had already been roasting for some hours filled the air.

"Wow! Smells great!" he said and drew close to her, then took another deep breath, "And so do you! Wow!"

Paul didn't want to appear too eager, yet his primal instincts were screaming at him to listen, to act in accord with their messages. Conversely, he felt that he had plenty of time—or maybe it was just his own fears. He also desperately wanted to talk at greater length about Roach. He needed Karen's professional clarity as much as he needed and wanted the personal.

Perhaps sensing the shift in his energy, Karen stepped back slightly and gave Paul a measured look.

"I need to do a couple of things more here, just a few minutes, and then we can talk."

He went into her consulting room. The Dallas Cowboys were already crushing the Arizona Cardinals by a score of 24-3, even though it was not quite the end of the second quarter. Paul was only mildly interested, not being an especial fan of either team, and wanted to focus more completely on Karen.

He fell asleep, ensconced in one of her matching wingback chairs. He was dreaming that he was napping in the very chair in which he was seated, when Karen gently called his name to awaken him from his brief slumber. He sat up, blinked his eyes, smacked his lips a few times and then smiled.

"Wow! That was awesome! How long was I asleep?"

"About forty-five minutes."

"Wow! I didn't mean to do that."

"It was perfect. Now, don't get weird about this, but you looked very sweet, kind of like a little boy."

Paul was discomfited by the comparison, as would be any mature male, but he heard the undertone of reverence in her voice. It touched him very, very deeply.

"I'm very...moved."

"I'm glad you didn't do the weird male macho thing."

"Thanks. I'm... I've always been..."

"I've always known. You're very sensitive."

"A friend of mine calls it 'SNAG: Sensitive New Age Guy!'"

320

"That sounds more like sarcasm."

"Yeah, he's a manly-man, or at least he ascribes to being one."

"Why do guys do that so much? It certainly isn't to impress women. It's a real turn-off for most women!"

"Many guys do it as a sort of threat display for other men. Guys walk around afraid of other guys; afraid we'll get attacked."

"That's weird!"

"I know. A lot of guys believe that it makes them more attractive to women!"

"And?"

"'And' what?"

"What lies beneath it? You obviously have some thoughts, Mr. Psychological Researcher!"

"I do as a matter of fact."

She made a twirling gesture with her right hand, and said, "So?"

"It's always early shame. Boys learn from their fathers what is and is not culturally acceptable, based on Dad's cultural experiences and the extent to which the Dad has been shamed or abused, and the depth to which he has internalized it or worked through it."

"Most men don't bother to work through it."

"It's certainly not encouraged or supported by contemporary society."

"The net effect then is that nothing really changes."

"Precisely! One of the worst things a young boy can be called is a 'girl.'"

"Pussy!"

"Exactly! The last thing any young man wants is to be considered effeminate. Boys learn early that they are supposed to be manly-men!"

"It's not only the basis of homophobia, but all of the isms: Defending one's position, no matter how irrelevant, no matter how ludicrous."

"I agree. We live in a totally toxic society where most of what is considered to be 'normal' is distorted bullshit!"

She slapped him lightly and playfully on his upper arm and said "And you guys have been promoting it for millennia!"

"And you women have been encouraging us!" Paul retorted.

"Because we've always been afraid of being attacked or assaulted by men!"

"That may be, but my question is, and always has been: How in the hell did all of this get started in the first place?"

"Now that is a very good question!"

"Do you have any good answers?"

"Developmental theory always postulates reinforcement through repetition."

"Yes."

"And so, somewhere, perhaps in the misalignment of physical size—men are generally bigger, taller, stronger; women, out of fear, agreed, maybe by default, with men's physical dominance."

"But women have other ways of attempting to even the playing field. I believe that women are far more intelligent than men."

Karen mock-preened and then did a Mae Westish vamp.

"I agree totally!"

Paul laughed out loud.

"This is one of many things I have always loved about you! We can talk about anything without things getting weird."

"Thanks. I think so too."

"You may be the least defensive woman I have ever known."

"I've been working on myself for a very long time too, you know."

"That may be the primary reason we get along so well. Neither of us have to grind on the other because of old emotional garbage."

Suddenly she lifted her head and exclaimed, "Oh!"

"What? What's wrong?"

"Here we sit, talking about how well we get along; how well we communicate." She paused for a moment, and then continued in a very subdued voice.

"There's something I need to tell you."

"OK."

"This is very difficult for me."

"OK."

"I…There's something I haven't told you."

"What? Are you physically ill?"

"No! Nothing like that!"

"Then what? Have you got a new boyfriend?" said Paul and couldn't keep the hurt out of his voice.

She came to him then and put a hand to his cheek.

"No! Never! Not that!"

"Then what?" answered Paul more gruffly than he had intended.

"Remember when I told you that Sinclair and I had split up?'

"Yes."

"That wasn't quite true."

"WHAT?"

"No! I mean we had split up, but not just when I told you."

"What do you mean?"

"I knew you were interested in me. At the time I told you we were a 'committed poly couple?'"

"Yes."

"That's around the time we split up."

Paul was stunned, shocked. Unable to speak.

She saw the look of shock on his face and just looked at him steadily, allowing him the space to absorb her revelation.

"But…why did you do that?"

"I was very upset when I found out he was cheating on me. With another guy. I felt shamed. Unlovable."

Paul took a deep breath and responded.

"And?"

"I knew you really liked me. And I knew I was attracted to you."

"Then why?"

"I was afraid! I didn't want to get involved again so soon! But I wanted to be near you, get to know you better."

"You could have told me the truth! I have been waiting all this time just to have a chance with you! Forcing myself to be restrained! Trying to not rush you! And it's all been a lie!"

"No! ever that!"

"Then what do you call it?"

"I was wrong! I should have trusted more! Trusted you more! But I was afraid!"

"Of me?"

"Not specifically. But you are a guy!"

"What the fuck does that mean?"

"Oh, come on! Admit it! I saw the tenderness in your eyes! The desire to comfort me! To help me 'forget' my pain!"

"I think that was pretty natural!"

"Maybe. But you would have robbed me of the opportunity to grieve and heal my own hurt!"

"By comforting you?"

"Yes! You would have lent me your strength and I would have accepted it. Loved it! Needed it!"

"Why is that bad?"

"It's not bad, per se. But now I am strong on my own. I have cried and cried and cried. Talked with my girlfriends about all of this."

"And?"

She took him by the shoulders and looked directly in his eyes.

"Now we have a possibility not based on you rescuing me! We don't have to play out all of that co-dependence!" She paused, and there was a tremor in her voice when she said to him, "If you're willing to forgive me. If you're willing to give us a chance."

Paul had never seen such raw beauty and vulnerability in any woman's eyes. He had never experienced such an upwelling of pride and love and admiration for any woman he had ever known. Her strength and wisdom so far outshone the petty juvenile hurt he had felt initially. Here clearly was a woman of depth and magnitude; of immense strength and intelligence; of the most magnificence of both heart and soul.

"If you'll have me, my dear, I will be delighted to have you."

CHAPTER THIRTY-SEVEN
THE BEAT GOES ON

San Francisco   **Monday December 25th, 1995: 1643**

They had embraced then, given each other as much love and intimacy as they could in that moment. They kissed, over and over, tongues dancing a kind of loving arabesque. Karen pressed herself against his stiffening manhood and they danced in place, absorbing all of the heightened energies—and broke apart simultaneously, as if sharing one mind.

"Wow!"

"Me too! But I want to eat! Today! I'm hungry…for food too!"

Paul laughed and stood unabashedly before her, face red, sweating, pants tented.

"Me too! That was just so…amazing!"

"And more to come! Just because we have opened the door, we don't have to go rushing through to the finale immediately!"

"I so trust your wisdom, but goddamn! I cannot wait to put hands upon you!"

"And I will welcome you even more for having love and respect enough to let me set the pace. It will be worth it!"

"It already is!"

"Beautiful man!"

"No question! I do not feel intimidated in any way. Just a little strange, trusting so much! I don't even feel diminished by not being a beast!"

"All in good time, my fine monster!"

"Ooooh! I love that!"

She reached over and kissed him again.

"Let's eat! I think the turkey has certainly had enough time to cool!"

"Maybe we can have a glass of that yummy looking wine you brought. You must have been saving that bottle for a long time."

"I bought a case way back when in 1979. This is the very last bottle."

"I'm honored."

"I wanted you to be. I mean, I do honor you. I think you are really special."

It was her turn to respond in a pseudo-accent. "Why, thank you, suh!"

Karen had anticipated him and had cracked the bottle just before Paul woke up. She presented the bottle to him like a sommelier, then turned and placed two Czech leaded-crystal wine glasses on the table. Paul poured a taste for both of them to sample—carefully inhaling the bouquet, then a sip washed around the mouth to excite the palate and under the tongue. They both raised their eyebrows, and smiled at each other.

"Exquisite! Worth waiting for!"

"Absolutely!"

"Shall we eat?"

"Excellent!"

Karen had taken the turkey out of the oven and allowed it to rest. Now it was ready to carve. Paul went through the knife drawer, chose the kitchen shears, and selected both a boning knife and a carving knife. He tested the edge on both of them, secured the diamond sharpening steel, and put a fresh edge on both of them.

"Why two knives, if you don't mind my asking?"

"Not at all. The boning knife," he said holding up the five-inch curved knife, "is perfect for dis-jointing the legs from the thighs, and the wings from the breast. The butcher's knife," he said holding up the ten-inch scimitar, "is perfect for carving the breast, and the thighs for that matter. Nice smooth, clean cuts."

"Excellent. Didn't know you knew so much about this. I always mess it up."

"I'll explain as I carve. Afterwards, I will de-bone the entire carcass so that you can boil the bones and make a good soup base."

"Oh, great! This'll be fun!"

Paul kept a running monologue as he trimmed the wing tips off and put them into a large bowl he had chosen for the bones. Then he cut through the skin intersection between the thigh and breast, pulled gently until he felt the joint resisting, cut through the joint and placed the leg on the platter. He did the same with the other side, then disjointed the thighs and placed them on the platter too. Next came the wings that joined the rest of that already cut.

"See how clean the breast is now, how much it almost invites being carved up?"

"You make it look easy!"

"Lots of trial-and-error. Plus carving beaucoup chickens when I worked in a meat department."

"Really?"

"Yeah, the Super K Market at 22nd and California. It was twelve years ago."

"There's a lot I don't know about you."

"And me about you. I'm glad we're going to change that."

"Me too."

Paul turned his attention back to the remaining turkey, and said, "See how easy it will be to carve nice thin slices now?" And proceeded to do so, laying them out in a fan-pattern on the other end of the platter. When he was complete, he gestured to the remains and said, "Before I leave, I'll clean off the rest of the meat, and debone it."

She had prepared broccoli florets in a sharp fresh cheese sauce, mashed potatoes, and a tasty, redolent pan gravy—and then presented it all with whole-berry cranberry sauce.

"Wow! I'm impressed!"

She simply nodded and reached for his hand.

"Do you mind if we do a little prayer of thanks and gratitude?"

"Oh, hell no! I was going to ask the same thing! You lead."

She sat up, straightened her back, and took a deep breath. He did the same.

"Oh, Great Mystery, Creator of All Universes, please hear our prayer! We give thanks for all of the grace and blessings we have been granted, especially for this wondrous meal, and all who have had a part in it coming to us. May it nurture our hearts and spirits and bring us ever closer to a deeper understanding and union. Ho!"

Paul echoed her and they continued holding hands, sitting in silence for a moment, then opened their eyes and smiled at each other.

"Wow!" they both said simultaneously.

The meal was extraordinary. Paul was delighted that Karen like white meat, thereby allowing him to shamelessly indulge in both thighs. The gravy was thick and rich with pan drippings, the potatoes whipped with heavy cream to an airy consistency. It was a remarkable meal, and Paul complimented Karen several times with great enthusiasm. The wine was an elegant compliment. They split the bottle between them and both realized they were very high, far beyond the effects of the fruit of the vine.

"I have a little treat for you!" she said at length.

"I don't think it's even possible to surpass the wonder of this meal!"

"Not 'surpass' so much as compliment."

"OK. What might that be?"

"Do you want to have an official session?"

"Why?"

"Maybe we should wait until after we have our session."

"Who's that?"

"Because I bought a small bottle of Drambuie!"

"Oh my God! Are you sure we're not related?"

"I know you really like it, and I decided I wanted to try it!"

"Let's sip a little snifter as we chat!"

"We can make an arrangement that doesn't violate the ethical code! After all, we're both professionals!"

She went to fetch the bottle and two snifters, and they made their way to the consulting room.

Did you ever consult with the Clinical Supervisor, the one you didn't like or trust?"

"You remembered! You really do pay attention!"

"Of course. I think you're a brilliant clinician!"

"Why, thank you ma'am" responded Paul in an affected, pseudo-Southern drawl.

Paul settled back more deeply into his chair, took a sip of his favorite liqueur and sighed. He felt very content, filled with joy and gratitude. His heart was racing, overflowing with the psychic and emotional embrace of all that was transpiring. His every breath was infused with the emotional and empathic scent of Karen.

"I am utterly and completely captivated by the day! I thank you so much!"

"You've been a wonderful presence today. It's not a one-way street!"

"Wow! So incredible!"

Paul sighed again and smiled.

"And now, the mystery client!"

"If you're up to it."

"I really want to tell you. I just don't want to shift the energy right now!"

"Me either."

Paul sighed again and smiled.

"I was in a conundrum. I really needed to consult about her, and

I had a supervisor I couldn't consult with, who didn't believe me; and who wouldn't be of any help at all. Where was I supposed to turn? I was only concerned about the client. We had a very good rapport. She was making progress with me, after years of being shuttled around between therapists who didn't have the slightest idea how to support her, help her grow and become more whole. All they could do was fill her full of goddamn drugs."

"You really are passionate!"

"I just wanted what was best for my client. I wasn't interested in clinical propriety!"

"But you had a responsibility to the clinic too!" she stated in a very harsh, almost confrontational voice.

"My ethical responsibility to my client was of a higher order!"

"And you felt trapped by circumstances?" Again, he felt the chill in her voice.

"Yes! Absolutely!"

"And so, you went ahead with what you felt was right?"

"Of course!"

"Despite what was legal and proper?" She sounded like a prosecutor.

"Of course!"

Karen looked at him for a moment, and then a small crystalline tear ran down her cheek.

"I am... I'm so proud of you!"

Paul went to her and they shared a tender embrace.

"You sounded like you became someone else there for a minute!"

"Just checking your dedication!"

"You could have asked!"

"It's not the same! I had to hear it in your voice!"

"And now?"

"I'm really getting to know who you really are!"

"What's that mean?"

"I just had to confirm my intuition about you."

"What's that mean?"

"I've always known you were brilliant. Now I know your heart is true."

"You keep...surprising me. You're becoming so much more real."

"'More real?'"

"I guess I've always had an intuition about you too."

She sighed, and they smiled.

"Then maybe we can have a strictly professional chat right now."

"Works for me."

"So, tell me about this client of yours."

CHAPTER THIRTY-EIGHT
MORE

San Francisco   **Wednesday December 27th, 1995: 0832**

They had had a second Drambuie, sitting quietly side-by-side, holding hands. They spoke little, but both communicated a shared sense of the other. Immensely turned on, Paul nonetheless restrained himself from acting on his carnal desires, though he had to renew his commitment every two seconds or so. He was aware that she was aware of how aroused he was. Paul created that it was a way for him to show here that he was indeed genuine. He too could manage to keep the deeply personal apart from the professional—at least for now.

They hugged for a long time and kept sharing deep, passionate kisses, with one or the other occasionally transgressing the professional altogether with hands and fingers too hungry to obey. They had resolved that clinical time would have to wait for another, purposefully specified time—though, they had laughed, it would be like drawing a line where the earth met the sky on the horizon to keep them from sharing their souls.

They called each other back and forth a dozen times the following day, sometimes connecting, sometimes just listening to the voice of the other since they had asked their respective services not to pick up for that very purpose. The sense of connection kept growing and growing, mad passion and something so much more. He felt like they were breathing essence when they spoke, each time they spoke.

"Hey! It's Paul. Can we talk?"

"I've only got a few minutes right now, but I'll call you back."

"Absolutely! I just wanted to make sure you're OK."

"Beautiful, actually! I'll call you."

Paul was elated, and thought briefly about taking a long walk, maybe though Golden Gate Park, but he wanted to be available when Karen called. Damn! He sincerely hoped he wasn't being a fool! But when he re-played the content of their conversations and her tone of voice, he knew this was right. The waiting was over!

It was a strange admixture of strength and desire that infused him, the one tempering the other. He felt such extreme desire to be with her, craving her touch, but more just wanting to know what she was doing, thinking, feeling. He fantasized about the sex, most assuredly, but more about just being with her, the sound of her voice, the touch of her hand, the feel of her against him, not speaking but deeply communicating, wanting that day-to-day interaction, the little touches and smiles, the small shared intimacies. His thoughts kept turning to her constantly. Patience had never been his strong suit, but he felt filled and full just thinking about her. He had said to her, "You're driving the car," and he had meant it with every fiber of his beingness, dedication and resolve. This was the "higher Love" of which Stevie Winwood had so rapturously sung. He was betting on him. He was betting on her. He was betting on them.

Paul felt himself fading like a slow wave receding from the shore, rather than experiencing the kind of crash he had always had when he hadn't eaten sufficiently, a true hypoglycemic crash. He decided to forsake all of his grandiose designs and just take a nap. He laid down, thinking to just relax and allow his mind to drift into an unstructured reverie.

Instead he fell into a profound somnolent state filled with Technicolor dreams. As he drifted off, he hoped he would dream of Karen, maybe even have an erotic interlude. Instead he dreamed of Jason, of Argonaut fame, only the intrepid hero wore Paul's face as he suffered through all of the incredible struggles through which he had gone to garner the Golden Fleece (previously owned by Hermes' ram) and return it to Iolkos, the capital city in Thessaly from whence it had been stolen. He wanted to claim the throne that had been usurped by his brother, who had demanded its retrieval ostensibly as a test of Jason's honor and courage.

Another version of Paul seemed to be watching from a platform high above, as if a dissociative self had split off and remained safe from all of the action, as Jason/Paul went through tremendous travails, only to escape stronger, wiser and more committed than ever—as if the only way to higher achievement were through pain; as if one could not simply envision a better position and assume it out of desire. It seemed as if the *via dolorosa*, the way of pain, were the only path that could be tread to reach the higher heights, at least at this point in humanity's slow, grinding path through the muck and the mire.

Within the dream, Paul identified with Jason's trials and triumphs, including being seduced by Medea to marry her. He was struck by the fact that, after successfully completing his Hero's Journey, Jason was granted the boon of a loving companion to share his life.

He jumped out of bed with the images still fresh in his mind. He had just loaded the coffee maker when the phone shrilled.

"Hey there! It's me!"

Paul felt a rush of the purest pleasure sweep though his body, and he knew his joy showed in his voice.

"It's so, so good to hear you. What are you up to?"

"I'm all caught up with my work stuff, and here I am!"

"Perfect timing. I just woke up from a very colorful dream."

"Oh, lucky you! Want to talk about it?"

"Uh, maybe later. I need coffee first."

"You sound like you're in a slower gear than I am. Want me to come over?"

"Absolutely! Should I make a pot?"

"No. Just take care of yourself, and I'll see you in about half an hour."

"I am <u>so</u> totally excited!"

Paul got aroused immediately with the sound of her voice, and he considered masturbating prior to her arrival, but practicality intervened. He drank half a cup of coffee, then jumped into the shower before dressing.

By the time she arrived a few minutes later, he was feeling totally refreshed. She handed him a small bundle of winter flowers—winter heath and winter jasmine, English holly, camellias, star magnolia and witch hazel. He blushed with pleasure, and tears filled his eyes.

"How delightful! It's absolutely wonderful to get flowers from you, my flower!"

"I wanted to brighten your day!"

He kissed her vigorously and whispered in her ear, "You are all I need for the day to be bright!"

They'd been standing on the front porch, so he bundled her in out of the clear and chilly day.

"May I get you a cup of tea? Anything?"

"No, thank you. You can give me another kiss, though" which he did with great vigor.

"I know this is going to sound silly, especially with me showing up at your house, but can we be a little more professional today, at least initially?"

Paul could not hide the disappointment from showing in his face.

She knew it immediately and reached a handout and touched his face.

"Sweetie, I've got a lot of questions today, clinical questions. I do not want us to just become a couple only. I love all the progress we have made professionally. It's part of how I've come to love you!"

"I love you too, baby!" he said, and they hugged deeply and long.

Paul then put a fresh edge on the flowers and arranged them in a clear glass vase.

"Thanks for being so sensitive. I'm not very used to it. But then, I guess you're finding that out."

"Your sensitivity is one of the things I like about you most."

"Wow! Thank you again, my lady!" he said and bowed. He so loved her directness and honesty. It was so soothing. He remembered a long period when he first got home from the 'Nam where he told his truth to everyone, using it like an offensive weapon while claiming neutrality. So many people found him to be "too honest." It had taken a long time for him to incorporate the more subtle shades of "truth."

They settled in sitting close and holding hands on the loveseat. She was literally bubbling with enthusiasm.

"I can't wait any longer to hear about your DID patient!"

Paul couldn't help but laugh. He loved her enthusiasm!

"So, where were we?"

"Your outside paid consultant was urging you to bring the Clinical Supervisor into the picture."

"Right. So, I decided not to do that. Despite all the potential fires I had put out for that clinic, I did not feel supported or honored at all. I knew my diagnostic choices were correct. I knew she was DID. There was no one else who had the clinical expertise to treat her properly."

She nodded her head, but then commented, "A little arrogant, huh?"

"I knew I was right. That is why she opened up to me. I was trustworthy. I didn't insist that she take useless 'medications!'"

"I'm sorry. I didn't mean it to sound as hard as it sounded."

"It did sound a little harsh."

"You went in the face of all the conventional wisdom. You did not send the information up the chain. You chose to keep treating her without the imprimatur of the 'clinical authorities.'"

"All true, and all for very good reasons. Did I tell you I got semi-reprimanded once for not referring enough of my clients to the psychiatrist for 'medication evaluation?'"

"No, but I believe it."

"I told the Director that I did not believe every client 'needed' drugs."

"He insisted that I call them 'medications' and 'look more closely at my client list!'"

"Oh my God! Sounds like a defender of the faith standing firm in the face of the heathen rebels!"

Paul laughed as she smiled at him and sent his heart thundering.

"He was just feathering his nest. He didn't want anything or anybody to be too radical, or to rock the boat of his little empire!"

"So, come on! Bring me up to speed!"

"I ended up working with her for more than a year. At one point I taped together two 11" x 17" pages, and drew a map of her alters—who connected to whom; who was protecting who; who mediated with the outside world best and who was hidden; who had sex and who was afraid of human contact. She even had several alters who spoke different languages, and one who was allergic to orange juice!"

"Wow! Pretty fascinating. Did you ever write her up?"

"Just for my personal files. I considered a journal article, but, at that point, without a doctorate, I would have had to find an MD or Ph.D. to front the paper. It would have been difficult, too, to get anyone else up to speed with my methodology. I created an idiosyncratic treatment method based on deep empathy and active listening."

"How did you terminate with her?"

"Actually, she terminated with me!"

"Really?"

"Yes. It was all very synchronistic actually."

"What do you mean?"

"I hadn't said anything to her, really to anybody, but I was considering leaving the agency. I wanted to have a private practice, even though I didn't have any idea how I might generate referrals, especially from insurance companies."

"It's tough these days, though there's never any shortage of loonies."

"'Loonies?'" Paul said, laughing

"Well, I'm in the presence of a fellow mental health professional. Aren't I allowed to let my hair down?"

"Most certainly, my dear!" Paul drawled.

She gestured with her hand and said, "Tell me."

"So, I'd been thinking about how I could approach her about leaving, maybe even take her on as my first private client—even though she was Medi-Cal and Medicare. It would have been almost impossible for me to take her insurance; and I knew I couldn't afford to work with her without getting paid."

"And?"

"She came into the office dressed-to-the-nines, makeup perfect, with a big smile on her face. She looked beatific."

"Wow! What happened?"

"First, a little back story."

Karen nodded and Paul continued.

"She had missed an appointment two weeks earlier. One of the alters called in and I had a brief conversation with her. She told me that the primary had been depressed and crying a lot the previous week. She told me that she thought that she was 'remembering a lot of stuff.' She didn't say what and I didn't feel I could push her too much. I knew she was delicate."

Paul took a deep breath and launched back in.

"I was astonished! And I told her so. I told her I had never seen her looking so good, and that I was proud of her. She kind of blushed a little and tittered, then started laughing out loud. Real belly laughter."

Karen raised her eyebrows and smiled.

"I was non-plussed. I didn't know what to make of it, so I asked."

"And?"

"She told me she had been having these 'powerful dreams.' What she described sounded like serious lucid dreaming episodes during which she was 'remembering' parts of her early life. We had earlier touched on her sexual abuse by her biological father; but now she told me about a whole series of encounters with her mother's boyfriends starting when she was a child. She told me her mother used to 'sell her' to these men for cash or drugs and alcohol."

"Jesus!"

"Yeah! No shit!"

"Was she clear about dreams versus remembering?"

"Vividly! I had never heard her tell her story without faltering! There weren't any cracks in tone. No shifts. None! I just sat there goggle-eyed! I didn't know what to say! She just laughed and laughed!"

"Wow!"

"I just kept looking at her! And I finally had to ask, 'What happened to you?' She just looked at me and told me she had remembered 'everything.'"

"'Everything?' I asked.

"'Well, maybe not everything yet. But I will.'"

"'How did this happen?'"

"She told me that our work had given her the confidence to accept her feelings as 'real.' She said, 'I've been feeling the truth all along. I just was too afraid to believe it.'"

"Oh my God!"

"Apparently when she 'let it in,' she was overwhelmed with an enormous sadness, and spent two weeks in bed crying! And having these amazing dreams! I've never seen such a transformation!"

"And it took all of the work you'd done with her to trust herself enough to listen to her own intuition."

"I guess."

"No, listen. You're not giving yourself enough credit for having held space for her week after week."

"That's what she said too, that she 'couldn't have done it without me.'"

"Thanks."

Paul Started crying then, tears falling without restraint. He had never told anyone this story and the feedback from Karen, voicing her perspective, just put him in awe and tremendous gratitude for his abilities, and for the opportunity of helping one of the most tortured individuals he had ever know regain a certain amount of strength and stability; to have freed herself from the abyss of her earliest horrendous years.

"It is just so rewarding, to know I really helped her; to know that she's going to have a better life!"

"Wow, Paul! You really contributed to her!" Karen said, then came over and hugged him.

Paul fell limply into her arms, and she held him tightly, rubbing his back and upper arms, kissing him on the top of the head and neck. He felt her love flooding through him, light illuminating all of the dark corners of his heart. He felt released from the shackles of his entire timeline. He noticed the rhythm of her breathing deepen and felt an increased degree of heat emanating from her sweet and beautiful body. She held him even tighter yet, and he felt his penis awaken and stiffen. She noticed immediately and moved he hand to lay lightly upon it. She looked him deeply in the eyes and conveyed such a look of love and respect that he almost had an orgasm on the spot.

Then she whispered to him, "Later. OK?"

He could only nod and shed more tears, now of immense gratitude.

"What you did was give her the very best of what we do as healer—especially after all of the swimming through the molasses!"

"So, what happened to her?"

"She and her husband left The City and moved to Northern California."

"What a blessing!"

"I know. The Universe gave her a special supporting cast."

"I'm inclined to believe that the Universe is actually benevolent."

Karen laughed and said, "I've always felt that way!"

"It's one of the many things I love about you. You radiate this core strength. It is so beautiful! You're so beautiful!"

Karen just looked at him with this enormous smile as a small tear streaked down her left cheek. Paul immediately jumped to the wrong conclusion.

"What? What? Did I say something wrong?"

"No, you silly. I'm just overwhelmed. And a little confused."

"I don't understand."

"I had thought this could be a professional meeting. And I'm sitting here wanting to have sex with you. It's confusing."

Paul sat up straighter and pulled her closer.

"I…Karen…I love you! I know we'll make love at some point. But right now, I don't care! I just love you!"

She closed her eyes and took a deep breath, then smiled.

"When a woman gives herself to a man, it's not as simple as it scems!"

She watched as he beamed at her, his face open and available.

"Sometimes a woman has sex because she likes a guy. Sometimes it's 'just sex,'" she said, making air quotes, "And sometimes, it's much more. But for any woman, it's always a commitment."

"And?"

"I'm really attracted to you. And I want to have sex with you."

"That doesn't sound like a problem to me," said Paul laughing, deflecting his own confusion.

"It's inevitable, we're going to make love," she said and smiled— "and it will be a commitment for me."

350

"And you want me to make a commitment too?"

"No! Absolutely not! I'm just asking you to wait, with me, for me! If and when you make a commitment to me, you will! I love you too!"

"I have this wild desire for you, about touching you, smelling you, feeling you next to me. I can't help it!"

"Do you think I don't?"

"And again, maybe it's the man-woman thing. Every day, many times a day, I have to stop myself thinking about you—otherwise I wouldn't get anything else done!"

"That's so sweet!"

Paul laughed, and asked, "You think?"

"I do. It makes me want you more!"

Paul adjusted his erection to a less painful position. Karen just smiled and replaced her hand.

"I feel committed to you already. It may not be 'the commitment' you were talking about, but God damn it, I have feelings too!"

"I'm not trying to make it more difficult for you. I just don't want us to lose our friendship."

"I hope I don't lose my mind in the process! I ache for you!"

She reached out and gently squeezed his engorged penis.

"Save this for me just a little longer, will you please?"

CHAPTER THIRTY-NINE
BATTER UP!

San Francisco   **Wednesday December 27th, 1995: 2133**

Paul was elated. Karen had left lingering threads of her infinite richness thrumming through him when she very reluctantly left his side. What a mind! What a body! Oh my God! He was practically drooling!

He had just settled, musing, into one of the leather chairs in his therapy office, wanting to just sit in Karen's glow—when the phone shrilled, sending a shock wave through him and he reacted, startled, nerve endings thrashed.

"WHAT?" in a very loud, angry voice.

"Dr. Marzeky? It's Darlene at your service."

Paul backpedaled quickly and apologized.

"I'm sorry. I was napping and the phone startled me."

"It's all right. I've heard worse."

"Thank you. You ladies don't get paid enough!"

She laughed and continued.

"I know you told us to hold all of your calls. Do you want us to continue?"

Paul's knee jerk reaction was to give a resounding "Yes," and just let it be, but he felt a strange prickling of his scalp that signaled an intuitive message for him.

"Let's see. Why don't you give me my calls to the moment, and then go ahead and hold them for the rest of the night."

"Works for me. You've had a total of five calls since this afternoon. Two hang ups, two from a fellow who simply said that you 'would know who it was' and refused to leave a name or number. And one just a couple of minutes ago from Karen, who said to call back before 10 PM."

"Oh. Good!"

"I know it's none of my business, but the last one sounded important, so I decided to call you and tell you."

"Excellent! Thank you for your initiative! Good night!"

Paul didn't even hesitate. He called Karen.

"Hi!" he said.

"Hi!" she said.

"I'm so glad you called. I haven't been able to stop thinking of you."

"Me either."

"I'm so glad we get to say 'Good night' again."

"Me too."

"Can we meet tomorrow? Maybe dinner?"

"That's an excellent idea!"

"Maybe some Greek food?"

"Asimakoupoulous?"

"A woman after my own heart!"

"Let's talk tomorrow. Late morning. I've got two early clients."

"Wonderful!"

"Good night, dear man!"

"Good night, dear lady!"

Paul's heart was soaring as he replaced the handset. Wow! What joy!

He brushed his teeth, measured water into the coffee pot, put in a filter and added enough coffee to make two good, strong cups. He had planned an entire morning of doing paperwork, and then hopefully, an afternoon devoted to writing. He often ran into opposition to his ideas about emotional expression with some practitioners who wanted to argue about "re-traumatization" and the "lack of necessity" for doing the reclamation work of releasing old and impacted traumas that he considered essential to healing.

He remembered Colman's definition of abreaction from the Oxford Dictionary of Psychology. "A release or discharge of emotional energy following the recollection of a painful memory that has been repressed...and may lead to a catharsis." The beauty of it lies in the unlocking of the mysteries of the past, and the bounteous riches that are contained therein; and can lead to ever greater awareness and personal enrichment. All of these are intertwined with the alchemy of art.

Erich Fromm chimed in from the archived recesses of his internal encyclopedia. "All great art is by its very essence in conflict with the society with which it coexists. It expresses the truth about existence regardless of whether this truth serves or hinders the survival purpose of any given society. All great art is revolutionary because it touches upon the reality of man and questions the reality of the various transitory forms of human society."

Paul decided to move, albeit somewhat reluctantly, to his writing office (he was actually tired and wanted to just curl up and muse on Karen from the warm confines of his bed). He quickly retrieved his place in the document and recorded all that had been running through his head. When he re-read it, he realized that there was another strain to follow, and went in search of the relevant material.

And found it in an archaic citation from 1751 by a fellow named Paul Jacques Malouin, who was a physician at the French Royal Court as well as an alchemist seeking the most profound of human powers through transformation of the Self. He called it "the chemistry of the subtlest kind" that allowed the practitioner to create extraordinary chemical reactions at a faster pace than that of Nature. It was all in pursuit of what he called the "Great Work" whose success would be proven through the manifestation of the fabled Philosopher's Stone; the transmutation of base metal (lead) into noble metal (gold or silver); or creating an elixir of life, which would confer youth and longevity.

It was a noble and inspiring ideal. It elevated Paul's aspirations to a higher level of desire for personal transcendence. He burned to experience the type of personal revolution that is both individual and collective, a true expression of the holographic paradigm—one's work on oneself creating a totally different range of daily interactions with others, and ultimately influencing the planet as a whole.

In retrospect, he was having what felt like a peaceful and dreamless night. At least that was the way his memory reconstructed it, until he was yanked from his slumber by the insistent, persistent hammering of his bedside telephone at 0310.

"Fuck!" he exclaimed and reached for the instrument.

"Dr. Marzeky!" he answered in a tone that was more akin to "What the fuck do you want?"

"Sorry, doctor. It's your service. I have one of your clients on the line who insists on talking to you."

"And?"

"He sounds...agitated. Incoherent almost. But definitely...kind of freaked out."

Paul knew immediately that it had to be Roach. All his other clients were stable enough that they would not call in the middle of the night.

"Thank you. Go ahead and put him through."

"Doc! Doc! You gotta help me!"

Paul immediately switched to crisis mode, emptying himself of all of his previous emotions, alert for the slightest of nuances.

"What's going on, brother?"

"They're coming to get me!"

Paul was reminded of the line from *Naked Lunch* in which William Burroughs, overamping on cocaine, screams, "I got the fear! I got the fear! I got the coke fear!" I'm being chased by ten thousand Chinese policemen."

"Who is 'they?'"

"I... they been following me!"

"Who?"

"I don't fucking know!"

"Then how do you know you're being 'followed?'"

"Goddamn it, doc! I'm not some fucking kid fresh out of ROTC!"

"Who's after you?"

"I don't know! Could be 'our' government! Could be OC (Organized Crime)!'"

"You don't know?"

"Could even be some old comrades of fucking Hoxley's!"

"What do you want from me?"

"I have to disappear."

"'Disappear?'"

"Go underground!"

"You're underground now!"

"Somewhere in Asia."

Paul took another deep breath and then re-assessed the situation. He was on the horns of a dilemma. If Roach were truly delusional, this could be an exaggerated panic, even manic, state. If, on the other hand he were not, and all of his stories were real, he could be in what was proverbially called "the shitter."

"Brother, we need to talk."

"We can't meet! What if they followed me and I led them to you?"

"Look! Take a deep breath. In fact, let's do two or three before we continue."

Paul followed his own instructions while his focus simultaneously shattered like myriad shards of a broken glass.

He was able to get Roach to take three breaths before the other man's voice exploded through the handset.

"Goddamn it! I've been safe all these fucking years! Almost died so many fucking times!"

Paul waited, sensing what was coming next.

"I knew I should just keep on keeping' on! Just fucking knew I shouldn't try to change!"

Paul maintained his silent vigil.

"Goddamn it, doc! I shouldn't have tried to change! I was fucking safe!"

Paul knew there was an element, no matter how small, of blame against him lodged in this sentiment.

"Brother, you've done good work! You're going to have a new life!"

"What good is it if I'm dead?"

"You said you wanted to change!"

"I'm not blaming you!"

"What do you want me to do?"

Paul was still harboring a tiny hope of getting through to him. He knew only too well how appealing it was to regress into former states of seeming safety that looked so much better in retrospect. They could become a screen for certain memory for some individuals attempting to prevent further psychic injury.

"I'm fucking sorry I got you involved!"

"That's not the issue. What can I do to help you?"

"I just hope they haven't traced me to you!"

"Can you be more concrete?"

"I'm going to disappear. Somewhere in Asia. I won't tell you where."

"How?'"

"I've got plenty of money. Other identities."

Paul was silent, seeking another avenue to open up.

Roach continued as if they had been conversing all along.

"Too many black helicopters! Too many faces, too many dark places!"

Paul kept silent, as his client further unraveled, revealing the parameters of his own personal safety zone against the intrusion of the world on his shame and trauma. Jung had once commented that each of us creates war outside of ourselves as a projection of the war we experience within ourselves—essentially the split between what one actually feels and how one is expected to act in accordance with the mandates of others. Such behavior was essentially the most telling indictment of a sick, and corrupt global society that underlay all of the machinations and manifestations of addictions and "mental illness."

He could feel his opportunity for meaningful intervention slipping by—was he delusional or severely traumatized or both?

If he were delusional only, his vast world of international drug dealing and sinister, dark figures seeking him, made eminent sense.

Delusions were always a kind of balancing out of a perceived or actual sense of deficiency, a kind of organic balance. The more severe the trauma, the more radical the internalized sense of loss and depreciation, and the more severe the delusional compensation.

He knew so many combat vets, and a significant number of black-ops people, who had told him variously through the years about recurring nightmares, visits by the ghosts of people they had killed, watching others die, ministering to the dying. He had also heard that the uncertainty of what may have happened to comrades-in-arms left behind. There had been no closure because one party or the other never returned to the tactical area of operations (TAOR).

"So. What do you want me to do?"

There was a long pause, and then Roach answered in a strangled voice.

"I know...we were on the right track."

"Roach, brother..."

"No! Don't. Maybe I'll get back in touch."

"Roach..."

"Oorah, brother!" said Roach, using the traditional Marine Corps phrase.

"Oorah, brother!" said Paul into the echoing sound of the dial tone.

CHAPTER FORTY
MORE QUESTIONS THAN
ANSWERS

San Francisco   **Thursday December 28th, 1995: 0703**

P aul woke up disoriented. He shook his head and wondered idly whether the early morning phone call from Roach had actually happened. As the film cleared from his eyes and the fuzziness of his brain lifted like the fog from the Bay, he realized that it was all true, all too true. Jesus! He started to castigate himself for not having done more, but then enumerated all that he had done, all of the very excellent work they had accomplished despite the restrictions imposed by Roach: not knowing his phone number or address; the irregularity of their sessions; and, most especially, not being able to complete their work. Then, he heard a silent voice address him that the work had been for his own benefit as well— and to be grateful, to give thanks, for all that they had shared. He realized the futility of trying to find him, a man who had successfully evaded the forces of the CIA and/or OC for twenty-five years!

He called his service and left a message to not be disturbed unless Roach called. Karen liked early morning appointments. She had even seen a client once at 0530 so the woman could go to work immediately afterward. Therefore, he was not concerned about missing a call from her. He knew they would connect. They were connected.

He had had another dream-filled night. The outstanding feature that stayed with him was a memory that looped through his now awake-brain like a highlight reel, one that he wanted to share at the earliest opportunity with his dear Karen, one that had brought him to consciousness in tears of joy, was of himself split into two main pieces or parts: one was the ravenous, raw sexual desire, the aching insatiable appetite for other that seemed to drive his waking life with loneliness and hunger for completion, while the other was the deep, richly feminine essence, the total embodiment of that which he sought. In the dream, these two seemingly disparate entities magnetically repelled each other while being intensely attracted simultaneously. In the earliest hours of the morning, they began to dance. The desire wore his face, and the essence wore the countenance of Karen. They whirled and twirled around the huge ballroom floor, and just before the dream ended, he went to a knee, took her hand and said: "I love you and invite you in." They hugged then and blended into a single fulfilled being. He couldn't wait to tell Karen.

He'd always been a "dreamer," a gift he had always mostly kept to himself since his earliest experiences with sharing his dreams had been mostly negative. But when he came home from the 'Nam, he was committed to what he called "radical honesty." Some saw it as a form of "mental illness." Since then, he had fought assiduously for his right to "tell his truth." It was part of his personal empowerment work that he shared with, and encouraged in, his clients. The very first step was telling the truth to just one person, and then expanding the field—though it was a potentially dangerous practice. He was reminded of the judgment against Socrates, who ended up drinking hemlock after being convicted of "corrupting the minds of the youth of Athens" and of "impiety," loosely translated as his failing to "believe in the gods of the State."

This latter charge was related to his questioning of the then (as now) collective notion that "might makes right," that was common to all of Greece at that time. Socrates believed that to uphold the status quo—and accept what he perceived as the development of "immorality" throughout his home country—was immoral for him.

Though it had all occurred over two thousand years ago, it seemed very contemporary. It was one strain of an underlying symphony that affected every artist, every human who was opposed to elitist policies, anyone who went counter to the "popular" ideology. Henry Miller said "Whoever uses the spirit that is in him creatively is an artist. To make living itself an art, that is the goal." Theodore Roszak had spoken to the larger context in *Voice of the Earth*:

Cultural creativity is always the province of minorities. My conviction is that those who contribute to the process of creative disintegration have diagnosed the ills of the age more keenly than the official experts or the professional planners or the heavy revolutionaries.

They are in touch with something contagiously and constructively idealistic. But their impact on our future, on the tastes and values of our society, will never be gauged by nose-counting sociology. Nor can they expect their efforts to be acknowledged or encouraged in the cultural mainstream, any more than we could have expected even the keenest political minds of dying Rome to recognize in their day that the next chapter in Western history would be written by the scruffy and uncivil likes of a St. Anthony ruminating in the wilderness, working, praying, building a new society out of the sweat and rubble beyond the horizons of their age.

This fueled what Paul called it his "morning rant." Even when the dreams had been psychedelic, Technicolor, inspiring love and beauty, he was often struck by the disparity of the other reality into which he awakened every day, and wondered "What exactly am I doing here?" It always felt as if someone had unplugged him from a higher dimension and glued him here like a child's cutout pasted into a cheap paper notebook. Sometimes the disconnect was greater, sometimes less, but it was always there. It was why he like to reserve the earliest hours to write (the first ones whenever he woke up), when he was most freshly returned from that more ethereal dimension—it was just more accessible, even though it all lay within him. "All" seemed like an exceptionally large order. He had been so addicted to what Walter Truett Anderson had called "the spectacle," whose entire purpose was to distract the population from "isness," usually to the benefit and profit of the modern day oligarchs and their greedy machine-like mentality. Such was the state of the

Empire in contemporary America.

The best part of it was being able to use the momentum to capture the intimations that were gifted by the ethereal forces. Sometimes he marveled at how long he had lived and the amazing experiences he had had. Even more, the people with whom he still maintained connections with whom he created true and enduring relationships.

It was in moments like this that he felt overwhelmingly grateful, to the point where he almost without volition started sobbing, to the point where he couldn't catch his breath. It had always been this ability and willingness to cry—to shun the common accepted wisdom that men should not cry—that had saved his life. That, and his almost innate ability to write. Emotional sensitivity and writing skills had kept him alive through all of the trauma and turmoil of his life. The former had allowed him to shed tears of agony and shame, releasing his neurochemicals to flow freely, to enrich his otherwise thirsty neurons. The latter created an emotional sanctuary for him, a haven in which to shelter from the storms of his violent repressive childhood; and to memorialize his feelings as well as giving him continuing opportunities to connect with himself and others; permitted him to step outside of the closed circle of chains and constrictions fashioned he had fashioned out of rage and violence— leading to endless complications, of mazes in a labyrinthine world, fueled by an insatiable nuclear core of self-inflicted punishment and derisive judgments against himself imprinted on his cell walls and DNA, a toxic taint that could never be healed, only relieved by dint of massive and continuous work on himself through the ensuing decades—unflinching, dedicated, tenacious and arduous. It was the penultimate sacrifice and yet it was the quintessential gift to himself that only he could render.

He had just wiped his eyes and blown his nose when the phone rang.

"Hello?" he croaked.

"Paul? You sound strange. Is everything all right?"

"Hi. Yes. Just recovering from a moment of deep gratitude. Sometimes they catch me off guard."

"Are you sure?"

"Actually, I'm great! Even better now that you called!"

Her laughter was like the trill of a bird echoing through him, a wave of joy, and he shuddered as if shot with shakti.

Into the silence, he exclaimed, "Oh God! I can't stop thinking of you! I have conversations with you when you are not here!"

"I love it that you are so open with me, so unguarded!"

"I am SO glad! Because I treasure your presence!"

"I'm so glad you don't think you have to act like a savage with me!'"

"I am so truly grateful! I really admire you!"

"What happened after I left last night?" she asked with a

crispness and clarity that was at odds with her innocuous question.

"Wow! Is it that obvious?"

"The sound of your voice betrayed you. I know you were glad to hear from me, but there was more to it than anticipation."

"My 'morning rant' led me to gratitude, and then to tears. Quite a journey!"

"I knew immediately that something was up."

"I should have waited until my tears stopped."

"The more real you are, the more I will love you!"

"Wow! Where did that come from?"

"Well, it's true!"

Paul's silence spoke volumes. Then he finally found his voice.

"I love how deep you are!"

Then he started sobbing again, overwhelmed by the memory of his last encounter with Roach juxtaposing itself with his rampant desire for Karen. Sadness and desire flooded his already tender nervous system. He started to share some of the details of his last session with Roach, but she stopped him.

"Can you come today? It sounds like we may need more than our usual hour."

"I agree. Does 1530 work for you?"

"That sounds good."

"Maybe we could have dinner after."

"Absolutely! Can't wait!

"You're beautiful!"

CHAPTER FORTY-ONE

REVELATIONS

San Francisco   **Thursday December 28th, 1995: 1533**

Paul felt confused and grief-addled about Roach. He continued to castigate himself for not having done more and worry about what might become of him. No matter what, he would always be a brother. The upside of the situation was that he had Karen with whom to discuss all of the twists and turns, all the vagaries of the case; and he got to enjoy her luscious self into the bargain. They were very soon going to have to resolve the personal/professional dichotomy. Maybe tonight!

They hugged briefly, at first in a friendly manner, and it quickly progressed as their mutual attempt to remain more-or-less neutral quickly dissolved. They both looked up simultaneously, smiled, kissed briefly, as if but not really ashamed, then settled into seats, more modestly side by side in the Bauhaus chairs. The look of love lingered in their eyes as the force field between them remained in force as Karen broached what she hoped was a professional tack. Paul felt acutely uncomfortable, and initially averted his eyes.

"So, tell me more about what happened?" prompted Karen.

Paul related his telephone conversation with Roach to her almost verbatim, becoming more animated as he spoke, and he the connection was like a thick cord between them pulsing with potential.

She couldn't keep the richness and depth of her innermost self from her eyes even as she made a stab at a more-or-less "appropriate" response.

"You look better already!" Karen exclaimed, almost gushing.

"I feel a lot better too!" he said, ditto.

He reached for her and they hugged deeply, and then she laughed.

"Doesn't that echo the basic tenet of what Freud called 'the talking cure?'"

Paul laughed, more heartily than he had proposed, and squelched his desire to be overtly sexual, choosing to stay with his feelings.

"I hope I get to work with him again!"

"Seriously, Paul? To what end? He seems committed to a toxic lifestyle."

"He had a toxic childhood, but he was changing!"

"You've told me your fantasies about the alternative childhood you never had—one with loving supportive parents! Is that resurfacing?"

"It's not new territory! I'm just pissed that I have to keep visiting it!"

"It's still valid!"

Paul sat back down and took a deep breath before he commented.

"No. I think mostly I'm just sad."

"It sounds like you were making good progress," she said and paused. "Your work seemed very comprehensive."

"You know the old saying: 'Therapy is only as good as the therapist!'"

"Absolutely! You cannot assist a client in going somewhere you haven't gone first!"

"Just because you see where a client might possibly go in treatment, doesn't mean that the client's either ready or willing to follow."

"Too true!"

"What are you taking away from all this?"

"It's funny. My own sadness came up several times when I was talking to him, but I didn't it let it show. It wouldn't have been appropriate. It reminded me of the etiology of PTSD.

"What about it?"

"During trauma, there's no opportunity to react in terms of what one is really feeling. If one were to stop and grieve in the moment, one might be injured or die. So, the moment gets dissociated, and one hopes to process and integrate it in a more optimal state after surviving."

"And?"

"Trauma increases the amount of emotional grunge you have to carry, in what I call the 'vault,' and that adds to the already-existing psychic burden."

"Is there more?"

"Oh! I forgot where I was going!" said Paul and cleared his throat.

"I knew I couldn't react appropriately, so I just let him have his own experience. It was a kind of final gift." Paul paused again, keeping eye contact, and then continued. "It really benefitted me to stay present and lucid for him in that conflicted moment. It allowed me to process my own stuff and not have to bury it. I got a valuable lesson. I'm…grateful."

Paul sat back, mildly spent, and Karen sat quietly too, both contemplating.

Then, without any precognition, Paul found himself crying, watching as if he were separate from himself—and yet he felt more deeply embodied. He fought to not feel uncomfortable or ashamed, choosing to be emotionally naked.

"It's always my goddamned father, no matter how much work I do!! I just wish I could be done."

Karen gazed at him with love and compassion in her eyes.

"Men's anger used to really trigger me. But with you, I feel compassion more than anything!"

"I still get triggered. I pray for the day I don't!"

"Ultimately, it's a matter of managing the triggering well enough that you 'magically' learn to turn your dissociative 'abilities' into positive use!"

She paused for a moment, and then graced him with a small smile.

"At least in theory!"

They both laughed.

"The worst is not knowing what's happened to him. I may never."

"Do you have a sense of what might lie underneath that feeling?" she asked, a little stiffly.

"Now you sound therapeutic!" quipped Paul, avoiding the question, the fact of which Karen reminded him almost immediately.

"I…it's been an underlying feature for much of my life."

She made a "Say more" gesture with her fingers when he again failed to answer.

"It's pretty universal, isn't it? Everybody feels incomplete."

"How specifically does this resonate for you?"

"Go deeper. I know you can."

"It's always been the perfect recipe, beating up on myself!"

"That implies that there's a standard against which you measure yourself."

"Isn't there always? I got caught up in the 'pursuit of the American dream' shit during my cocaine days."

"You're avoiding the question! Come on, Paul! Where's your transparency?"

"I'm afraid!"

"Of being abandoned?"

"Well. Maybe," Paul said, shrinking from exposing the dark core of his shame. He suddenly felt it open up in the field between them. Karen responded immediately.

"Paul! Don't hide from me! Whether we're being professional or personal, we're still us! There's still" she gestured, waving a hand back and forth between them, "all this. It's real, goddamn it!"

"I…don't know what to say! I feel it too! Goddamn it, I love you!" he said and dissolved into a welter of tears. She let him be for a moment, let him have his own emotions before she moved next to him, put her arm around his shoulders and let him sob. Tears of love and compassion rolled down her cheeks in complete simpatico with him.

At length they sat, and, more composed, she spoke.

"It seems to me that you might be experiencing incomplete grief."

"'Incomplete grief?'"

"You're still carrying around old grief, unexpurgated grief. It's part of your psychic burden, working against that self-imposed standard of perfection, trying to make it 'right' somehow."

"I've always had to work hard to feel worthy!"

"And?"

"'And,' I don't know, maybe this whole situation re-stimulated me!"

She smiled at him, and asked, "What would you tell yourself if you were your own client?"

Paul laughed, and in a moment, so did Karen.

"That was beautiful! Brilliant!"

"So? Answer the question!"

Paul's face imploded slightly as his concentration deepened, and he turned more deeply inward.

"I…I would tell me just to feel it, to embrace it completely and then let it go!"

"So? Do you think you can manage a dose of your own therapy?"

Paul hesitated, and then said "Sure. When?"

"Now?"

"'Now?'"

"'Now?'"

"Wow!"

"'Wow!'"

Paul shook his head and laughed.

"I trust you! Can you…would you…?"

"Of course."

Paul looked up with a mixture of fear and gratitude.

"How…Is it going to affect…us?"

"We've got kind of mixed boundaries anyway. This is therapy! It doesn't mean there's…nothing personal too!"

"Can you really manage your boundaries that well? Are you really…that strong?"

"You've always said I was 'brilliant?'"

"You are!"

"And I'm telling you, straight up, that I am strong enough, focused enough, that I can handle whatever comes up. And no matter what, I will still love you!"

CHAPTER FORTY-TWO
A NEW WORLD APPEARS

K aren's words had been simultaneously a balm for his heart and soul and a relentless driving force like an archeological wedge, prying loose his deepest fears and shame—but he was unafraid. He had had an incredibly distilled moment of the utter clarity. It felt a little like an end-of-life review, as if he were dying. He had a horrible moment when he doubted Karen's truth about continuing to love him, and instantly dismissed his trepidation as invalid, to set his fears aside trusting in the light Karen held, the light she she was, and decided that she was bringing great truth into his life.

It was imperative! He had to heal his heart! It was his core issue!

And he told her so, looking into her beautiful liquid eyes, sharing the sum of all his fears with her in a completely unguarded manner, sharing everything with her in a welter of tears that loosened all his hardened edges, the ones he had had carried since he could first remember. It just all poured out and he did not try to hide, could not hide, let them pour out like a wave restrained too long, grown too strong. He released it without restraint, all limits and limitations washed away in the completely unconditional love that now filed him, given unrestrainedly, without reserve. The pure experience of it superseded anything he had ever known. It was everything he had ever wanted, everything he wanted, now and forever!

He collapsed to the floor, heaving as his sobs diminished, feeling as if he were a newborn child—as indeed he was in his heart of hearts. He felt radiant. Radiant and peaceful. Empty and fulfilled at the same time. He felt resolved, complete. He lay there and breathed for what seemed like eternities, all time and space stretching out around him as he lay in primal innocence.

Then, at length, he felt Karen next to him, felt her warm, sinuous, loving self-slide in next to him, cushioning his head on her breast, soothing him with her gentle touches.

He could not speak. Did not feel any need to. Her presence was enough.

She seemed to feel the same. She held him silently as he basked in the glow she emitted, that surrounded them both. He had always believed that such a thing was possible, even that some people were blessed to live their whole lives with a memory of such abundance as the core material that sustained them. And now he knew, just knew, that he would forever after be one of those! It was a gift of transmission that he felt inside of himself now, that could never be taken away, that was his forever! No matter what! The greatest gift he had ever been give—bestowed by the most beautiful and loving woman he had ever known! He felt so, so incredibly blessed!

CHAPTER FORTY-THREE
A NEW BEGINNING

San Francisco   **Friday December 29th, 1995: 0301**

P aul awakened, completely disoriented, his memories of the events of the previous evening vaguely recalled like the most extraordinary dream he had ever had. He lay in bed in a gelid state, reacquainting himself with his fingers, toes, arms, liver. And suddenly, he knew. Who he was. Why he was. Where he was. And then, with a tenderness that swept through him, a small tingle that became a wave that developed into a tsunami of monumental proportions in which was dissolved yet maintained his integrity. He knew.

And felt the warm, sleeping form of Karen next to him!

It was with a mixture of joy and wonder that the awareness penetrated his every cell, though he did not remember how they had gotten there, not the tiniest scintilla. Part of him didn't care. The fact that she was there, there, was both overwhelming and just perfectly enough.

He moved gently to take a crick out of his arm, not wanting to disturb the sleeping beauty by his side—and rejoiced, echoes of joy quietly screaming through him as the incontrovertible fact of his presence in her bed spoke volumes.

It was all true! He was really there! Oh my God! Oh my God!

As he breathed more and more deeply into his gradually warming body, and the memories flooded back in, he was immensely delighted to feel the full-bodied awareness of the insights of the previous night, the harvest of the work of the previous night, facilitated at the hands and with the heart of his beloved who lay by his side. He crept his newly liberated hand down slowly toward his waist and, while encountering his boxer shorts, was delighted to acknowledge that he was alive and well, his penis throbbing in a glorious salute to the enormity and freedom of what he had uncovered, in homage to this amazing woman sleeping peacefully, smiling, by his side. It became an instant "favorite memory of all time," one he knew he would cherish if he were to live a million years!

With a smile as big as his face, echoing and rippling down into the infinite reaches of his soul that was dancing in exhilaration even as his most corporeal body released its tenuous hold on being awaken and fell into contented slumber.

CHAPTER FORTY-FOUR
MOVING ALONG SMARTLY

San Francisco   **Friday December 29th, 1995: 0711**

They awoke holding hands, simultaneously coming aware in the same moment together, both immediately engulfed in an immense sweet shared love that, with squeals of delight, erupted into a deep and restrained hug that annealed them into a single being sharing all of the senses of both of them, sharing all of the nerve endings, fingers, tongues and genitals of the both of them, sharing without restraint or any sense of need to hold back anything from the other as they explored freely, giving and taking exquisite pleasures each to the other, sharing heart and soul and body fluids in the ever-expanding, luminous, numinous joy-filled tenderness that emanated from and returned to the essence of each other without deliberation, repeatedly, infinitely. There was no separation, nothing but the most permeable of boundaries between them, flowing and retreating as if to and from the shores of an ancient primeval sea, inexhaustible, infinitely powerful and immensely aware of every zeptosecond passing, coming to them, through them, in the utter sweetness of each shared sensation, every possible sensation flashing between them and mirrored back through an undefined chamber, ever reflecting the infinite goodness of the other, and radiating out to the edges of the City and County of San Francisco, to the boundaries of the State of California, indrawing

382

North American, then the entire planet Earth and the Milky Way, flowing beyond to embrace infinite space, the Great Central Sun at twenty-five degrees of Sagittarius, to its Great Central Sun even further out in the Universe, to the billions, quadrillions, uncounted and uncountable stars beyond reach—and back into their own hearts filled with the sublime joy of lovers discovered, uncovered, recovered, ignited, reunited, whole and forever.

When they next surfaced, as if from a deep, deep pool of crystalline waters that had enriched and refreshed all their cells. They embraced for a long time, skin-to-skin melting together, smile-to-smile embracing, heart-to-heart, soul-to-soul merged and indissoluble—and broke apart slightly, each breathing deeply of the essence-infused air, deeply into lungs newly-awakened to the joie de vivre infusing each moment with anticipation of the next touch, the next kiss, the next look between them, and simultaneously anticipating the inevitable separation, no matter how poignant or painful it might be, required by the functional separation of being in two bodies, the needs of physical separation such as eating, sleeping and working. It was this last that drove Paul to broaching the topic. He wanted to write, to take some of the joy-infused ecstasy he was feeling and channel some of it into his current manuscript. He also had a client session scheduled. (One that he would not have made if he had anticipated, had any glimmer, of what was going to transpire with the lovely Karen).

"Baby, I've been laying here contemplating that very topic!"

"You, of course, have sessions and such too, don't you?"

"I knew what was going to happen between us. I just didn't expect it to be so quick."

"I had flashes of us too, but I didn't think it would happen so soon either. I hoped, but I really was, am, committed to your driving the bus. So, what'll it be, my sweet?"

Her smile was radiant. She put a hand behind his neck, pulled him closer and kissed him full on the lips.

"I'm not going away! No matter what!"

"I love you so!"

"And," she said, arching an eyebrow, "if we are to have a working partnership—and I want that too—we're going to have to re-formulate all of the rules to suit us! Rethink everything, absolutely everything, that we have ever believed."

"We've done a lot of the groundwork already. All of the sessions we've had, no matter how we define them, they benefitted both of us. We've sorted through so much material—and we've discovered we have so much in common, so much that we share—all the basic stuff, plus you speak Psychologese!"

Paul teared up hearing her summarize the data of their relationship. It was so powerful to hear his innerness echoed through her lips and heart. She really was the woman of his heart! The one for whom he had waited through all the decades of loneliness and anguish, all of which had sharpened the divine white-gold sword of his consciousness, given him the strength and purity to maintain his journey in the face of the tremendous challenges he'd faced, especially all those for which he'd had no precognition, no prescience.

"Oh, my darling! I am SO, SO grateful to know you! I just love you SO!"

It seemed like even the slightest puff of air could stimulate one or the other or both. They kept attempting to function, but even during the making of breakfast, they had had to have a lovemaking break on the kitchen table. After innumerable kisses, hugs and mutual stimulations of various sorts, Paul managed to leave for his place by 1421. Karen offered to give him a ride, but he was very aware that she had duties to which she had committed too, so he made his way home, stoned on thoughts of her as he rode the #5 Masonic to Kearney and Market, and then walked the rest of the way up Powell.

He and Karen had agreed to talk on the phone later in the evening after they had each gone about their individual tasks. He had a strong desire to write, but only made it as far as the leather couch in his therapy office, having decided "to rest for just a little bit." He awakened, chilled, at 1723. He called Karen and left her a message that he was heading directly to bed after brushing his teeth. He slept deeply, filled with dreams of Karen—as a radiant goddess, as an angelic being and sometimes inhabiting hundreds of glassy, translucent spheres filled with an incredible variety of amazing details, whole lives in full glory, she in multiple bodies (male and female) with an enormous diversity of characteristics and qualities, all overflowing with enormous love and vitality. He felt infused, brimming, supersaturated with her love, her divine energy.

He woke very early the following morning as the sun's cutting through the stratified layers of fog and mixed-rain clouds filled the eastern sky. Literary thoughts ran at dynamo-speed through his neurons, and he said a prayer of gratitude, giving thanks for his holy body (remembering St. Francis always called his body "Brother Ass," and feeling immensely more grateful than that). When he recalled Roach's abrupt departure for real or imagined reasons, he allowed himself a few moments of sadness, and then remembered Karen's brilliant healing words that calmed him again. He gave himself the gift of the morning to have coffee and write, before preparing the final draft of another court-ordered psych eval. This one had been far more clear-cut to diagnose and to write an initial draft. He took forty-five minutes to do a line-edit and print it up for the client who was due at noon

The guy was not going to be happy. He knew he was hoping for an exotic diagnosis that would pave the way for him to be psychiatrically hospitalized versus going to prison, but Paul had studied his psychological testing extensively. The first time he administered the MMPI-2, it yielded a pronounced K-score, one that was so high that it totally invalidated the entire test. When he confronted the client with this findings, he was greeted with the usual denial, pseudo-confusion and bewilderment—until Paul told him it was impossible for his to have scored as high as he had on the Validity Scale (sometimes called the 'Lie Scale"), unless he were deliberately trying to present a false image of his mental status.

"Sir, the test is designed to point out any deliberate attempt to present a false picture!"

Five useless minutes later denials became protestations of innocence, and repeatedly blaming Paul for mis-scoring the test. When Paul declared that he wanted to call in another psychologist to verify his own findings before submitting the current test results to the judge as is, the man broke down crying, and then begged for another opportunity.

"I don't want to go to prison!"

"Sir, I cannot do anything about that! Whatever crimes you committed will be adjudicated by the court. My only job is to render to the court my expert opinion as to your psychiatric diagnosis and the implications thereto."

"But I'm paying for it!"

"Court-ordered, sir."

"I'll give you double!"

"I'm going to pretend you didn't just try to bribe an officer of the court!" That was not strictly speaking true, but Paul always loved the sound of it.

"Can't I take the test again? And tell the whole truth this time?"

"I do have the leeway to re-administer the test, but I would have to charge you for the extra time required.

"Yes! Sure! Anything!"

"And I will have to submit a statement to the court that you requested a re-test in addition to the original findings."

"Please! Anything!"

The man was highly likely going to prison, though Paul wasn't going to tell him that. As for the retest, he would make some sort of sidebar explanation, and tell the judge privately first. He would—in fact, he felt duty-bound ethically—tell the judge about the man's attempt to feign mental illness, though he would skip the attempted bribery, especially since it was "he said, he said."

"I was so pissed!" he had told Karen.

"Why?" she had asked in an inquisitive manner that nonetheless managed to sound a little laconic.

"I was insulted! As if my professional opinion were for sale!"

She smiled. "Well, it is, kind of."

He smiled back. "Yeah, but I'm not accessible to a bribe! It hurt my feelings!"

"But why, exactly? Can you pin it down?"

"He thought that money could sway me to be unethical."

"And?"

"That would make me like all politicians and lobbyists!"

"And you disown that association?"

"Of course!"

"But we all have a price! We all sell ourselves for money to some extent!"

"But there's a huge difference!"

"There are other ways of viewing his rather clumsy attempt."

Paul felt a frisson of anger inching its way up his legs.

"Like what?"

"Oh, for example, you could've seen it as funny."

"'Funny?'"

"If you look at it in a certain way, it is pretty comical."

"'Comical?'"

"I'm sorry. I was not there and I was making a sort of cartoon out of the interaction. If you were to do that, you might see that his effort was pitiful, even comical, in a certain light."

"But he implied I was for sale!"

"Does that imply to you that he thought you were a prostitute?"

"In a sense, yes!"

"And what exactly is so insulting about that?"

Paul again felt angry and defensive, but he knew the depth of her love. She was just being therapeutic, probing one of his tender spots. He knew she would never attempt to hurt him, to exacerbate a bad situation.

"I...it felt like I was just an ordinary human being!"

"And you're not?"

"No! I'm goddamn better than that!"

"How exactly?"

"I... I'm spiritually aspiring! I'm not down in the fucking abyss anymore! I been clean a long time!"

"And you're associating his attempt at bribery with you being one of the dregs of Life?"

"Wow! Where did you get that one? It's a phrase I used to use!"

"It just came to mind."

"We're becoming telepathic!"

"Funny. It did feel more like your thought than my own!"

Paul laughed. "Maybe that's what happens when the psychic barriers come down!"

"Could be. But, more to the point, do you still believe any of that's true?"

"I don't know. Maybe."

"Did your father ever call you that?"

"No! His favorite phrase was 'piece of shit!'"

"Why do men always make such a thing out of feces?"

"I guess it's the lowest, most disgusting thing we can think of."

"Just like calling another guy a 'pussy!'"

"No! That's as far from being a manly-man as you can get."

"It is _so_ sexist!"

"It just a way for guys to further distance themselves when they claim to want to be closer! Usually it's all about sex anyway!'

"It _is_ a big driver! But it's not fair to lump all men together! Some of us aspire to a more intimate, loving relationship!"

She sat for a minute and allowed him the space to feel his own feelings, and then reminded him of a line from Rilke: "I hold this to be the highest task of a bond between two people: that each should stand guard over the solitude of the other...Love and friendship are there for the purpose of continually providing the opportunity for solitude."

She moved over next to him and put an arm around his shoulders as he continued his emotionally release.

"I love it that we've transformed a dual relationship into a working partnership!"

When he got home, he had quickly and efficiently did a line-edit of the eval, then read through it again and printed five copies—one for the client, one for his own files and three for the court. He didn't like the guy. He had the mottled complexion of a heavy drinker and smelled strongly of cigarette smoke. Paul had had a weird premonition that this particular client would be a problem, especially if he pushed Paul into telling him what he called "the larger truth," rather than the more "limited truth" he intended to tell him. The former contained his own "off the record" comments and conclusions which were not included in the official document. But he had a weird feeling about this client, and prepared himself mentally to be attacked, at least threatened.

It was not that big of a deal overall. He had been attacked many times during the years he had worked on psychiatric units. Of course, then he always had backup. Nonetheless, Paul always kept some plastic zip ties in one of the middle drawers of his office desk, just in case, though he had never had to use them. The bad feeling kept coming uninvited, though he never acted on his intuitions until he got the "hit" three times.

He knew that he should not focus too strongly on that possibility if he were truly interested in keeping the situation cool. Too much wrong could come out of his having to physically intervene: he himself could get hurt; the client could get hurt; the guy could file a complaint alleging impropriety of all sorts (it was his house as well as office); he could claim Paul had attacked him and he was only defending himself. Paul affirmed to himself that he would maintain his composure unless he were actually attacked.

He had no sooner decided this than there was a knock on his front door. Just great! The guy was fifteen minutes early. For him, it was as bad as being late.

When he opened the door, Paul was immediately greeted by the twin smells of stale alcohol and cigarettes. Paul suppressed his revulsion and took a breath of the more relatively fresh air in his house before stepping back and allowing the man to come in.

Arnold T. Jones (he always insisted on his middle initial) was a short stocky man with short blonde hair and several days growth of beard. The reek only got stronger once the man was inside. Paul suppressed his gag reflex and stood aside for the man to proceed him. That was another mistake as it gave him an up-front and personal whiff of the man's intense body odor.

Paul took the furthest seat at the far end of his leather couch when the man chose one of the leather chairs.

"So, doc, what's up?" he said in a very bad imitation of Bugs Bunny.

"Mr. Jones, I have a copy of your evaluation for you," Paul said, and handed him his copy. The man held the paperwork close to his face and squinted as he mumbled and seemed to read what was written. After a couple of minutes, he stopped and looked up, anger glinting in his eyes.

"'Adjustment Disorder?' That's the best you can do?"

"Mr. Jones, I chose that diagnosis because it most closely describes what I see as a pervasive pattern to your behavior."

"What the fuck does that mean?"

"It means that, according to the history you provided and court documents I received, you tend to have crises in your life that seem to develop from the circumstances of your life."

"What the fuck? I never seem to get a break. Things have always been difficult for me!"

"Sir, that is what is meant by 'adjustment.' You seem to have difficulty adjusting to your changing life circumstances."

"So, fucking what? It doesn't make me a criminal!"

"According to court documents, this is not your first encounter with the criminal justice system."

"So, fucking what? I've made a few mistakes."

"'A few mistakes?' Sir, I hasten to remind you I have a copy of your criminal record here! Please do not lie to me!"

"They're lying! I... they made all that up!"

Paul procured another document, a long yellow sheet with computer-printed wording. His client looked up, angry and defensive at the same time.

"That's all bullshit!"

"So, you're saying that these," he paused and counted, "six, seven, eight different times you've been arrested...these are all made up?" Paul asked mock-incredulously, knowing that he was being provocative, but unable to resist.

The man jumped up from his chair, arms down at his sides, fists clenched, face creased by crevasses of rage as tears poured down his cheeks.

"You're all a bunch of motherfucking liars!" he said and took another step.

"STOP!" said Paul in his most commanding voice, left hand palm open and facing outward. He fixed the man with what he called his "laser beam look," harsh and intense at the same time. It froze him in his tracks.

"Sir, I think you'd better take your copy of the eval and leave my premises immediately!"

The other man started to speak again, and Paul spoke forcefully again.

"NOW!!"

The other man looked at him for a milli-second as if he were going to go ahead with his plan, but Paul's stance—feet spread and balanced, arms wide, palms open and steel in his voice—stopped him. He gathered up his paperwork and made for the door. He hesitated just before he got there, but Paul was ready.

"GO!!"

When he was alone, Paul double-locked the door and took a deep breath as if through the top of his head, held it for a two-count and released it as if down through his feet. Then he started to shake, as he knew he would, as he always had after confrontations when working on psych units. His adrenaline had amped, given him the power to stay calm and react appropriately, and then released when the action was over and he was safe, as he was now. He again realized how truly magnificent his body was and gave thanks!

He sincerely hoped he wouldn't have to testify against Arnold T. Jones. Not that he minded testifying. In fact, he really quite enjoyed it. But that asshole would, in all likelihood, stiff him for his court appearance fees, even if the judge mandated it. Oh well!

Even though it was early afternoon, and he never drank alcohol that early in the day, he went to the cabinet and poured himself a shot of Drambuie in a small crystal snifter (Czechoslovakian, of course) and sat in his writing office chair, looking out at the view of the Bay, the Bridge and the East Bay hills, reflecting on the beauty and majesty of Mount Diablo in the far distance. Although it featured prominently in both the Miwok and Ohlone Indian (the original inhabitants) creation myths, the conventional view is that the peak derives its name from the 1805 escape of several Chupcan Indians from the Spanish in a nearby willow thicket. The natives seemed to disappear, and the pursuing Spanish soldiers gave the area the name "Monte del Diablo", meaning "thicket of the devil." It had a magnificent view plain that stretched all the way to the Sierra Nevada Mountains, especially visible after a strong winter snow storm.

He sighed, and sincerely wished (as he did from time to time) that he were both old enough and had money enough to simply retire and move to Hawaii (despite his longstanding invocation that he would "never leave San Francisco"). Sometimes he just got worn down by the daily grind, even with his self-defined schedule, his great office and the work that paid so well. He dismissed the idea of raising his rates as not really constituting a solution for his nagging angst. It wasn't about money. He had sussed out the trap of the monetary, one that so many people fell into, convinced that more was better; and even, that it was possible to have enough money. (Some of the cheapest and greediest people he had ever met were multi-millionaires).

The primary difference, if he had "plenty" of money, was that he would write full-time, at least until the urge abandoned him— although he seriously doubted that would ever really happen. Like Anais Nin, for him it was akin to breathing. He did not feel alive without it. He knew so many people who claimed to be "writers," a recently chic appellation that anyone scribbling with a crayon in a spiral-bound notebook now seemed to believe they could claim. He had even had people tell him that "It's all in my head!" when asked to see what they had written, "I haven't written it yet!"

It irritated him, who had been writing since he was eight (admittedly he considered that early work "scribbled-drivel," but still). It had become *en vogue* now, much as being a Viet Nam vet had in the late 1970's when it was finally "safe" to claim status, especially for those who had not been there. Just like all of the ignorant goddamn clowns who were justly accused of "false valor," for wearing medals and claiming military experience with no basis in fact. He had heard from vets who had fronted such people (wearing Army decorations on a Marine Corp uniform, for example) who tore their medals from their chests. All he could say was "Good on them!" and wished he might have such an opportunity!

Paul believed in his work, even that he was writing superior fiction. After all of his years of "practice," he felt that he had eminently publishable material, though he seemed (once again) to always run afoul of a plethora of "rules" and bureaucracy attendant to the process. Non-artists seemed always to take delight in inserting themselves into the process as a kind of power-grab, to aggrandize themselves, as if their interference in the process gave them pseudo-artistic status. There seemed to be an eternal disconnect between art and business, related to what Paul called "the artist's schizophrenia": plenty of time and not enough money; or plenty of money and not enough time. He had always seemed torn between the two horns of the dilemma, especially when he focused on money, hoping to diminish his sense of deficiency, which, of course, was innate and would never yield to any eleemosynary (loved that word) considerations. The only real relief he got was to dive more deeply into releasing more of the internalized poisoned emotional materials. He was only forty-eight years old! Living another thirty or forty years, especially alone and impoverished, his broken dreams in ashes, filled him with angst and dread.

The goal of being published professionally felt like a huge

sinkhole that threatened to eat his soul. There seemed to be so many "necessary" steps required to see his work published. He wanted strongly to share his thoughts widely, the distilled wisdom of his journey. It was doubly frustrating that people with machine-like mentality insisted that a concretized adherence to "the rules" was imperative, despite the beauty and vision of his art.

In the current dystopic world-society, the machine wogs had taken over, making bureaucracy its "god," denigrating all human feeling to feed The Great Machine. It reminded him of a long poem called *Eco-Promise* he had written in 1982, that encapsulated his discontent with a contemporary society without empathy. The opening stanza read:

There is a day of reckoning coming

for all who for so long have worshipped the great god Techno;

have knelt in obeisance at his gleaming polished metal shrines.

have bent our knees in fear and awe and trepidation

at his massive mechanical altars

seemingly promising more and better, yet even more and better

of all that which we have been conditioned to crave

by the insensate and uncaring forces which guide the inner lives

of those who serve in his dark temples of devotion,

advertising the wares of the insensitive brutal god

whose smooth skin is so seductive, whose touch so evocative, that we have invited him and all the spawn

of his creaking mechanical loins into intimate relations with us,

and we abandon ourselves in techno-ecstasy,

in a pseudo-mystical trance of surrender.

CHAPTER FORTY-FIVE

OASIS

San Francisco   **Saturday December 30th, 1995: 0820**

Karen was such a balm for his soul, a true delight! So lovely, and what a mind!

Even thinking about her evoked in him a higher, more deliciously enriched state, awakened a tenderness, a softness and mental/emotional availability that he usually seemed unable to express. He gave thanks now for his ability to cry, to express deep, often conflicted emotions that had contributed to his mental constipation and emotional misery.

He'd once had a very arrogant client (male, of course) who boasted that he hadn't cried since he was eight years old, and told pseudo-prideful inflated stories about his physical abuse and the strength he had developed as a result—able to pick up hot skillets and pots from the stove without burning his hands (he was a chef and a tyrant in the kitchen); manage his migraines without medication, even going so far as to have cavities in his teeth fixed without lidocaine! He had come to Paul "seeking advice" (he refused to call it therapy) because he had come close to being arrested for getting into an altercation with a stranger walking past his property who, he claimed, had "sneered at him." The police had been called and intervened. Only the fact that the other fellow had been a martial artist—and had easily fended off his aggressive attacks—saved him from being arrested. (There were three witnesses against him).

Paul asked him to commit to a rigid schedule of twice-weekly sessions for a month and guaranteed he would "have him crying" by the end of that time. With great bravado, the man agreed. He boasted through the first three or four sessions about his vainglorious deeds (featuring himself as a kind of superhero), and deflected any topic that touched on his own vulnerability. Paul attempted to penetrate his façade, using his father as a lever, but it evoked only more anger and even greater re-trenchment. He seemed proud of his father's violence, even that it had been directed at him. One day, Paul casually mentioned his mother, and it evoked a defensive reaction. The man's initial outburst was intended to intimidate.

"Motherfucker, I loved my mom!" he shouted and started to rise from his seat.

"Sir, I'm asking that you refrain from cursing."

"Fuck you, man!"

"If you keep it up, I'll terminate this session!"

"But you said my mom was guilty of abusing me too!"

"No, sir. I said your mother allowed 'your father to abuse you.' That's totally different."

The other man's face paled and seemed to implode, cracking into a thousand small fractures like the craquelure of an Old Master's painting. He stopped abruptly and stood transfixed, as if branded on his feet, looking like a giant guppy as his mouth opened and closed in a series of "Os."

Paul remained alert to the possibility that the man might become violent and stood watching silently. As time elapsed, Paul grew more curious about what he had elicited.

The client's eyes remained unfocused and he flapped his hands ineffectually as if attempting to wash Paul's words, and his own interpretations, out of the air; to erase them as if they had never been uttered.

"My m-m-m-om," he stuttered. "What the fuck? I haven't stutt-t-t-ered since I was a kid!"

The man seemed genuinely perplexed. His face contorted, stricken as by a rictus, and tears started pouring down his cheeks. He sobbed, and a deluge poured out of him. He shook as if he were having a seizure, then collapsed, falling to the floor, crumpled in a heap. His body assumed an involuntary fetal position, falling short only of sucking his thumb.

Paul was thunderstruck, frozen. Paul felt his own intransigence melting as he realized that he had perhaps gone too far, pushed this client beyond what now seemed like his very fragile boundaries. He had worked so hard to break the man down, surges of power branching through his nervous system, inspiring what was turning out to be a false flag of enthusiasm and bravado. He was suddenly swept by a wave of regret and contrition the more his emotions thawed. He was forcibly returned to the present by his reaction and chivvied himself into action.

He knew from long experience to maintain a certain distance; not to touch the man; keep his voice quiet and steady; listen attentively and actively, allow himself to absorb the other man's words as if an actual touch; and give minimal feedback, only focused on whatever material the man might present. He took a deep breath and let it out through the bottoms of his feet, then took two steps closer and squatted, not saying a word.

His client lay curled on the floor of his office. He looked like a wounded young boy, no longer a robust, healthy adult. Slowly, his breathing calmed, though he did not speak. Paul continued simply to observe, until at some length, his client's eyes first the left, then the right—opened, blinking as if in the new light of day. He had not yet spoken and Paul told him he was going to get him a glass of water, and would return shortly.

When Paul returned, his erstwhile client shifted slightly and grunted, a sound that approximated a "Thanks," drank the entire glass thirstily and then lay back, condign.

"What the fuck did you do to me, man?"

"What do you mean?"

"Nobody's made me cry since I was eight! Not even my bastard father!"

"I've just been pointing out the truth as I see it."

"B-b-b-ut my m-m-mom?"

"For me, it seemed obvious that she had had to play a part in your abuse!"

"S-s-s-she saved me!"

"'Saved you?' Watching your father beat you?"

"K-k-kept him from k-k-k-killing me!"

"Did she really? Why didn't she stop him?"

"S-s-she did! He would have k-k-killed me! F-f-fucking s-s-s-stutter!"

"I was going to ask about that, when you were ready."

His client closed his eyes and sat up slowly. He took a very deep breath and sighed.

"Do you feel up to talking about it?"

"I...I... never thought she..."

Paul sat silently and waited for him to continue.

"Do you really believe...what you said?"

"I don't ever lie. Ever."

"B-b-but mom...?"

"What?"

Suddenly the other man found his anger again and lost his stutter.

"Goddamn it! She was my mom!"

"See? You just stopped stuttering!"

"What does that mean?"

"You don't stutter when you're angry!"

"So?"

"What happened just a minute ago?"

"I... you..."

"Yes?"

He lowered his head to his hands and did not speak. Neither did Paul.

"You reminded me."

"Of?"

"Of...her."

"Your mother?"

Nod.

"And?"

"You bastard! You can't be right!"

"See? No stutter!"

"But..."

"I've gone all these years!"

"And then I reminded you of your mother. The woman you've always considered to be a saint!"

"She is fucking was!"

"Didn't you just consider it for a moment?"

He nodded.

"And you stuttered."

Another nod.

"And you cried!"

"Fuck! I hate it!"

"Why?"

"I'll have to change everything!" He paused and seemed to reconsider.

"Or I can just just walk away and pretend it didn't happen!"

"But why?"

Ignoring Paul's question, he stood and threw a pair of hundred-dollar bills on the mahogany table.

"And you're bound by confidentiality! You cannot tell anybody about this! Nobody!"

"But..."

"Get this, man! I do not want to change!"

"But..."

"I'm leaving!" and he did, slamming the front door.

Paul still wondered what had happened to the man, all these years later. He did not believe he had ever met anyone who was so strongly defended that he would not change. He shook his head, realizing how that that experience had reinforced his opinions and attitude about cognitive only work, or at least cognitive work before doing the emotionally cathartic work for which changes the cognitive is best suited to frame.

He decided he had to call Karen. Go have a good dinner, somewhere special, just to celebrate their beauty.

CHAPTER FORTY-SIX
A NIGHT OFF?

San Francisco   **Friday December 29th, 1995: 2025**

Paul decided to sit for just a few minutes, swept by a sudden wave of nostalgia for what he called "The Lost San Francisco," his own version of Herb's Caen's flashback journeys into the happenings of the 1930s and 1940s, that were now forever lost to the merciless tides of time. Sometimes Paul felt grief for the loss of places and people—Golden Gate Park; the Fillmore; the Fats Waller Commune; Quicksilver Messenger Service—whose passing he sincerely missed, and for which he occasionally, and indulgently, allowed himself to pine—Sufi Sam Lewis; the Straight Theater and Stephen Gaskin's Monday Night Class; Berkeley Community Theater; the Original Henry's Hunan; Jefferson Airplane—but it was a good thing, contrary to the more ordinary use of the word, allowing himself both gratitude for having had the experiences that had enriched his life and write about, but also the precious opportunity to grieve that which was irretrievably lost— The Golden Gate Bridge; Asimakoupoulous; Matrix; Cable Cars (the only moving object on the List of Historical Monuments); Country Joe and the Fish—thus dumping some of the frequently heavy burden of carrying forward memories of the past. There was a level on which he believed that it was this ability to off-load aspects of the past that led both to his looking much younger than his years and permitted him both extra memory space and the ability to remember with greater clarity and depth—Coit Tower with frescoes by Diego Rivera; Twin Peaks; Family Dog; Fior d'Italia; Steve Miller Blues Band (with Boz Skaggs on bass)—during what may have simply been ordinary experiences during out-of-the-ordinary times—The Filbert Steps; Henry Africa's; Sweetwater; The Rose Pistola; Santana—all of the extraordinary (maybe they were simply ordinary in out-of-the-ordinary times), people and events— the roller-coaster drive down Seventeenth Street from Twin Peaks; Lion's Share; Palace of Legion of Honor; The Original Tandori on Van Ness; The Three Kings: Freddy, Albert and B.B. (all on the same bill)—and there was no discounting the cleanest, purest, most powerful mind-blowing drugs ever made. His mind kept popping like a pinball on steroids, bouncing from memory to memory to memory in a kind of eclectic electric freefall that lit and jolted his neurons—The Ferry Building; Vesuvio's (founded by the "Mayor of North Beach" Henri Lenoir in 1949); Winterland; Basque Family Restaurant; Creedence Clearwater Revival—a montage of pictures flashed through his mind's eye, images flowing and swirling as he sank ever more deeply into his reverie—The Conservatory of Flowers and the Botanical Gardens; The Great American Music Hall; Enrico's ("The Banduch"); The House of Prime Rib; The Grateful Dead—The psychedelic surge caught him again, memories of locations driving him from place to person (and often to the drugs he had taken) in a flowing stream of the richest memories in his vault—The Postermat; The Saloon; Palace of Fine

Arts; Tosca Café; The Youngbloods—it seemed unending, eternally unfolding, burgeoning exponentially as he traversed the superhighway of his neural network, taking him ever-deeper into the accumulated wealth of his mind and heart—The de Young Museum; Leon's BBQ; Gump's; The Youngbloods—All of the extraordinary altered states to which he had been initiated and he had embraced, substance-induced and otherwise: the entire alphabetical panoply: LSD, STP, DMT; psilocybin; mescaline; "uppers"; nitrous oxide and pure O_2; and sweet sister *cocaina*, in all of its forms and fashions— Mt. Davidson; Inn of the Beginning; Le Central (whose cassoulet has been cooking continuously for 16,069 days); Janis Joplin and Big Brother and the Holding Company; La Chateau—

He recovered his sense of presence and took a deep breath just moments before he started crying, filled with an almost impossible gratitude, overflowing with an unspeakable, perhaps even non-formulatable uplift of spirit, that gave rise in him to a soaring swell akin to an infamous "sneaker wave" at the beach that seems innocuous before swamping you with its immensity.

When he "returned," he was sodden, his clothing soaked through by the neurological baptism he had just experienced, an initiation as real as any he had ever experienced, a gift from the Universe that had come to him from the utter depths of the eternity, triggering a fecund and profound awareness, so much more than he could even begin to comprehend or acknowledge. It had been a clarion call to awakening, to embracing the Higher Sense of Order that underlay everything in Creation. to come and to re-member himself literally and figuratively, joint and juncture, reuniting parts and pictures to generate an entirely new image of essence that was simultaneously brand new and ancient, fresh and enduring, bringing all power and wonder into the Living Present.

CHAPTER FORTY-SEVEN
SOUL COMPANION

San Francisco   Saturday December 30th, 1995: 0142

P

aul woke up feeling disoriented, and paradoxically clear and numinous. He found himself laying stretched out on the leather couch in his therapy office, the quiet stretching out around him like rays of invisible light in all directions. He felt like a junior-sized G-2-star pulsing from within and radiating glorious light. The telephones rang, and immersed in his own glow, he chose to ignore it, and waited for his service to pick up. Its incessant (and increasingly intrusive) shrilling started to carve into his equilibrium.

At some length, he realized that someone must be asleep at the switchboard because the phone kept ringing. What had started as a mild irritation soon moved to a supreme nerve-jangling annoyance. With a cavernous sigh, he levered himself up from the couch and picked up the handset.

"Hello?" he croaked.

"Paul? Is that you?"

Paul Realizing it was Karen, Paul switching gears swiftly. He turned his face away from the handset and cleared his throat.

"Hey! Glad to hear you!"

"You too! Are you OK?"

"Yeah, I'm fine actually. I'm sorry I didn't call you earlier."

"That's OK. I didn't call you either," she said and laughed.

"I just woke up. I had this incredible ...kind of dream, I guess you could call it. Didn't even know I fell asleep. I ...I don't believe it was a dream. There was an entirely different quality to it."

"I had kind of a weird night myself. I... can we talk?"

"Of course!"

"No! I mean now. Right now!"

"Absolutely! I need a few minutes. I'll get a cab."

"I'm hungry. Are you?"

"Me too! Where do you want to go?"

"There's really not a lot of choices, even though The City's still wide awake!"

"Let's meet at The Grubstake! It'll be a lot quicker if I take a cab directly there."

"Works for me! I'm on my way!"

"See you soon!"

The Grubstake was the best possible choice. Otherwise it was Zim's (which was pretty good) or Denny's (which was mezzo mezzo), but neither of which would or could provide a quality breakfast or salad at this hour of the morning. Plus, their coffee was superior.

The Grubstake was a series of completely refurbished old railroad cars, "serving love since 1927," as their motto says. The food was consistently excellent, and they drew an extremely eclectic crowd that went far beyond their Polk Gulch location—especially after midnight. Staying open every day until 0400 was a huge bonus. He ate there with frequently, even when it wasn't for early morning breakfast, his favorite meal. He loved their salad with bacon and hot tuna accompanied by a side of crispy French Fries. And coffee. Always coffee.

Paul called a Luxor cab. One had been dispatched to his house and arrived before he had completed changing his clothes. He often used their service, as did many of his clients, and the drivers knew he tipped well. He arrived at the restaurant before Karen and secured a table in the back section furthest away from the counter and the kitchen so they could have maximum privacy. There was a decent after-hours crowd of mixed individuals—some gay, some straight—mostly centered at the counter and towards the front of the establishment. Some had obviously been drinking, but no one was rowdy or obnoxious. There was an unwritten code about such behaviors.

Paul was savoring his first cup of freshly brewed coffee when Karen appeared, her face slightly ashen though she brightened considerably when she saw him, and came rushing down the aisle to embrace him heartily.

After she sat, he said, "You look pale."

As he mirrored awareness of her feelings, tears flooded her face and dripped slowly down her sweet cheeks.

"I've had horrible day! I tried to deal with all of the stuff that's been coming up today by myself!"

"You're not alone anymore, baby!"

"I know. I know. But I'm scared too!"

"I'm here for you!"

"I know. I'm just…I…since Sinclair, I've been having…it's been hard for me to be too open!"

"But baby, you have been so open with me!"

"Remember when we talked about sex and commitment?"

"Yes."

"This is a perfect example! I was…I'm so very attracted to you! I love having sex with you! You're awesome!"

"I love you too!"

"Sinclair's betrayal came up again!"

"In what way?"

"Being so honest with you, so open," she blushed, "letting you inside of me…triggered letting you into my heart. And I balked!"

"How? Why?"

"I realized I want you in my heart! And I was afraid! I realized I...he was still in my heart!"

Paul felt immediately conflicted and flooded with a paradoxical admixture of emotions that clearly showed on his face as he flashed from confusion to sadness to joy and excitement. Karen saw it immediately and put her hand on Paul's face.

"Thank you for that! That was beautiful!"

Paul was stopped momentarily by her honesty and the possibility that he had invested himself to quickly; but then, he quickly rallied himself, feeling an incredible deluge of love for the beautiful, wonderful woman sitting next to him.

"I don't care! I don't care! We can work it out! No matter what!" Paul started crying, completely emptied of fear and shame, not caring what might come next—other than the deepest and most profound hope that she would give him an opportunity to live up to his words and prove to her the immensity of his love. She sat there quietly for a moment, simply gazing at him, then she too started to weep.

"Do you...do you really mean it?"

"With all of my heart! I love you so!"

Then she reached over and slithered her arm around his neck, pulling him closer into a firm, tight hug, then whispered in his ear, "I love you too!"

They both started to speak at once, then Paul smiled and nodded to her.

"Since we have been consulting professionally," she said, and Paul's head jerked slightly, and Karen responded immediately.

"I know. I know. There's this whole other level too. I guess we're crossing the divide tonight."

"'*Ālea iacta est*,'" quoted Paul.

She squinched up her face and asked, "What?"

"'The die is set.' It's what Caesar said in 49 BCE, when he crossed the Rubicon in defiance of the orders of the Roman Senate."

"I do feel like we are crossing a boundary of some sort here. We've had such…we've been such good friends. And now…Wow! I wasn't expecting this!"

Karen looked at him for a long moment, searching his face for any form of inconsistency or insincerity. Seeing none, she smiled, the notion moving from her eyes to her lips the longer she looked.

"Once we cross the Rubicon, we can't pretend we didn't."

Paul laughed and said, "Karen, I'm a lot stronger than I look."

"Paul, I know how strong you are."

"OK, then. Tell me."

She took a deep breath and sighed.

"I've been so raw! Ever since Sinclair!"

"I don't blame you."

"But I've been blaming me! I can't forgive myself!"

"I've struggled with that too!"

"I know. I'm proud of you. Of the progress you've made."

"Why, thank you, ma'am!" he said in his drawliest drawl.

"You silly!" she said and smacked him on the arm with her hand.

Paul smiled his richest, most profound smile.

They both sat back dreamily, fingertips touching as their meals arrived. She had elected to have the Classic French Toast and a glass of milk. He had ordered Joe's Special: 3 large eggs (he asked for them poached in a separate container—could not stand the excess water) with ground beef, onions, garlic, mushrooms, and topped with parmesan cheese. And a side order of crispy French fries with Grey Poupon mustard (made in Dijon since 1866) for dipping.

They both fell to heartily, sharing intimate looks, smiles, small grunts and other sounds of satisfaction. When, at length, they had each sated their appetites for food, they sat back peacefully and sighed, then smiled at each other, again linking hands on the table top. She now ordered a coffee and they both declined desert.

Paul laughed and then said, "If it's not too bold of me to say, that was amazing foreplay!"

She squeezed his hand and said, "That's not all the foreplay we're going to have this morning!"

CHAPTER FORTY-EIGHT
INTO THE MYSTIC

San Francisco   Saturday   December 30th, 1995: 1131

T hey had languished in bed, waking to make love several times and falling back into peaceful slumber over and over. When they awoke this time, they awoke, they took turns using the bathroom and returned to bed. They held each other silently, then turned to each other and smiled, kissed and sighed again.

"It was so helpful to get your perspective! I had no idea how stuck I was!"

"I'm so glad we have an open doorway between us."

"I want complete transparency!"

She leaned over and kissed him long and deeply. She reached over and took his turgid manhood in her hand. They had just started breathing heavily when her phone rang.

"Just leave it!" she said vehemently, as Paul's body tightened, and he reacted involuntarily to reach for it.

It already felt like lovers of longstanding, each seeking and pleasuring points and places of pleasure in and for the other. Soon there was an audible energy, like the palpable hum of a high-speed dynamo, as their bodies joined, and their spirits flew to ever-higher

420

dimensions.

At one point, when they were deeply interpenetrated—each looking deeply into the other's eyes as they experienced the exquisite sensations rippling through the both of them, filled with the joy and tenor of their mutual pleasure, each nuancing their movements so as to give her greater pleasure and the building, increasing prescience of orgasmic vibrations. Their eyes were locked and he absently wondered how incredible it must be to be her, to be a woman receiving him sexually and emotionally. Then in a sudden blinding flash, he found himself in her body receiving his hot penis, with increasingly urgent waves of joy and excitement flushing and gushing along fully opened nerve channels and he/she started to shake as if in a high decibel earthquake that swiftly turned increasingly into full tremors that approximated petit mal seizures, escalating vertically into a massive shaking that signaled the pre-ordained release of a gigantic, engulfing orgasm masquerading as a grand mal earthquake seizure.

In that moment, he was she and she was he, united now and forever. They were inseparable, molecules, nerves, cells, emotions resonating in total harmony to the point of absolutely no difference in quality or essence, conjoined in soul and spirit, eternal and forever. He saw the flash of recognition in her eyes too, acknowledging and mirroring the total verisimilitude of the experience. They shared it in totality, nothing in that brilliant quark of comprehension and awareness that was separate from their intimate commonality. Nothing. They were each of them functionally whole simultaneously embracing an infinitely greater wholeness that was eternal and numinous, uninterrupted and luminous.

They were both pulsing with the exquisiteness of their telepathic bond as they rearranged themselves in the bed, still touching each other on every level.

They exchanged a gaze that was confusing because momentarily neither really knew who was whom.

"Me too" they said simultaneously. And laughed.

"Did we...?"

"...really experience...?"

"...that?"

"Oh my God!" Simultaneously.

"Is this...?"

"...really true?"

They both laughed again and tears of gratitude welling their eyes.

"I... I don't know what to make of all of this!" he said. "I am... overwhelmed!" she said.

Then she slithered hand sinuously around Paul's upper arm and looked him directly in the eyes.

"This is all new for me too!"

"Does this enhance or eliminate our professional relationship? Especially after last night?"

Paul had spent the better part of two hours helping her work through some of her thorny issues around Sinclair, and her childhood antecedents. They were equally experienced though divergent in their paths, so he was able to apply areas of his skills and training to assist her in sorting out her lingering patterns to explore. She was far more intuitive than him, but he had more technique-based training than she, especially in Voice Dialogue.

"I think that great conversation is the best kind of foreplay" Paul laughed.

"I've been saying that for years!" she said, again amazed at the congruity of their thinking and their beingness.

"I've always thought you were brilliant. I just had to call you. You've been so sweet. I realize what a great healer you are."

"I think our mutual skills and training can assist us both, personally and professionally. Maybe we could even share a private practice office."

"You're moving awfully fast!"

"I'm just thinking…maybe we can work together, and you know, be together too!"

She smiled and his heart opened even more completely, a rushing wave of love and gratitude pulsing through him. He thanked the Universe again and again for his miraculous strength and forbearance. As far as Karen was concerned, "I got a heart full of soul" as the Yardbirds song once said.

"I've noticed something," she said with a smile, and Paul knew she wanted to broach a difficult subject, "I want to talk to you about."

She saw the look of minor dread pass across Paul's face, and she put a hand on his forearm.

"It's nothing bad!"

Paul smiled and leaned over to kiss her sweet full lips.

"Usually, when women say that, it's a criticism."

"We agreed to be transparent. Remember?"

"I wouldn't have it any other way. Besides I've been emotionally naked with you already!"

"I know. But now we're on a different level!"

Paul openly admired her naked breasts and she laughed as she followed his eyes.

"That's not what I'm talking about…right now!" she said and casually covered herself.

"You win. What is it you want to talk about?"

"Well, it's kind of a supervision topic, but personal too. Not a bad thing. In fact, I kind of admire it in you."

"Oh good, let's hear it!"

"From some of the stories you've told me, you're really attracted to danger."

"Hmm. Maybe."

"You run toward danger, not away from it."

"In that sense, yes. I agree with you."

"I was wondering how you developed your counterphobic stance."

"Wow! Great question!"

"Thank you."

"Let's see. Probably goes way back. My father used to visit the scenes of fires."

"Like an arsonist?"

"No. He was always careful to differentiate between being a 'fire buff' and being a 'fire bug.' The first term is said to go back to the early 20th century, when people turned out to attend emergencies during wintertime wearing buffalo robes, thus coming to be called 'buffalos' or 'buffs.'"

"He just liked to watch fires?"

"I know it sounds a little goofy, but yes. He and my uncle both, the one who lived a few doors away. They both had radios attuned to the Fire Department."

"Never really heard of that before."

"I grew up with it, especially when I was younger. I'm not talking brush fires. They would usually only go out after the second alarm, calling in more equipment and men (it was always men in those days), or if it was a well-known building."

"Why?"

"Near as I can track it from this distance in time, they had a fascination with fire and destruction, but not in starting them."

"But why?"

"I guess he was kind of counterphobic at one remove. Another thing," Paul paused and took a deep breath, "is the classic information from the literature that speaks to the correlation between fire and sexual excitement."

"Maybe in the 'serial killer triad,' but buffs don't start fires, do they?"

"My father used to say that a buff is not trained but born. He used to tell me about chasing after the horse-drawn fire engines when he was a kid. He always played fireman, looking at pictures of fire engines and going to firehouses when he was a kid, even later too. He always wanted to be a fireman, and his original excitement and interest never diminished."

"Did you ever go with him?"

"When I was a little bit older. A few times, starting at age eight or nine. He even bought me coloring books and little child's books featuring fireman."

426

"Wow!"

"So maybe I got an early hit from him, but I think my stuff woke up later, probably in Vietnam."

"Did you see a lot of guys on the front lines?"

"'Front lines' is kind of a WWII concept. In the 'Nam, there were no 'front lines.' Usually they would just go somewhere and build a base wherever they wanted. We were almost always surrounded by civilians, some of whom were VC or NVA."

"But you told me you used to deal with a lot of guys 'straight out of the bush,' I think is how you termed it."

"I did. What that means is they were coming in from patrols or even longer campaigns when they were out a month or more."

"Oh. OK."

"And sometimes they would come in and head right for me, even before being debriefed."

"What does that mean?"

"They would download their information—and their emotions, especially vital military information to the appropriate personnel, before they were released. But sometimes, I had guys come right out of the boonies and tell me they had to see me. They wanted to talk about traumas in the field, buddies killed, shit like that."

"And that was your job?"

"Yeah. I kind of got a taste for it. That is why I worked five years in crisis clinics. How I got into in-patient psych when I first got home. I needed the intensity. I suppose it was why I started using speed and LSD too."

"You're still that way!"

"Not as much as I used to be."

"But you're still counterphobic. Most people run from danger."

"That's true. But I used to dun myself for not having been in the infantry."

"I think you were in exactly the right place."

"Me too, now. But it took a long time for me to get that sorted. I used to feel that I had never gone far enough, never been intense enough!"

"Whew! I'm here to tell you, baby, you are plenty intense!"

"Why thank you ma'am!"

"In fact, why don't you give me some of your intensity, right now?" she said, uncovering her swelling breasts and rigid nipples.

"Wasn't there something else you wanted to talk about?" he said, purposely teasing her.

"Oh, shut up!" she said and moved herself over him.

CHAPTER FORTY-NINE
ANOTHER AWAKENING

They had both awakened several times during the night, and, after using the bathroom, found themselves stimulated again and again, the very nearness and presence of each other being all of the stimulation required for them to rush to the gateway of lovemaking over and over. They both seemed to have an unquenchable desire for the deepest intimacy on offer. They shared without thought of receiving or fear of lack of reserve. The gates were wide open, and they were partaking fully like a pair of wild horses set free from the confines of a corral.

They awakened simultaneously. They both seemed almost shy turning away slightly as if strangers. Paul rubbed the sleep out of his eyes and realized that his penis was erect again. He reached over and gently touched Karen on the shoulder and she turned to him with a smile that would have caused the Sun to put on sunglasses.

"And good morning to you, my dear!"

It broke his heart open to see the raw desire and the burning welcome in her eyes. It jolted him to the very depth of his being, lifted him on a rising wave of love and admiration that seemed as if it would not, could not possibly ever, peak. It seemed as if it had no summit, and he started crying out of love and a sense of finally being found, of being seen and recognized, of being wanted and needed and loved. She slipped over closer and held him in her strong arms. She didn't say a word, did not make a sound. The sheer power of her physical presence was so strong that she resonated volumes with her touch. He felt so...found was the only word that seemed to fit. Recognized. Validated. As if his lifelong search had been fulfilled, and here he was in her bed, wrapped in her arms, being held and consoled in releasing his joy and grief, with no recriminations, judgments or criticism. He felt no shame, no fear, no sense of loss of face as the tattered remnants of his façade fell away from him into the Great Void. He no longer had to pretend. Ever again. He was home, safe in the arms of love. And he knew, just knew, somehow, that no matter what difficulties they might encounter through the years, that they would always be able to work things out. There was such an essential sense of connection, of relatedness, of bond. It was indisputable. It was indissoluble. He knew he need never again hide; not ever again have to tell less than the full and total truth. He could live now illuminated by the radiant light of love and truth and beauty.

They held each other for a timeless time, until hunger for food stirred them both to action.

"How about waffles and sausage?" she queried, and Paul immediately agreed, especially since she had a real old-fashioned waffle maker. She, like he, preferred sausage patties to links, so he knew he could count on delicious meat with the waffles.

"How about I whoop up an omelet to go with?"

"Excellent! I've got some of that Bulgarian feta you like so much!

"Damn! I'm starving!"

Without further ado, and while appreciating the others' nakedness and sex appeal, they chose to put on bathrobes and head to the kitchen. It felt so connected to be doing what they were doing, so intimate that it had a sexual tinge to it. Then again, Paul reflected, if intimacy were the key, then everything they did would feel sexy and intimate. It was as if they were living an orgasmic life in which everything had the potential to be exciting and fulfilling on a cellular level.

She made two medium-sized patties and started them sizzling. Then, pulling out various bags and containers from kitchen cabinets, said "This is my special waffle mix." Securing a large mixing bowl, she gave a monologue as she prepared.

"I use one-half whole-wheat pastry flour that I sift, one quarter brown rice flour and one quarter oat flour."

"Wow! That sounds exotic!"

"It gives a special lightness to the inside and crispiness to the outside!" she said, pouring and stirring. "I like a little heavy cream in the mix too."

"I can't wait. I'll wait until you've got them pretty much ready to make the omelet. That way everything will be hot at the same time."

"Sounds right! This is fun!"

"It is! Do you mind if I check my service really quick? I'm not going to call anybody. I just want to check in. After all, it's been a day since I have," he said and they exchanged a deep, rich smile, followed by an air kiss to each other.

Paul called his service on a special number given to clients. It was answered almost immediately.

"Oh Dr, Marzeky, I am SO glad you called!"

"It's good to know I'm appreciated!"

"No, seriously, Doctor, the SFPD has called several times!"

"Any messages?"

"A Lieutenant McLaren. He left his number. Wants you to call him as soon as you get this message!"

Paul jotted down the number and thanked the young woman.

Karen looked at him with arched eyebrows.

"Phil McLaren. He's Homicide. Wonder what he wants?"

"I would guess somebody's died!"

"Elementary, my dear Watson!" replied Paul with a smile.

"Aren't you going to call him?"

"Not right now. It can wait until after we've eaten."

"Really? Are you sure?"

"Homicide investigates not only murder, but any 'suspicious death.' So, it could be anything."

"Aren't you curious?"

"Not right now, I'm not."

She flipped the waffle to cook on its opposite side as well as the sausage. She turned to tell him he might want to start preparing the omelet, but he was already up and striding toward her across the floor of what he considered one of the best features of her house— a farm-style kitchen with many bins and cabinets as well as pull-out shelves for kneading bread or other kitchen tasks. Paul swiftly secured a large ceramic bowl and a wire whip. He took five eggs from the container and returned it to the fridge. He opened one of the pull-out shelves, centered the bowl and cracked the eggs. Then he grabbed a cast iron skillet from the drawer under the stove, poured some of the grease from the pork sausage pan into it, and lit the burner.

"Oh God, this is just so wonderful! I love it that we can get along so well together even in the kitchen!"

"Why not? We really cook together!" she smiled, and they hugged briefly, then kissed.

They dawdled over breakfast, both having dismissed any sense of urgency related to time, stopping frequently to touch hands or kiss. At length, Karen, being practical, reminded Paul that the police were anticipating a call from him.

"I know. What a drag! I'd much rather just keep ignoring them and hang out with you."

"Me too. But it's your duty to respond."

"You're right. But I have a feeling that when I call, it will be the end of our idyllic day."

She got up from her chair and sat on his lap.

"We'll have more of these!" she said and kissed him deeply. When she felt him starting to become aroused, she jumped up and declared "Phone call!"

He laughed and went to the instrument. He hit the appropriate buttons, after re-reading what he assumed was Phil McLaren's direct number.

He was rewarded with an answer on the first ring with a gruff "McLaren."

"Phil? It's Paul Marzeky."

"Where the fuck have you been? I've been trying to reach you!"

"I have been off duty and out of touch!"

"You and I need to talk forthwith! Where are you?"

Paul dodged the direct answer, and replied "I'm in The City."

"No shit, Sherlock! Where?"

"First tell me why you need to talk to me so urgently."

"Do you know someone by the name of Donald Hoskins? DOB:

04/17/46?"

"Never heard of him. Why?"

"He was found with your business card in his wallet."

"I give out a lot of those."

"Five foot ten inches, Caucasian, long white hair, slender build."

"Maybe."

"We need to talk."

"Again, Phil, why?"

"We recovered his body at a Penthouse Suite at the Fairmount."

"So?"

"He was dead of a heroin overdose, but we're looking at it as suspicious."

"How does that relate to me?"

"Your business card was the only thing we found on his body. He had twenty thousand dollars in fifty-dollar bills in a money belt around his waist."

"No shit! I still don't know who he was."

"I'd like you to come look at the body. See if you recognize him."

"Sure, Phil. When?"

"Right now. I'll send a squad car for you."

"Negatory! Are you at the Medical Examiner's Office?"

"That's right."

"I can be there in twenty minutes."

"Why all the mystery, Paul?"

"I have a right to a private life too!"

"I'll see you there."

Karen was tucking a white linen blouse into her blue jeans when he hung up the phone.

"I've got to go to the Medical Examiner's Office."

"I heard. Get dressed. I'll take you."

"I can grab a cab."

"No, silly. This way we can stay together longer!"

"Duh!" he said and mock-slapped the side of his head.

She pulled up outside the Medical Examiners' Office (more commonly referred to as "the morgue"), located underneath and behind the Hall of Justice. He marveled at the beauty of the facility that, in an emergency, could (and had) doubled as a surgical facility. Though the ME's ultimate instruments were his hands, a Crusader seeking the often-obscured Grail called cause of death, was here assisted by the wonders of modern medical technology. Here was a Mass Spectrometer, and there a Gas and Liquid High-Performance Chromatograph—either capable of analyzing 40,000 drugs and chemicals.

Roughly 8000 bodies that passed through the portals of the ME's demesne. Of these, approximately one-quarter required his office to determine cause of death. The law was very clear: Anyone who died in custody; from suspected Sudden Infant Death Syndrome; a "suspicious death"; or anyone who hadn't seen a doctor in the previous 20 days, were automatically remanded to him. He could routinely complete an autopsy in thirty to sixty minutes, while the far more detailed Medical/Legal Post Mortem could take as long as two full days—not counting the distinct possibility of a prolonged wait for detailed laboratory findings and reports, especially if it were for a tox screen asking for exotic poisons and chemicals. The M.E. always had to be especially mindful of yet another court appearance.

Phil McLaren met Paul as soon as he had checked in at the thick-glassed Reception Office. Paul had done research there for a previous book, and shook his head reflecting on the long history of the coroner's office. He imagined how amazed would be a time-travelling coroner from the 12th Century (when the job was first created), who could see the wonders of his modern kingdom—a long way from being *custos placitorum coronae*, or "guardian of the Crown's pleas," charged with keeping local records of legal proceedings in which the Crown had jurisdiction. This included suicide which was adjudged to be a "crime against the State," for which all property would be forfeit—it being the duty of the family to prove otherwise. His ancient antecessor would have also been required to raise money for the Crown by funneling the property of executed criminals into the king's treasury; and to investigate any suspicious deaths among the Normans (in order to assure that deaths amongst the ruling class were not taken lightly). At one point, all criminal proceedings in England were the coroner's responsibilities.

They went down a long hallway to a "cold room" wherein sat stacked rows of pull-out drawers housing the assigned condign inhabitants, past a large room where a crème colored ceiling reigned twelve feet high above a waist-high tile line. Five stainless steel tables dominated the main room, each featuring a drain and a hose connected to a water source operated by foot pedals. A scale that could accommodate up to six hundred fifty pounds sat in a corner, while a decontamination shower and sinks with eye flushes, were in every one of the working areas.

One of the ME's assistants stood sentinel by a drawer about halfway down the aisle. When Phil and Paul came abreast, he slid out a drawer to expose a wrapped corpse. At a nod from Phil, the man pulled back the talon of the zipper on a plastic body bag to reveal the placid, flaccid face of Roach (aka Donald Hoskins).

CHAPTER FIFTY
AFTERMATH/A PRELUDE

San Francisco   **Sunday, December 31st, 1995: 2001**

After Paul identified Roach's body, Phil insisted that he accompany him upstairs to his office in the Homicide Bureau. Paul had severe concerns about doing so, having a flashback from a time some years before when he'd been summoned to the Homicide Bureau after there'd been a murder on the locked psychiatric unit where he'd been working.

San Francisco   **Saturday September 24th, 1988: 1643**

The City itself had come under intense media scrutiny. The hydra-headed media had declared it a homicide before the M.E. issued his ruling. Sensational stories filled with innuendo and outright lies designed to stir up public attention appeared in all kinds of publications. Organizations as diverse as The Network Against Psychiatric Assault, the Patients' Rights Advocacy Office, and even the American Civil Liberties Union had applied vaingloriously for court orders. The hospital and agencies of the city, the county, and the state were deluged with thousands of phone calls and letters, even telegrams. Splinter groups each with their own agenda, who generally saw benefit in rabble-rousing of any sort around any

439

possible topic, clamored for more public attention.

Several staff members had been approached with offers of "untraceable" cash to tell their version of the story, as if the death of a patient had a "side;" or as if individuals had already been named as culpable. Paul had screened his telephone calls and deleted any that had no personal connection. Fuck the media! They were a vicious bunch of intrusive, greedy jackal assholes who wanted to aggrandize themselves through, and profit from, the misfortune of others. They could all rot in hell!

He was pissed off at having been so rudely summoned, and purposely arrived fifteen minutes late for his appointment. He had refused to get there on time, carefully showering and shaving while keeping his mounting rage under wraps. He was gruffly greeted by the grizzled-looking desk sergeant who told him to "take a seat." Paul propped himself up in a corner with the 1934 Dashiell Hammett novel The Thin Man. Most of those waiting in the lobby were handcuffed to steel rings arrayed around the walls. The cloying scents of human rot and human waste allied with unbathed funk, cigarette smoke, alcohol fumes, and utter despair, warred with the disinfectant fumes, and resembled nothing so much as the odors of Battle of the Somme. Although not appropriate, the phrase "Black Hole of Calcutta," kept running through Paul's brain. He put a clean handkerchief to his nose to filter out some portion of the offending odors.

Whether as payback or by design, he was kept waiting—ten,

fifteen, twenty minutes, as he grew growing increasingly restless and irritated. At length, he told the burly man at the desk that he was going to step outside for some fresh air. He started to protest until Paul asserted himself and asked, "Am I under arrest?" When he received a negative reply, he went immediately to the door and let himself out. He hoped that his not wanting to further endure the miasmic odors would get some action. He had far, far better things to do than hang out at a shitty ass police station!

The oppressiveness of the situation continued to weigh on him. He cast his thoughts into the wind like a fisherman's hand net and caught yet another glimpse of the myriad twisting pathways that seemed to branch and re-branch like a tree of neurons from him as the Alpha point of his entire excursion, seeking solutions to issues far too large and convoluted to be approached directly, being as they were all tied to one another in thousands, perhaps millions of ways; solutions that might not be approachable until he left his body, and was no longer tormented by the everyday tedium of embodied life. The problems of the world seemed deeply intertwined with and inseparable from all that was good. He was convinced that there had to be a way to be at least 99% true to oneself and still manage to live in the world, perhaps even live well, enjoying good food and drink, having fun, with exciting, inspiring friends and lovers—and still not lose one's spiritual path, one's way home without having one's internal, eternal compass permanently shattered.

"Mr. Marzeky? Won't you come in?"

The seemingly polite approach belied the appearance of the man addressing him. He was five foot six inches tall with a thick, bushy moustache that did little to hide a razor-thin scar that ran from his left ear to the tip of his chin (possibly a souvenir of his days as in undercover narcotics).

As he re-entered the building, the energy went even further downhill. Paul was shown into a small, airless, stench-drenched, pale-green painted room that was already occupied by Detectives Timothy Ryan and Ladislaw Kubicek, neither of whom got up from their chairs facing the door. They simply looked at him with an air of skepticism.

"What? What? Why are you looking at me like that?" asked Paul.

The two detectives shared a glance but said nothing.

"Why am I here? What do you want?"

Still no response.

Paul's deeply encysted well of rage burst open as he raised his voice even higher.

"If I'm not under arrest, I'm fucking leaving!" he said, and turned to the door which was, of course, locked.

"Let me the fuck out of here!" said Paul slamming the door with his right hand, and then kicking it brutally twice.

As Kubicek approached, arms spread wide, with a grim look on his face, three uniformed cops burst through the door.

442

Suddenly, Paul felt like a desperate five years old struggling to survive.

"Motherfuckers! Leave me alone! I didn't do a goddamn thing!"

His whole world turned red, and he thrashed wildly as ten arms attempted to restrain him. The tender edges of his mind collapsed and snapped. He reverted to a time when he was trapped, stuck under a bookcase and unable to move, while struggling madly to free himself from the onerous weight. His paranoia index shot through the roof, and a claustrophobic rage burst through the top of his skull. They held him tightly as he screamed incoherently—biting, screaming, fighting, fighting for his life, and then the he that was he disappeared, swallowed and swirling into the blackest black hole in the heart of his life, in the heart of All Life. He floated in a dark void populated by billions of stars, his consciousness of being a separate self, of having semi-osmotic membranes, disappeared. "He" floated for an interminable, indeterminate amount of time, the very concept itself meaningless.

As he suddenly became aware of having bodily outlines and his internal organs began to coalesce, he noticed having fingers and toes, the vague outlines of his body re-emerged and he began to appraise the artifacts of the "he" that "he" might be infiltrated through the flimsiest translucent veil. The void swirled and closed, winking like a mechanical iris. When his eyes flickered open, he was greeted by the most horrible stench he had ever encountered yet it seemed to be emanating from him. He tried to move what had become his hands, he found he was handcuffed to a hospital bed and with leg chains attached. His head ached like a beach ball overinflated with helium. Every muscle, tendon, and thew complained with pain. Rippling waves and intense nausea shot through him no matter how miniaturized, or minimalized, the motion he made.

"Somebody! Help me!" he shouted, shouted, shouted— until his voice croaked hoarsely and extinguished.

He squeezed saliva into the interstices of his throat, and tried calling out again, sputtering ineffectually, even as a rumbling clanking sounded in the distance. He couldn't see, but he tried again and again to speak, spluttering as he repeatedly cleared his throat and mis-spit twice.

"Hey! I need some help here!

A uniformed sergeant looked through the peephole of the door and walked away. Very shortly, Ryan and Kubicek entered, and, standing as far away as possible, observing him as if he were a laboratory specimen.

"What the fuck am I doing here?!" he squeaked.

"Maybe you should tell us that." Ryan.

"What the fuck do you mean?"

"You freaked out in the interrogation room. We had to restrain you for your own safety." Kubicek.

"Fuck that shit! I want a fucking lawyer! I'm gonna sue your asses off! I didn't do a goddamn thing wrong! You fuckers are harassing me!"

Ryan stepped closer, and said, "Well, Paul, you came in voluntarily for further questioning, and then you started screaming and fighting before we even had a chance to talk to you."

"That's bullshit! You fucking locked me in a room, and then took me down and put me in handcuffs!"

"I have the statements of five police officers that contradict what you just said."

"I don't give a fuck! That's bullshit! I want a lawyer!"

"You're not under arrest, so that means you will have to call one, and pay for engaging his services."

"If I'm not under arrest, then what the fuck am I doing in handcuffs? And why in a jail cell and not a hospital? You fuckers triggered me! I had a flashback!"

"We considered a 5150 for 'Danger to Self' and 'Danger to Others,' but we thought we'd give you a chance to regain your composure, maybe talk to us."

"About what? I've already answered your fucking stupid questions four or five times! At least a half a dozen people saw me at the time you claim the murder happened! So, let me the fuck out of here!"

"Murder is a very serious business. And it happened at your workplace."

"It's not my fucking job to figure out who did it!"

"We thought you might like to assist the police in their investigations."

"Fuck you! This is harassment! I want a lawyer! I want Shirley Stephenson!"

Ryan raised an eyebrow at the mention of the name. She had represented and won handsome settlements against the SFPD, The City and County of San Francisco, and the State of California, all for a variety of infractions related to civil liberties violations.

"So, you know Miss Stephenson?"

"I want to call her! She'll be really interested in what's happening to me!"

"I guess that means you'll have to get out of cuffs first," said The Kube, laconically.

"Fuck you! This is bullshit!"

"Until we're reasonably sure you won't harm yourself or anyone else, you're staying in cuffs."

"And how would you determine that?"

"Your attitude and willingness to cooperate."

"With what? Goddamn it, I have answered the same-same fucking questions, over and over! I'm not a fucking dummy! I know

446

you fuckers are trying to pin this one me!"

"Why would we want to do that?"

"Because you fuckers don't have a clue, and you want a quick solution!"

"You been reading too many detective novels, Paul."

"Fuck you too! I been in a whole lot of worse situations than this and survived!"

Ryan stepped closer, and said "In the 'Nam?"

"What do you know about the fucking 'Nam?"

"I was an MP! 196th Infantry Brigade. 67-68."

"No shit?" Paul asked, softening despite of his resolve not to cooperate.

"No shit! I have no reason to lie to you."

Paul burst into tears as a large frozen wall of ice melted the glacier of his heart; all of his pent-up rage was spent; and he could finally surrender to a higher level or measure of himself, one that had lain hidden, and was now emerging out of the dark mists to reveal clarity. He sobbed and sobbed as eons of anguish washed away. He felt he might be dying, assaulted by wave after wave of pictures and images flashing; memories of his very first incandescent moments flashing like neon signs from the time before he even had a hippocampus to store and release fleeting pre-verbal images of a deep past, surrendering all of the prohibitions of his limbic system as they collapsed in the hormonal conflagration triggered by his pituitary gland.

A fluorescent brightness flared behind his closed eyes, and he separated from his body again and again, a body that no longer struggled against the metal restraints but simply lay there melted, unresisting, in lost thrall to the greater forces of the Universe. Gout after gout of healing tears fell unimpeded from an inexhaustible well. He felt himself to be those tears, impelled by Creation's providence in extremis, giving him an ally, a brother who had been there, done that—no matter that he had been responsible for being restrained in the first place. He prayed that someone might be listening, might potentially believe him, even be willing to add some strength and force to his continued assertions of innocence.

He was grateful. He knew someone was listening.

CHAPTER FIFTY-ONE
INTO THE NEW

San Francisco   Sunday December 31st, 1995:   2301

When Paul was finally (and gratefully) been escorted out of the HOJ, he made a quick call to Karen and grabbed a cab to her house.

She greeted him at the door with a full body embrace and a deep, luscious kiss. They held each other silently for several long minutes, communing in the shared energy.

At length, Paul started to speak, to tell her about what had transpired since he had last seen her, to share more with her more about Roach. He sputtered as he spoke and his tears fell, safe in the embrace of her loving arms.

She shushed him and stroked his back, neck and arms until he quieted. At length, he went slack in her arms. Then she took him by the elbow and led him to the couch.

They sat silently, wrapped around each other, both seemingly waiting for the other to speak.

At length, Karen spoke softly.

"Was it him? Your client, Roach?"

"No doubt about it. He looked...more peaceful I've ever seen him."

"Was it an overdose?"

"That's what they're saying."

"And?"

"I'm not sure I believe it."

"Why not?"

"I think he may have been murdered."

"Why?"

"My diagnosis now is leaning more toward psychopathy than delusion."

"Why, all of a sudden?"

"Seeing him lying there really moved me."

"You've seen dead guys before!?"

"Of course. But this was different."

"How? Tell me, baby."

The term of endearment sounded sweet.

"He was clean for thirteen months. We'd made such good progress."

"But he stopped coming!"

"Doesn't matter! He had a giant breakthrough!"

"Maybe that was the problem. Maybe he freaked out and he started using again—because he didn't want to face it."

"Maybe. That just doesn't feel right."

"Maybe you don't want it to."

"Probably not, but something just feels off about this whole thing."

"Why don't you tell me more about it."

Paul stopped and took a deep breath. Sharing his concerns with Karen made a lot of sense. He was shaken after they closed the morgue drawer, but it didn't deter Phil McLaren from boring right in.

"So, how did you know him?"

Paul gave him a brief précis of his long but interrupted association with Roach.

"And how long were you treating him?"

"A number of months. I'd have to check my files to be more precise."

"How often?"

"Usually every other day."

"Why?"

"Why what?"

"Why was he seeing you?"

"You know that's confidential."

"He's dead."

"Doesn't change anything, unless you get a court order."

"I'll subpoena your case files."

"I didn't keep any case notes at the client's request."

"And I suppose he paid you in cash too."

"That's correct."

"Did you keep track of it? For tax purposes?"

"Of course, detective!"

"Any idea why he might have killed himself?"

"It would all be speculation on my part. It's still confidential."

"Was he an experienced drug user? Could it have been an accidental overdose? He seemed to have gotten a hold of some really strong stuff!"

"Can't comment, detective."

"If you knew him in the 'Nam, then you have deep background on him that could be really helpful."

"No comment."

"Come on, Paul. What if it wasn't suicide? Don't you want justice for him, for your fellow vet? One you knew!"

"No comment."

"I'll get a court order, Paul. Compel you to reveal what you know."

"Good luck with that."

"I will."

"I'll see you in court then!"

Karen had sat silently while he recounted the encounter, then she asked.

"He was addicted when you first met. Right?"

Paul affirmed it, and she continued.

"And he was selling heroin for a living, right?"

"For decades apparently."

"So, you think he might have been murdered? That his story about being stalked by government agents was true?"

"Or organized crime."

"Either or. Have you abandoned the idea of delusions?"

"No. But I'm leaning more toward him having told the truth."

"Why?"

"More just a feeling than anything else."

"But he was a junkie! A drug dealer!"

Paul was well aware of her prejudices. She had never really been a big drug user. She has smoked a fair amount of pot and tried cocaine once or twice, took some LSD. But overall, she was essentially straight. Paul saw it as a kind of character fault, that she was somewhat rigid and short-sighted despite her otherwise exceptional intelligence and extraordinary empathy. It was this latter to which he appealed now.

"Dear, I want to ask you a small favor."

"Of course."

"Please don't be offended, sweetie. But I want you to look at his life choices as traumatically driven."

"And?"

"And consider too, that there was a long time when you would have called me a 'junkie' too! Yet, I've changed!"

She flushed as the implication struck her. She lowered her eyes and said, "I see."

"I believed in him! He was a brother! I really believed he was going to have a different life!" said Paul and started to sob.

Karen hesitated for just a moment, still swept up in her own emotions, then took Paul in her arms and held him, allowed him the space to embrace the long process of his grief and release it as the new year came in.

CHAPTER FIFTY-TWO
THE GEARS KEEP TURNING

San Francisco   **Monday January 1st, 1996: 1030**

They had awakened early, holding hands. Paul immediately started to apologize, but she shushed him with hugs and kisses that he happily returned.

"Don't be silly, silly! That old bullshit macho crap does not turn me on!"

"You won't think the less of me because of my grief? My tears?"

"I've known from the beginning the kind of man you are! You'll never be the hard guy you've always wanted to be!"

"How could you know?"

"I saw beyond your façade immediately! I knew you were a gentle man."

"Is that why it took us so long to get together?"

'Well, there was Sinclair."

"How true!"

"And for a while, I thought I might actually be polyamorous."

"I'd really love to hear some more about that," he said, and then hurriedly added, "but not now, if you don't want."

She smiled and kissed him.

"I love it that you're considerate."

"Thanks."

"At first, I thought I might really be one of those who just really weren't destined to find one real solid love, who needed multiple lovers to fulfill multiple desires and needs."

"And?"

"For a while, it seemed exactly right. I was having sex with different people—women too—and felt like the entire philosophy made sense."

Paul nodded and stayed silent to encourage her to go on.

"But the longer it went on—and then when Sinclair and I decided to be a poly couple—I thought I would have the best of all worlds."

"So, what happened?"

"One of the primary principles, if you're a couple, is asking and getting permission from the other partner, if one is going to have sex with someone else. It's just a sign of respect."

"I can see that."

"Plus, Sinclair started having sex with a lot of guys. At first, I didn't really care too much, figured he was just breaking out of his old mold, getting more and more free."

"And?"

"I have to admit I was getting concerned about AIDS."

"Was he having unprotected sex?"

"He said not, but he always wanted to have sex with me without protection."

"Hmmm."

"I know! I know!"

"And?"

She sighed, then suddenly started crying.

Paul moved and embraced her silently.

"I really loved him! I believed all his lies!" She sobbed and then said, "He lied to me!"

"How? What did he lie about?"

"I totally believed him! He was fucking all of these guys—and didn't tell me!"

"That's pretty scary!"

"Then he told me he wanted to be exclusive! The biggest lie of all!" she said and started crying again.

He held her silently and felt himself flowing into her, his inner resources awakening in response to her needs. He wanted to comfort her, to give her the sort of peace she had been bringing to him without restraint, completely and fully, filling him. In that moment, he felt a new level of commitment being forged, one he had never before approached—an inner marriage, a merging of his inner male and female, animus and anima, joining and linking indissolubly—and the wholeness of who he was now merging into eternal wholeness and flowing out to meet her soul's needs creating an even greater completeness, comforting and soothing, healing and annealing. His own work was complete and he was now available to use to help heal the wonderful, blithe spirit he held in his arms. He breathed in from the depths of the Earth and silently allowed his exhale to move without restraint into her.

CHAPTER FIFTY-THREE
CLARITY?

San Francisco   **Monday January 1st, 1996: 1543**

It seemed the perfect day for new beginnings—of the year, for their relationship; and of endings, of Roach's passing on, though Paul could not so easily dismiss it. It bothered the hell out of him, and he had had a long conversation with Karen about the ethics of divulging confidential information when the client was no longer living.

"Of course, confidentiality survives death."

"I agree."

"Did you know that Lizzie Borden's records are still held in confidence by her primary attorney's law firm?"

"Really?"

"Yes. Absolutely!"

"You are full of trippy information."

"If the SFPD subpoena's you, I would suggest you check with your liability insurance carrier before you comply. The way I read the law is that you can refuse. Only a judge can compel you with a court order to divulge it."

"You continue to amaze me!"

"I hope I always do!"

He leaned over and kissed her lightly. "I have faith in you!"

She blushed mildly, and encircled his neck with her arms, pulling herself into a tight embrace.

"I love you!"

"And I love you so!"

Their embrace deepened and he scooped her up and carried her into the bedroom. He knelt and gently deposited her, then fell to her opposite side. They reached simultaneously for the other and their lips locked sealed together. The phone started ringing then, and Karen immediately said, "Fuck that!"

Paul laughed and said, "My sentiments exactly!"

Paul felt her heat burning through him, and managed to whisper, "I want to go slow, baby, but I don't think I can!"

"Don't you dare! I want you!"

They tore at each other's clothing, and quickly immersed themselves each in the other. Paul's phone started ringing. They both laughed and simultaneously said, "Fuck that!"

Later, much later, they staggered from the bed and checked their phones.

Paul had a message from Phil McLaren; and Karen had a message from the SFPD dispatcher trying to locate him.

"Shit! I don't even get a break on New Year's Day!"

"Are you going to call him?"

"Maybe after we have dinner. I don't owe him anything!"

"Do you like Moroccan food?"

"I haven't had it much. You?"

"Really like it. Ever been to El Mansour? On Clement?"

"No. Wanna go? Do we need reservations?"

"Usually not. But this is New Year's Day."

"Oh god! I almost forgot! There's so much new in my life now!"

She walked up to him, snuggled close and kissed him softly but deeply on the lips.

"I'm so glad..." she started.

He responded, "I'm so glad."

And then together they sang, "I'm so glad I'm glad I'm glad!"

They laughed, and she called to confirm that they could get seating for that night. They were expected in forty-five minutes.

The setting was authentic and the exotic cooking aromas surrounded them as they walked in. They were seated on plump pillows on the floor. They perused the menus and decided to share the harira (lentil) soup appetizer, followed by two five course price fixé dinners, one Moroccan Seafood and the other Lamb and Chicken (with Almonds). Both came with home-baked bread, couscous and vegetables. Paul asked for a side order of spicy eggplant, which he especially loved. It was perfect. They finished their meals with mint tea and shared a keneffa (filo dough filled with house-made pastry cream).

By the time they got back to her place, all they wanted to do was crawl into bed and snuggle. Phil McLaren had other plans though. Karen had three more calls from the SFPD and Paul's service had logged five from the persistent lieutenant

They giggled and sniggered, feeling silly and childlike, disparaging of authority, thinking themselves quite smart.

"Do you think you should call?"

"Probably. Otherwise he might think up some kind of bullshit charge and have me arrested!"

"I thought you were kind of friends."

"We've encountered each other before," he said and then told her how much Kubicek seemed to really despise him. The man had been a part of the Czech Secret Police.

"I thought you told me he was a brother vet?"

"Phil actually released me from my cell. That fucking Kubicek wanted to keep me in custody and keep interrogating me until I gave him what he wanted—even if I didn't have it!"

"Our tax dollars at work!"

"Typical!"

"Let's have a coffee first. Maybe a Drambuie."

"Let's."

They brewed a fresh pot and had a Drambuie as they relaxed on the couch.

"Shouldn't you call him?"

"I guess. I just really don't like cops. And he's going to be pissed!"

"I know," she said, putting her hand on his forearm, "but the sooner you deal with it," and now she smiled, "the sooner we can get to bed!"

He firmly kissed her and said, "Righty-O!"

McLaren's phone had barely rung when he shouted at Paul.

"Where the hell are you?"

"I'm having a life. Thank you very much."

"I have been trying to get a hold of you! I need more information!"

"You could have asked!"

"I am asking!"

"No, you're shouting at me!"

There was a protracted silence and then the man spoke again in a totally different tone of voice.

"Look, your friend Hoskins may have been murdered."

"What's changed since yesterday?"

"It's still officially a suspicious death. I'm Homicide. I investigate."

"Why are you being so hostile?"

"Are you still refusing to divulge what information you might have?"

"Do you have a court order?"

"I have applied for one. Should have it tomorrow."

"Fine. Then I will gladly respond. But, as I said, I have no written case notes."

"Fine. Then you'd be willing to come in and give a recorded statement that can be transcribed?"

"Of course."

"I'll call you. And answer your goddamn telephone this time."

Then the tone of his voice shifted dramatically yet again.

"Listen Paul. The goddamn FBI, the CIA and the DEA are all on my ass for information. I've been keeping them off you, but I don't know how long I can keep it up."

"OK, man. I understand. I really appreciate it."

Karen looked at him for a long time without speaking, then asked, "What did he say to you? Your voice changed."

"It seems that all of the government agencies I most despise are pressuring Phil to get information out of me."

"Oh shit!"

"No shit"

"Now what?"

"I need to call Shirley Stephenson. I'm not going in there without legal representation."

"I think that's wise" she said, and he put in a call to her. He left a message with her service, then called her home number. Karen could only hear his end of the conversation.

"Maka hike hou, Shirley!"

"Well, of course it's you! Who else speaks Hawaiian to me on the New Year?"

"I've had a new year's invitation to visit the Hall of Justice tomorrow!"

"Tell me more."

He explained the circumstances, and then replied to her next question, saying "It is my fondest wish. I would so appreciate your being there."

"Excellent! Excellent! You want me to pick you up. Or...?

"No. I'll see you in the lobby. Thanks again!"

"Wow!" said Karen, "she agreed just like that?"

"We're old friends."

"Must be."

"Plus," I have her on retainer!"

"Oh you!" she said, a slapped him on the upper arm. "Let's go to bed!"

CHAPTER FIFTY-FOUR
A WALK INTO THE GAPING MAW

San Francisco   Tuesday January 2nd, 1996: 0943

There was a proverbial media circus out in front of the HOJ. Paul dismissed it as a response to yet another so-called "celebrity case." Bu Shirley dashed up to him and re-routed him to the Attorney's Entrance, an extraordinary concession by the Sheriff's Deputy manning the gate. She was wearing a well-tailored navy-blue business suit, with a fuchsia-toned blouse and a multi-colored Hermes scarf, an outfit that was in stark contrast to the fog-shrouded sky and the dense humidity that was portending rain

"How did you get me a pass through the Attorney's Entrance?"

"You saw the media scrum?"

"Of course."

"They're here for you. Somebody alerted them. Maybe your buddy Phil."

"Oh, shit!"

"I mean, I hope not. But somebody did."

"Jesus! What could they want with me?"

"I spoke to a female reporter I know, and she told me they'd gotten an anonymous call, telling them that you were going to be 'interviewed' by the FBI and the CIA!"

"Oh my God! Why"

"They all think you have information that may be 'vital to national security.'"

"Oh my God!"

"Don't worry. I'm here to keep things as clean as possible."

"What does that mean?"

"They may try to put you in 'protective custody.' Or claim that your withholding confidential information is 'obstructing justice.'"

"Because I won't tell them something I don't know?"

"They seem to think that you may be harboring key names in a massive international drug operation!"

"Oh, sweet fucking Jesus!"

"Just stand pat on your right to maintain confidentiality. Don't be swayed by any references to 'patriotism!'"

"You know me better than that!"

"I'm just saying that they may try that too."

"What a fucking mess! I'm sure glad I kept a rough estimation of what he paid me in cash!"

"Do you think they have any way of knowing exactly?"

"Roach claimed that he was being 'stalked.' It could have been federal surveillance."

"At this point, I don't think so, even The Fed is trying to overshadow the local investigation."

"Why?"

"If they had that kind of information, they might have pressured you to come to 450 Golden Gate."

Paul turned to Shirley, fear and exasperation chasing each other across his face, and said, "Look. I really do not have any information about his drug dealing!"

"I understand, and I believe you. I'll do my best to keep them off you, but it'll be the FBI fronting for the CIA if The Fed get involved!"

"I'd still have the same things to say!"

"I understand. I'm just saying..."

The further they got into the bowels of the building; the darker Paul's thoughts turned. By the time they were ushered into the Homicide Bureau anteroom, he felt depressed. He was having second, even third thoughts, about what he was doing there, though he didn't really have a lot of choice. This was the crux of the emotional energy that was triggering a virtual tsunami of flashbacks about feeling helpless, powerless, with no direction home. It was a poignant reminder of his every encounter with "authorities" that were themselves always memories of his father's autocratic manner, and his own long-delayed desire to retaliate in the present for past crimes. The creepy Sergeant Kubicek was a key target of his misgivings about being here, an experience he was loath to repeat. Thank God for Shirley! He reached over, gripper her upper arm and thanked her.

"Don't explode! If you start to get overwhelmed, ask for a break—or I will."

"I'll likely get bored with their incessantly asking the same questions over and over!"

"It's one of their tactics. You know that. They are so used to dealing with hard-core criminals that they're disinclined to believe anything an honest person tells them!"

"But the truth is so simple!"

"Just stick to it. Don't lie. Don't embellish!"

"That'll be easy! I don't know anything!"

Of course, that didn't matter to his obsessively-minded interrogators who seemed to have a script that revolved around his being willing to sacrifice any and all ethical principles in order to ameliorate their urgently preoccupied, almost addictive demand for information to which they assumed he was privy; and was petulantly choosing not to reveal—despite the fact that they'd been granted a court order.

"Tell us again, Mr. Marzeky, what your client Donald Hoskins revealed to you about the source of his income."

In spite of Shirley's many admonitions, Paul felt a wave or white-hot rage rising up through his spinal process and burning up out of him like the flare of natural gas from a well head. It always reminded him of his father's Gestapo-like techniques.

It was Shirley who spoke up, a true advocate.

"I am again going to insist that you at least have the courtesy of addressing my client by his proper title! It's <u>Doctor</u> Marzeky!"

After which Paul went through the entire litany of his knowledge of Roach, reciting yet again his very minimal knowledge.

"But you knew he was a drug dealer?"

"Again, he claimed to be a drug dealer. He also claimed to be being pursued either by organized crime or 'elements of our government.' From the beginning, I questioned whether or not he was telling the truth or was simply delusional."

"And?"

"I vacillated between the two. I never came to a firm conclusion. I kept seeing elements of both."

"Was he using?"

"He told me he had been clean for thirteen months when we first started working together. That is a perquisite of my taking on a client."

"You never saw him use? Never saw him loaded?"

"No! Never!"

"'Never?'"

"Never!"

"Then, how do explain him dying from an overdose?"

"I can't. How do you?"

"He was your client. He died of an overdose. You say there's no connection?"

"No."

"I think there is."

"What does that mean?"

"I think you know far more than you're telling me."

"Like what?"

"Like the names of his confederates. His connections here and in Asia."

"Oh, fucking please!"

"What does that mean?"

Shirley intervened this time.

"Asked and answered numerous times already, detective."

"And I want an answer again."

"Same answer. And," he said, turning to Shirley, "I believe that if I am not under arrest, I am free to leave. Is that correct?"

"Absolutely, Paul. Detective?"

"Sir, I believe you are obstructing justice! That's a felony!"

"So, arrest him, detective, if you have any proof!"

"Shirley!" said Paul reprovingly.

"No, Paul! Enough of this bullshit! We've been here almost three hours and you have repeatedly, and quite politely, answered the same questions! Let's go!"

Paul rose as the detective scowled at him.

"I will be seeing you again!"

"Not without me!" said Shirley resoundingly.

"Oh. By the way, would you mind submitting a urine sample?"

"WHAT?" From both Paul and Shirley.

"You say you're clean from drugs for a long time. So, I just wondered if you wouldn't mind submitting to a tox screen. Just to prove it."

"Why exactly in the fuck should I have to?"

"Just to prove you were not using heroin!"

"WHAT?!"

"You are completely ridiculous, detective!" Shirley's face had bloomed bright red, and she furiously stalked toward the suddenly flummoxed detective, who stepped back two steps behind his desk chair.

"It's nothing official. It just occurred to me that..."

"If you want something as intrusive as that, I strongly suggest that you get a court order!

"Yes, ma'am!" he said.

As they were walking down the stairs, eschewing the elevator for more privacy, Shirley was angrier than Paul had ever seen her.

"That pretentious asshole! How dare he suggest that you were using heroin! Ridiculous!"

He was touched by her response and told her so.

"I know how proud you are of your long-term clean time."

"I am. Thanks."

"Do you have me on your speed dial?"

"Of course."

"I just want to make sure. You call me any time they call you want to talk. I don't care what time of day or night."

"It's a deal!"

As they parted at the base of the stairs to go separate ways, Paul went home with Karen on his mind, even knowing he still needed time to further process this day, and that it was best done alone, at least initially. There was a kernel there of something that could or would enrich him. He wanted to document today's events at the keyboard, to allow his thoughts and ideas to pour out of him like a deluge from his brain to the paper. He was reminded of Henry's Miller's line from *Tropic of Cancer*: "What need have I for money?

I am a writing machine. The last screw has been added. The thing flows. Between me and the machine there is no estrangement. I am the machine."

CHAPTER FIFTY-FIVE
REFLECTION OR RESOLUTION?

San Francisco   **Tuesday January 2nd, 1996: 1345**

Paul left a brief message for Karen.

"I need some time alone right now, my sweet, but let's have dinner tonight. Call me when your sessions are completed."

Paul was again feeling the grief he was carrying had over Roach, wishing he had had just a little more time, just a few more sessions. The man had changed significantly through the arc of healing that they had initiated. He knew he had done his part in assisting him as much as he could. The more he reviewed the course of treatment, the less he dunned himself.

He loved this work. It was the most rewarding occupation he'd ever had. He enjoyed the money and prestige, of course, but it was the service that really lit him up. Seeing intimate changes in the lives of his clients was such an inspiration. He was always enriched and uplifted by seeing them overcome their struggles and triumph.

He honestly didn't know what he might do, if for some reason, he was unable to continue practicing his healing work. The very thought of it saddened him immensely. He tracked his grief for the loss of Roach, and he released it with relish and gratitude; that he had the freedom and the permission to release, to express himself without fear of shame or retribution; relieved of the burden of the terrible violent proscriptions of his childhood; to be freed now at last to walk the Earth a new man, to feel what he really felt, to see what he really saw, to be who he really was. It was of such magnitude that he felt slabs of leaden gray emotion falling off of him, like an iceberg calving. He shook the heaviness from his hands, and shot out of his fingers like lightning bolts, feeling the weight of decades, ages, eons of loss now forgotten and ignored. At length, he closed his eyes and fell into a soothing dreamless slumber.

A timeless time later, feeling himself blessed to be a San Franciscan, he opened his eyes to the reflected oranges, pinks, salmons and golds of the sunset splaying out across this great city of his far to the west, radiating out above Ocean Beach into the sky above where Playland-by-the-Sea had once stood, and the holy site where the closing concert of the Family Dog with Quicksilver Messenger Service was held (and all of them Virgos! Jesus!).

The telephone rang as he sat up and reached across to the nightstand to answer it. He absolutely knew it was Karen.

"Hi, dear. I just woke up. Did you have a busy day?"

"Back to back to back all afternoon. Just barely had time for a couple of cookies and a cup of coffee around 1400. How are you feeling, baby? Hungry?"

"You bet! What appeals to you tonight?"

"I know you are almost always up for ethnic of some sort! What haven't we had recently?"

"Sweetie, I just so flat out love you! If you want mud pies, I will gladly eat them with you!"

"Wow! Maybe you should visit the cop shop more often! You are really mellow!"

"Just joking. I want some real food! How does The Tandoori strike you?"

"I love it! But why don't we go see your friend Mr. Kapur at The Maharani?"

"Excellent thought! I love the food and it's such a trippy atmosphere. I'll call and see if we can have the Fantasy Room."

"Great idea! Want me to come and get you?"

"That would be awesome! See you, what, half an hour? Forty-five?"

"Make it forty-five. I want to take a shower first." He knew how much Karen like a freshly shaven face.

"Beautiful, baby! See you soon."

Twenty-five minutes later he emerged from the bathroom and spied a thick manila envelope lying on his therapy office desk. It had not been there before.

The front door was locked, as were the windows. Then he went back to his office to inspect the envelope. It looked new and felt heavy for such a relatively small size. Curious, he opened it cautiously—and was astonished to find a thick stack of fifty-dollar bills spilling out of it!

"What the fuck?" he could not help but exclaim.

CHAPTER FIFTY-SIX
CURIOUSER AND CURIOUSER

San Francisco   Tuesday January 2nd, 1996: 1921

He read the hand-written poem he found in the envelope with the money without counting the latter.

Do Not Stand at My Grave and Weep (© 1932, Mary Elizabeth Frye)

Do not stand at my grave and weep.

I am not there; I do not sleep.

I am a thousand winds that blow,

I am the diamond glints on snow,

I am the sun on ripened grain,

I am the gentle autumn rain.

When you awaken in the morning's hush

I am the swift uplifting rush

Of quiet birds in circled flight.

I am the soft stars that shine at night.

Do not stand at my grave and cry,

I am not there; I did not die.

Roach wasn't dead! Roach wasn't dead!

He'd faked his death!

The man he identified looked exactly like Roach, but the autopsy report said he had had Stage Four pancreatic cancer that had metastasized to his lungs and bladder. The ME hypothesized that the man had only had four to eight weeks to live at best.

Roach could have easily paid someone an enormous amount of money, someone of roughly his shape and size, to have plastic surgery and subsequently take an overdose of heroin—the perfect solution for Roach. It would effectively get his enemies off his back. It might satisfy the alphabeted governmental entities seeking to silence him—and he could simply disappear forever into the jungles or back streets of Southeast Asia.

Jesus! Paul thought he might be going fucking nuts! But then, where in the hell had the money come from? It was only then that he thought to count it.

He went to his desk and grasped the stack of bills. One thousand fifties! An even fifty thousand dollars. Oh my God!

It had to have been a gift from Roach! But that was crazy! Utterly crazy! A very extreme gift indeed!

He quickly dressed and readied himself for Karen's arrival. He pondered briefly how much, or even whether, to tell her right now.

She immediately noticed his preoccupied look as soon as she kissed him.

"What's up baby?"

Paul knew he could not hide from her. Did not want to, yet part of what he was thinking was so outlandish it was more appropriate as a plot for *Twilight Zone*.

He bundled her into the car before he spoke. Then he took a deep breath and launched into the story, citing the money, but without sharing the poem.

"But where did it come from?"

"I have no idea! I came out of the shower and there it was!"

"And the front door was still locked? And the windows too?"

"Absolutely! I checked."

"It was fifty thousand dollars? In fifties?"

Yes."

She took a deep breath, holding silence for the length the next block. Coming to a stop sign, she turned to him.

"You told me Roach always paid in fifties!"

"Too true. And I have some speculation about this, but I don't want you to think I've developed a mental illness!"

"If you try to withhold from me, I will apply the electrodes personally!"

He laughed, partly because he loved her humor and partly out of relief. He felt like they had passed through a shared tunnel.

"I don't believe Roach is really dead."

482

"WHAT?"

"You asked what I thought."

"I thought you identified the body."

"I did."

"And?"

"Phil McLaren told me the autopsy report indicated that the body I identified had Stage Four pancreatic cancer. He would not have lived another month."

"So?"

"I don't believe that Roach was that sick!"

"So, what? He paid somebody to overdose for him?"

"He had plenty money."

"But why? How?"

"I don't know how. But if, and I emphasize if, he did pull it off, it would be the perfect way to disappear somewhere and get everybody off his trail."

"So, now you're saying that he was not delusional, and you believe his story?"

"There's something I didn't tell you. The cops found twenty thousand dollars in a money belt around his waist."

"Wow!"

"Yeah. All in fifties."

"Wow!"

Paul sat quietly as she motored toward their location, on Post just beyond Polk. If he were ever on Death Row, he fantasized that he would choose Indian food as his final meal.

"If you haven't already decided to put a 5150 on me, I'll tell you more."

(Welfare and Institutions Code 5150 mandated that individuals who were: A Danger to Self or Others; or who were unable to provide for themselves due to mental disease or disorder, and were considered to be Gravely Disabled, could be placed on a psychiatric hold for up to seventy-two hours against their will).

"No, baby. I think you're crazy, but not mentally ill."

When he shared the poem with her, she read it aloud. She added special emphasis to the last line: "I am not there; I did not die."

"Did he ever tell you any of this?"

"No! I swear! This was a total surprise to me."

"What are you going to do?"

"I haven't gotten any further than deciding to talk to you."

"What do you want to do?"

"I don't feel inclined to report it."

"I agree."

"But what about the cops?"

"Shirley made it noticeably clear that I am supposed to call her anytime day or night. I am not to talk to the cops by myself ever."

They had good parking karma that night and found a parking spot on Post just steps away from the entrance. Mr. Kapur greeted them effusively as they entered and seated them in the Fantasy Room. They took off their shoes and put their feet up. One of his nephews/waiters came over, and they were soon supplied with water and chop sticks. Next came an off-the-menu appetizer, courtesy of the house, along with the menus.

They were enjoying samosas, Tandoori Chicken, Curried Lamb, Saag Paneer, two sides of raita and a basket of Garlic Naan (why not? They were both eating it!) Since they were both so hungry, the meal gave them a chance to digest both the food and Paul's revelations.

"Sweetie, I've been thinking about your conclusions. And I believe you're right."

"I am?" he said incredulously.

"Yes. If he had that much money, and incredible connections with both government agencies and organized crime, it would have been easy for him to pull off that kind of deception."

"What's your take on the money he left me?"

"Seems like a 'Thank you.' Maybe he knew somehow that you didn't sell him out!'

"I couldn't have even if I wanted to! I did not know anything! I stayed focused on wanting to help him to start a new life!"

"Maybe it was a reminder that you are bound by confidentiality. You actually can't report it."

"I didn't think of it that way!"

"Personally, I am going to imagine that Roach is still alive, running around the world, living the high life!"

"Actually, I hope you're right!"

CHECK OUT DR. STEFAN MALECEK LATEST BOOK

Crucible of Shame: Healing the Societal Roots of Addiction and "Mental Illness"

Guilt says *"I did something wrong."* Shame says, *"I am something wrong."* The experience of *shame* is a direct negative evaluation of the self. In *guilt*, the self is focused on negative behaviors, but the self is not the focus.

Shame is built into every society, every culture. Shame factors into all addictions, all "mental illness. *Crucible of Shame: Healing the Societal Roots of Addiction and "Mental Illness"* discusses the self-destructive force of shame as it has infiltrated every aspect of the contemporary world. Over time, toxic shame causes us to hide our struggles which often end up leading to emotional and psychological trauma. In this book, the author discusses the causes of mental illness as well as mental health counseling and finally, techniques for healing shame.

Get The Book Here

https://www.amazon.com/author/stefanjmalecek

ABOUT THE AUTHOR.

Stefan J. Malecek, Ph.D.

D r. Stefan J. Malecek has worked extensively with Trauma-affected clients, including 100% PTSD Veterans. He spent nearly 2 decades working on in-patient psychiatric care units in the San Francisco Bay area and nearly a decade in community mental health out-patient facilities, followed by 5 years in a private psychotherapy practice. He taught psychology at the community college level for 7 years.

He is the author of the acclaimed Paul Marzeky Mystery series: *Crazy Tales of Combat Psychiatry, Unwitting Witness, Alchemy's Angels, Spirals of Time, The Gilded Edges Of Shadow and his latest, Excelsior.* The Crucible of Shame: Healing the Societal Roots of Addiction and "Mental Illness" and Trauma and Transformation are his first published non-fiction books.

All are available now at: amazon.com/author/stefanjmalecek/

Dr. Stefan J. Malecek was born in St. Louis, Missouri, and left there in 1966 after high school to join the US Army. He initially trained as a Combat Medic at Fort Sam Houston, Texas, and worked as Social Work/Clinical Psychology Specialist at Fort Riley, Kansas. After a year there, he was transferred to Vietnam. He spent 1968-1969 in-country partly with the 14th General Dispensary/85th Evac Hospital, and then flying all over "I" Corps with the 326th

Medical Battalion of the 101st Airborne Division, doing interview evaluations, and counseling many men, often fresh from battle.

Stefan returned to school and got his BA from New College in 1992, and soon thereafter moved to the Oregon Coast. He continued to work in various aspects of mental health and got his master's degree from the Institute of Transpersonal Psychology in 1998; and a Ph.D. in Psychology from Saybrook University. His graduate work was devoted to recovery from trauma, addictions and dissociation.

Learn about the Author at his website:

https://www.stefanjmalecek.com/home-page

Get A Complimentary Therapy Session with Dr. Stefan

www.ingramcontent.com/pod-product-compliance
Lightning Source LLC
Chambersburg PA
CBHW020917020726
47495CB00002B/224